HKJC

D0617906

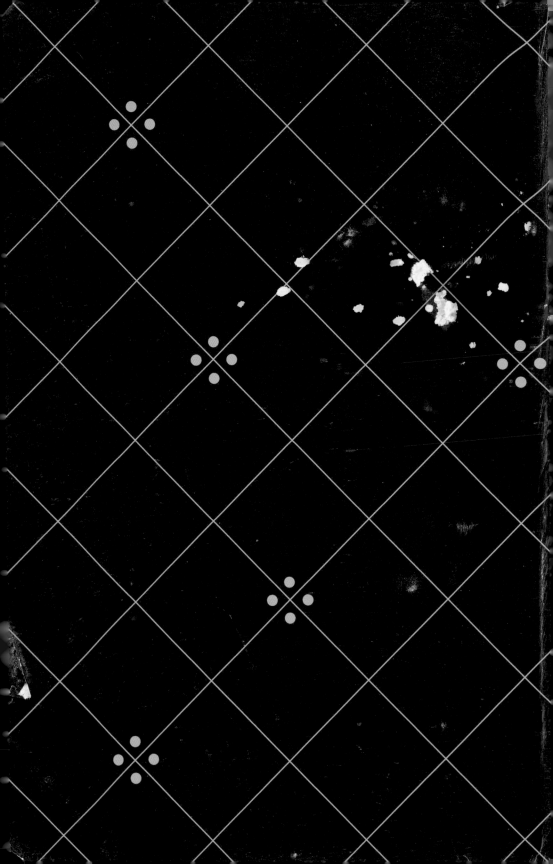

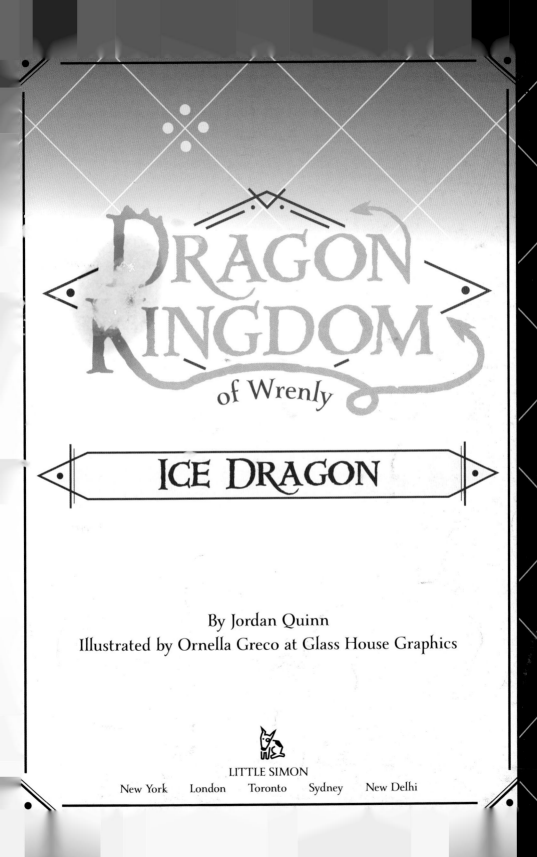

DRAGON KINGDOM
of Wrenly

ICE DRAGON

By Jordan Quinn
Illustrated by Ornella Greco at Glass House Graphics

LITTLE SIMON

New York   London   Toronto   Sydney   New Delhi

This book is a work of fiction. Any references to historical events, real people, or real places are used fictitiously. Other names, characters, places, and events are products of the author's imagination, and any resemblance to actual events or places or persons, living or dead, is entirely coincidental.

LITTLE SIMON

An imprint of Simon & Schuster Children's Publishing Division
1230 Avenue of the Americas, New York, New York 10020
First Little Simon edition November 2021
Copyright © 2021 by Simon & Schuster, Inc.
All rights reserved, including the right of reproduction in whole or in part in any form.
LITTLE SIMON is a registered trademark of Simon & Schuster, Inc., and associated colophon is a
trademark of Simon & Schuster, Inc. For information about special discounts for bulk purchases, please contact
Simon & Schuster Special Sales at 1-866-506-1949 or business@simonandschuster.com. The Simon & Schuster
Speakers Bureau can bring authors to your live event. For more information or to book an event, contact the
Simon & Schuster Speakers Bureau at 1-866-248-3049 or visit our website at www.simonspeakers.com.
Designed by Kayla Wasil
Text by Matthew J. Gilbert
GLASS HOUSE GRAPHICS Creative Services
Art and cover by ORNELLA GRECO
Colors by ORNELLA GRECO and GABRIELE CRACOLICI
Lettering by GIOVANNI SPATARO/Grafimated Cartoon
Supervision by SALVATORE DI MARCO/Grafimated Cartoon
Manufactured in China 0921 SCP
2 4 6 8 10 9 7 5 3 1
Library of Congress Cataloging-in-Publication Data
Names: Quinn, Jordan, author. | Glass House Graphics, illustrator.
Title: Ice dragon / by Jordan Quinn ; illustrated by Glass House Graphics.
Description: First Little Simon edition. | New York : Little Simon, 2021. | Series: Dragon kingdom of Wrenly ; 6
Summary: Ruskin and his friends travel to Flatfrost for the Winter Festival where the legendary ice dragon has
appeared–she who unknowingly holds an important piece to the puzzle of who are the dark forces are that have
been plotting against Ruskin all along.
Identifiers: LCCN 2020048829 (print) | LCCN 2020048830 (ebook) | ISBN 9781534484801 (paperback)
ISBN 9781534484818 (hardcover) | ISBN 9781534484825 (ebook)
Subjects: LCSH: Graphic novels. | CYAC: Graphic novels. | Dragons–Fiction. | Fantasy.
Classification: LCC PZ7.7.Q55 Ic 2021 (print) | LCC PZ7.7.Q55 (ebook) | DDC 741.5/973–dc23
LC record available at https://lccn.loc.gov/2020048829
LC ebook record available at https://lccn.loc.gov/2020048830

Contents

Chapter 1

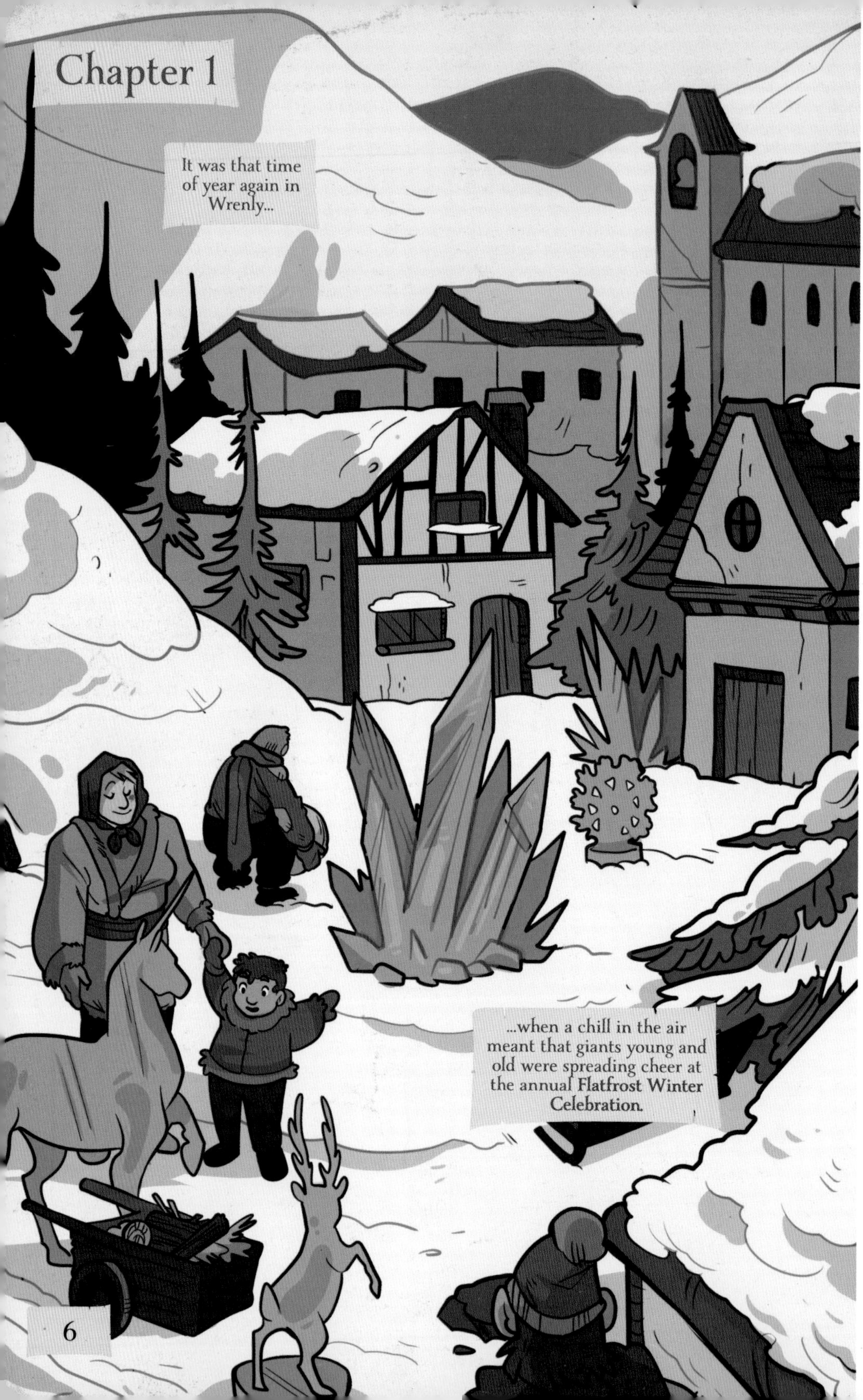
It was that time of year again in Wrenly...
...when a chill in the air meant that giants young and old were spreading cheer at the annual **Flatfrost Winter Celebration.**

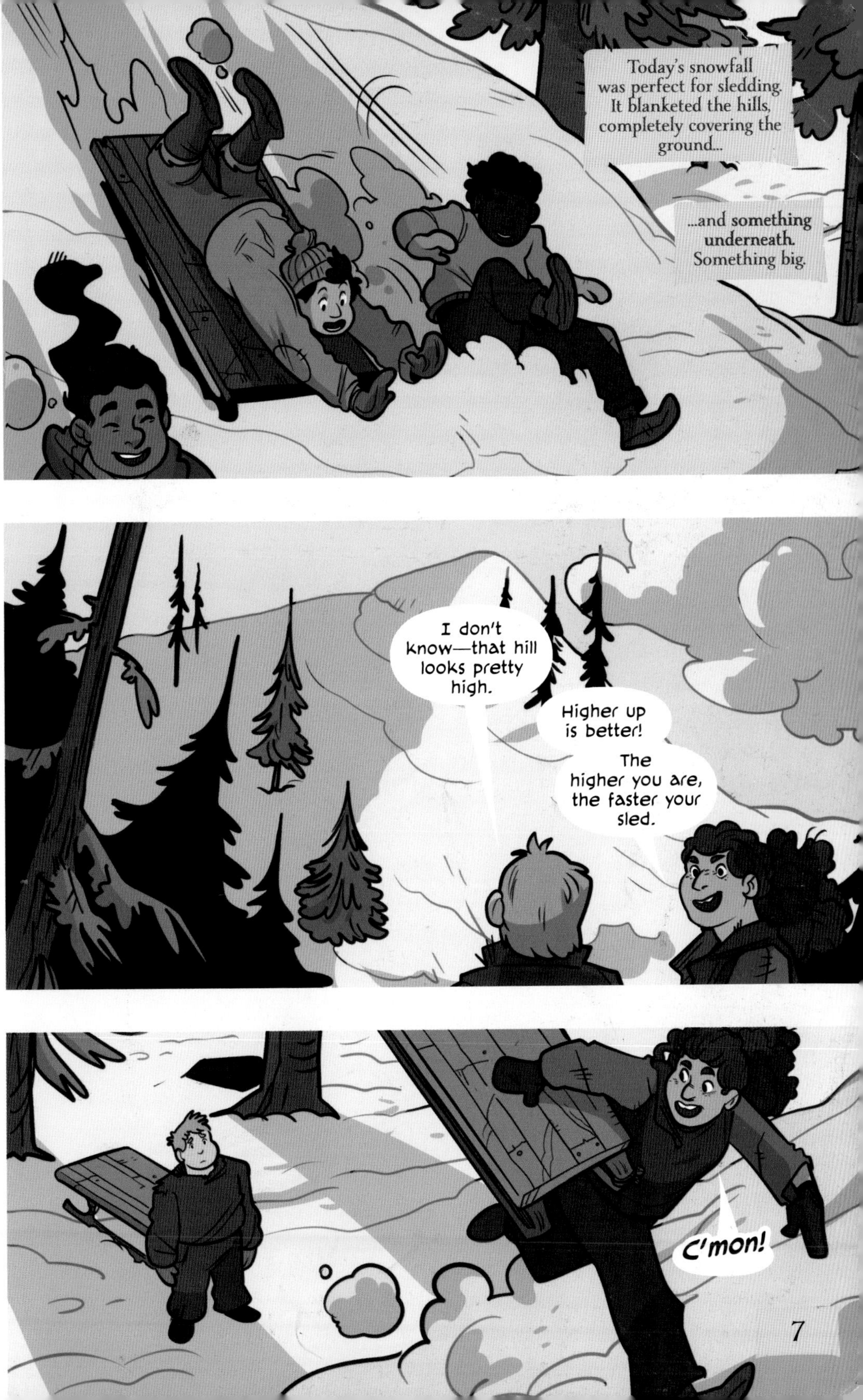
Today's snowfall was perfect for sledding. It blanketed the hills, completely covering the ground...
...and something underneath. Something big.
I don't know—that hill looks pretty high.
Higher up is better!
The higher you are, the faster your sled.
C'mon!

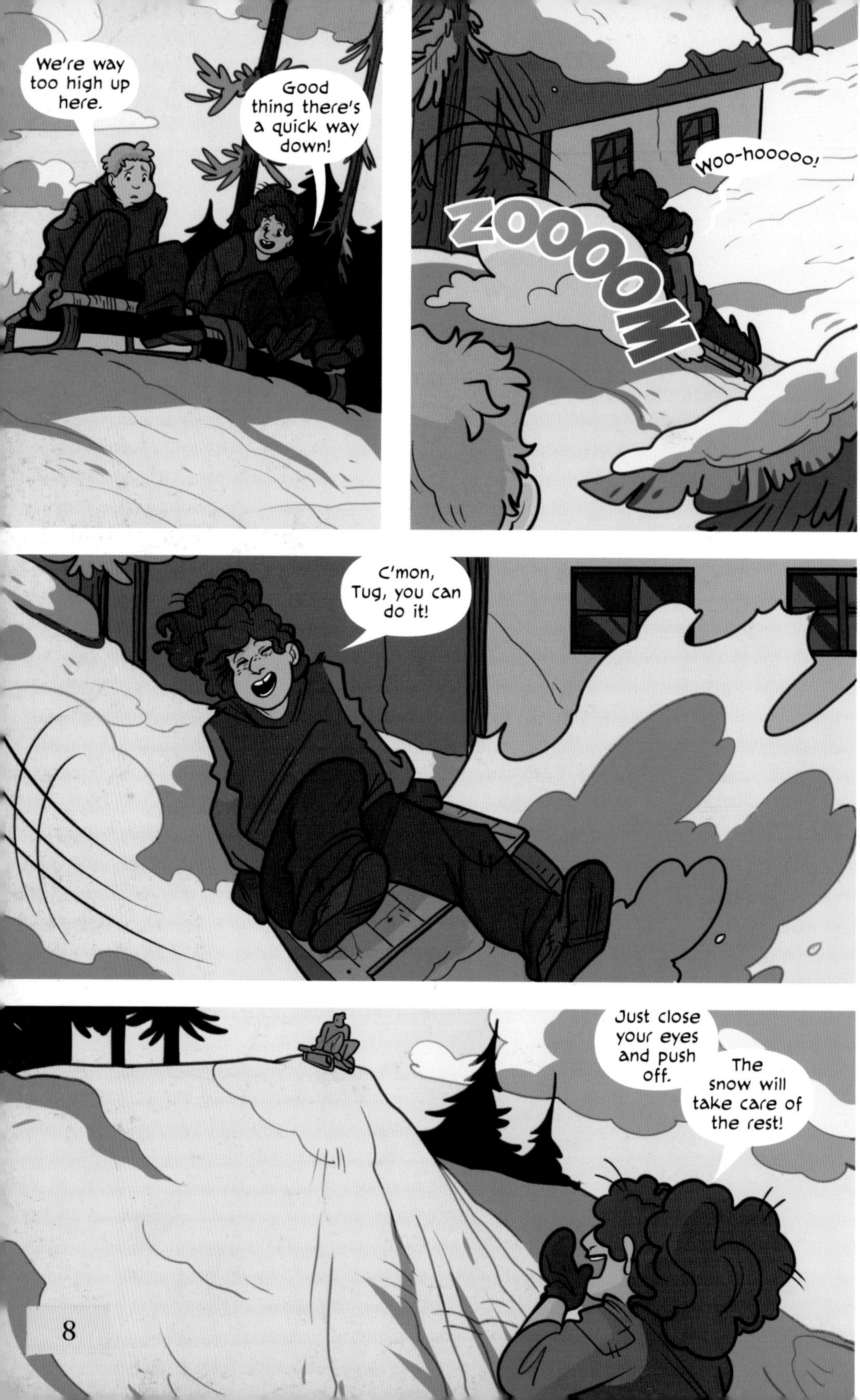
We're way too high up here.
Good thing there's a quick way down!
ZOOOOOM
Woo-hoooooo!
C'mon, Tug, you can do it!
Just close your eyes and push off.
The snow will take care of the rest!

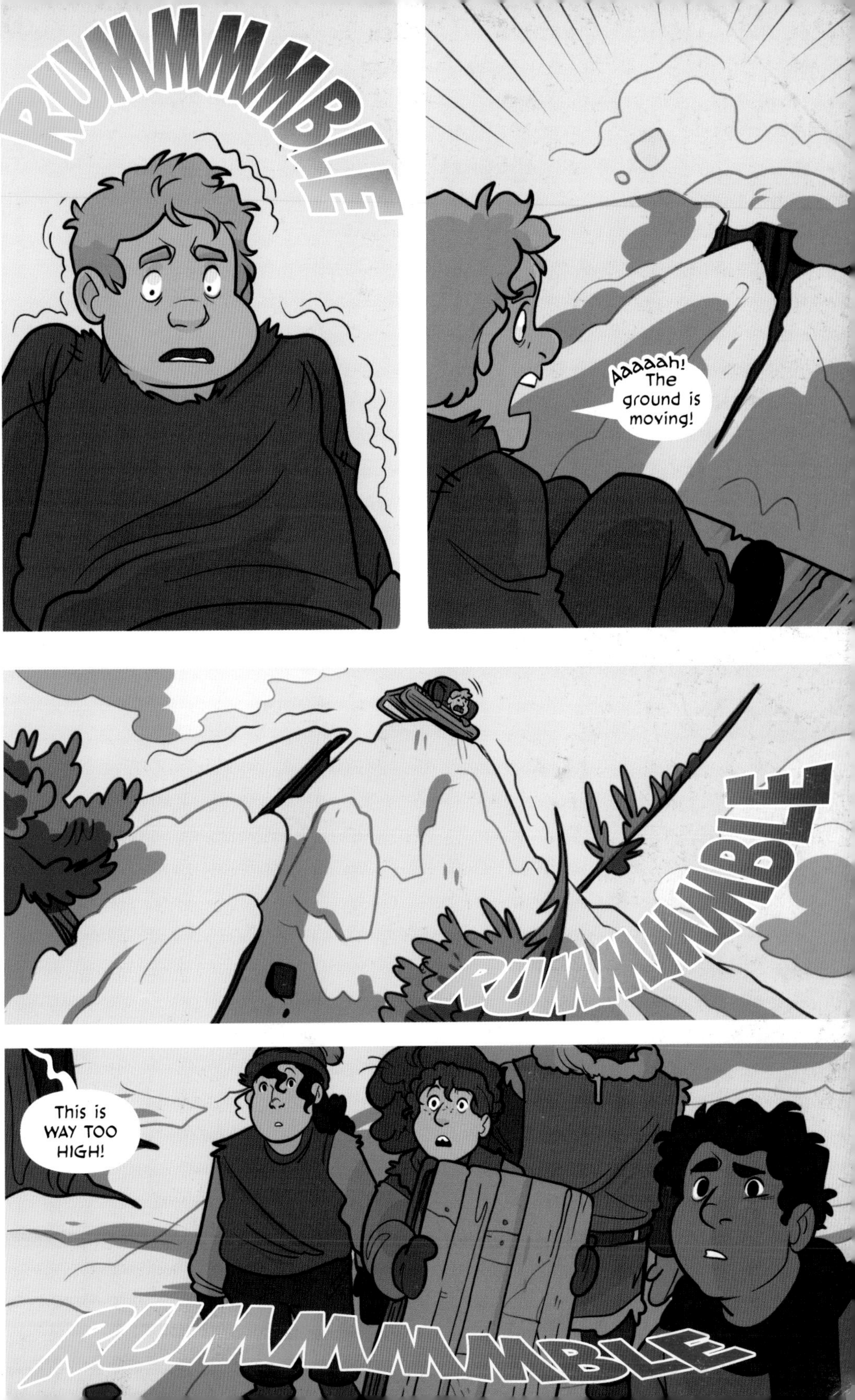
RUMMMMBLE
Aaaaah! The ground is moving!
RUMMMMMBLE
This is WAY TOO HIGH!
RUMMMMMMBLE

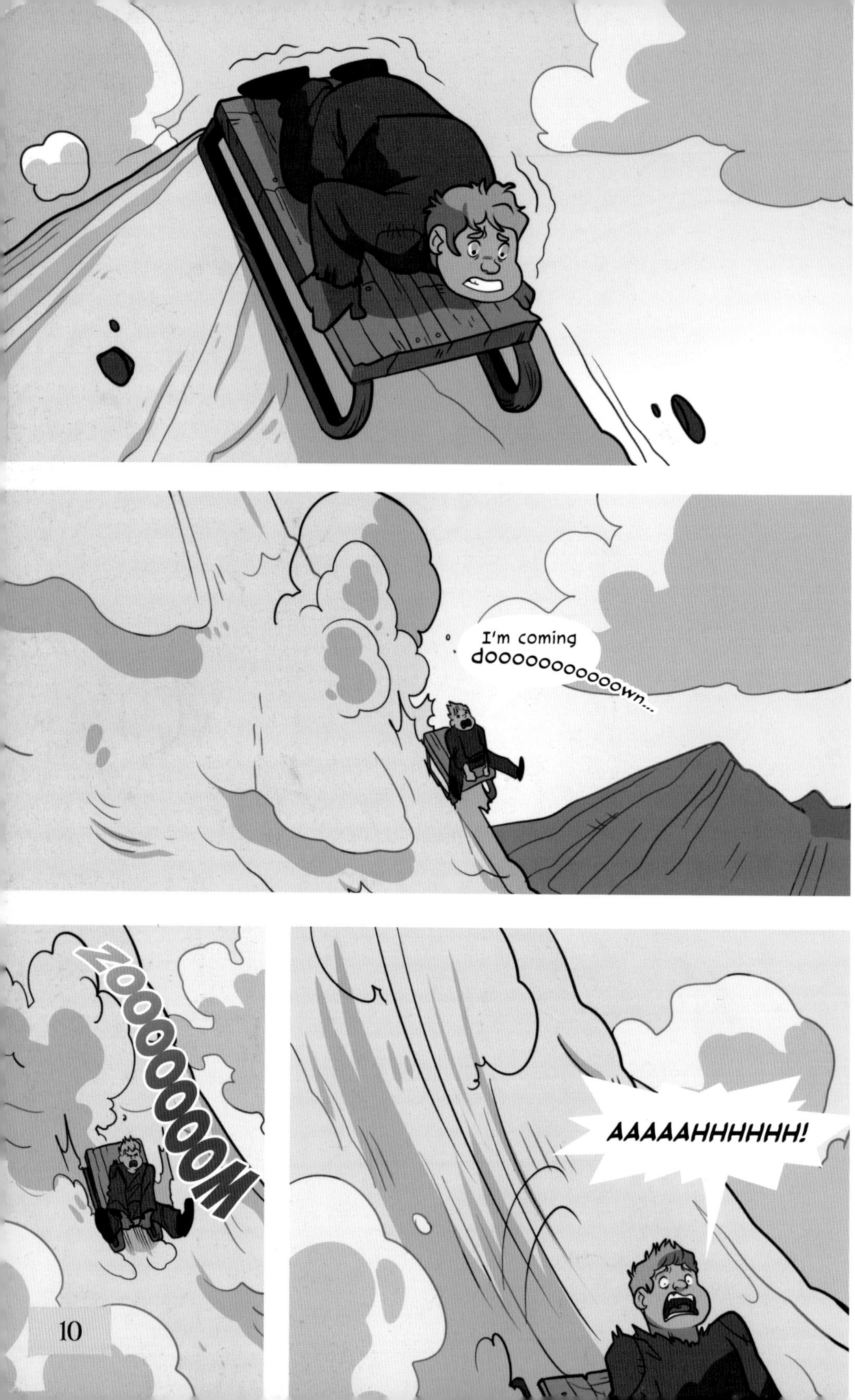
I'm coming doooooooooooown...
ZOOOOOOOM
AAAAAHHHHHH!

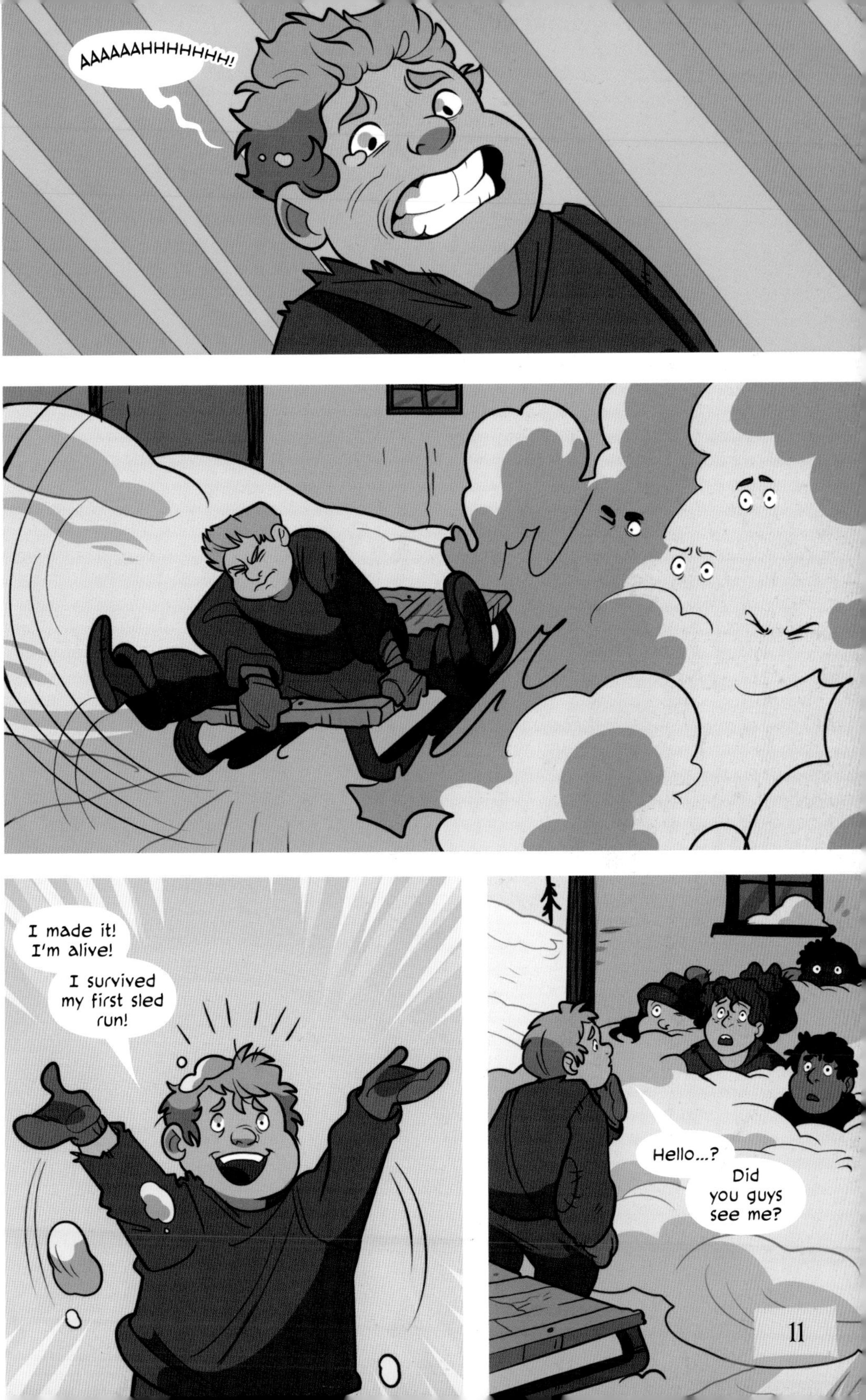
AAAAAAHHHHHHH!
I made it! I'm alive!
I survived my first sled run!
Hello...?
Did you guys see me?

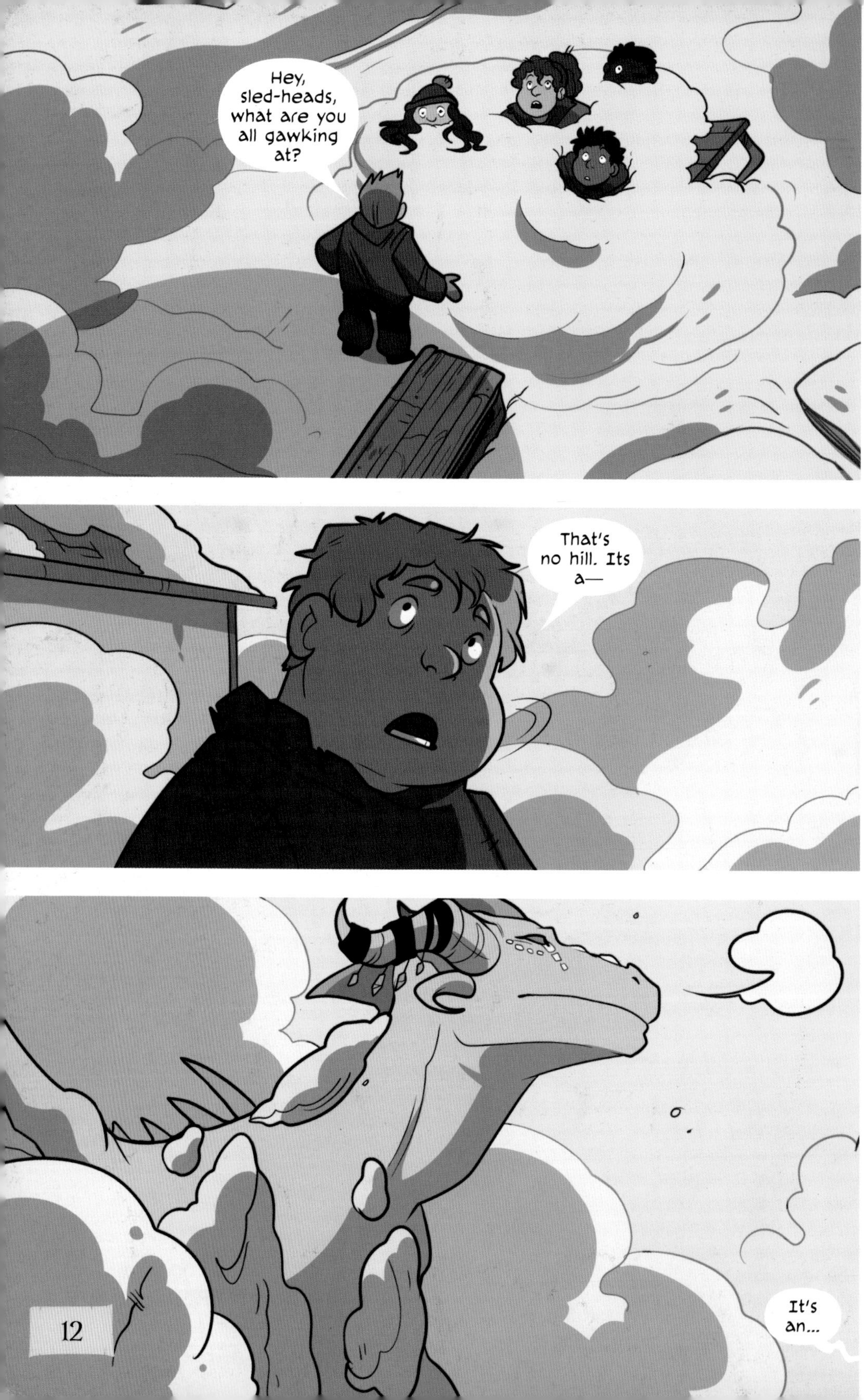
Hey, sled-heads, what are you all gawking at?
That's no hill. Its a—
It's an...

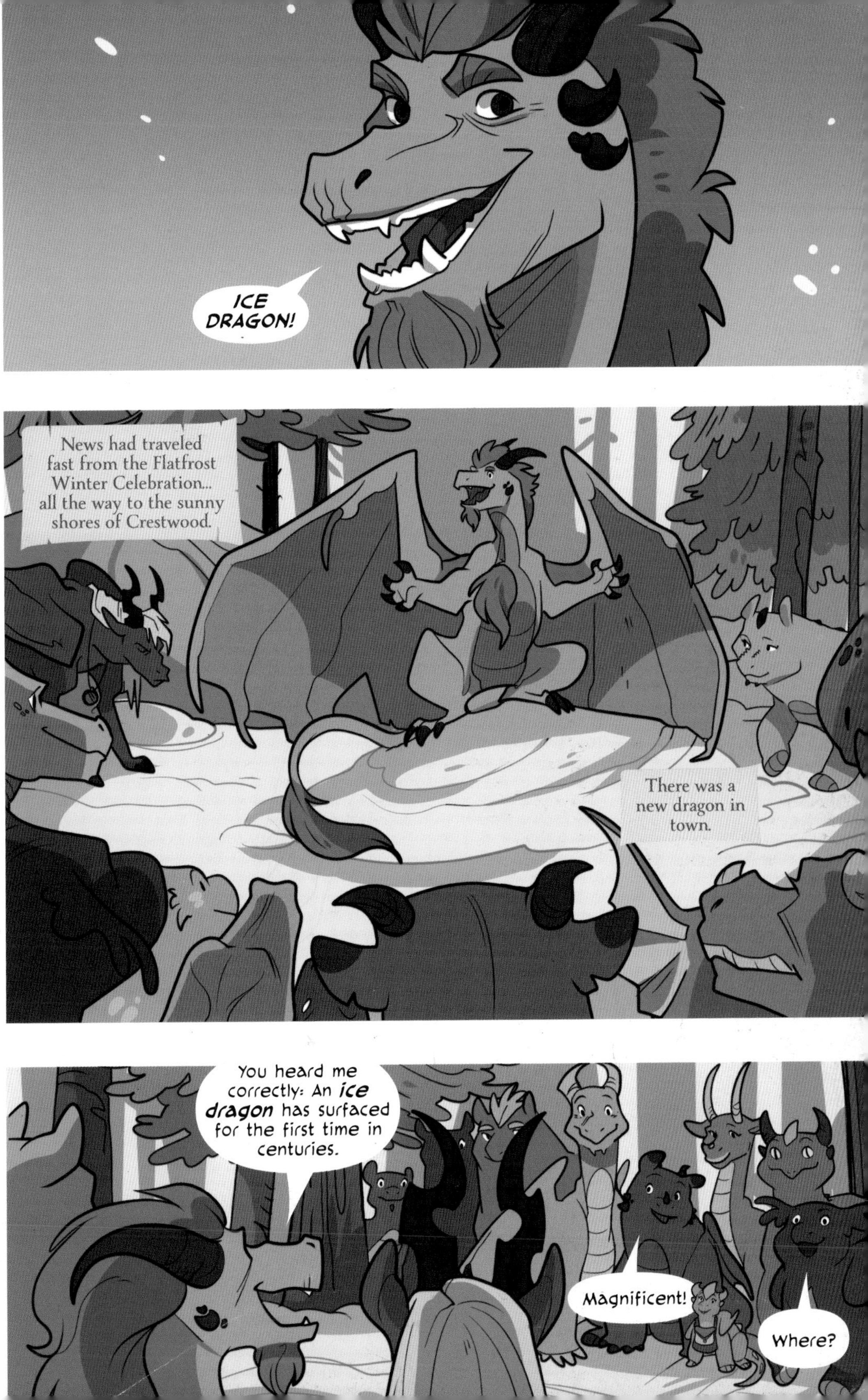
ICE DRAGON!
News had traveled fast from the Flatfrost Winter Celebration... all the way to the sunny shores of Crestwood.
There was a new dragon in town.
You heard me correctly: An *ice dragon* has surfaced for the first time in centuries.
Magnificent!
Where?

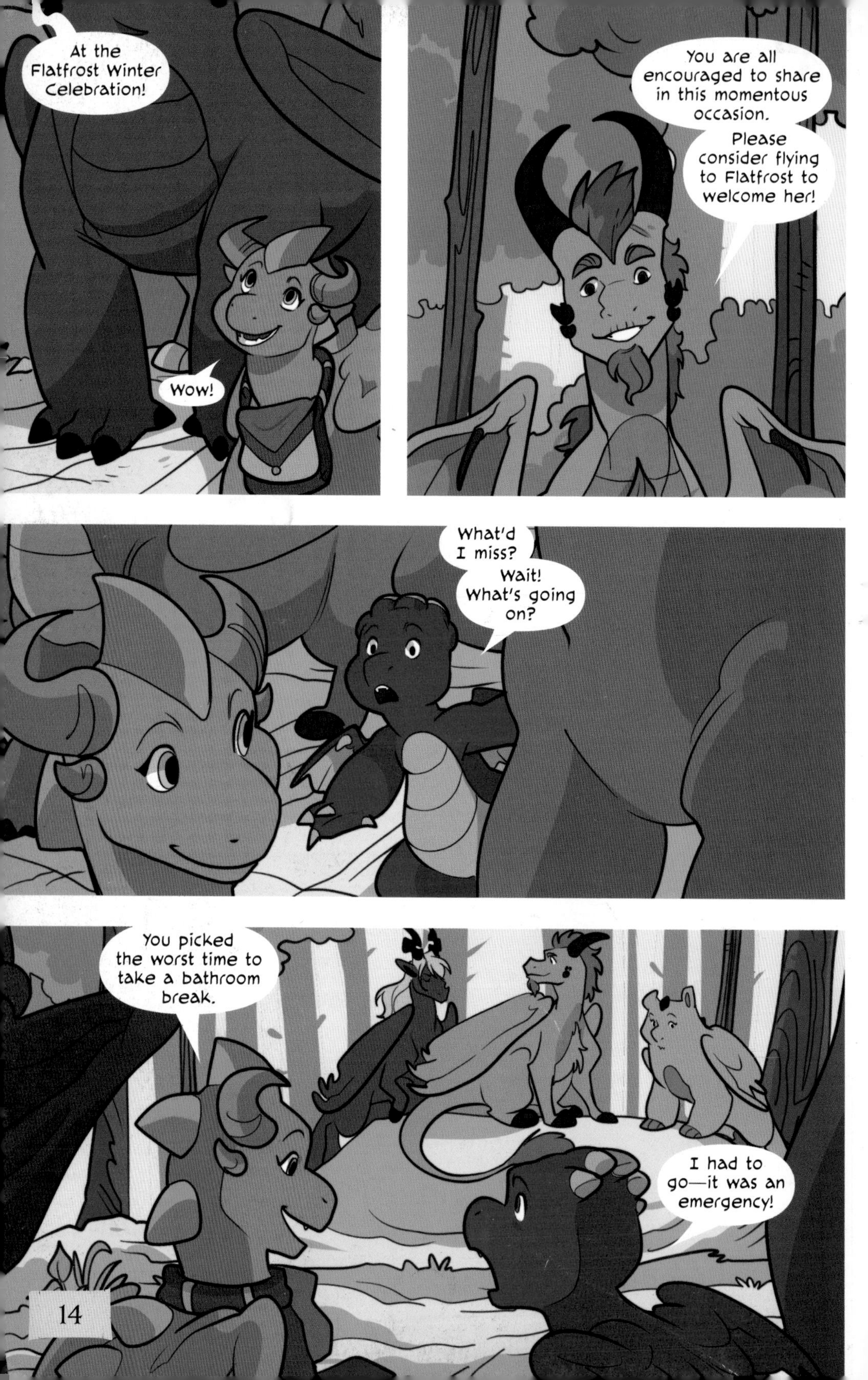
At the Flatfrost Winter Celebration!
Wow!
You are all encouraged to share in this momentous occasion.
Please consider flying to Flatfrost to welcome her!
What'd I miss?
Wait! What's going on?
You picked the worst time to take a bathroom break.
I had to go—it was an emergency!

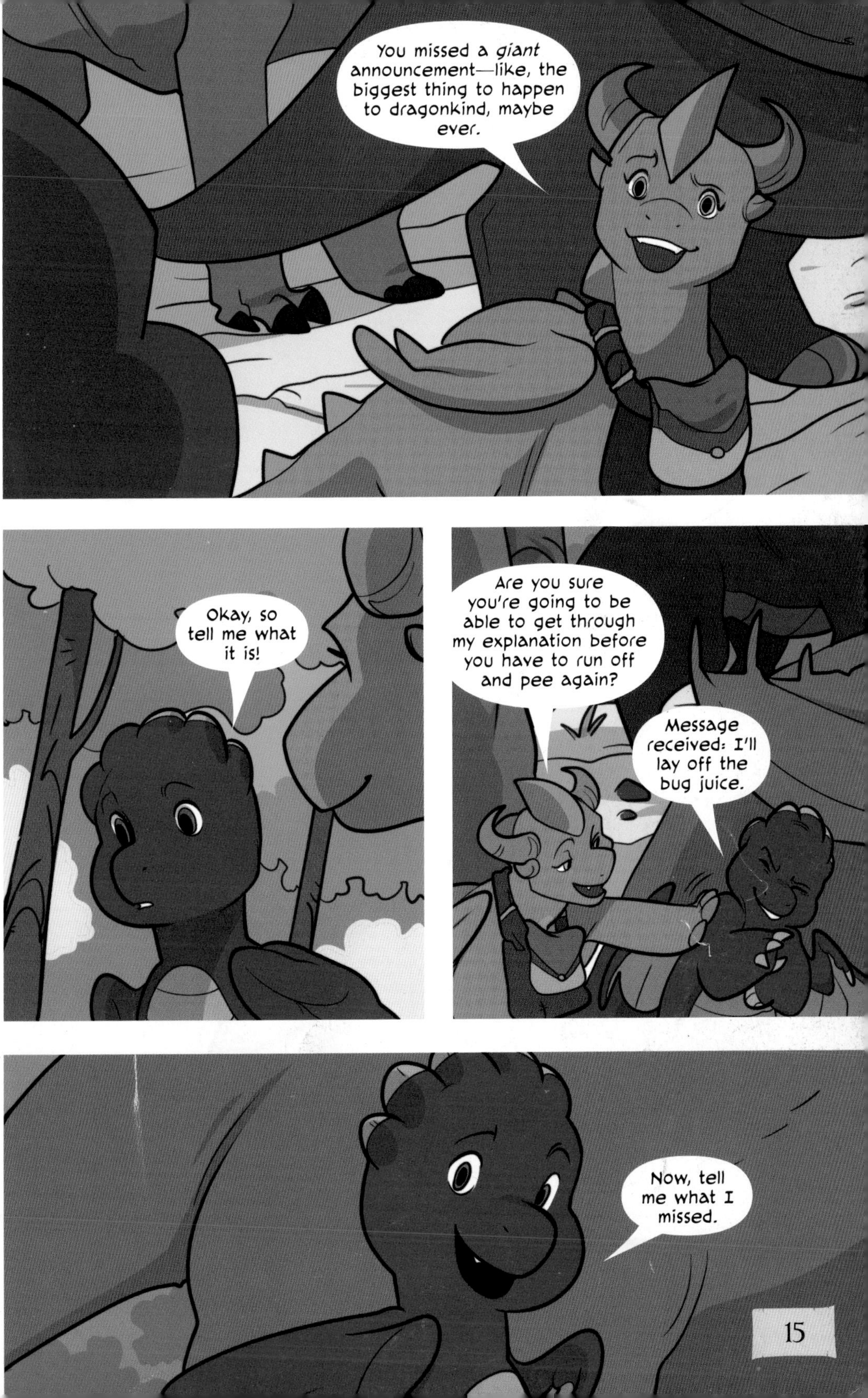
You missed a *giant* announcement—like, the biggest thing to happen to dragonkind, maybe ever.
Okay, so tell me what it is!
Are you sure you're going to be able to get through my explanation before you have to run off and pee again?
Message received: I'll lay off the bug juice.
Now, tell me what I missed.

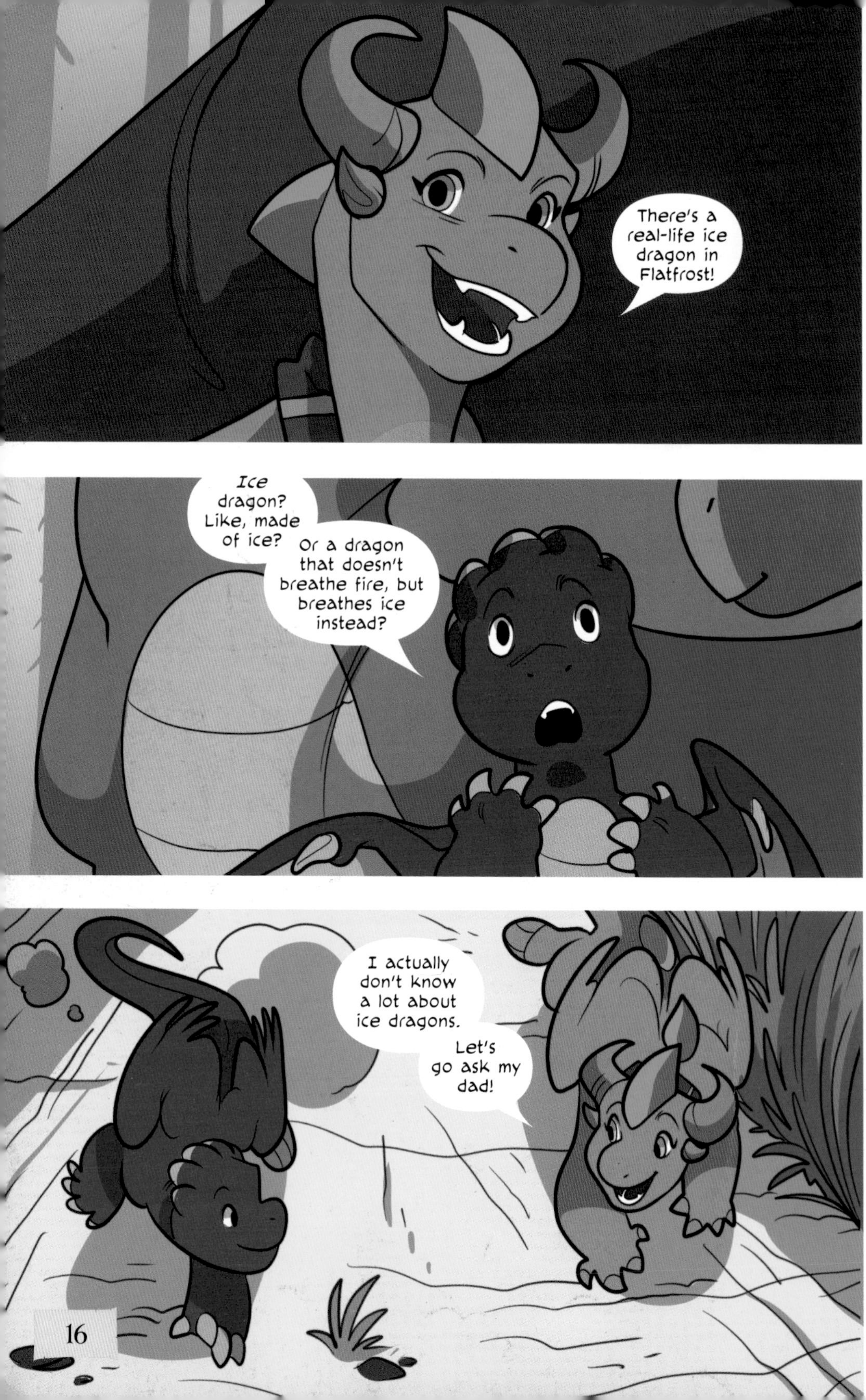
There's a real-life ice dragon in Flatfrost!
Ice dragon? Like, made of ice?
Or a dragon that doesn't breathe fire, but breathes ice instead?
I actually don't know a lot about ice dragons.
Let's go ask my dad!

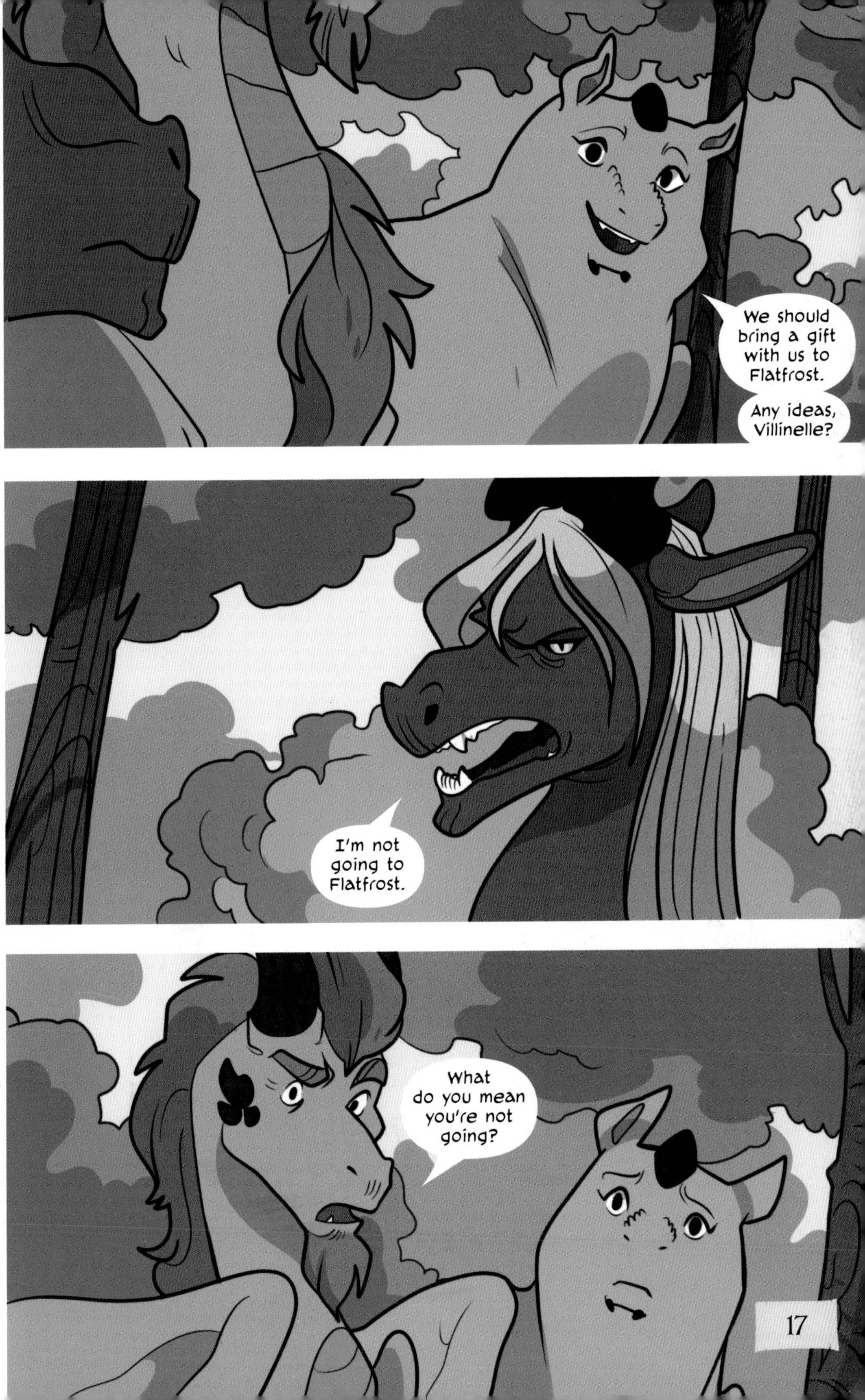
We should bring a gift with us to Flatfrost.
Any ideas, Villinelle?
I'm not going to Flatfrost.
What do you mean you're not going?

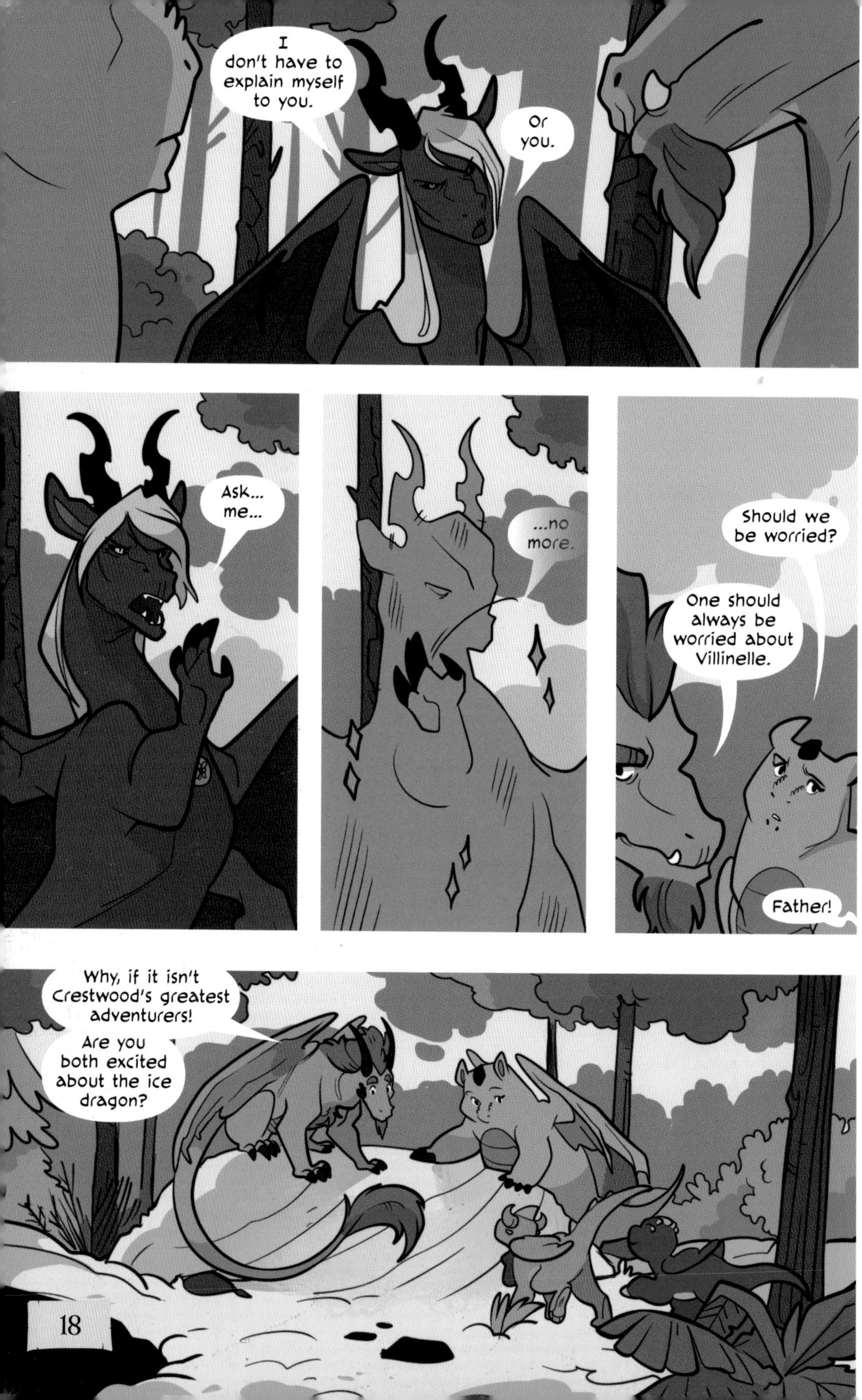
I don't have to explain myself to you.
Or you.
Ask... me...
...no more.
Should we be worried?
One should always be worried about Villinelle.
Father!
Why, if it isn't Crestwood's greatest adventurers!
Are you both excited about the ice dragon?

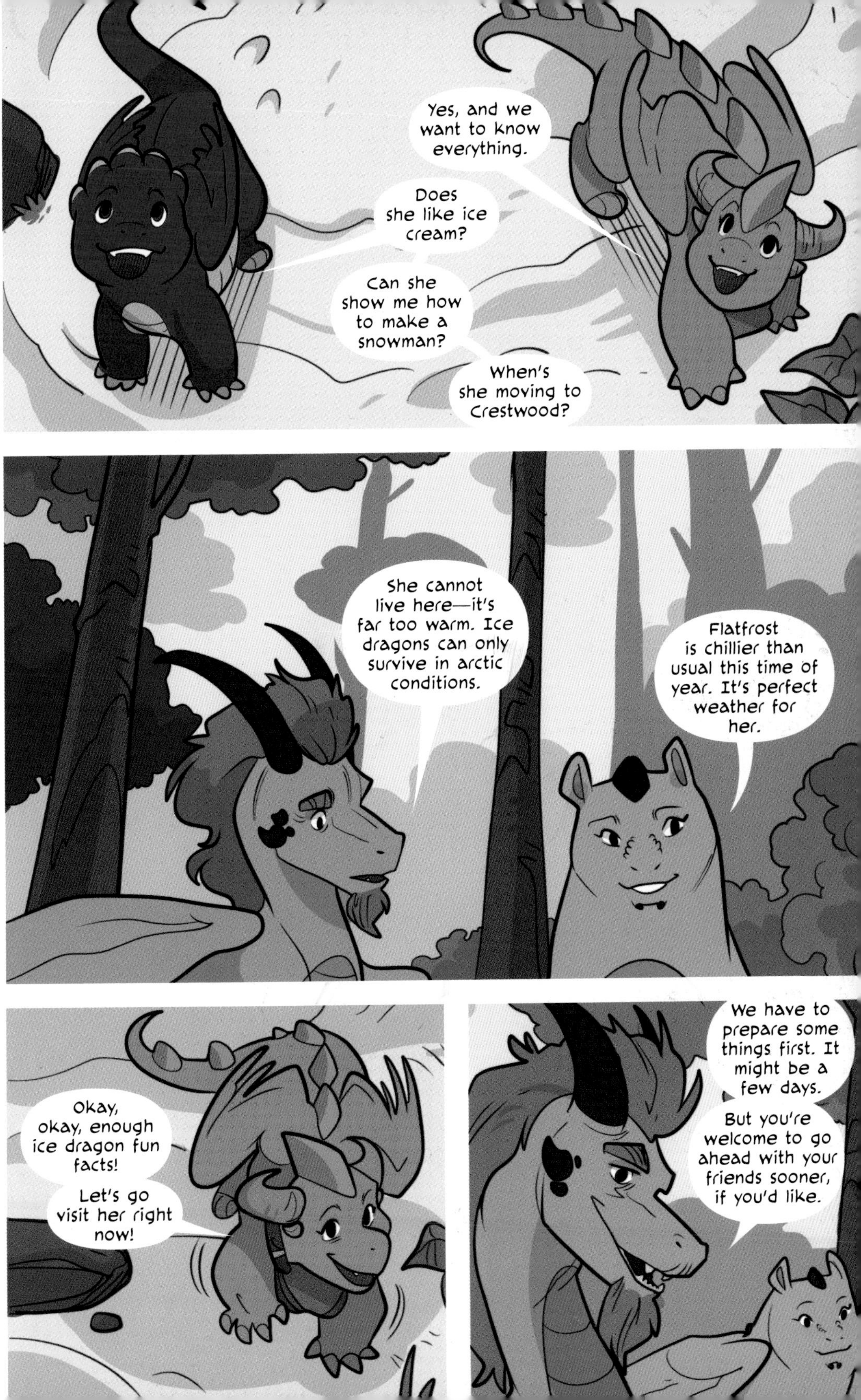
Yes, and we want to know everything.
Does she like ice cream?
Can she show me how to make a snowman?
When's she moving to Crestwood?
She cannot live here—it's far too warm. Ice dragons can only survive in arctic conditions.
Flatfrost is chillier than usual this time of year. It's perfect weather for her.
Okay, okay, enough ice dragon fun facts!
Let's go visit her right now!
We have to prepare some things first. It might be a few days.
But you're welcome to go ahead with your friends sooner, if you'd like.

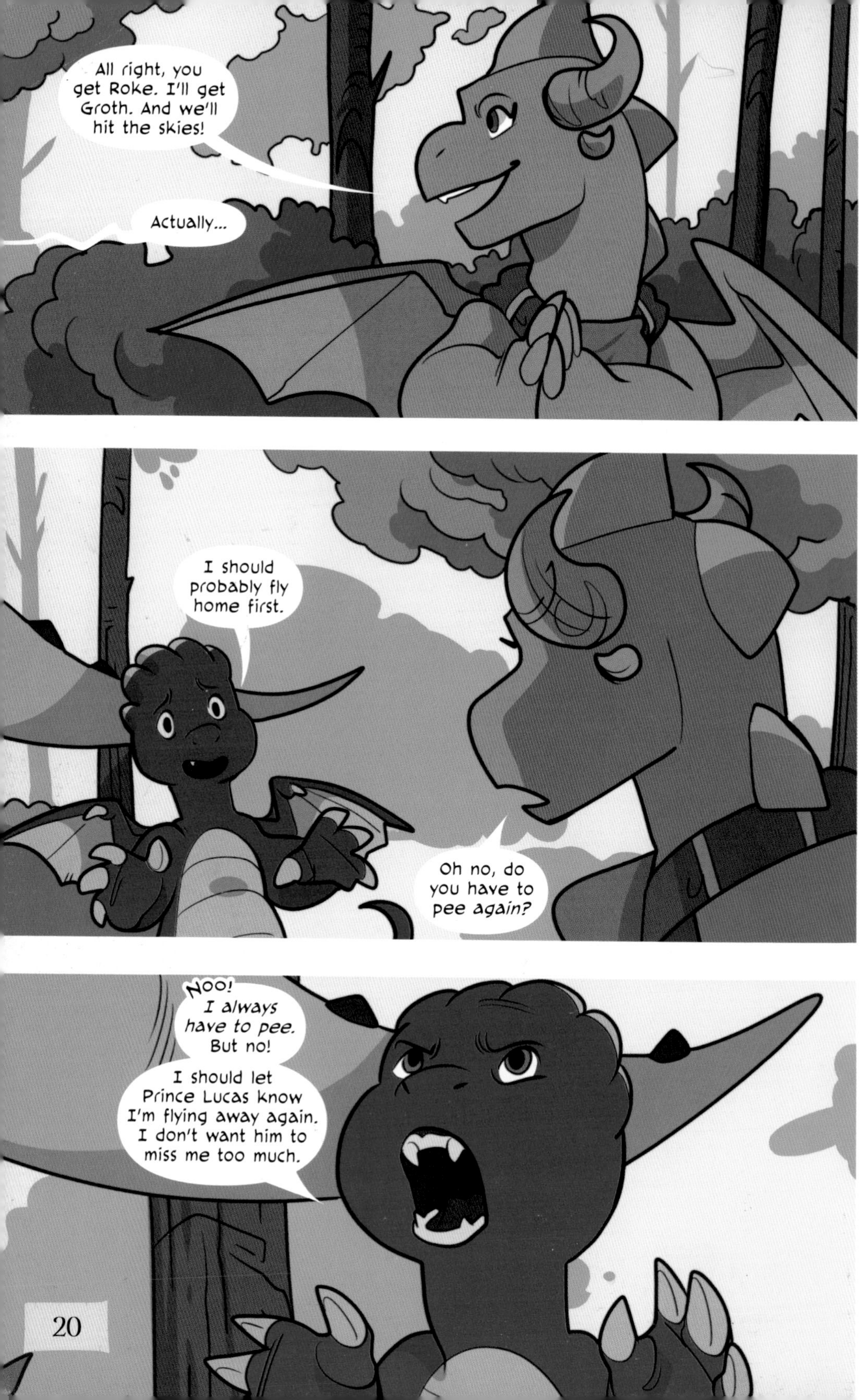
All right, you get Roke. I'll get Groth. And we'll hit the skies!
Actually...
I should probably fly home first.
Oh no, do you have to pee again?
NOO! *I always have to pee.* But no!
I should let Prince Lucas know I'm flying away again. I don't want him to miss me too much.

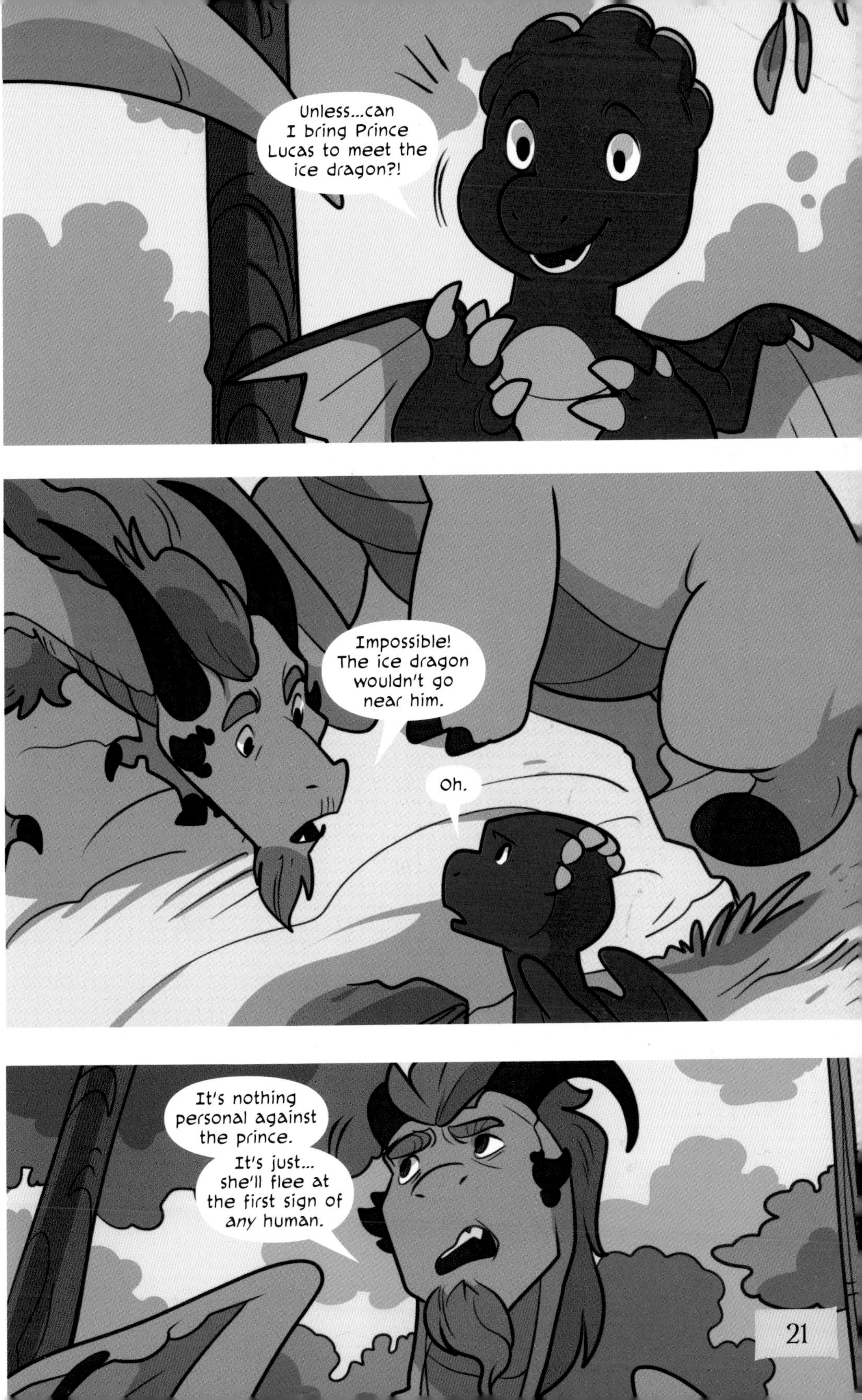
Unless...can I bring Prince Lucas to meet the ice dragon?!
Impossible! The ice dragon wouldn't go near him.
Oh.
It's nothing personal against the prince.
It's just... she'll flee at the first sign of *any* human.

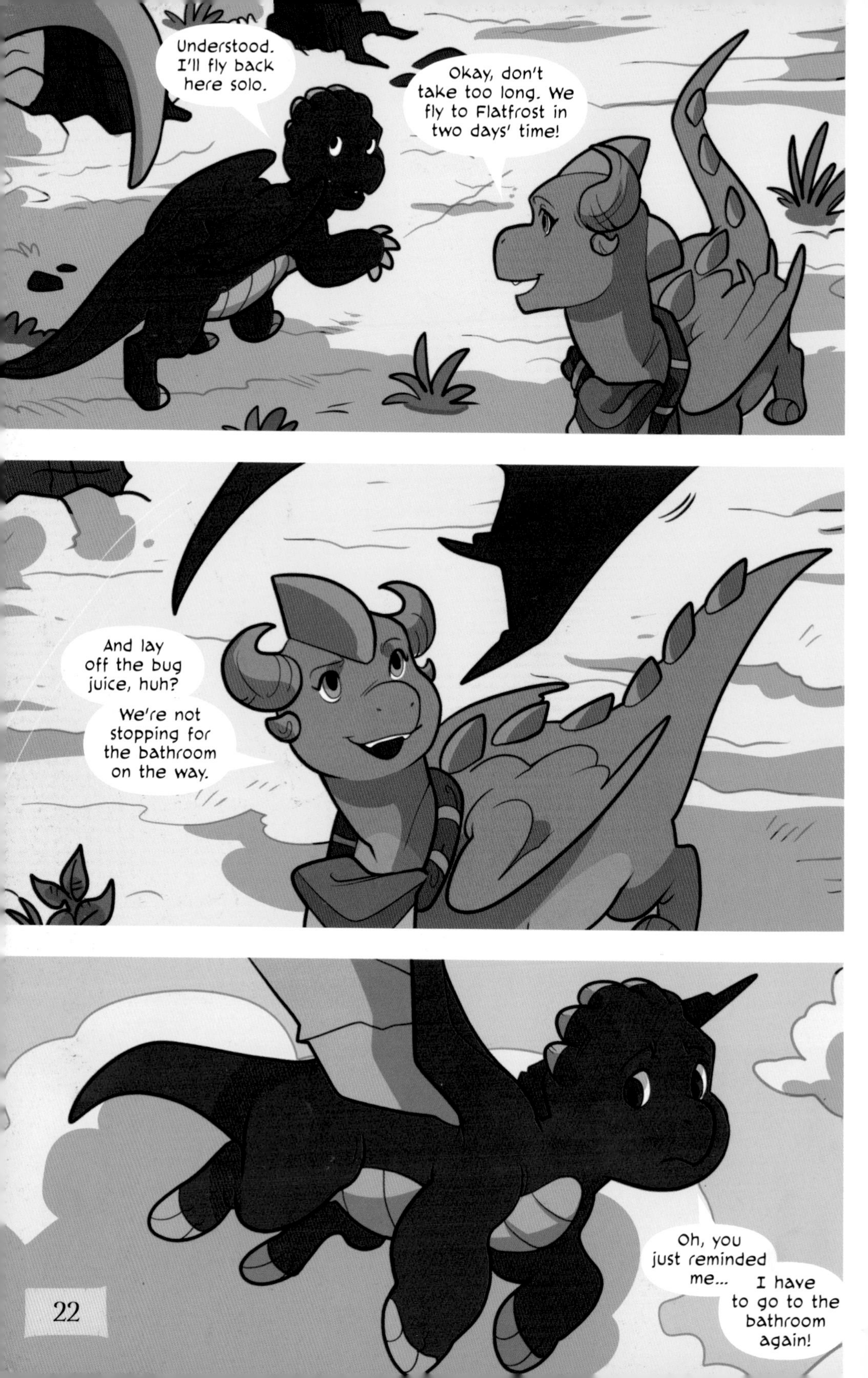
Understood. I'll fly back here solo.
Okay, don't take too long. We fly to Flatfrost in two days' time!
And lay off the bug juice, huh?
We're not stopping for the bathroom on the way.
Oh, you just reminded me...
I have to go to the bathroom again!

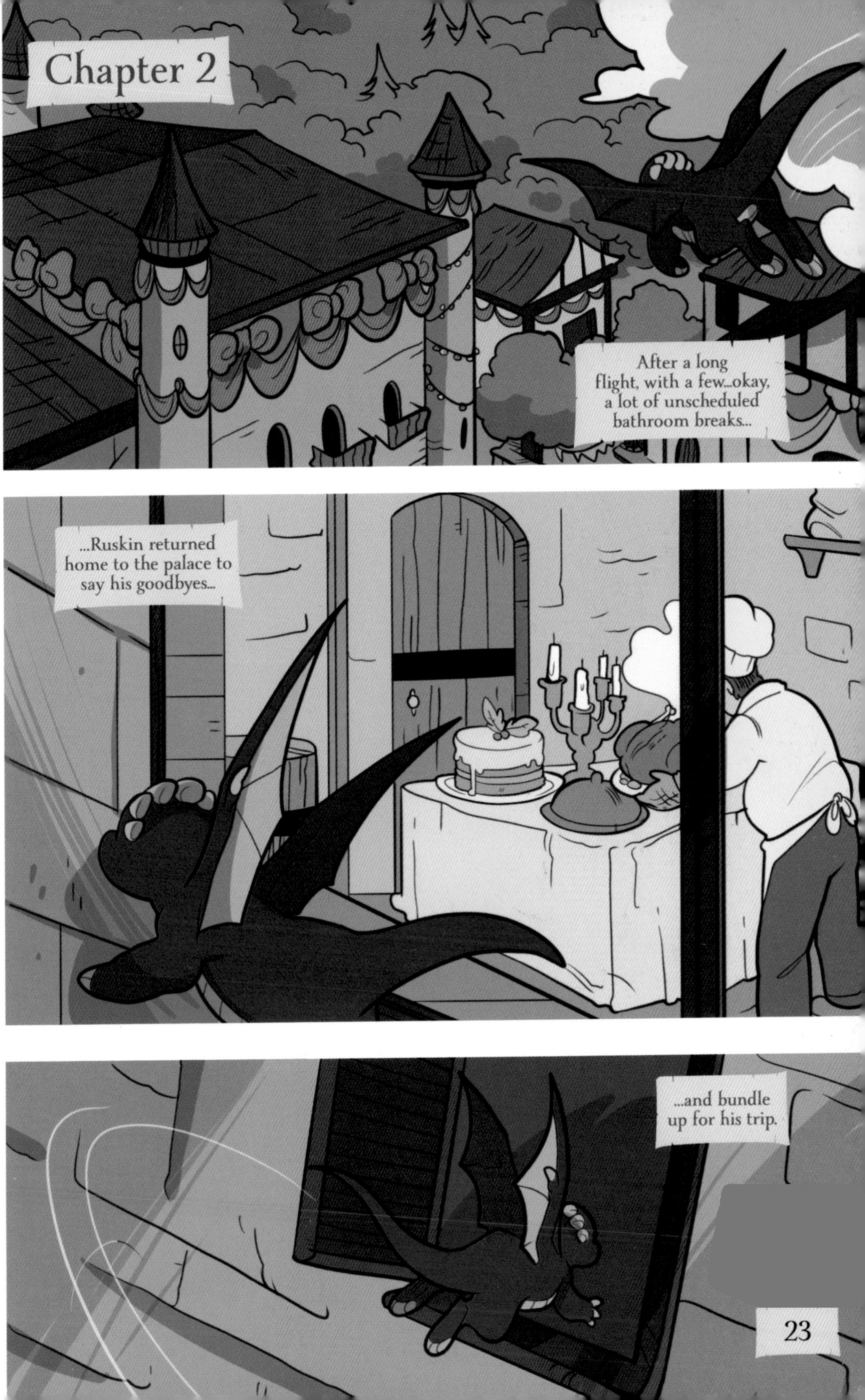
Chapter 2
After a long flight, with a few...okay, a lot of unscheduled bathroom breaks...
...Ruskin returned home to the palace to say his goodbyes...
...and bundle up for his trip.

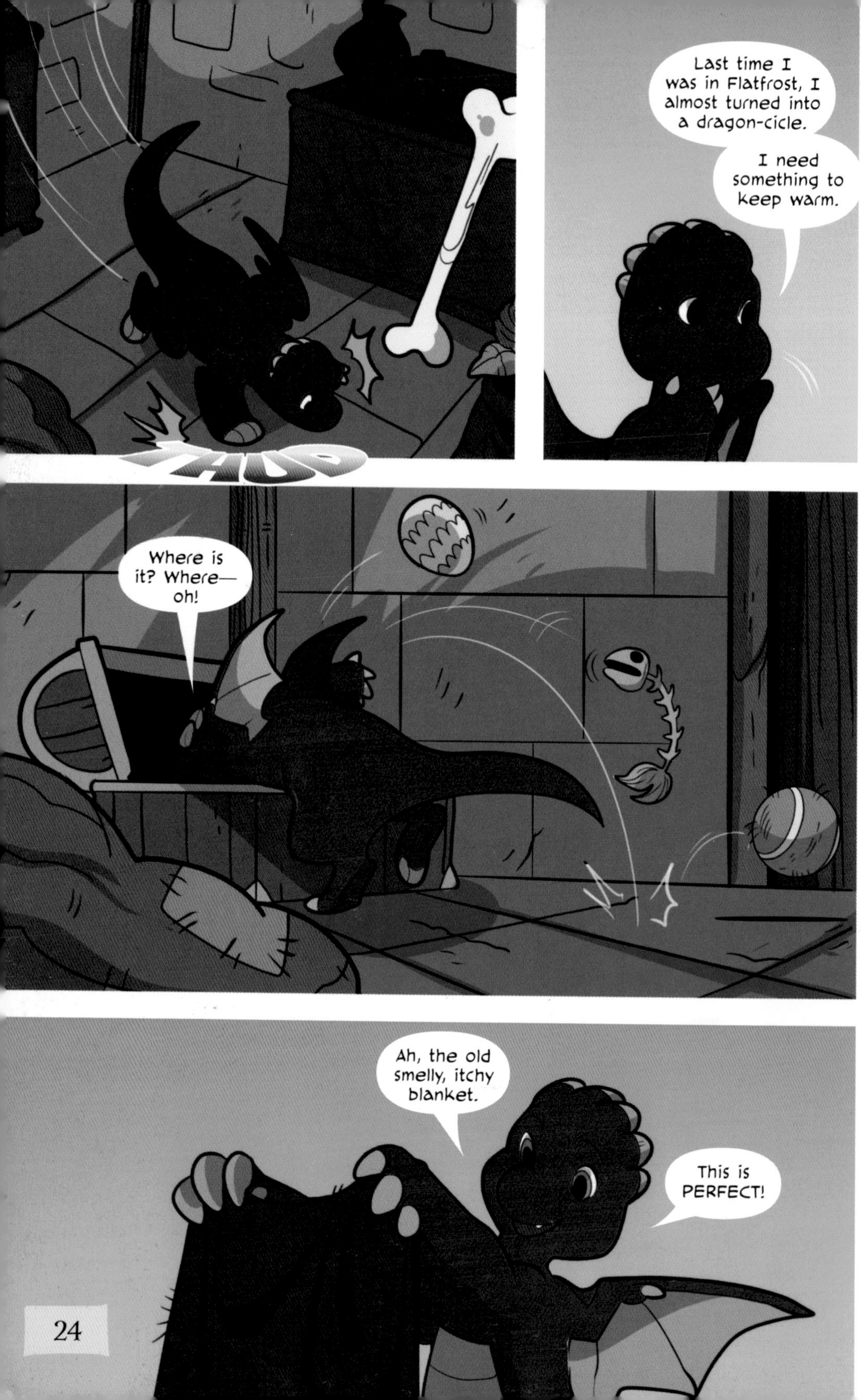
THUD
Last time I was in Flatfrost, I almost turned into a dragon-cicle.
I need something to keep warm.
Where is it? Where—oh!
Ah, the old smelly, itchy blanket.
This is PERFECT!

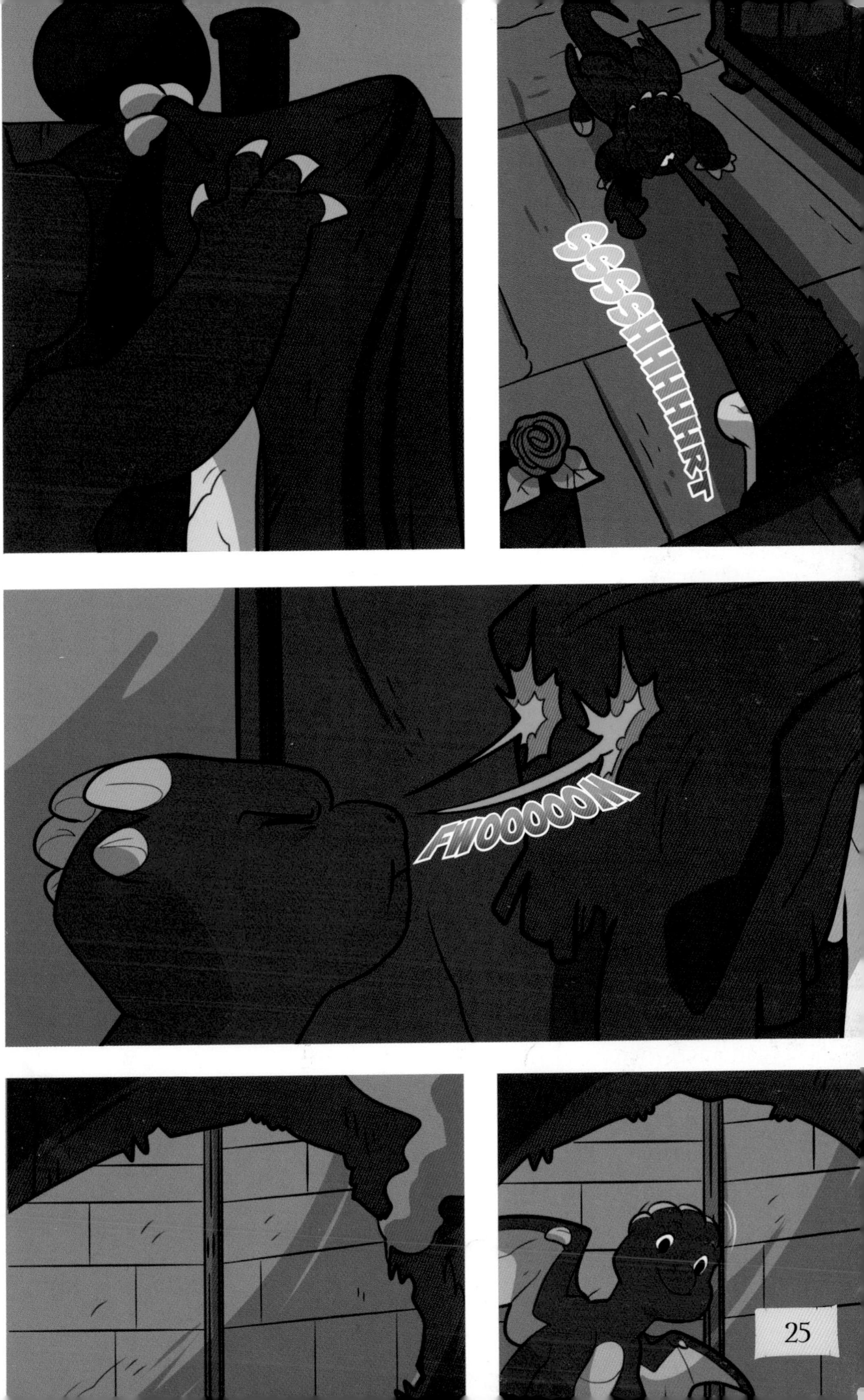
SSSSHHHHHRT
FWOOOOOW

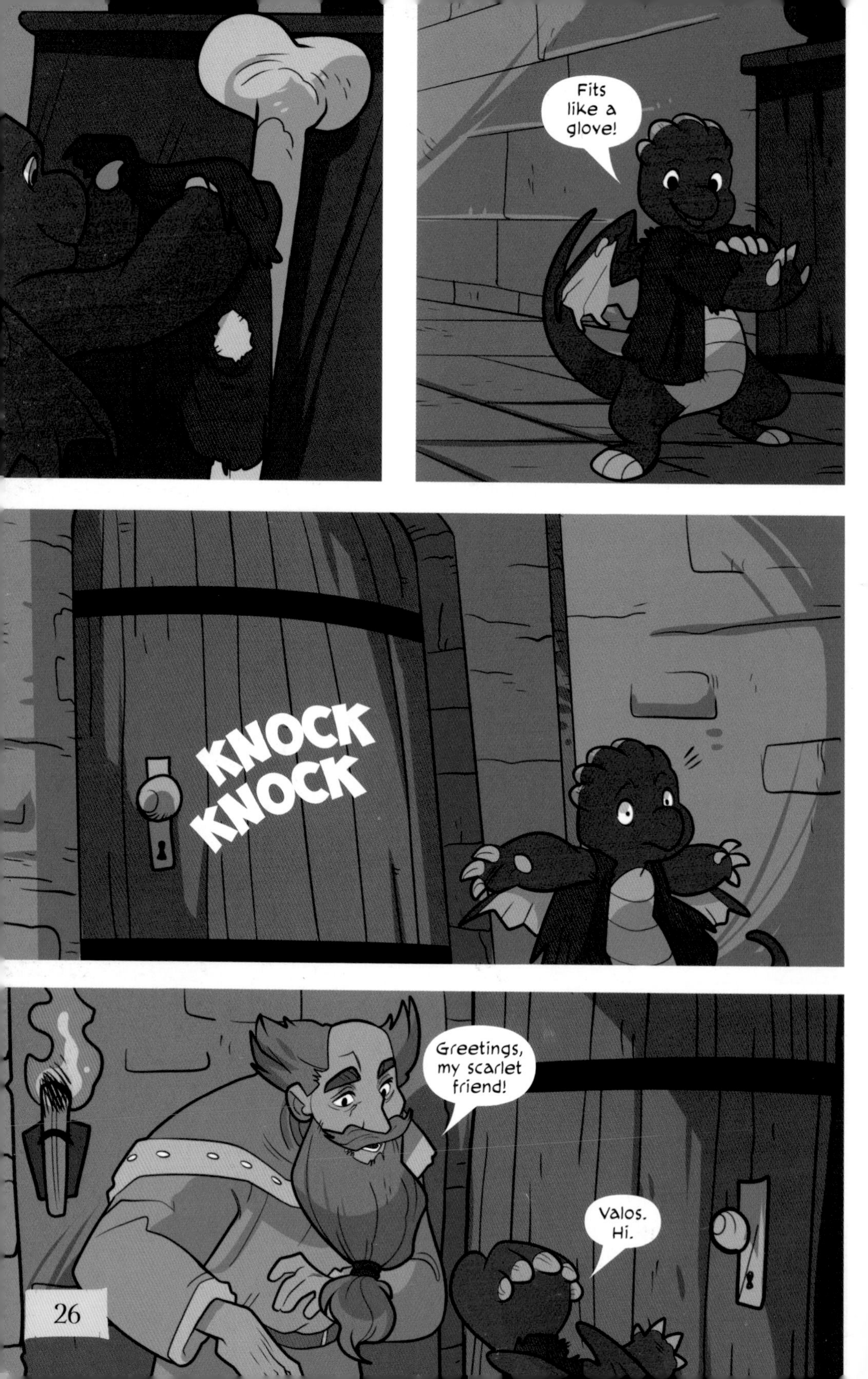
Fits like a glove!
KNOCK KNOCK
Greetings, my scarlet friend!
Valos. Hi.

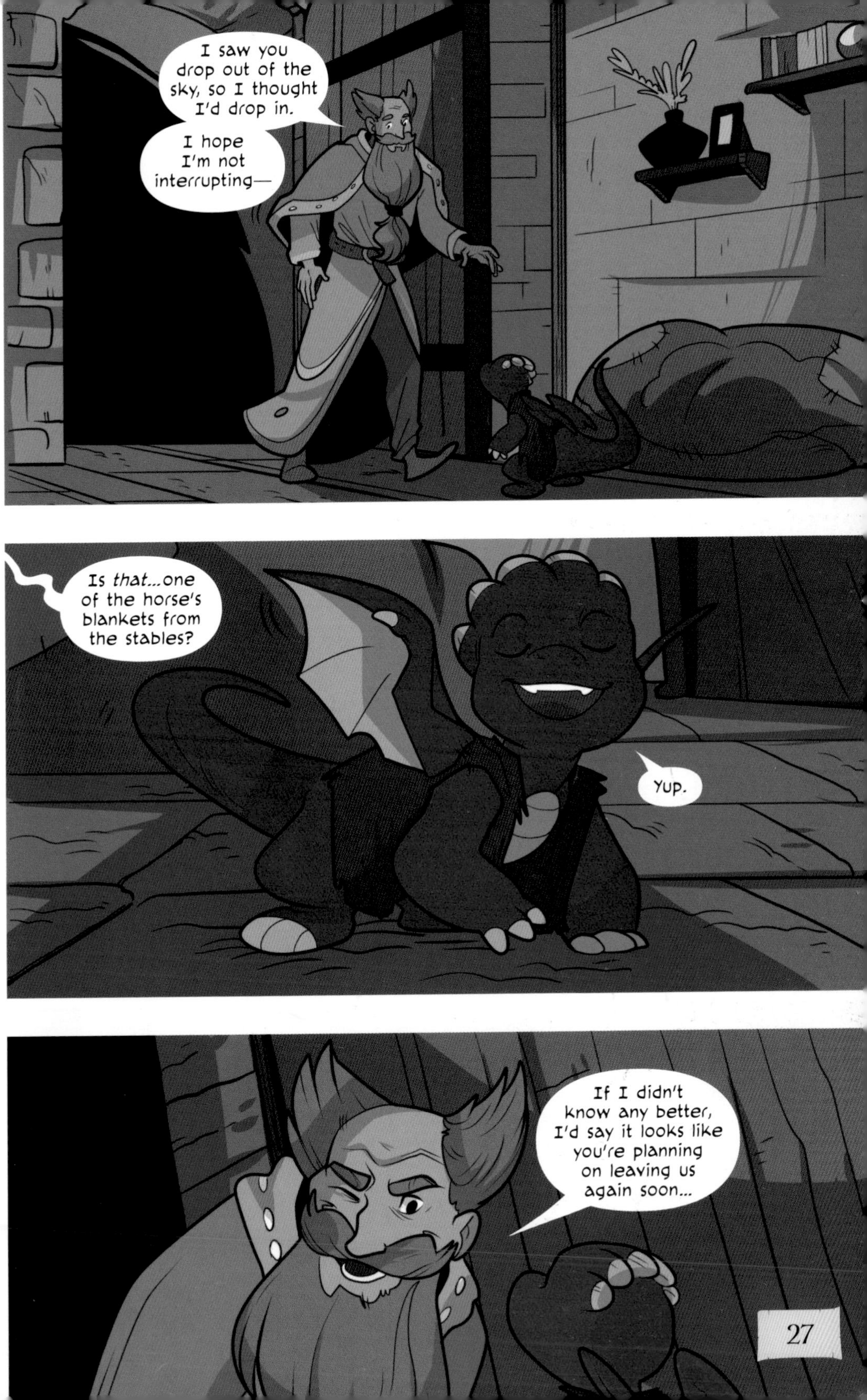
I saw you drop out of the sky, so I thought I'd drop in.
I hope I'm not interrupting—
Is *that*...one of the horse's blankets from the stables?
Yup.
If I didn't know any better, I'd say it looks like you're planning on leaving us again soon...

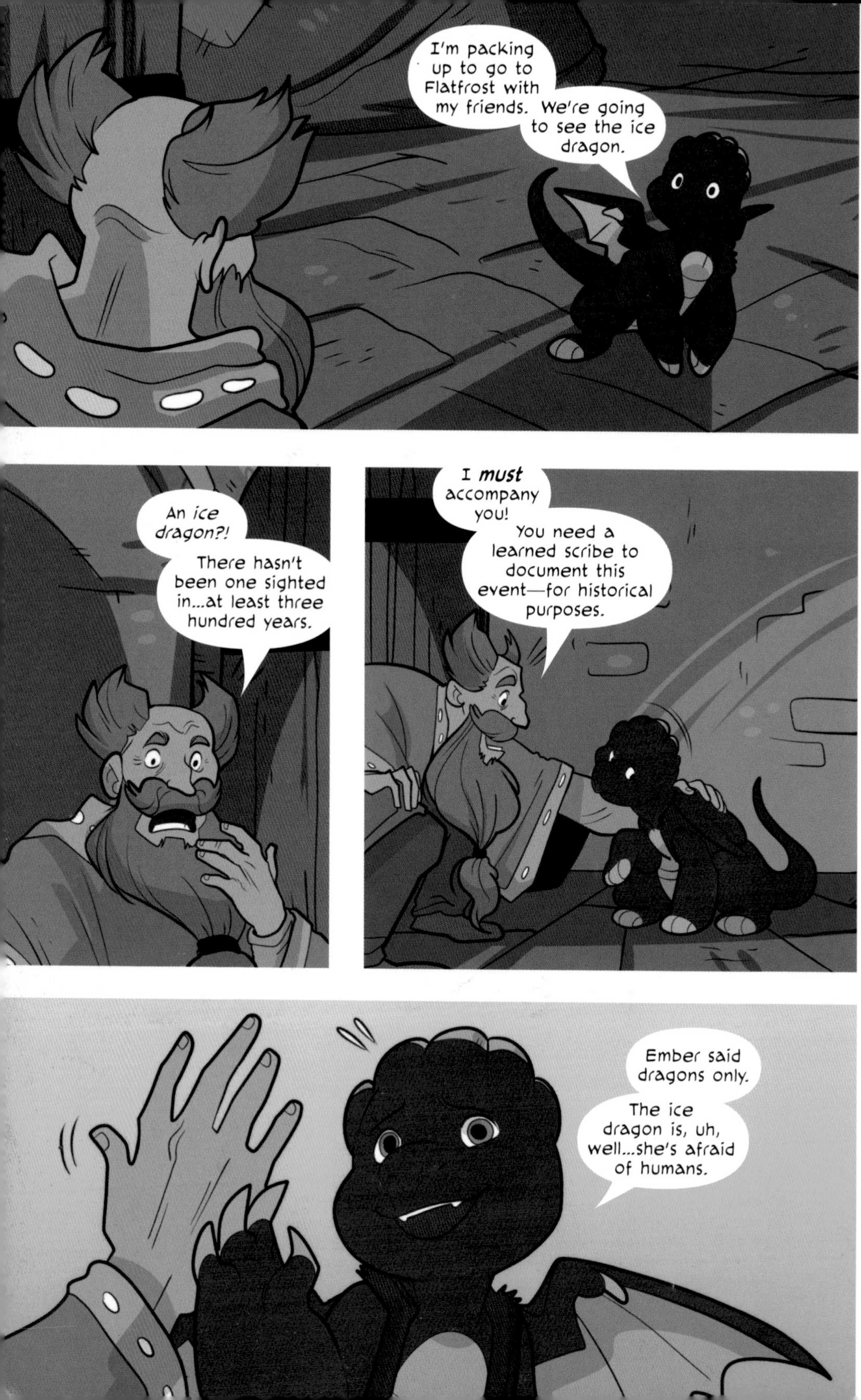
I'm packing up to go to Flatfrost with my friends.
We're going to see the ice dragon.
An *ice dragon?!*
There hasn't been one sighted in...at least three hundred years.
I ***must*** accompany you!
You need a learned scribe to document this event—for historical purposes.
Ember said dragons only.
The ice dragon is, uh, well...she's afraid of humans.

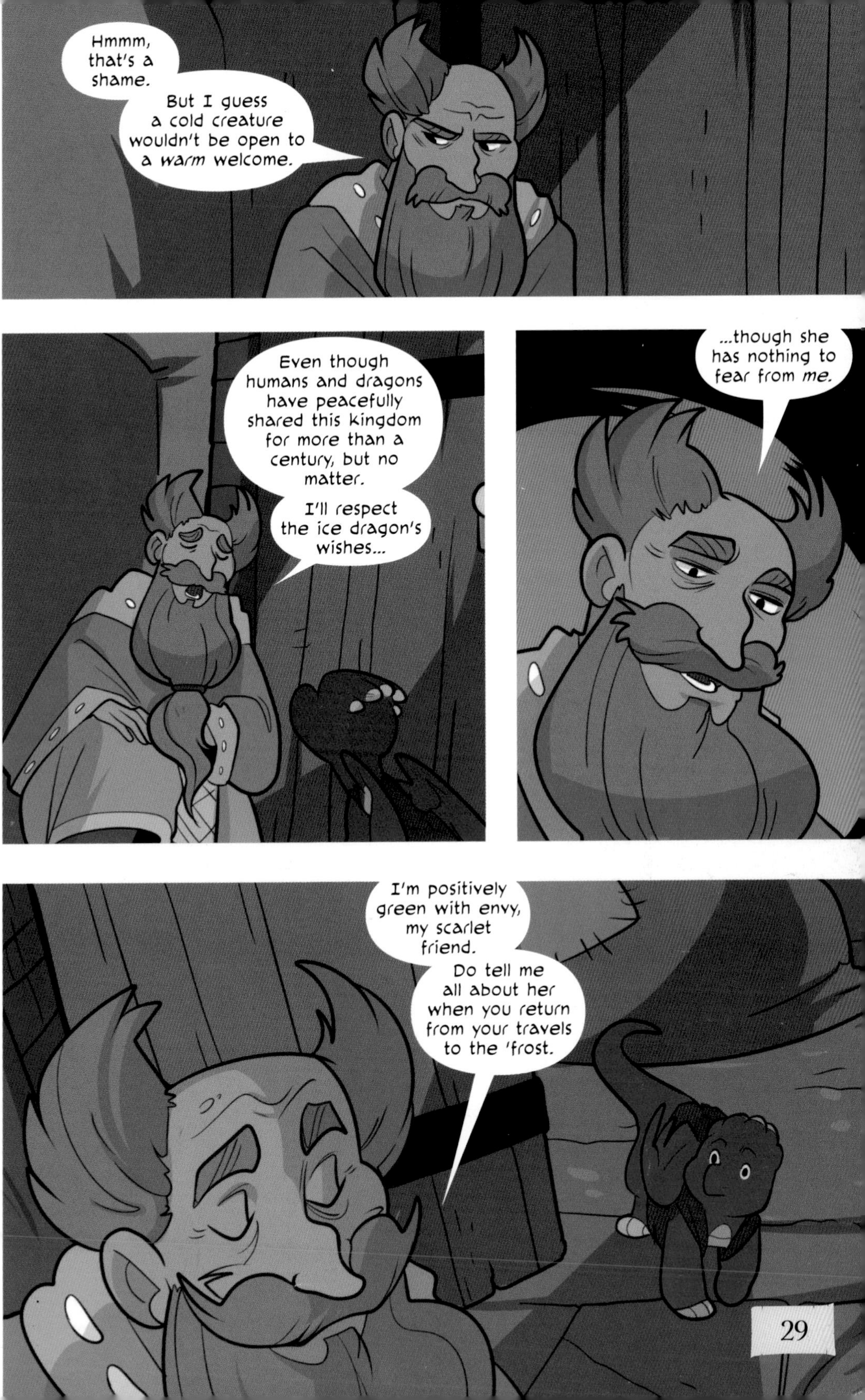
Hmmm, that's a shame.
But I guess a cold creature wouldn't be open to a *warm* welcome.
Even though humans and dragons have peacefully shared this kingdom for more than a century, but no matter.
I'll respect the ice dragon's wishes...
...though she has nothing to fear from *me.*
I'm positively green with envy, my scarlet friend.
Do tell me all about her when you return from your travels to the 'frost.

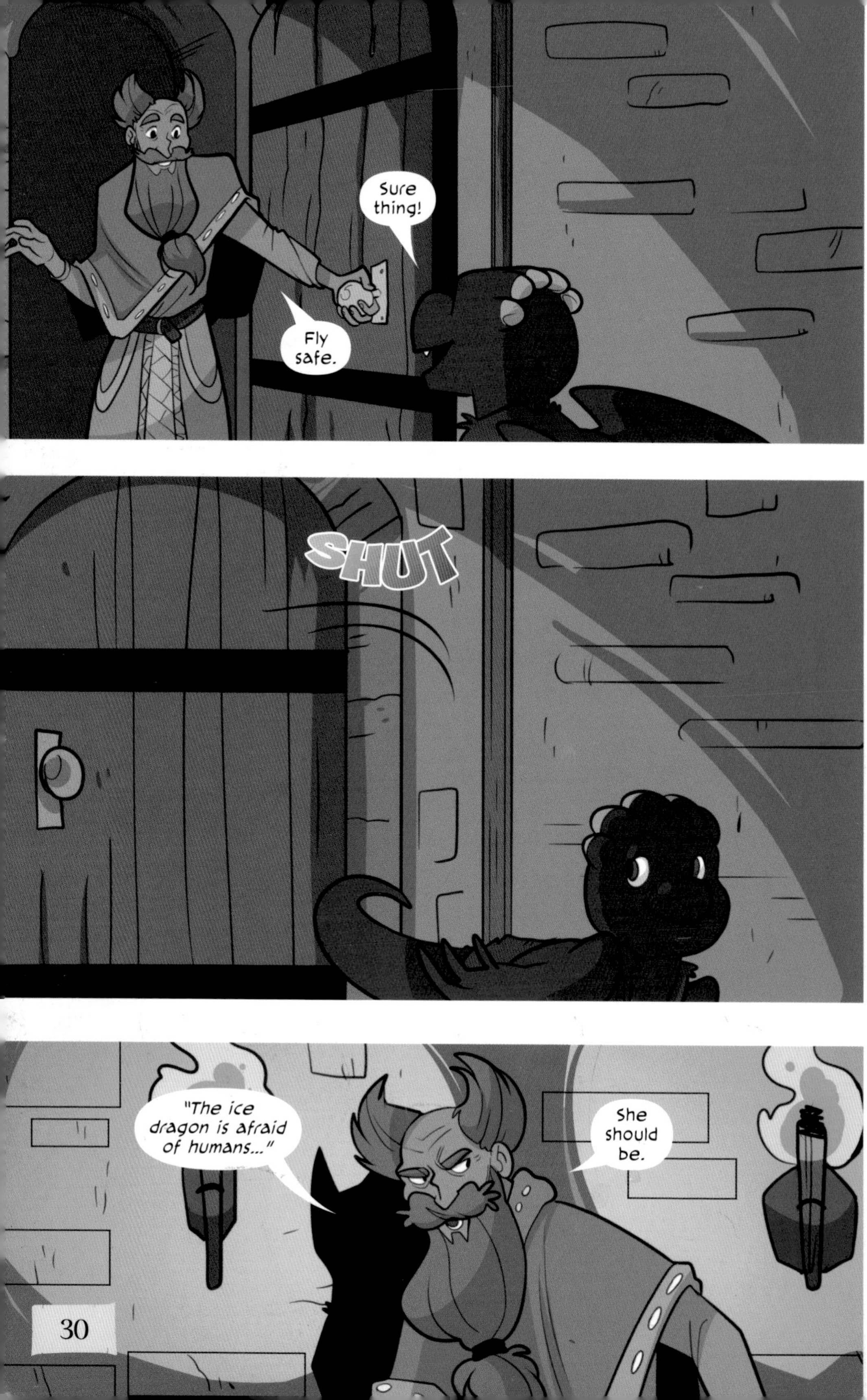
Sure thing!
Fly safe.
SHUT
"The ice dragon is afraid of humans..."
She should be.

Moments later, in the royal library...

...past the history books and fables and ancient scrolls...

...was a secret book in a magic safe.

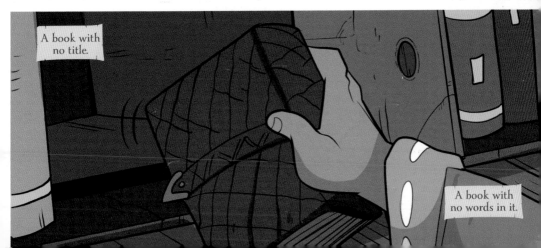

A book with no title.

A book with no words in it.

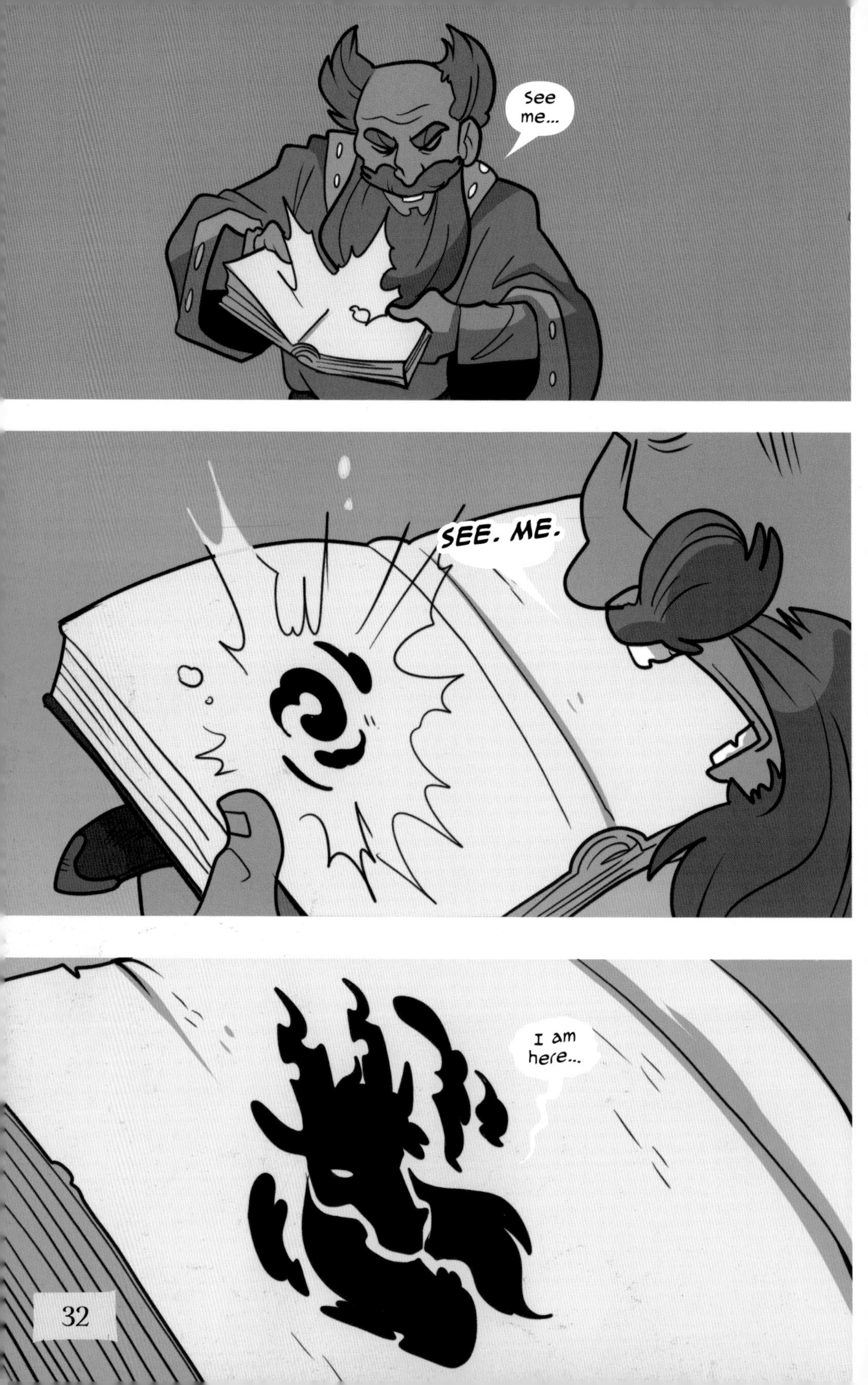
See me...
SEE. ME.
I am here...

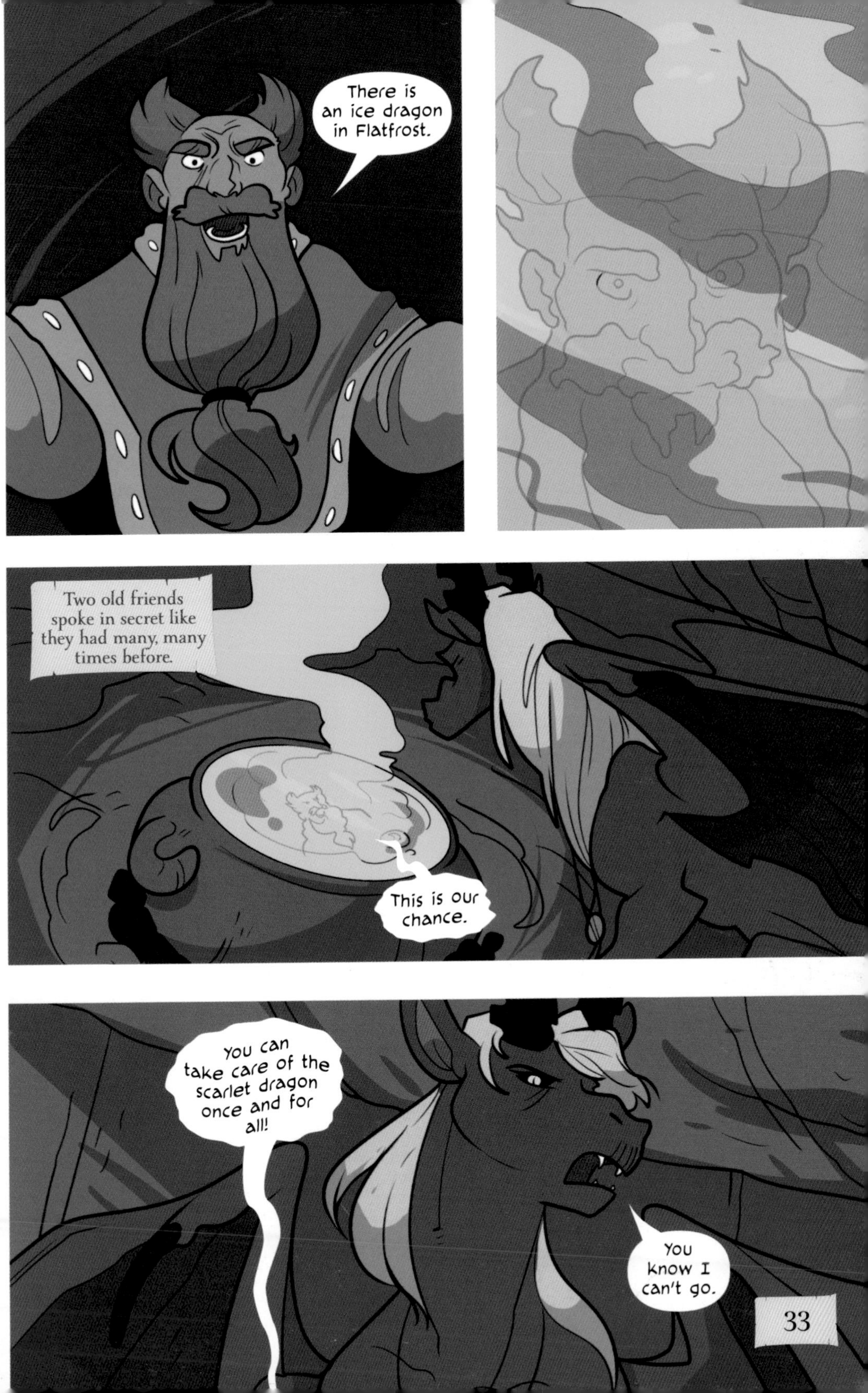
There is an ice dragon in Flatfrost.
Two old friends spoke in secret like they had many, many times before.
This is our chance.
You can take care of the scarlet dragon once and for all!
You know I can't go.

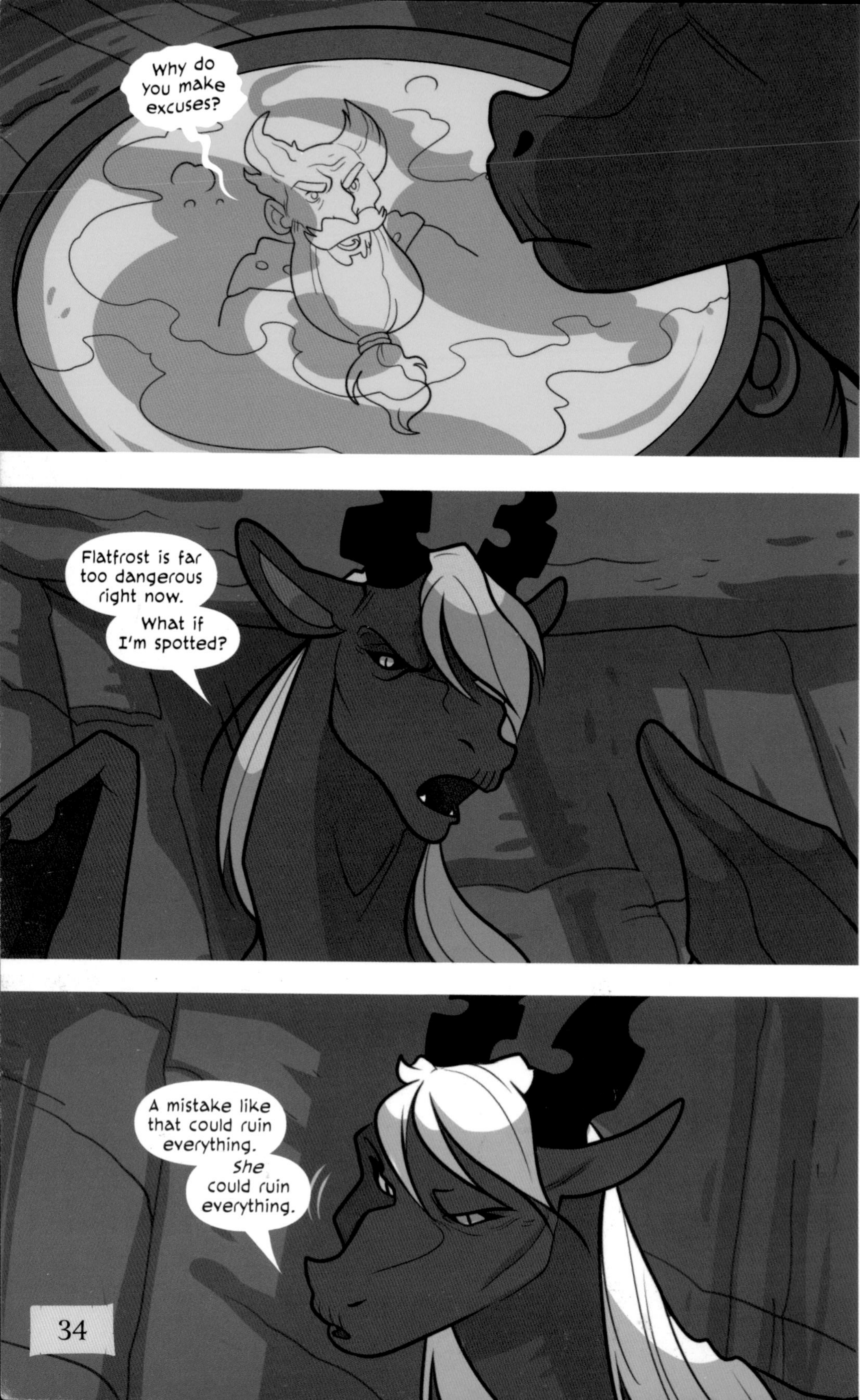
Why do you make excuses?
Flatfrost is far too dangerous right now.
What if I'm spotted?
A mistake like that could ruin everything.
She could ruin everything.

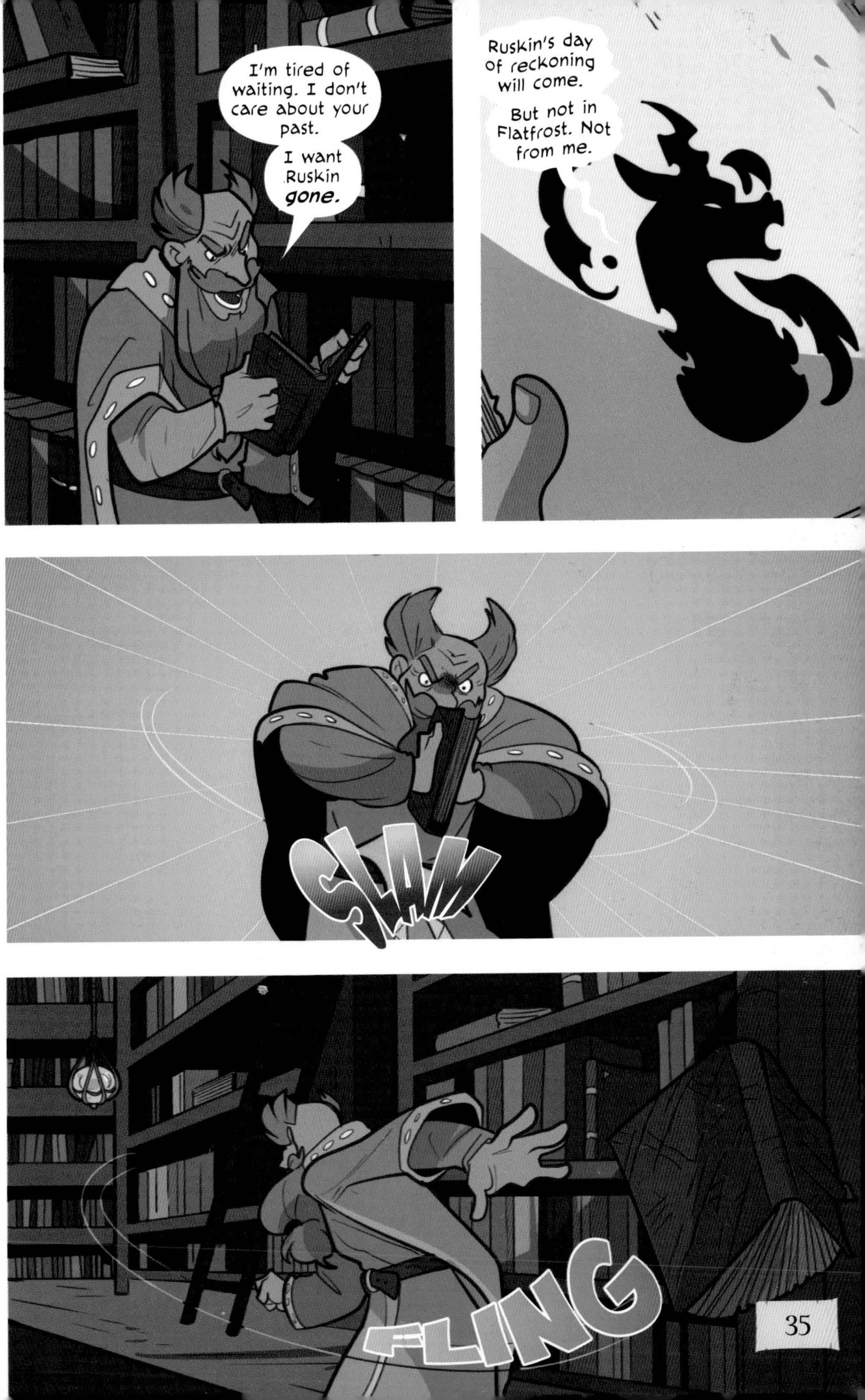
I'm tired of waiting. I don't care about your past.
I want Ruskin *gone.*
Ruskin's day of reckoning will come.
But not in Flatfrost. Not from me.
SLAM
FLING

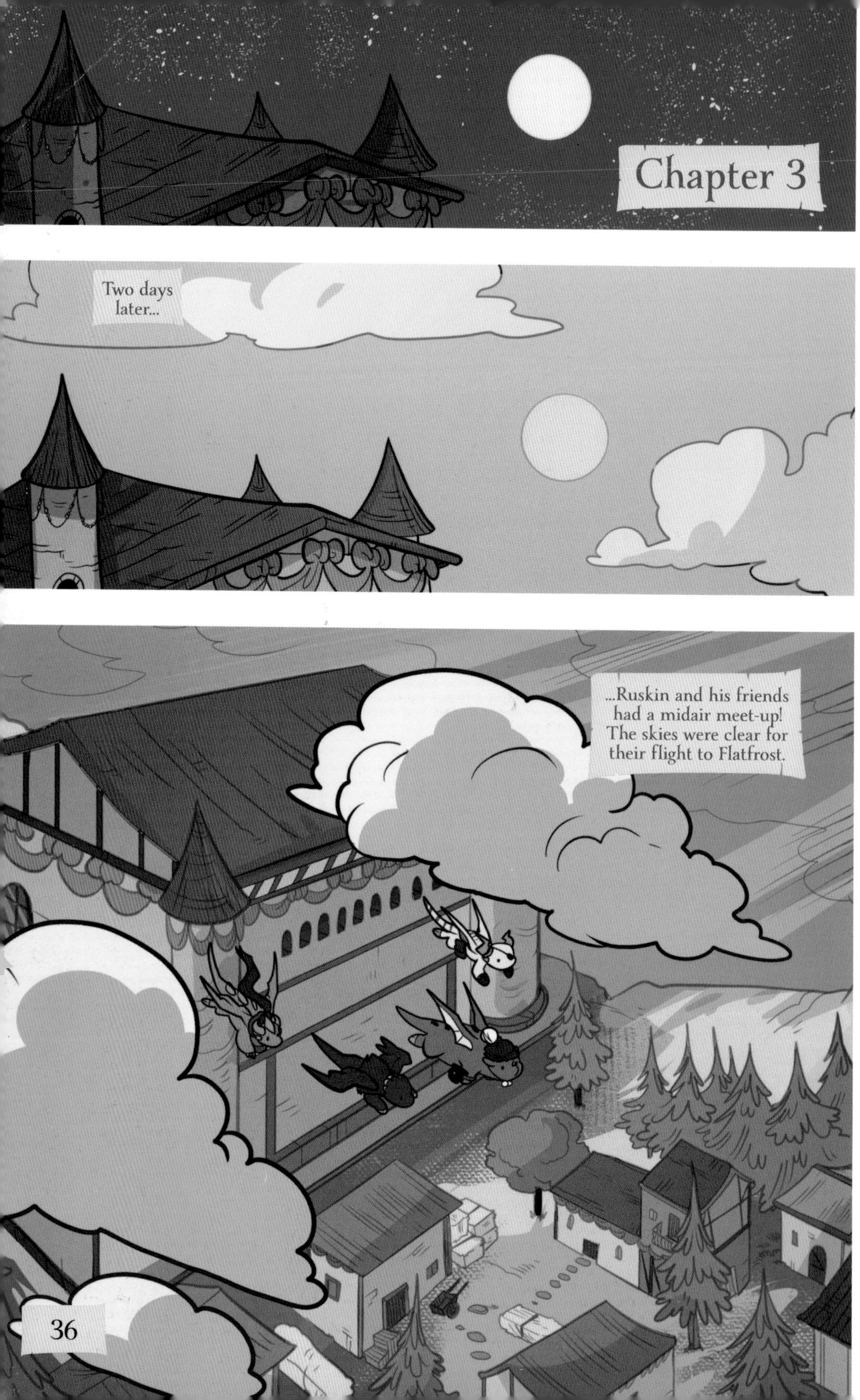
Chapter 3
Two days later...
...Ruskin and his friends had a midair meet-up! The skies were clear for their flight to Flatfrost.

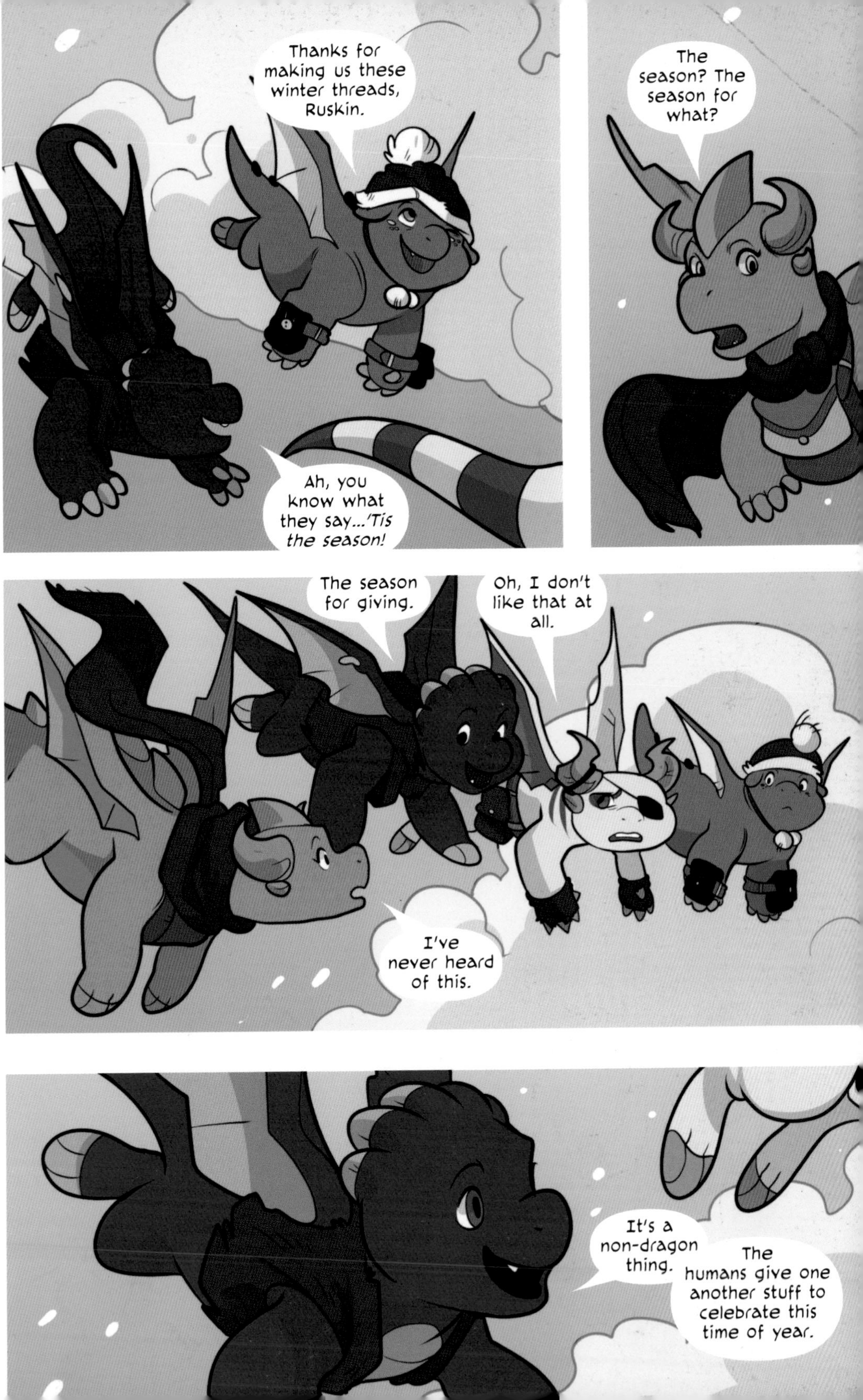

Thanks for making us these winter threads, Ruskin.
Ah, you know what they say...*'Tis the season!*
The season? The season for what?
The season for giving.
Oh, I don't like that at all.
I've never heard of this.
It's a non-dragon thing.
The humans give one another stuff to celebrate this time of year.

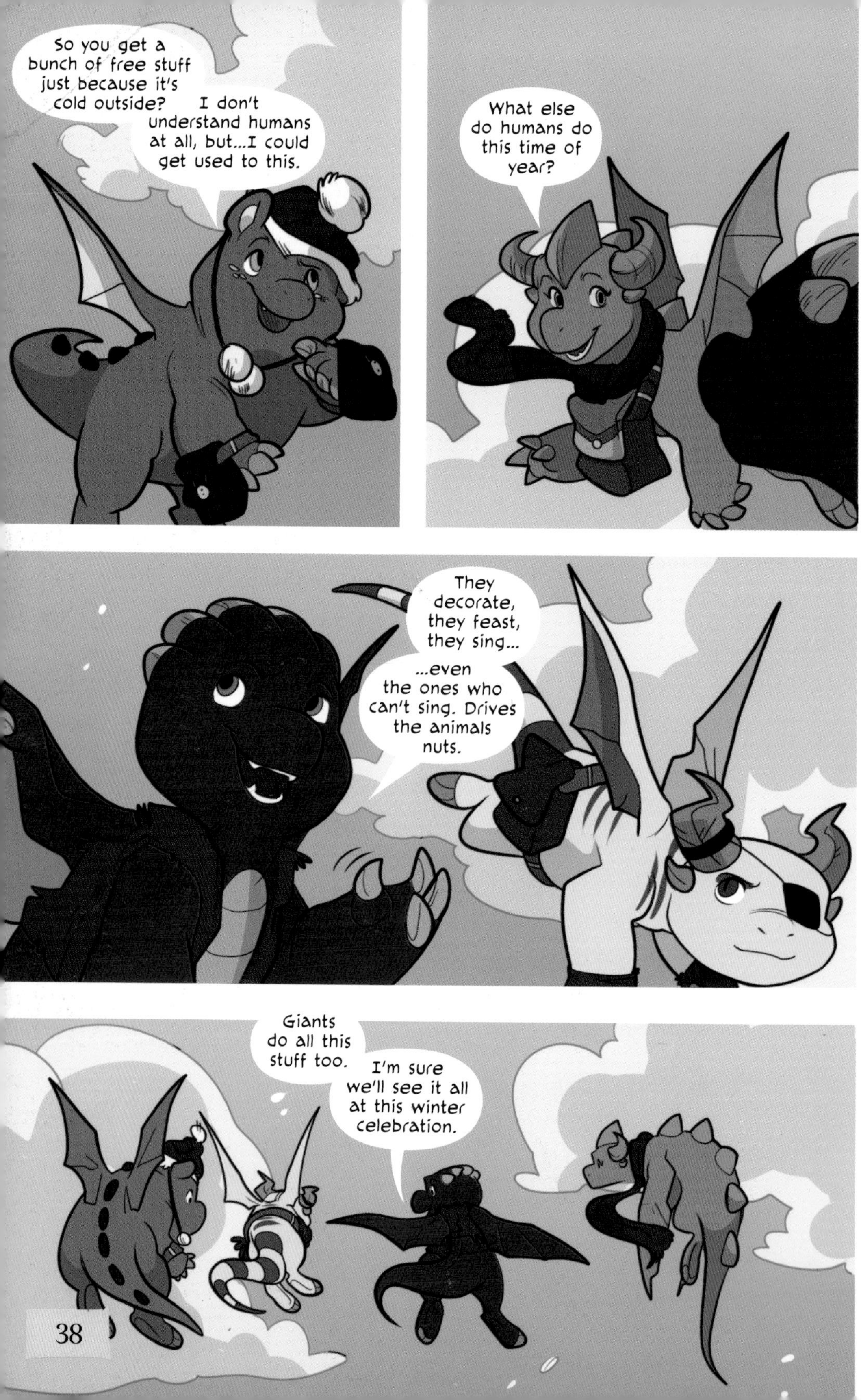
So you get a bunch of free stuff just because it's cold outside?
I don't understand humans at all, but...I could get used to this.
What else do humans do this time of year?
They decorate, they feast, they sing...
...even the ones who can't sing. Drives the animals nuts.
Giants do all this stuff too.
I'm sure we'll see it all at this winter celebration.

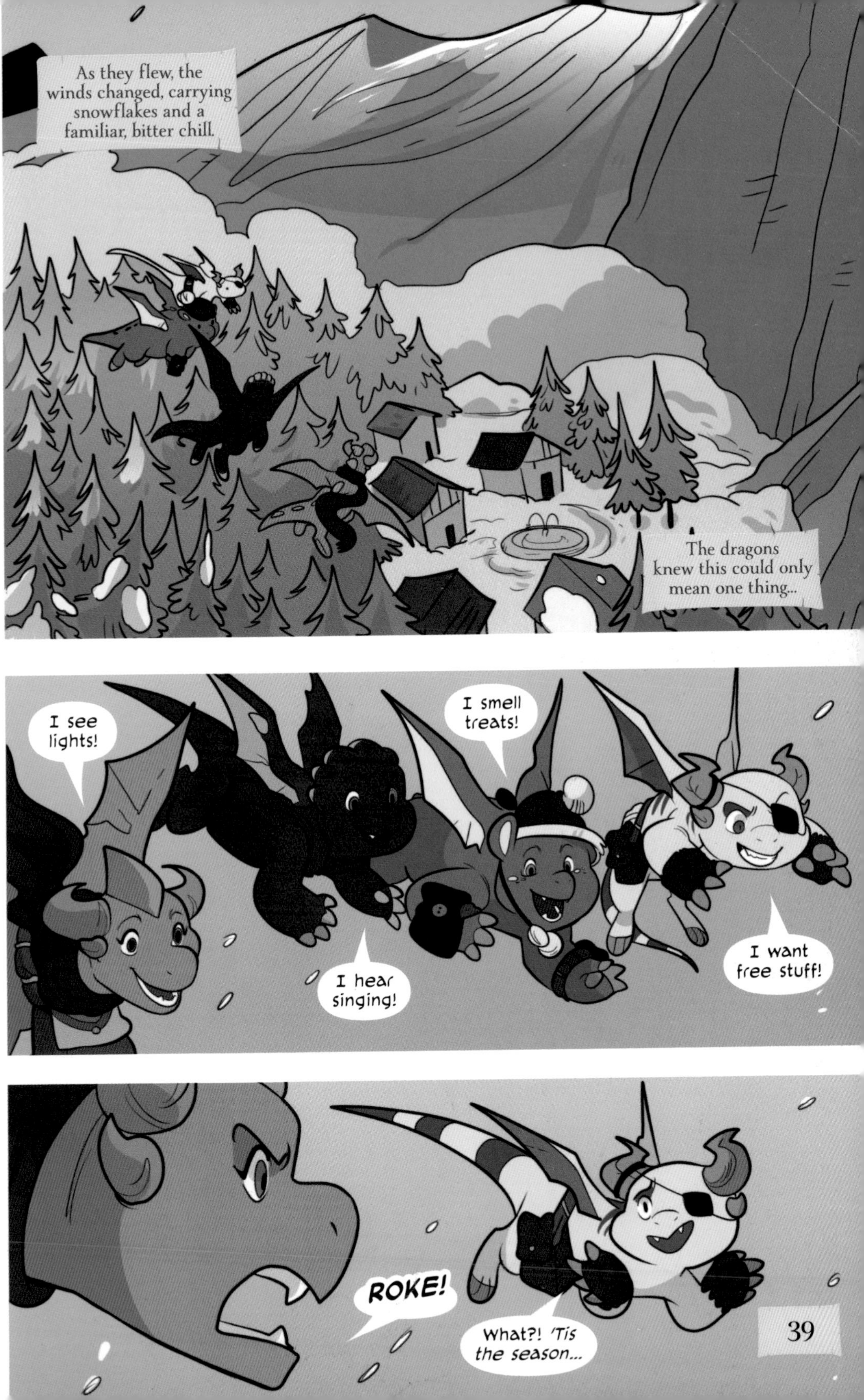

As they flew, the winds changed, carrying snowflakes and a familiar, bitter chill.
The dragons knew this could only mean one thing...
I see lights!
I smell treats!
I hear singing!
I want free stuff!
ROKE!
What?! 'Tis the season...

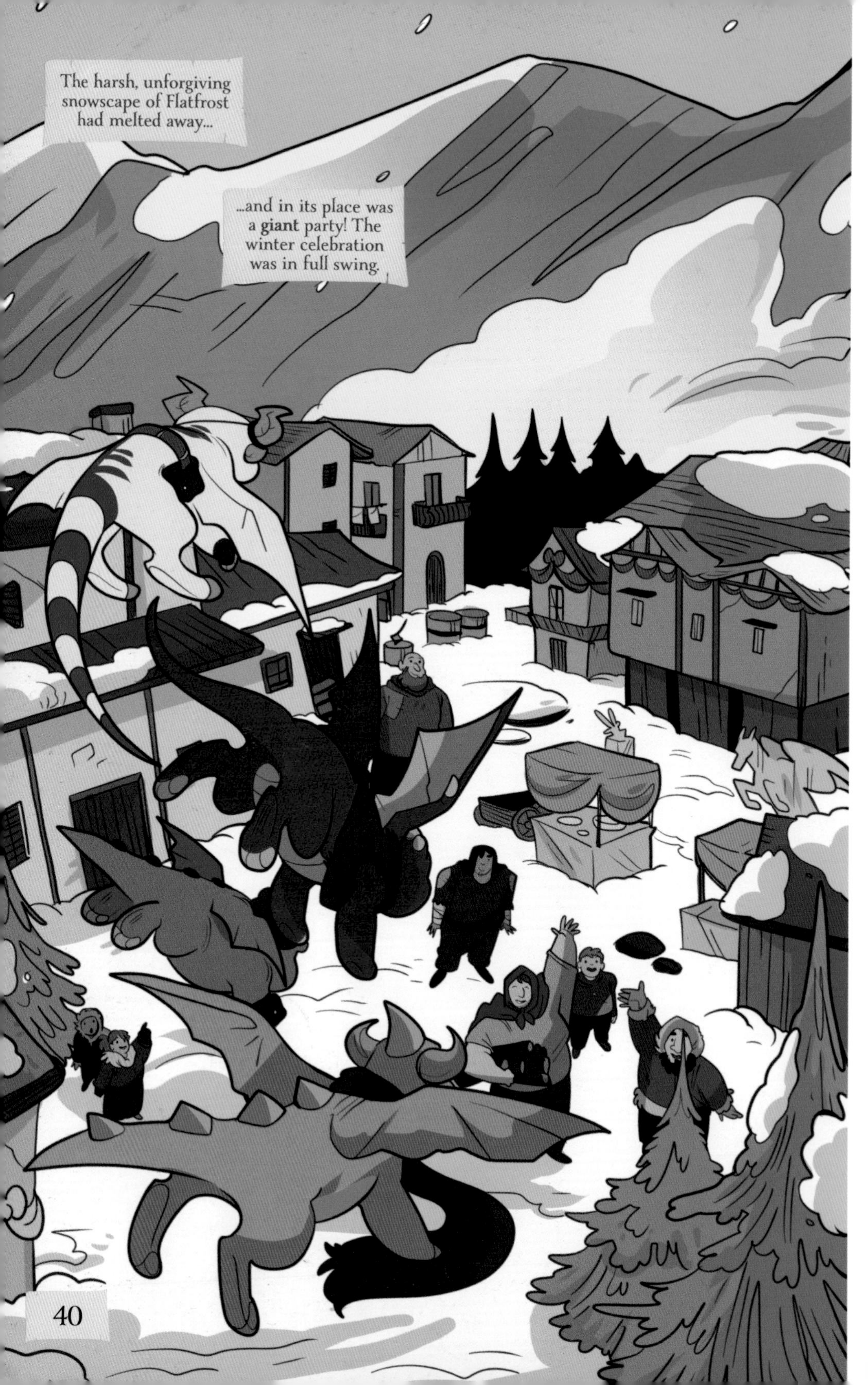
The harsh, unforgiving snowscape of Flatfrost had melted away...
...and in its place was a **giant** party! The winter celebration was in full swing.

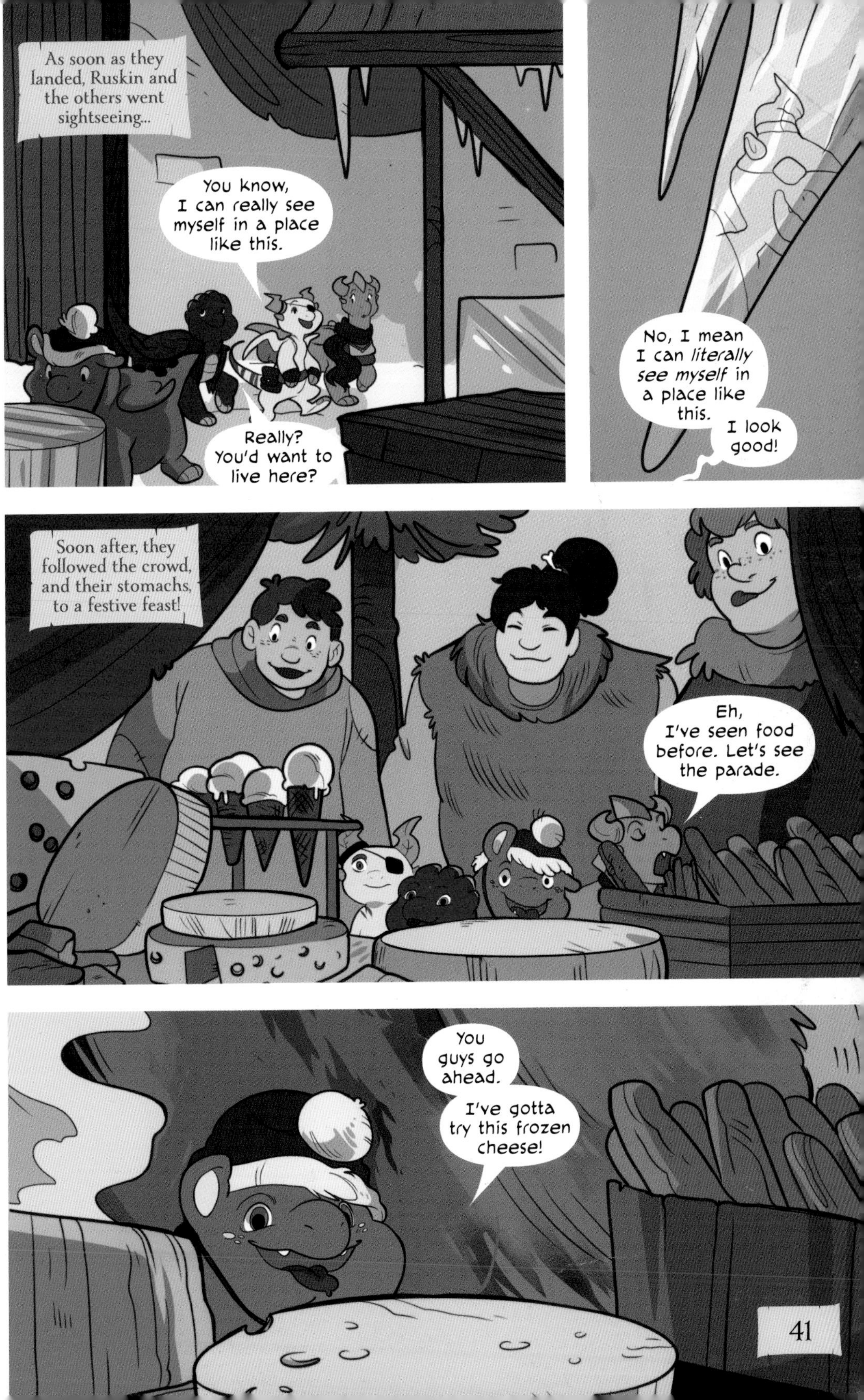
As soon as they landed, Ruskin and the others went sightseeing...
You know, I can really see myself in a place like this.
Really? You'd want to live here?
No, I mean I can *literally see myself* in a place like this.
I look good!
Soon after, they followed the crowd, and their stomachs, to a festive feast!
Eh, I've seen food before. Let's see the parade.
You guys go ahead.
I've gotta try this frozen cheese!

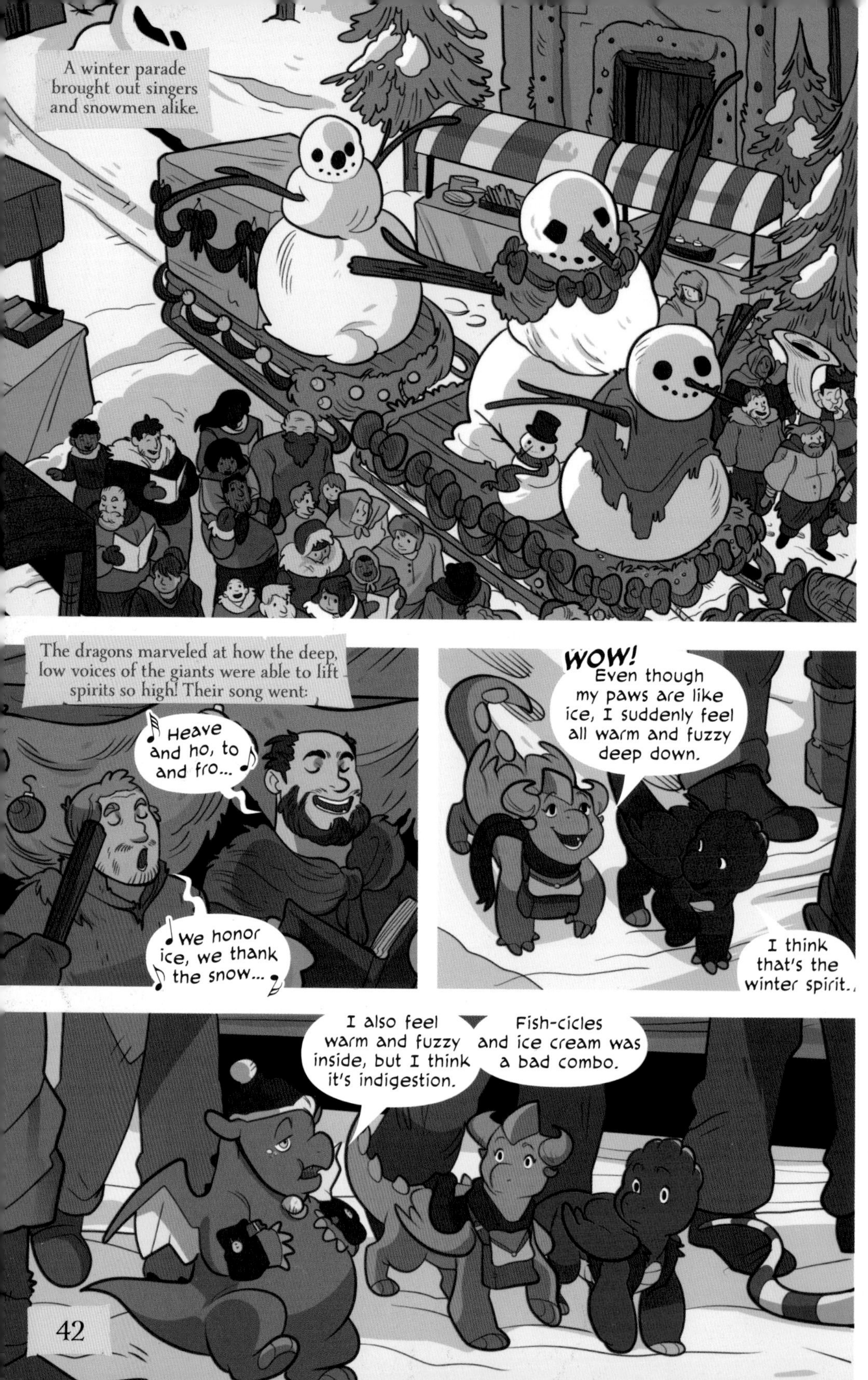
A winter parade brought out singers and snowmen alike.
The dragons marveled at how the deep, low voices of the giants were able to lift spirits so high! Their song went:
Heave and ho, to and fro...
We honor ice, we thank the snow...
WOW! Even though my paws are like ice, I suddenly feel all warm and fuzzy deep down.
I think that's the winter spirit.
I also feel warm and fuzzy inside, but I think it's indigestion.
Fish-cicles and ice cream was a bad combo.

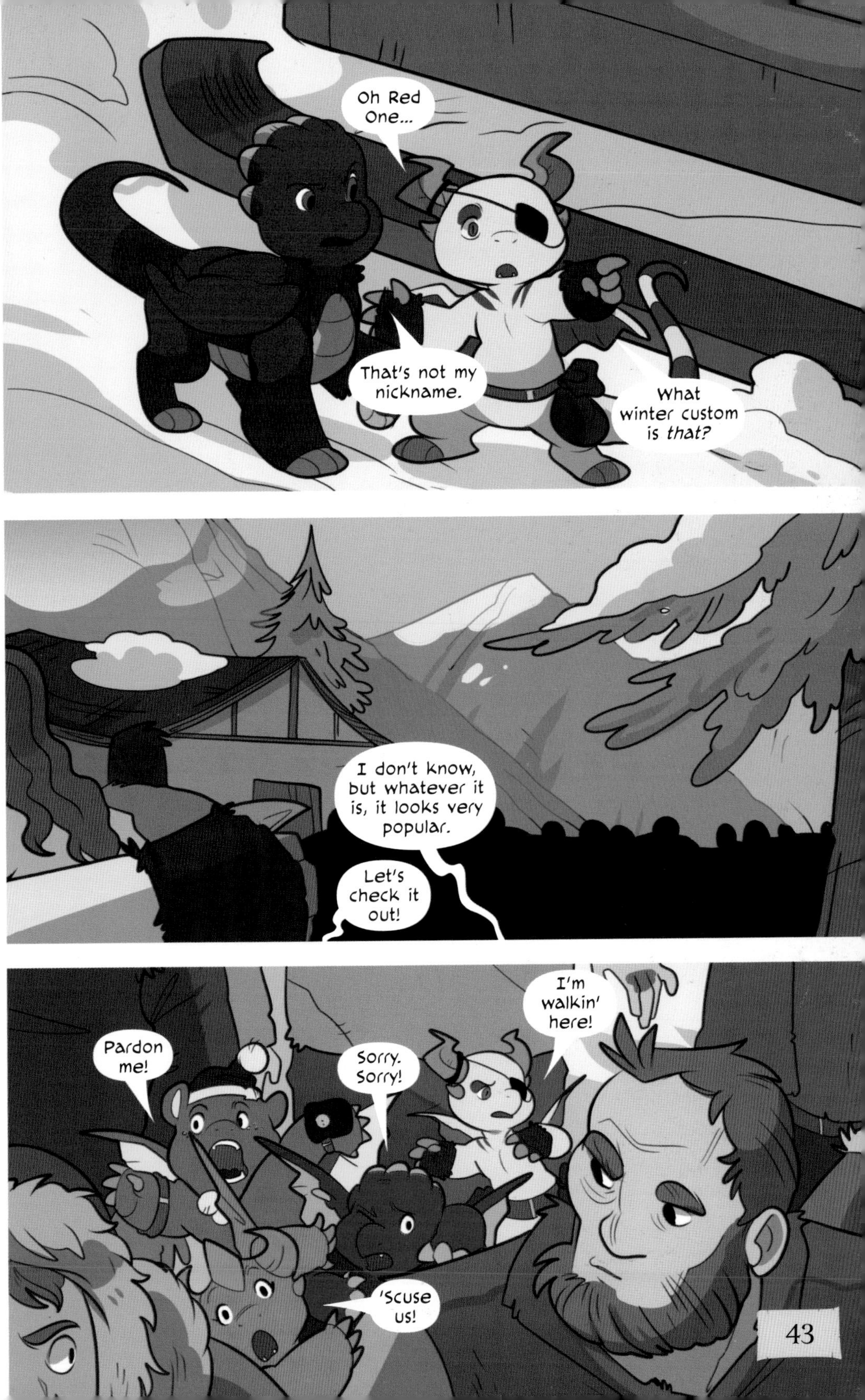
Oh Red One...
That's not my nickname.
What winter custom is *that?*
I don't know, but whatever it is, it looks very popular.
Let's check it out!
Pardon me!
Sorry. Sorry!
I'm walkin' here!
'Scuse us!

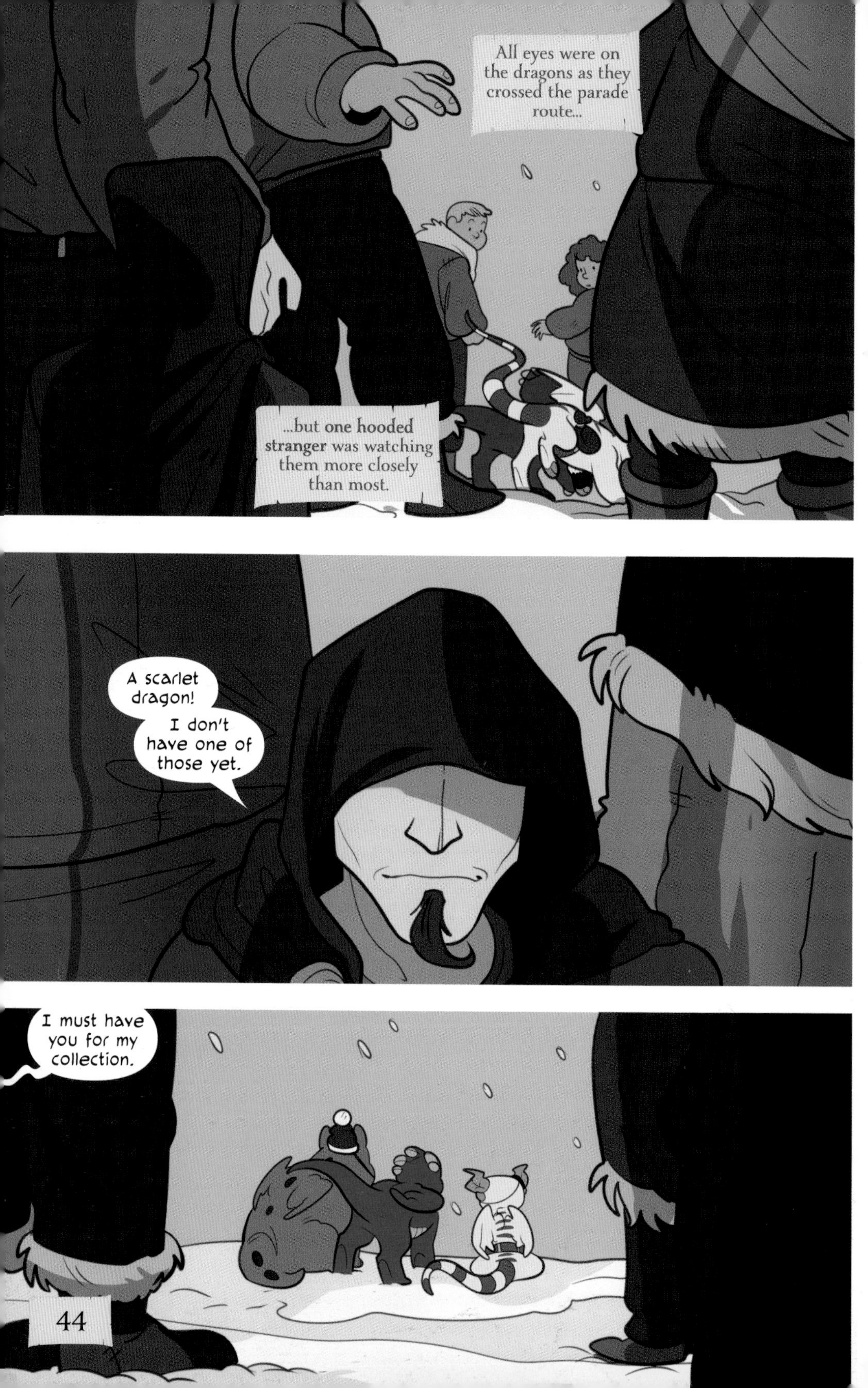
All eyes were on the dragons as they crossed the parade route...
...but one hooded stranger was watching them more closely than most.
A scarlet dragon!
I don't have one of those yet.
I must have you for my collection.

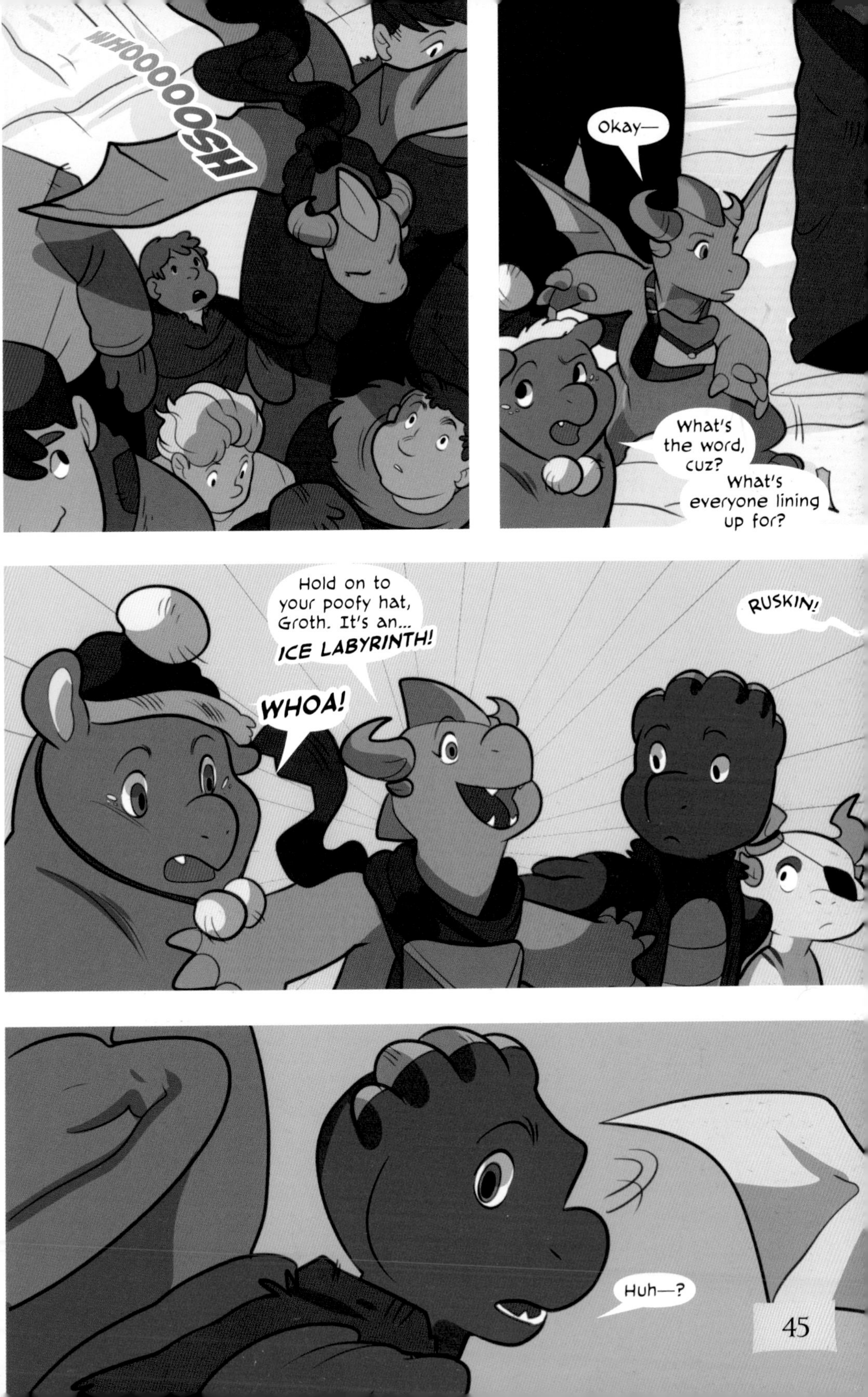
WHOOOOOSH
Okay—
What's the word, cuz? What's everyone lining up for?
Hold on to your poofy hat, Groth. It's an... ICE LABYRINTH!
RUSKIN!
WHOA!
Huh—?

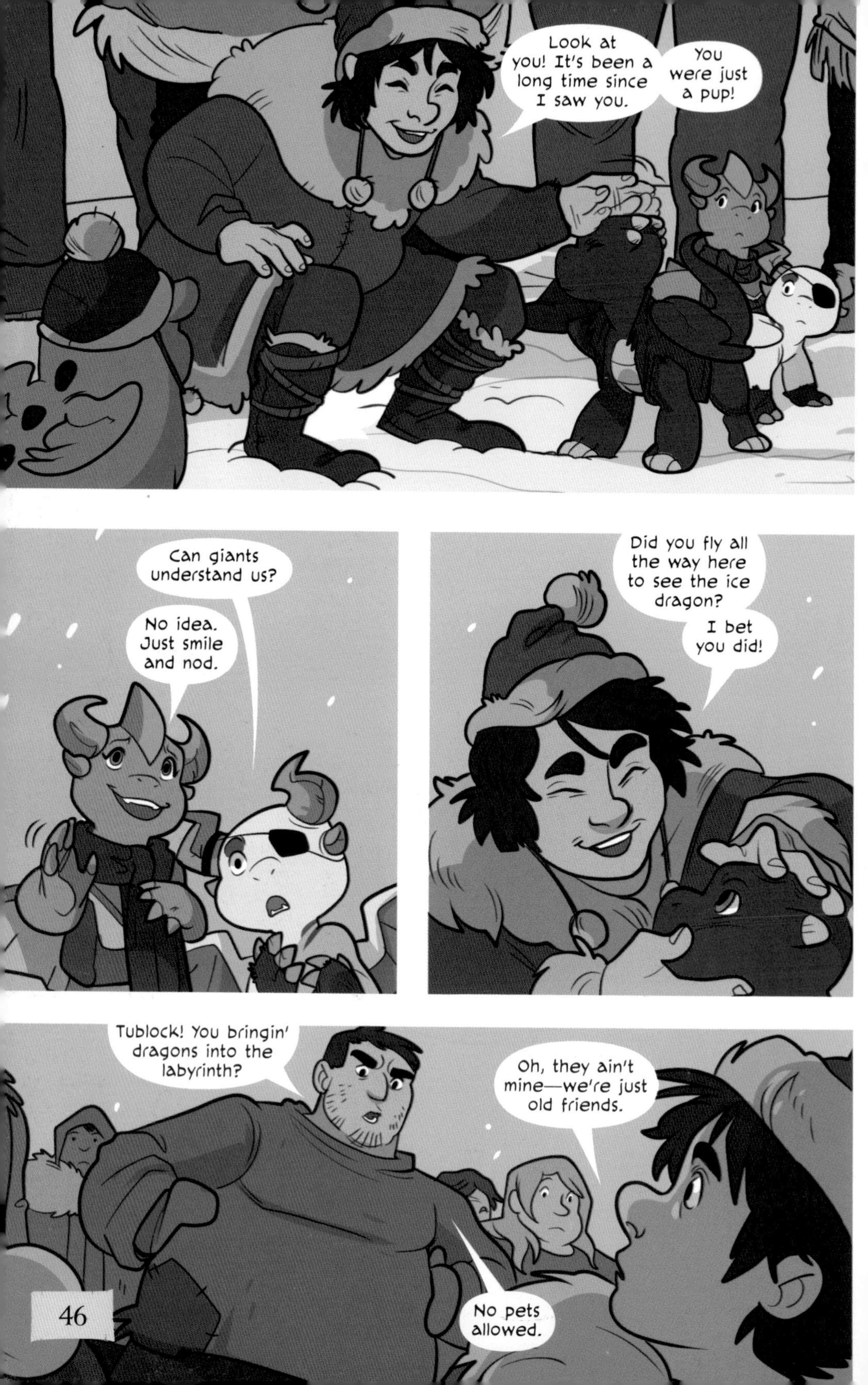
Look at you! It's been a long time since I saw you.
You were just a pup!
Can giants understand us?
No idea. Just smile and nod.
Did you fly all the way here to see the ice dragon?
I bet you did!
Tublock! You bringin' dragons into the labyrinth?
No pets allowed.
Oh, they ain't mine—we're just old friends.

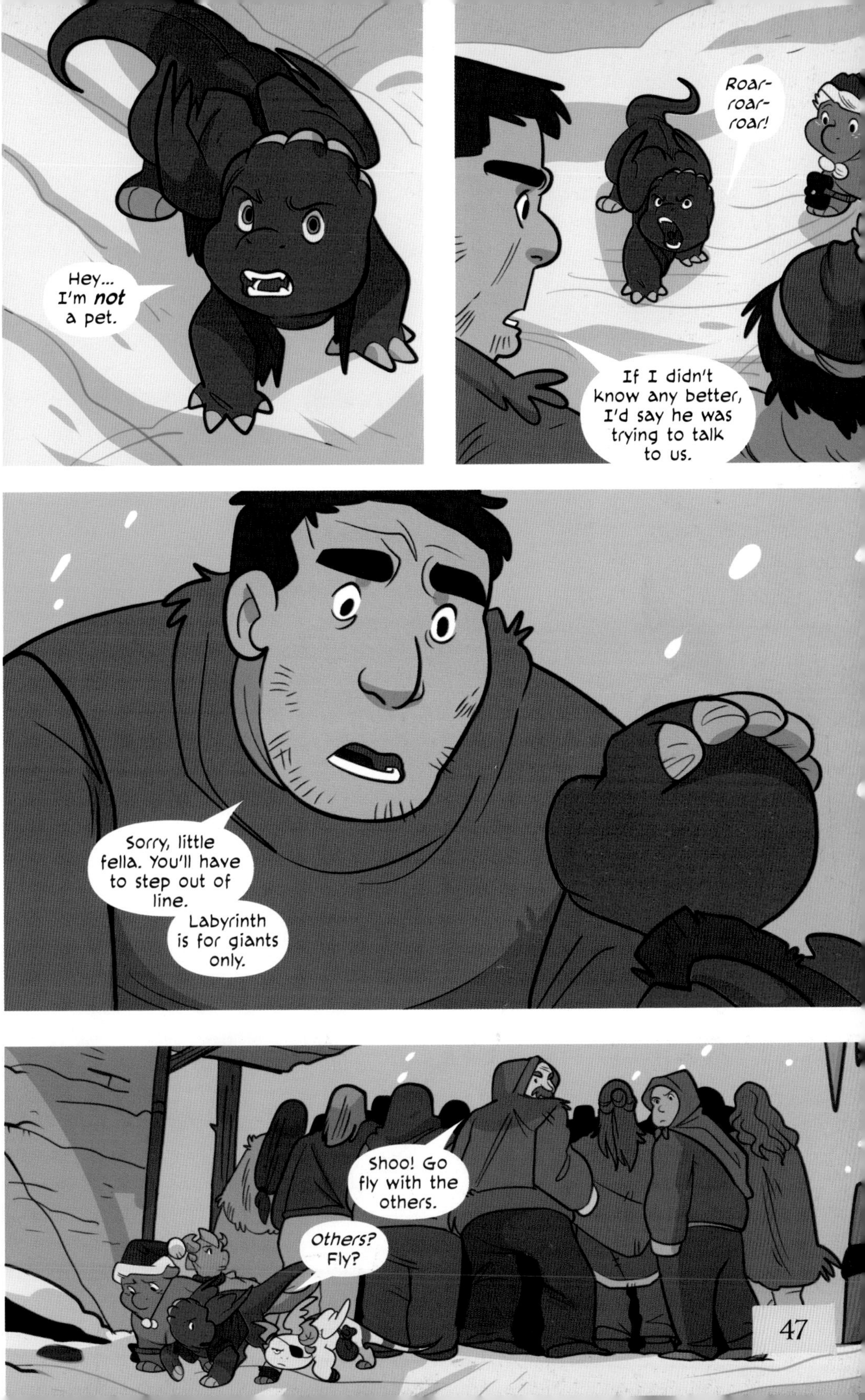
Hey... I'm **not** a pet.
Roar-roar-roar!
If I didn't know any better, I'd say he was trying to talk to us.
Sorry, little fella. You'll have to step out of line.
Labyrinth is for giants only.
Shoo! Go fly with the others.
Others? Fly?

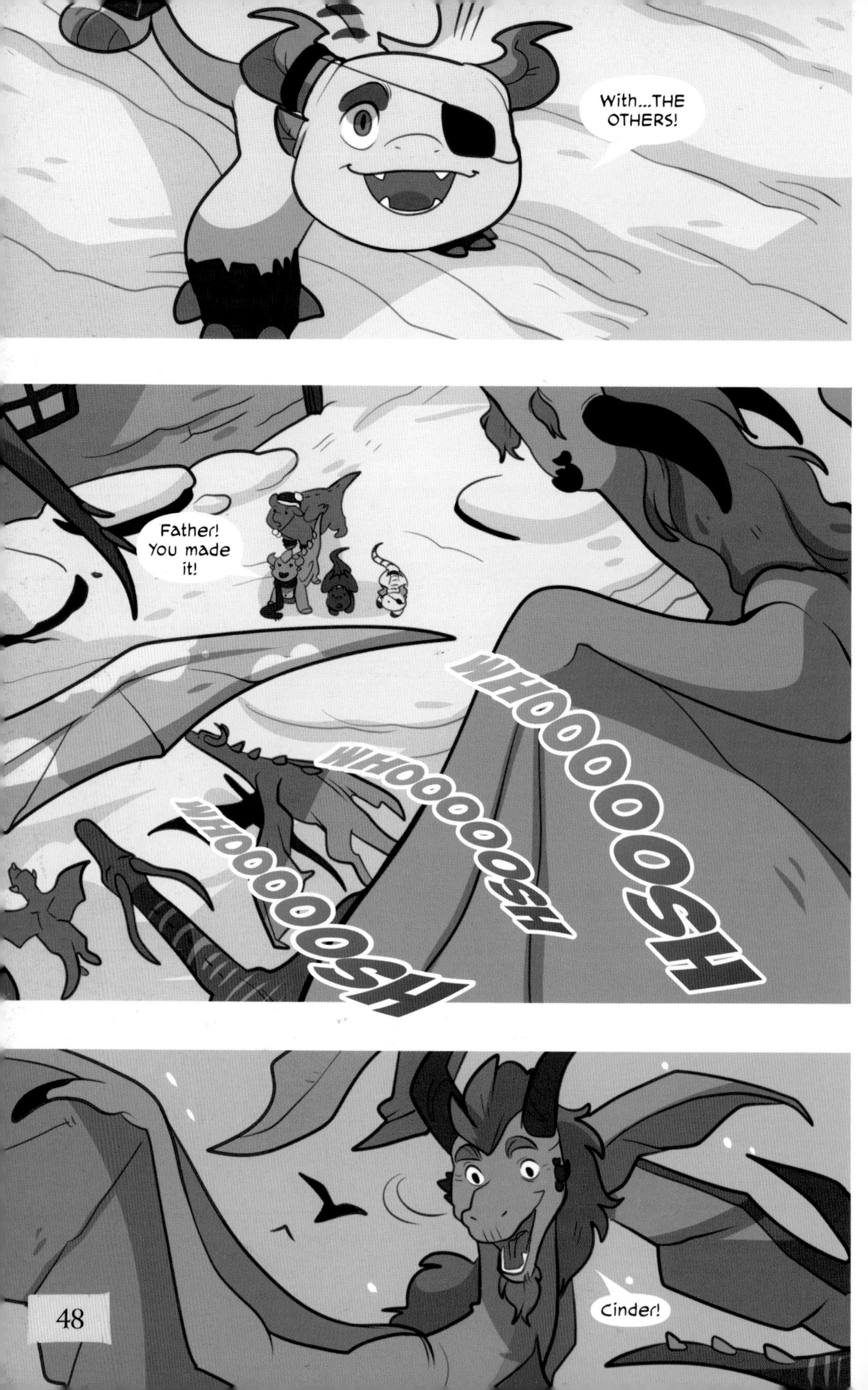
With...THE OTHERS!
Father! You made it!
WHOOOOOSH
WHOOOOOSH
WHOOOOOSH
Cinder!

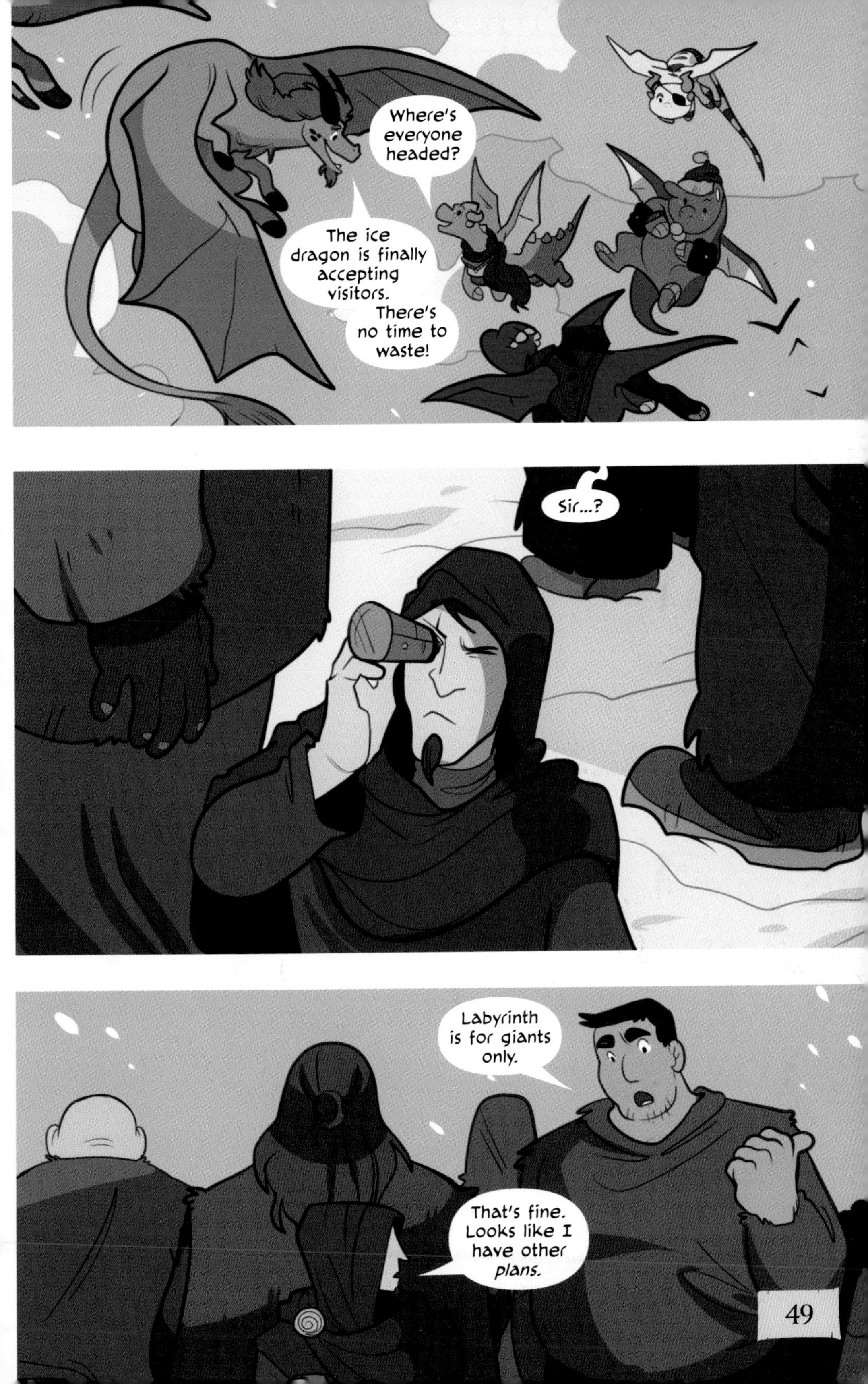
Where's everyone headed?
The ice dragon is finally accepting visitors.
There's no time to waste!
Sir...?
Labyrinth is for giants only.
That's fine. Looks like I have other *plans.*

Chapter 4

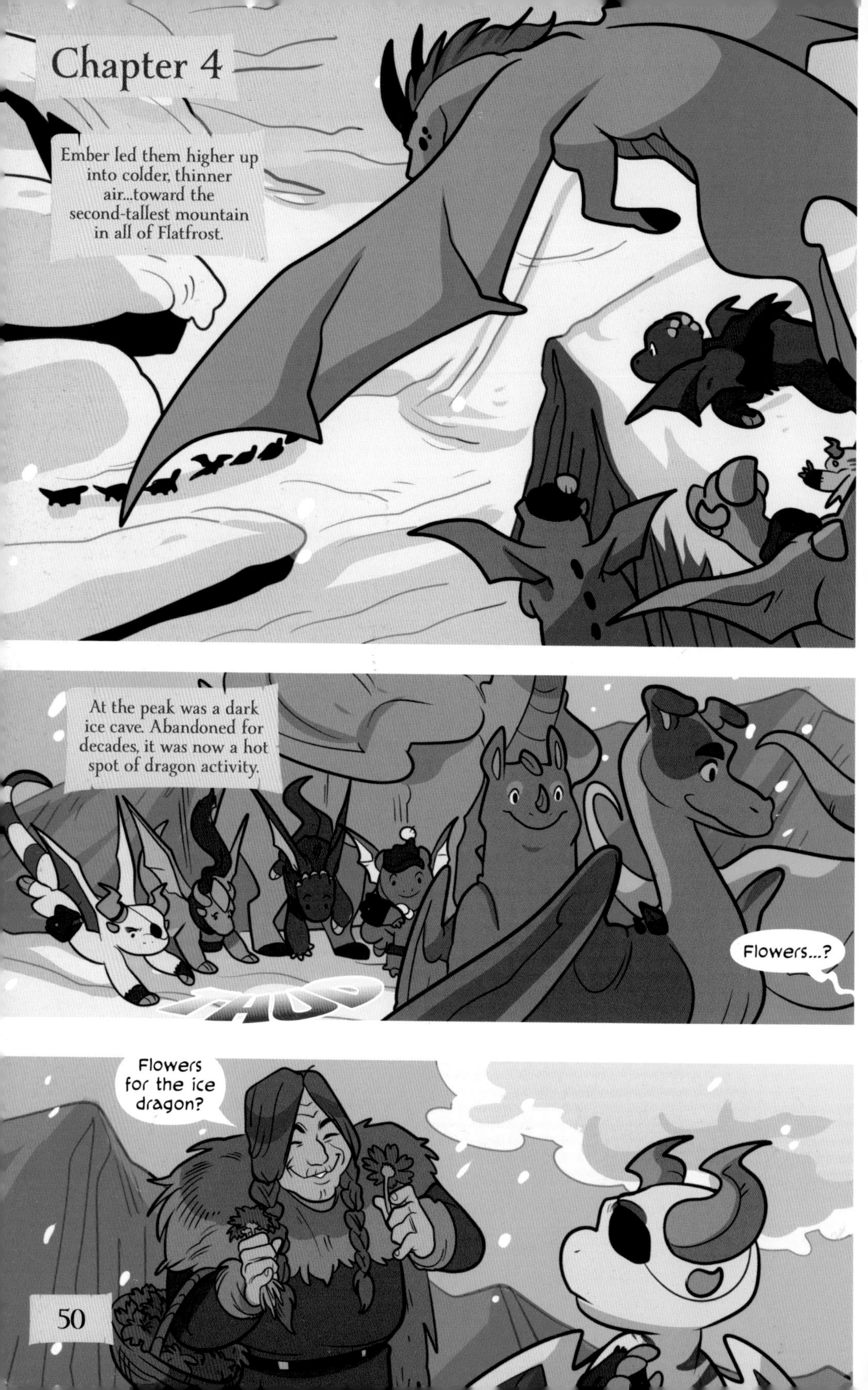
Ember led them higher up into colder, thinner air...toward the second-tallest mountain in all of Flatfrost.
At the peak was a dark ice cave. Abandoned for decades, it was now a hot spot of dragon activity.
Flowers...?
Flowers for the ice dragon?

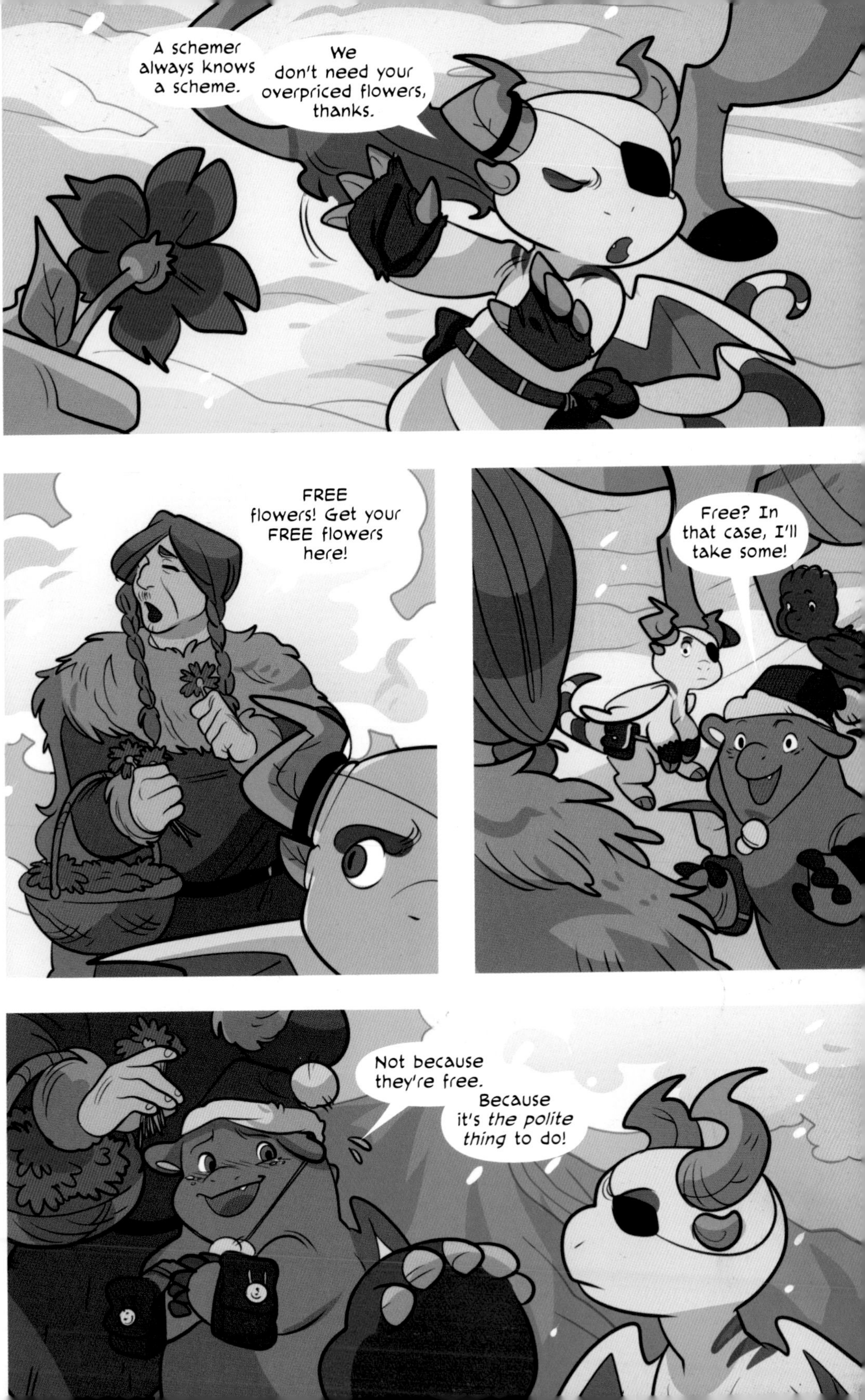
A schemer always knows a scheme.
We don't need your overpriced flowers, thanks.
FREE flowers! Get your FREE flowers here!
Free? In that case, I'll take some!
Not because they're free.
Because it's *the polite thing* to do!

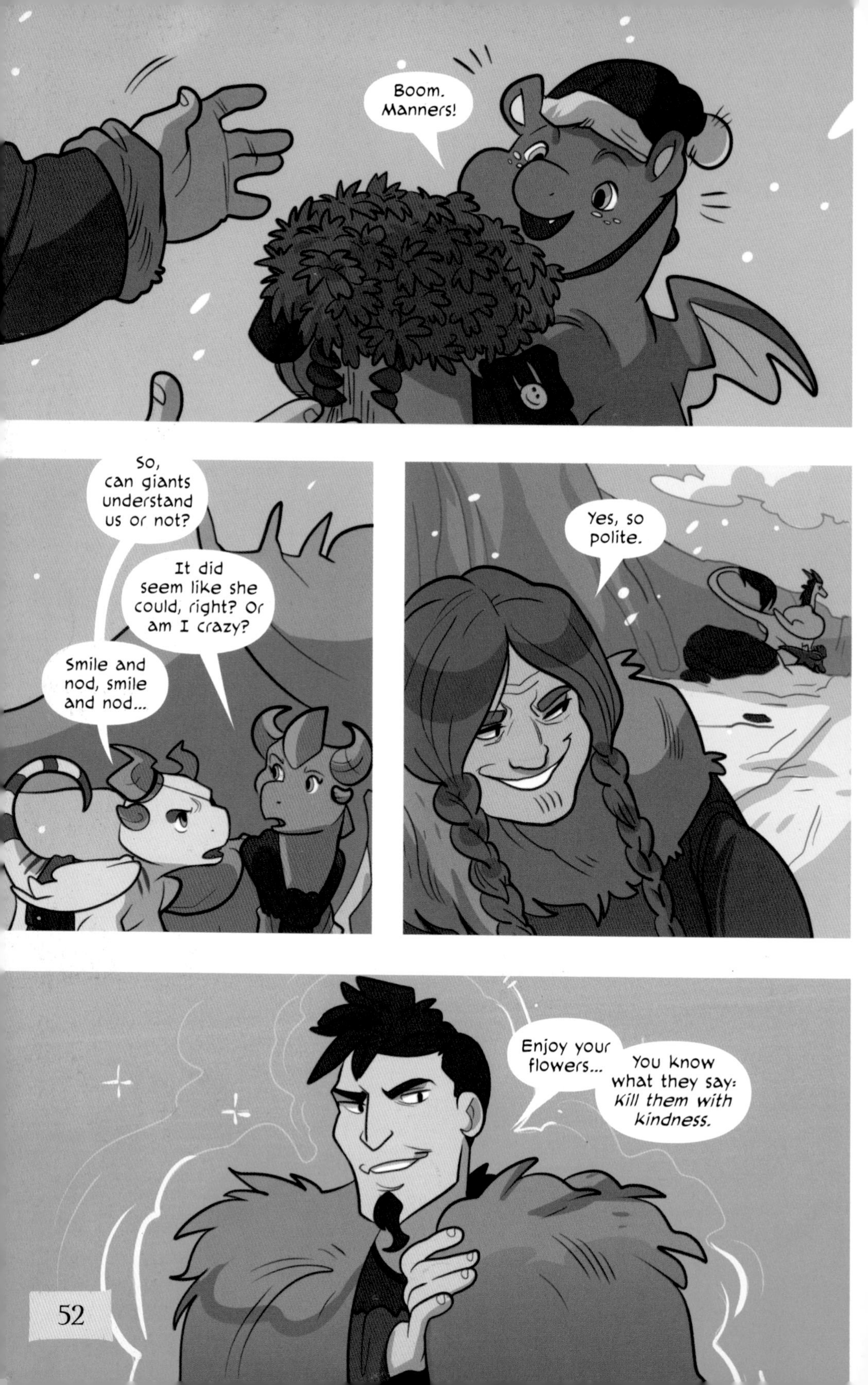
Boom. Manners!
So, can giants understand us or not?
It did seem like she could, right? Or am I crazy?
Smile and nod, smile and nod...
Yes, so polite.
Enjoy your flowers...
You know what they say: *Kill them with kindness.*

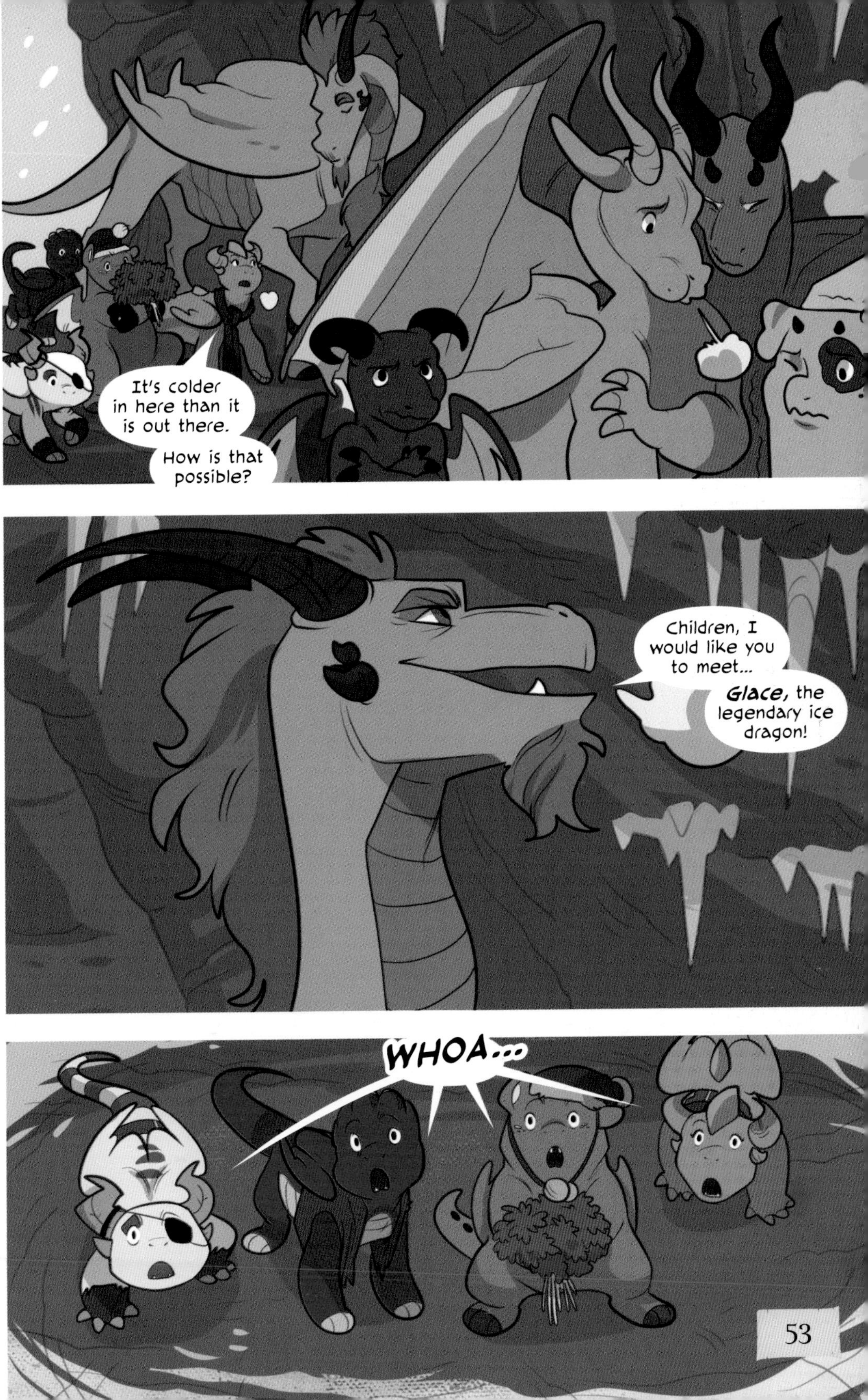
It's colder in here than it is out there.
How is that possible?
Children, I would like you to meet...
Glace, the legendary ice dragon!
WHOA...

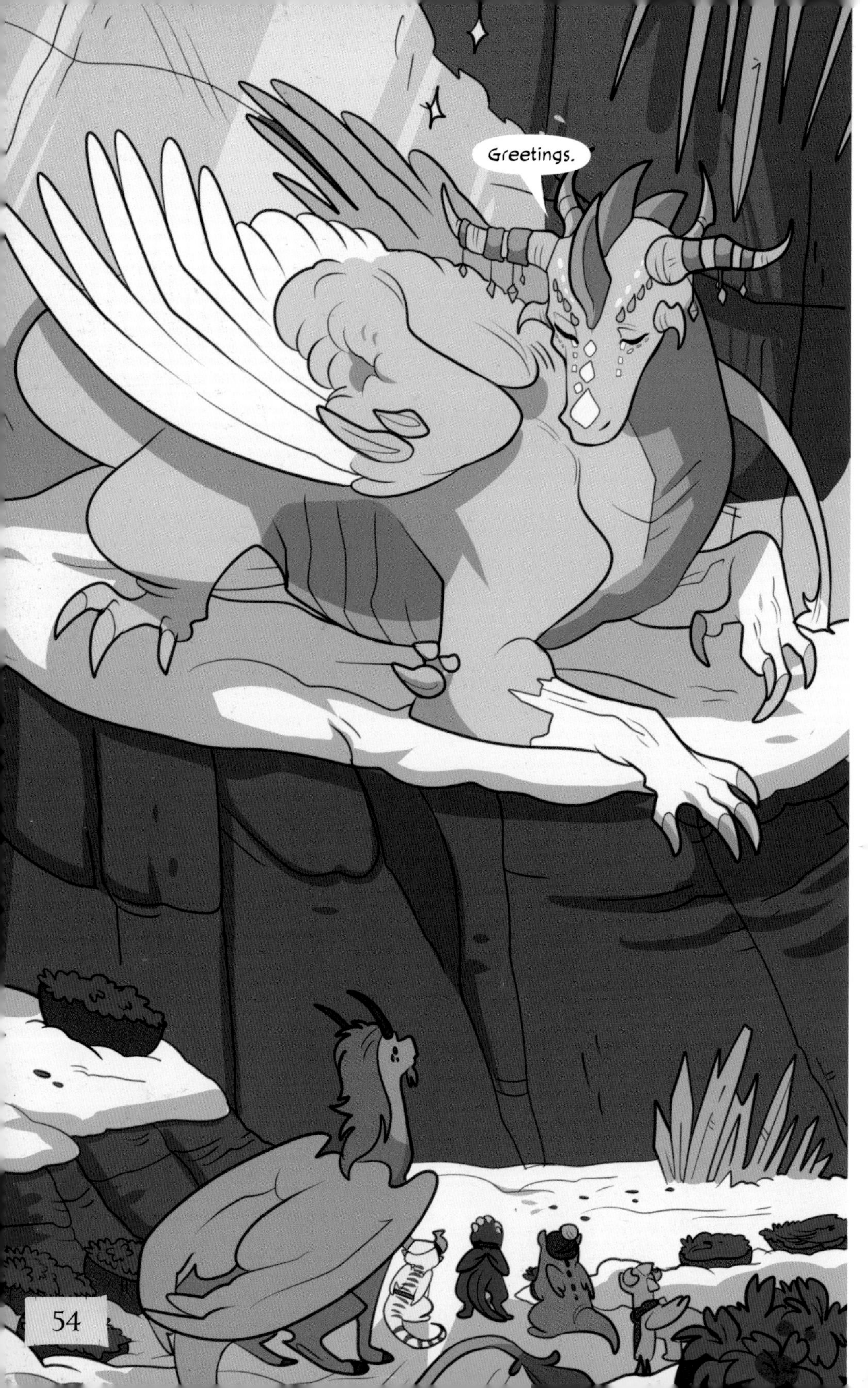
Greetings.

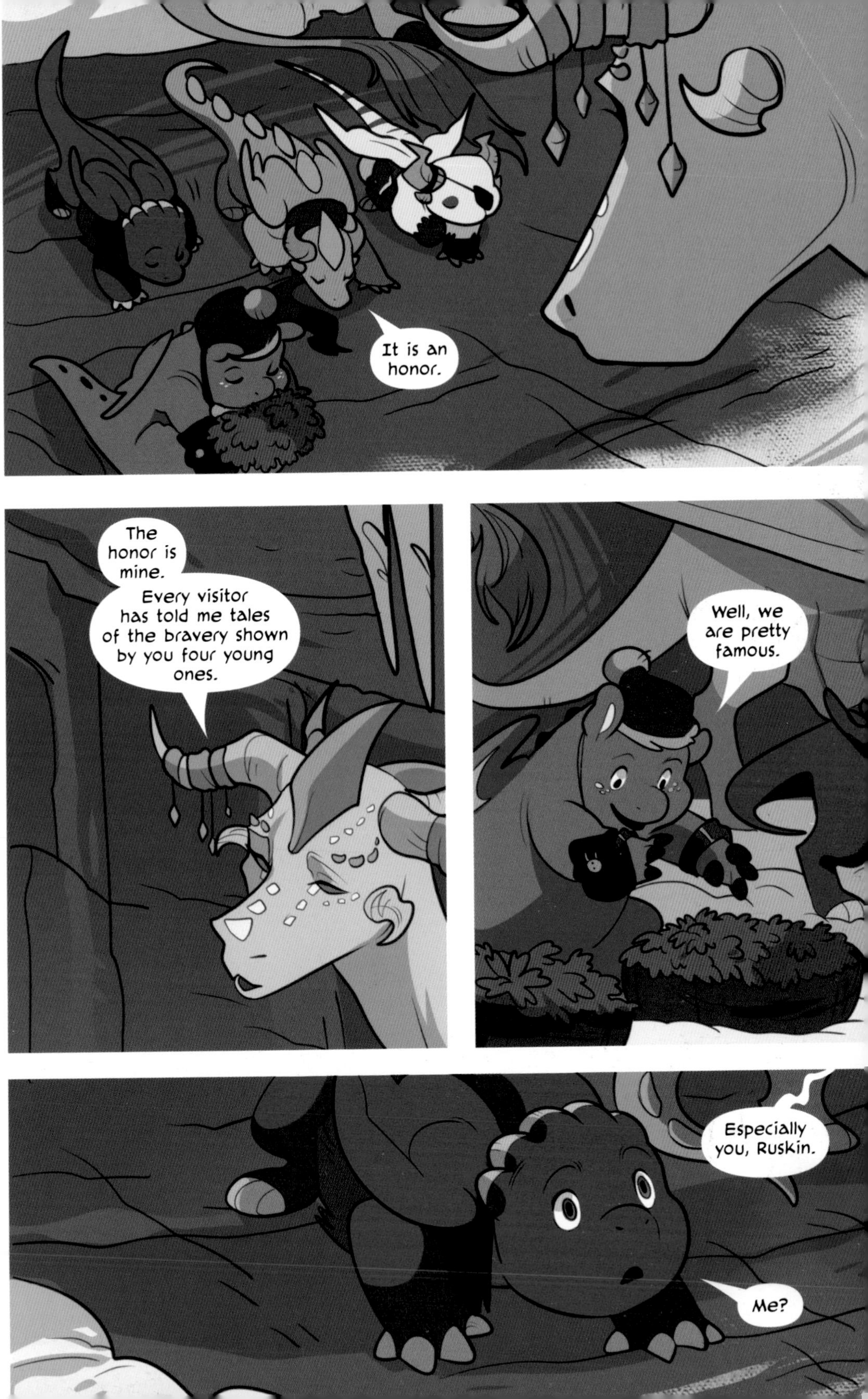
It is an honor.
The honor is mine.
Every visitor has told me tales of the bravery shown by you four young ones.
Well, we are pretty famous.
Especially you, Ruskin.
Me?

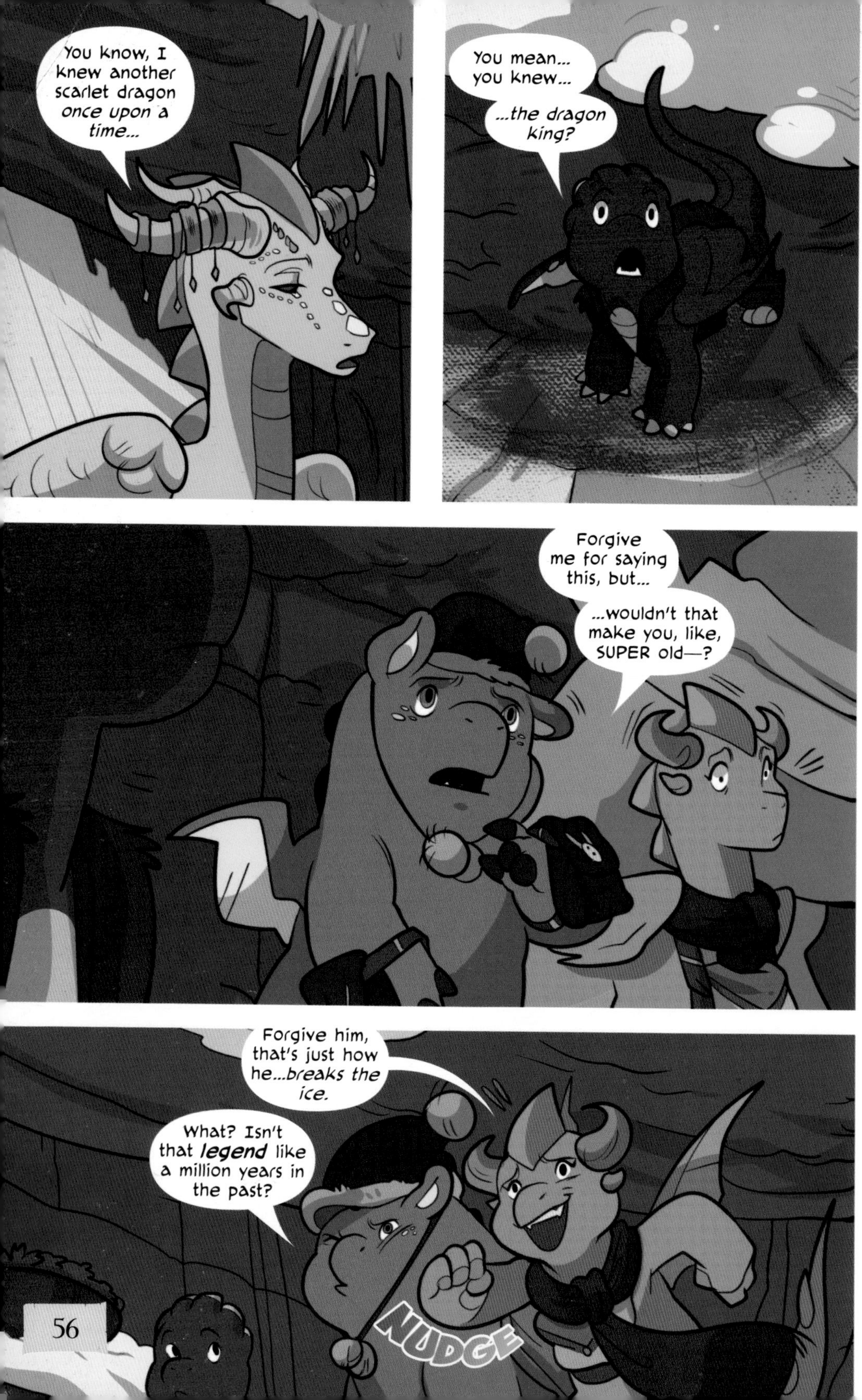
You know, I knew another scarlet dragon once upon a time...
You mean... you knew...
...the dragon king?
Forgive me for saying this, but...
...wouldn't that make you, like, SUPER old—?
Forgive him, that's just how he...breaks the ice.
What? Isn't that legend like a million years in the past?
NUDGE

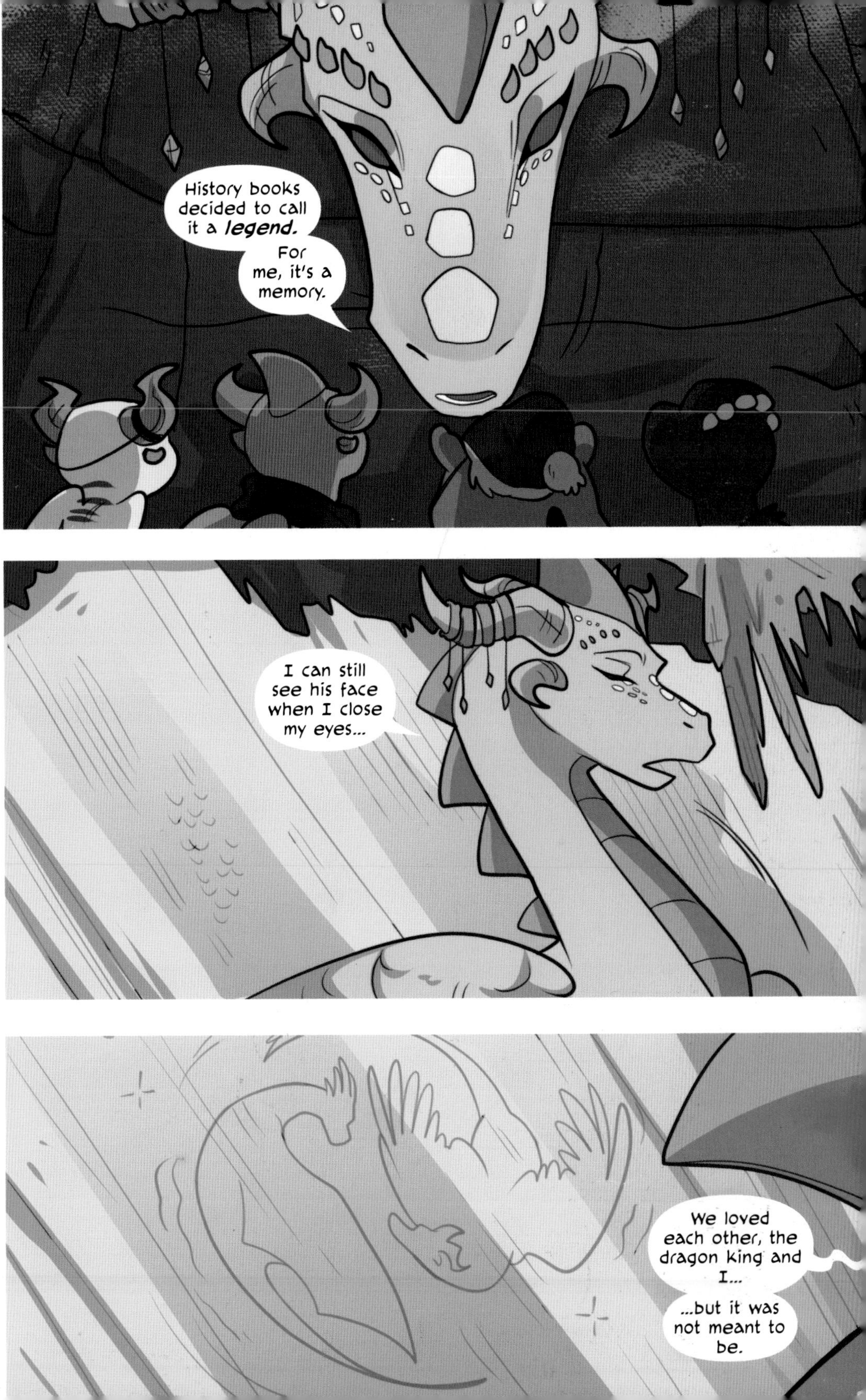
History books decided to call it a *legend.*
For me, it's a memory.
I can still see his face when I close my eyes...
We loved each other, the dragon king and I...
...but it was not meant to be.

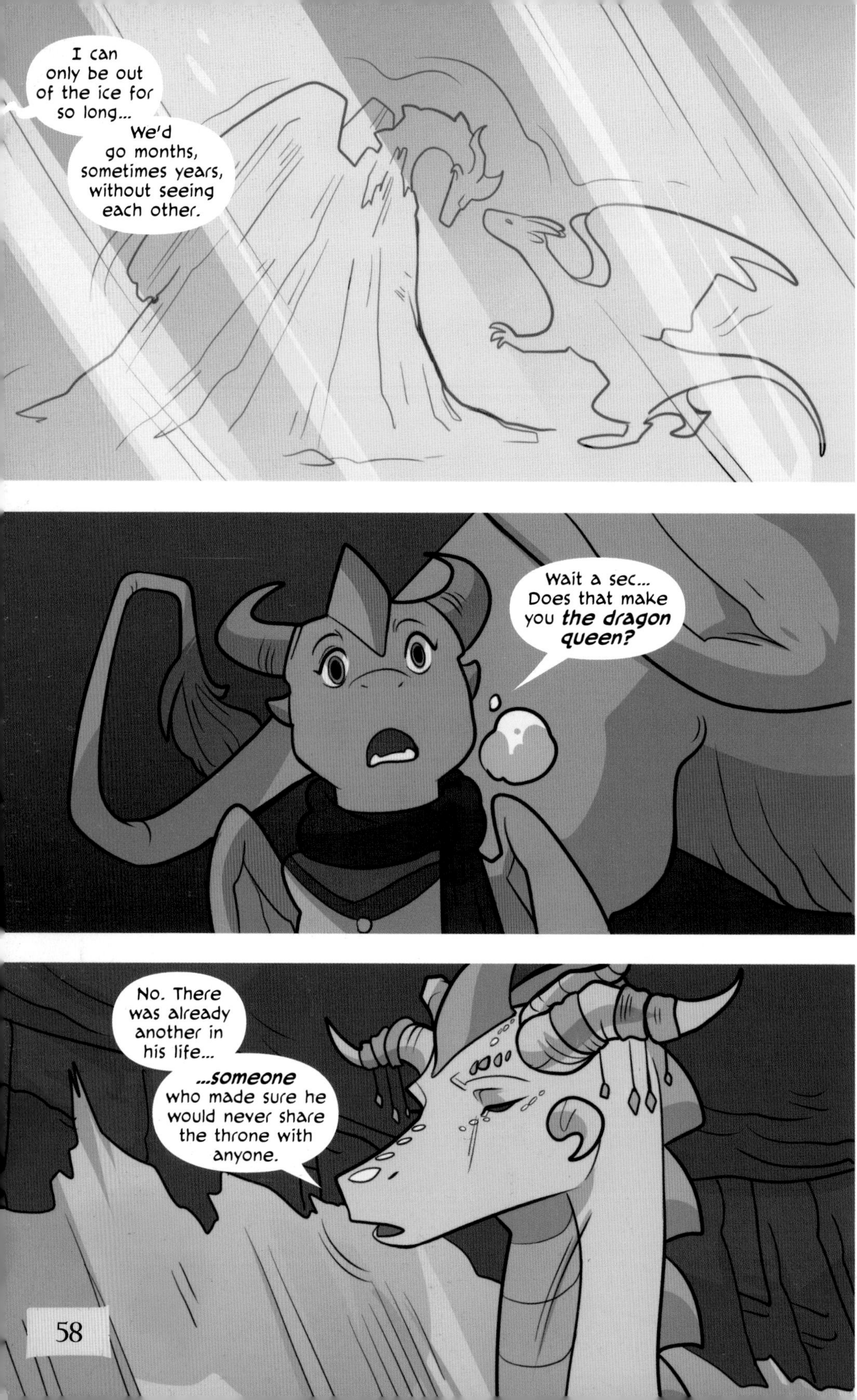
I can only be out of the ice for so long...
We'd go months, sometimes years, without seeing each other.
Wait a sec... Does that make you ***the dragon queen?***
No. There was already another in his life...
...someone who made sure he would never share the throne with anyone.

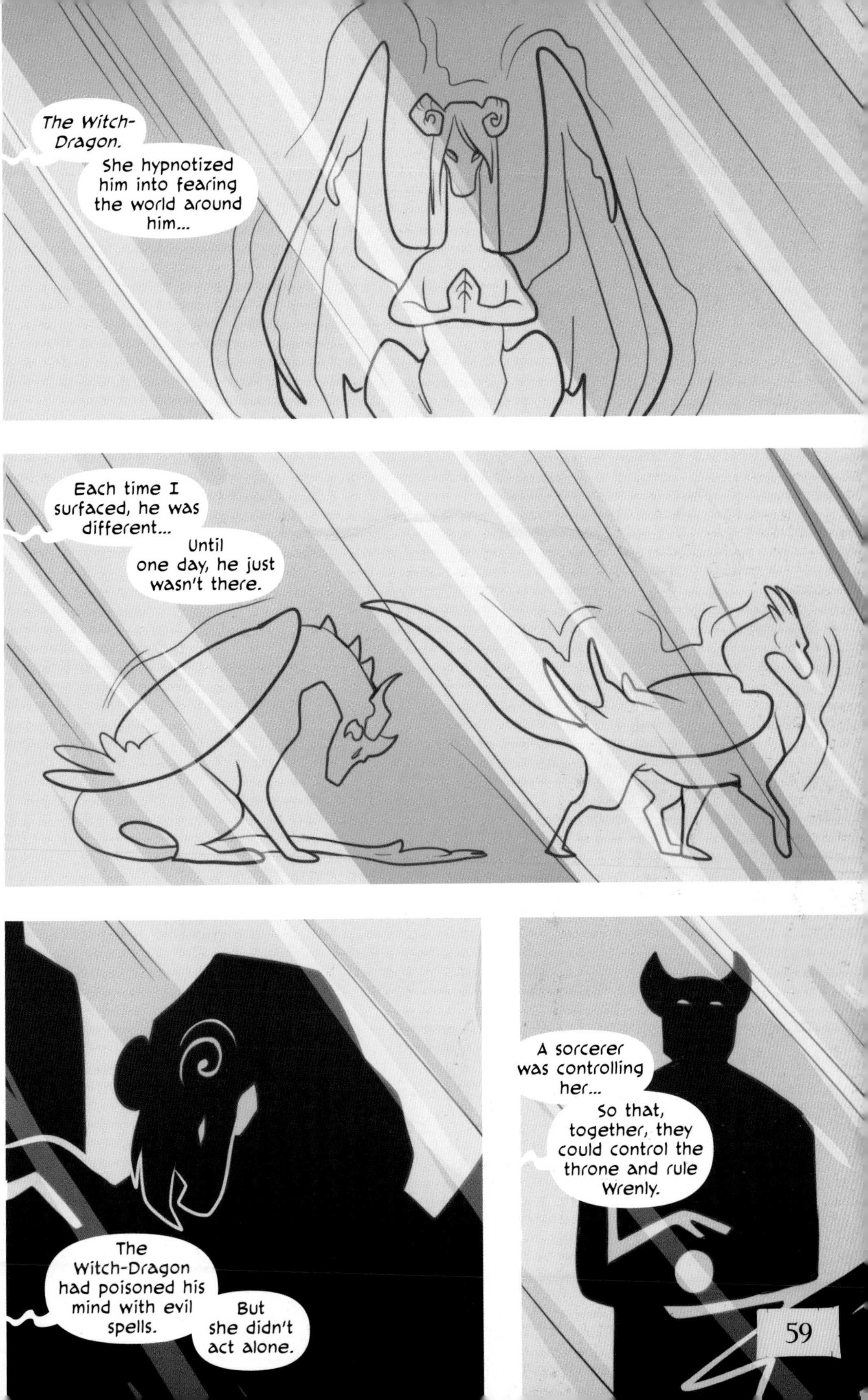
The Witch-Dragon.
She hypnotized him into fearing the world around him...
Each time I surfaced, he was different...
Until one day, he just wasn't there.
The Witch-Dragon had poisoned his mind with evil spells.
But she didn't act alone.
A sorcerer was controlling her...
So that, together, they could control the throne and rule Wrenly.

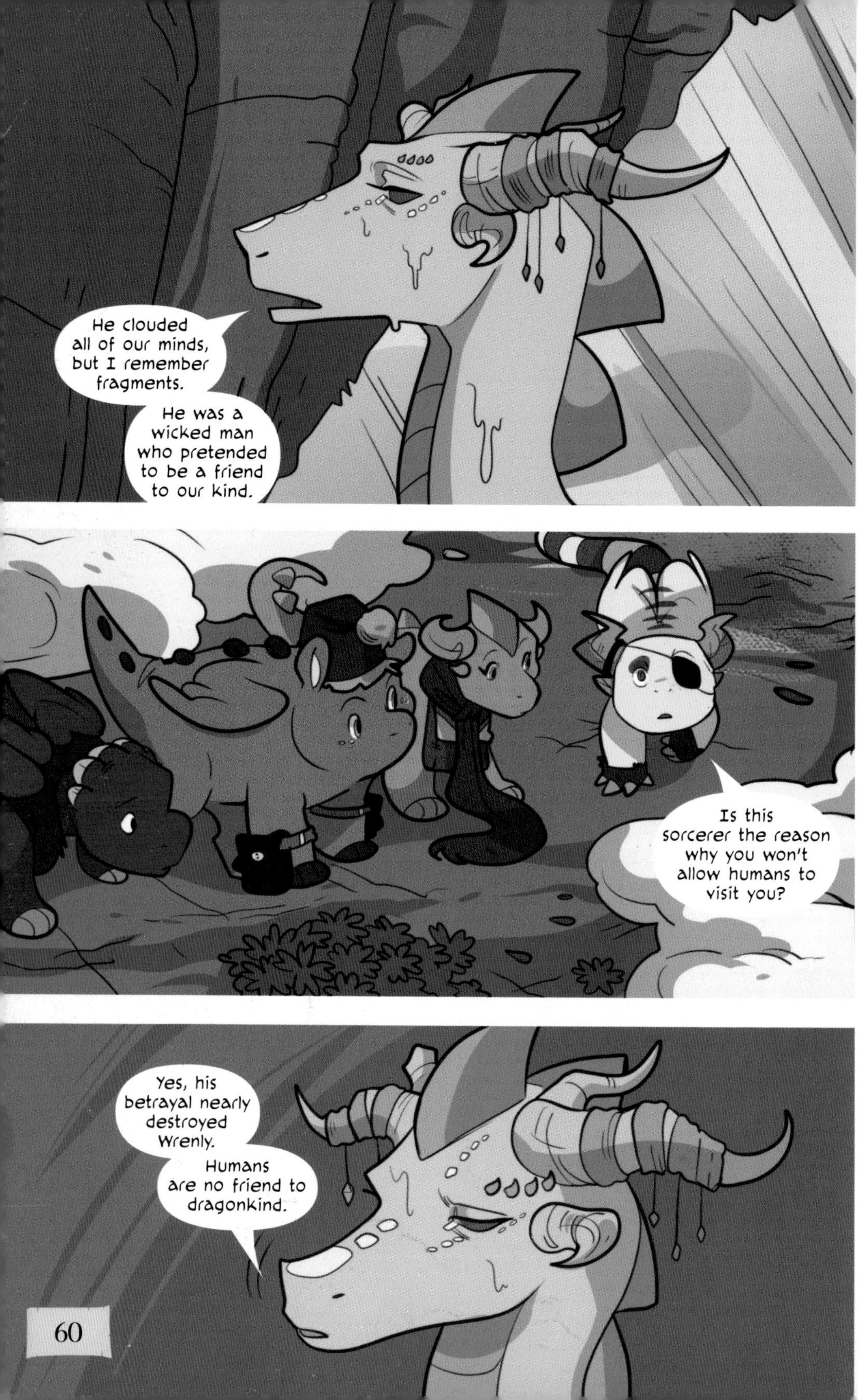
He clouded all of our minds, but I remember fragments.
He was a wicked man who pretended to be a friend to our kind.
Is this sorcerer the reason why you won't allow humans to visit you?
Yes, his betrayal nearly destroyed Wrenly.
Humans are no friend to dragonkind.

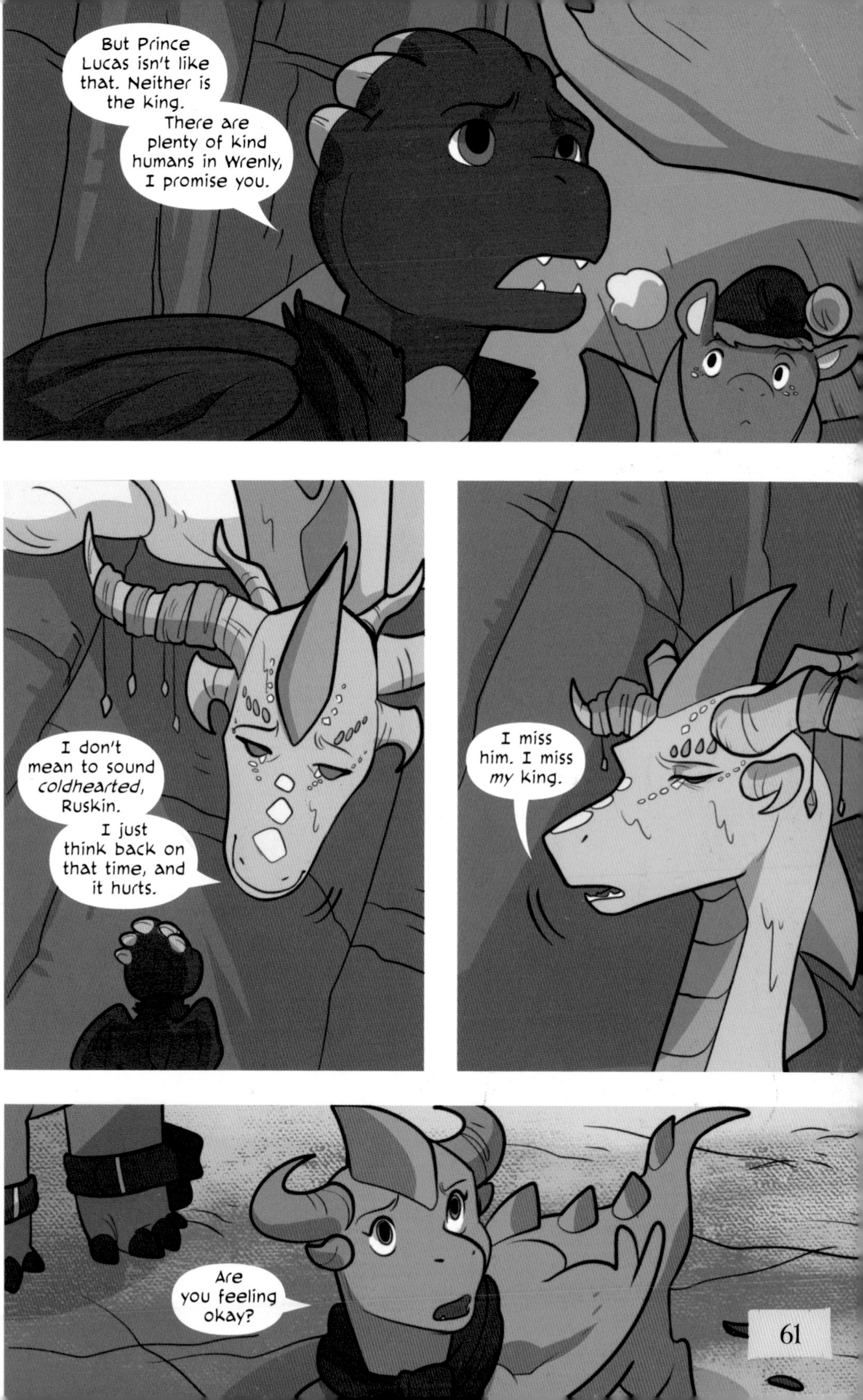
But Prince Lucas isn't like that. Neither is the king.
There are plenty of kind humans in Wrenly, I promise you.
I don't mean to sound *coldhearted*, Ruskin.
I just think back on that time, and it hurts.
I miss him. I miss *my* king.
Are you feeling okay?

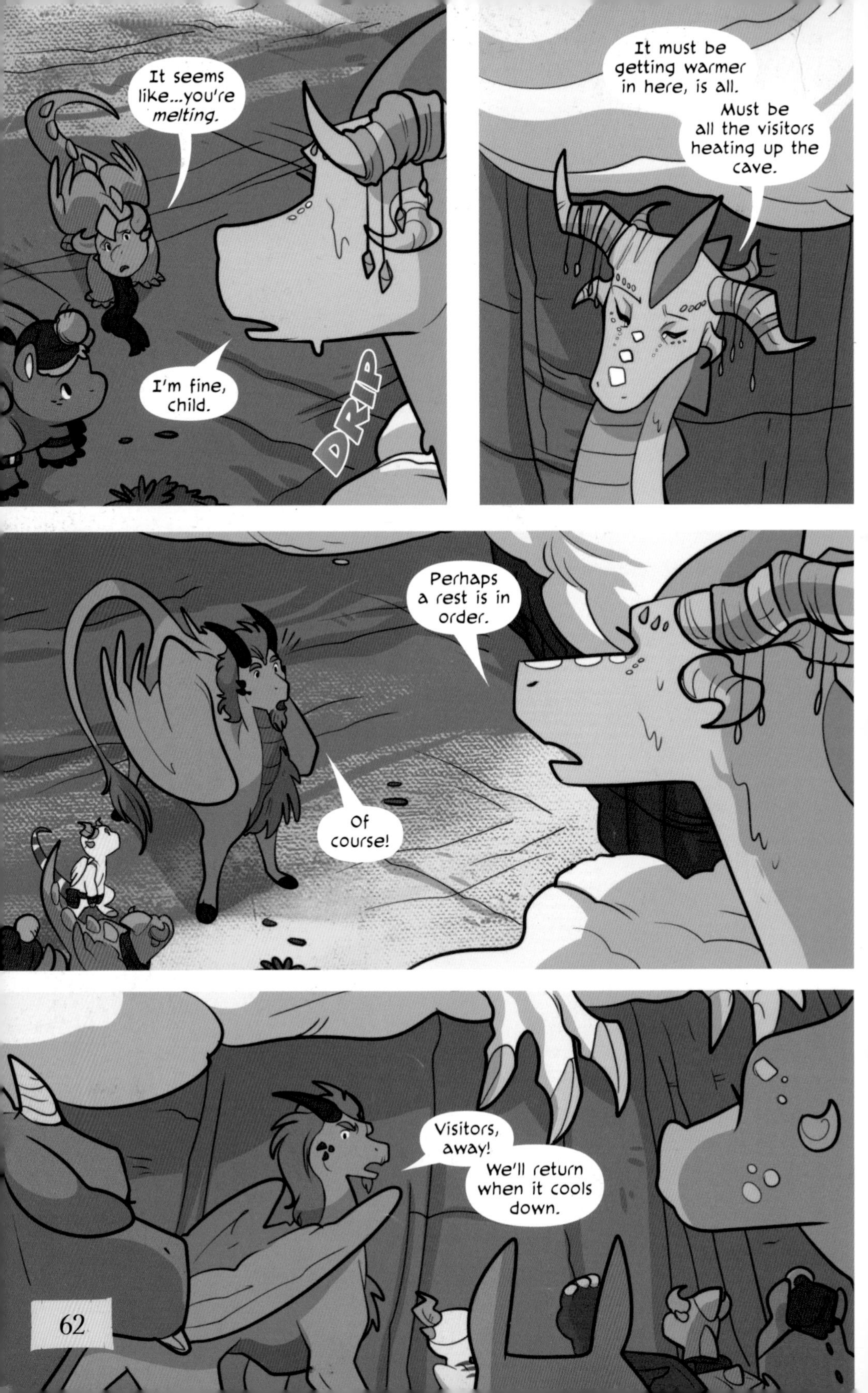

It seems like...you're *melting.*
I'm fine, child.
DRIP
It must be getting warmer in here, is all.
Must be all the visitors heating up the cave.
Perhaps a rest is in order.
Of course!
Visitors, away!
We'll return when it cools down.

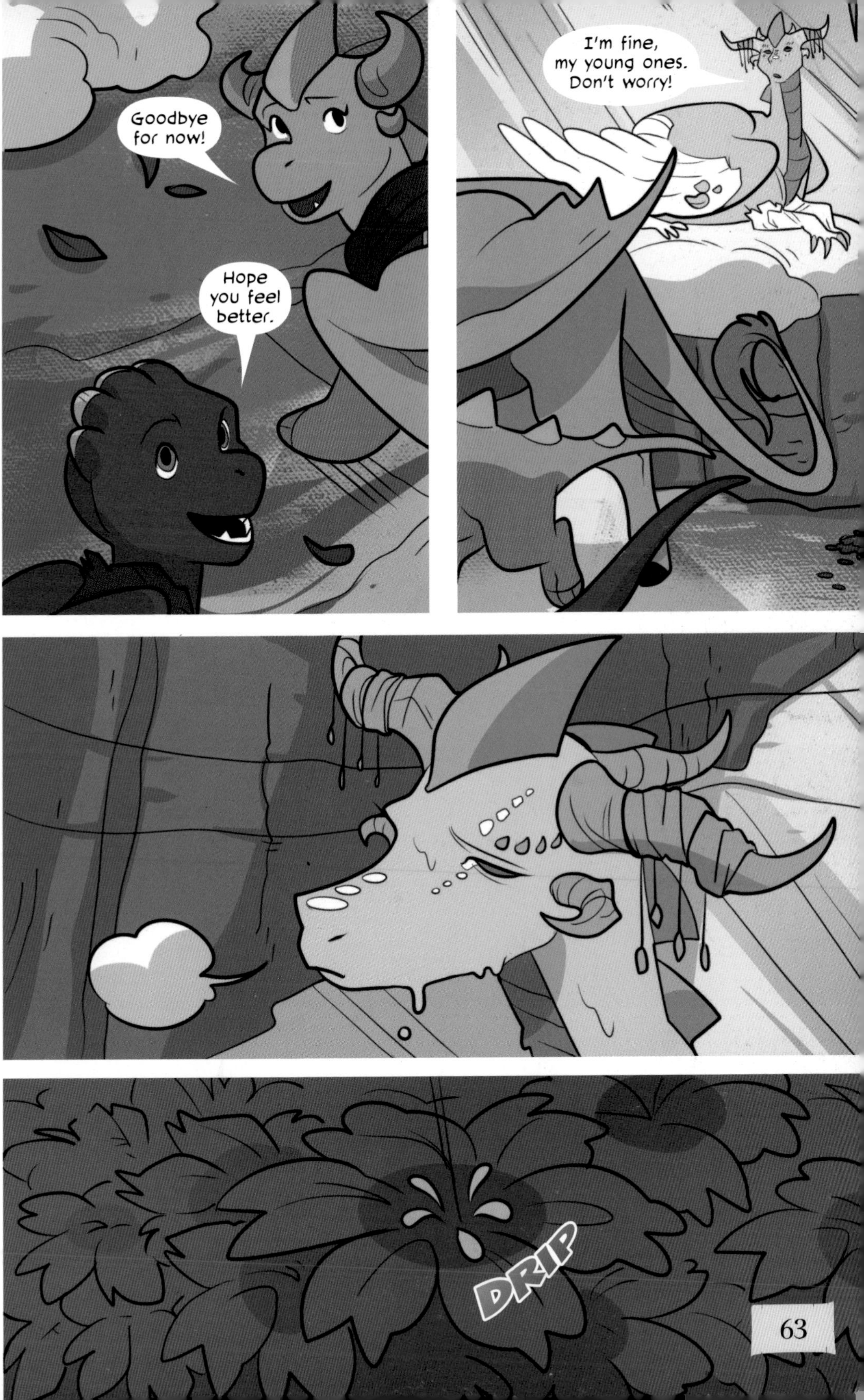
Goodbye for now!
Hope you feel better.
I'm fine, my young ones. Don't worry!
DRIP

Chapter 5

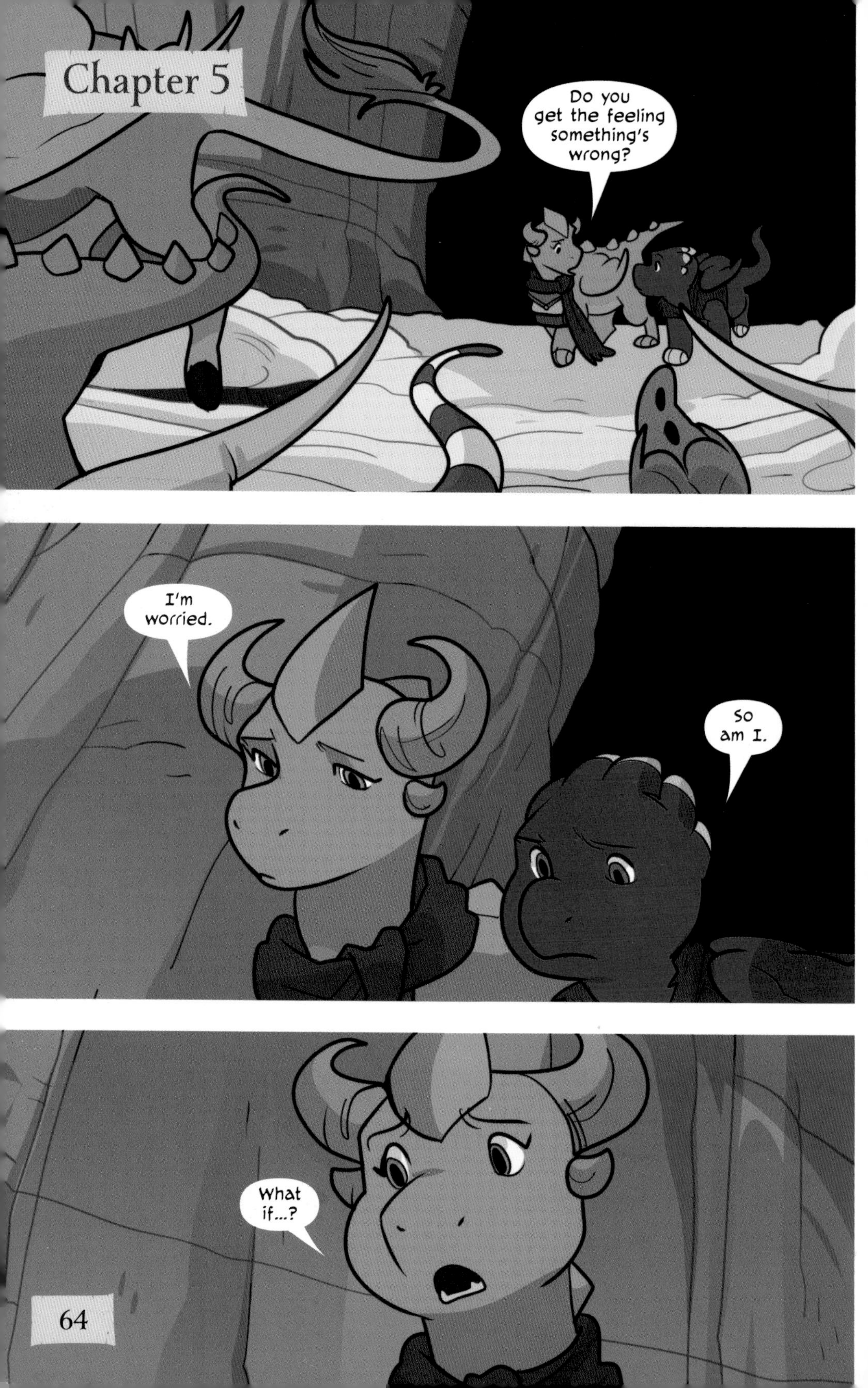
Do you get the feeling something's wrong?
I'm worried.
So am I.
What if...?

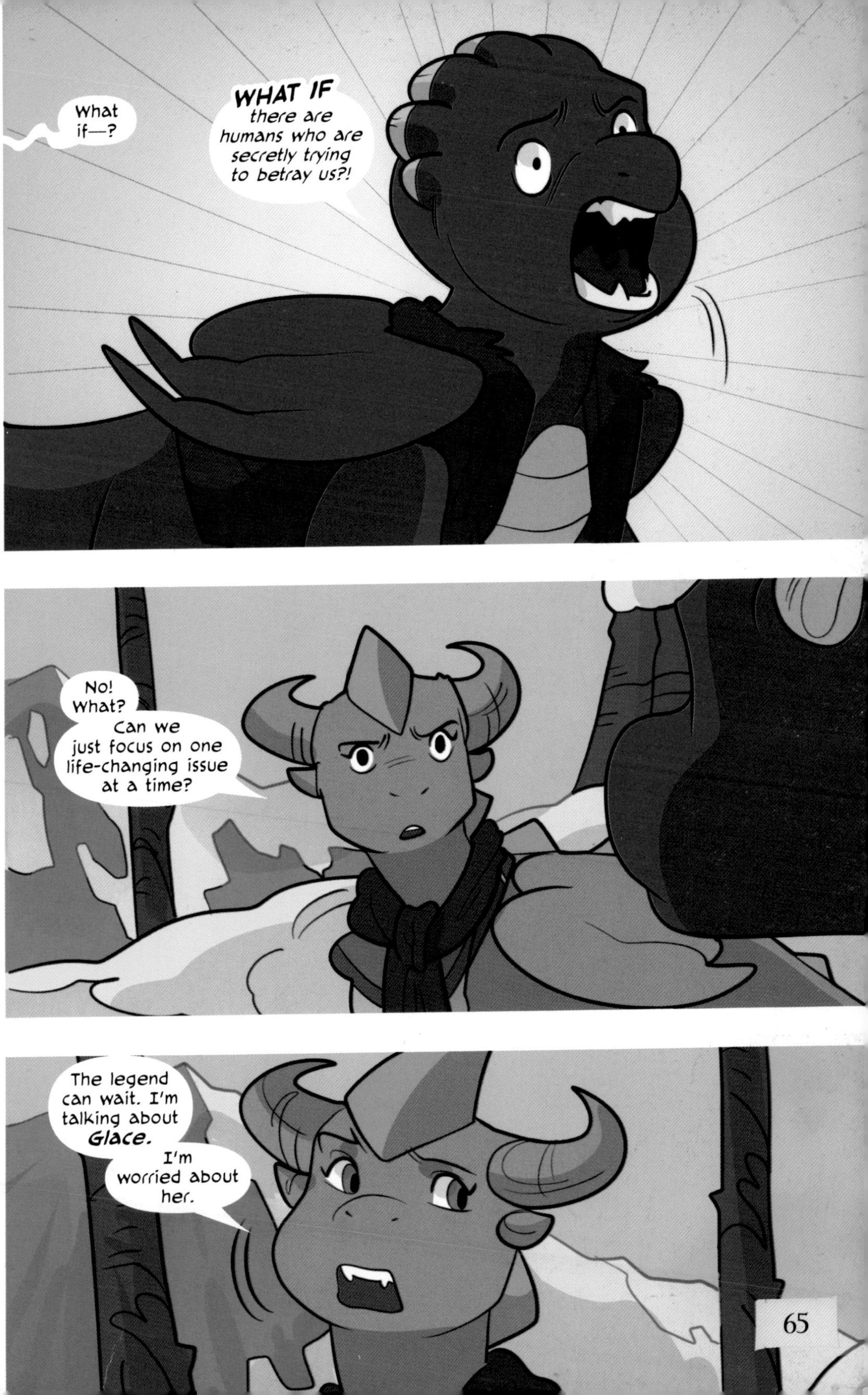
What if—?
WHAT IF there are humans who are secretly trying to betray us?!
No! What?
Can we just focus on one life-changing issue at a time?
The legend can wait. I'm talking about *Glace.*
I'm worried about her.

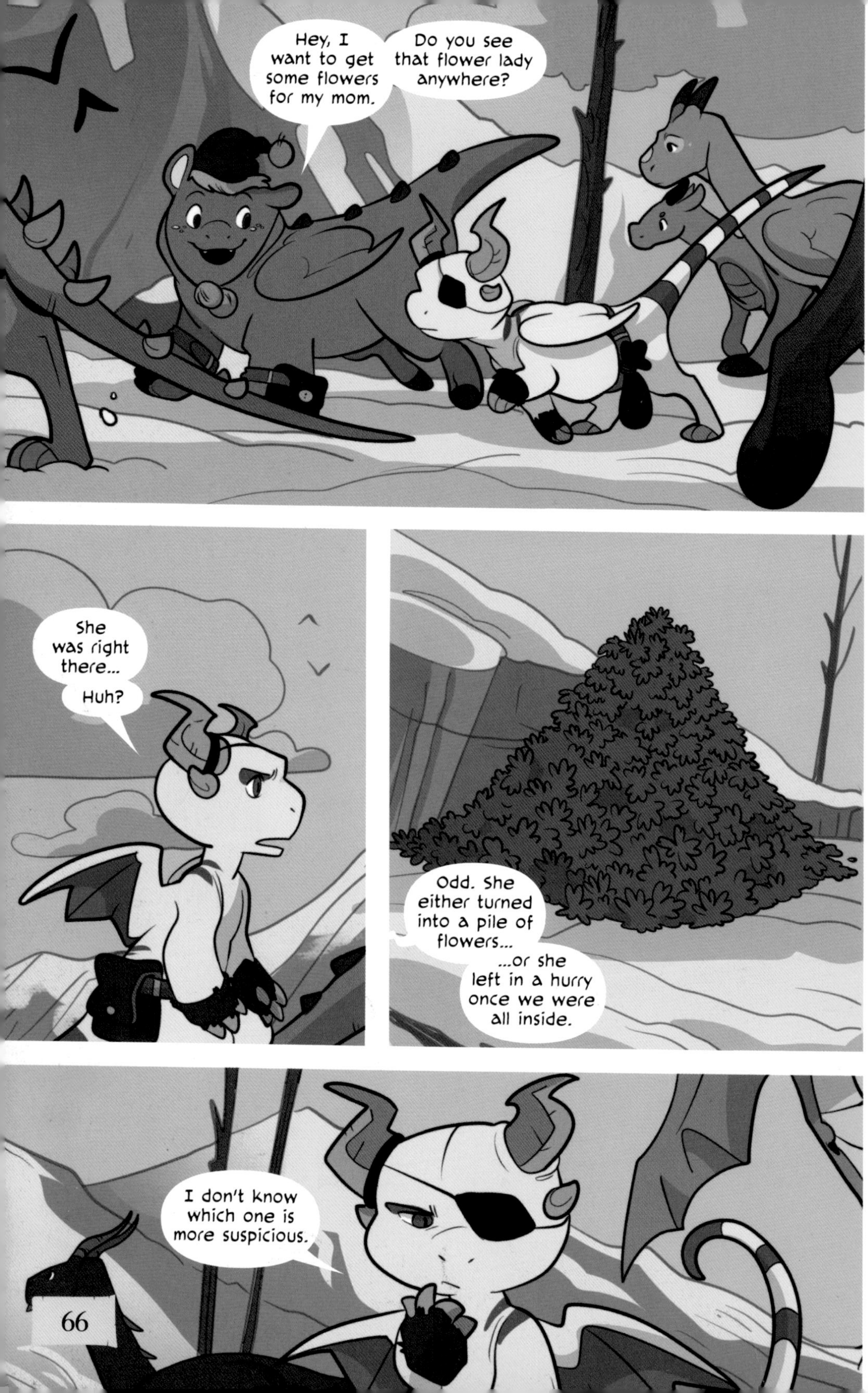

Hey, I want to get some flowers for my mom.
Do you see that flower lady anywhere?
She was right there...
Huh?
Odd. She either turned into a pile of flowers...
...or she left in a hurry once we were all inside.
I don't know which one is more suspicious.

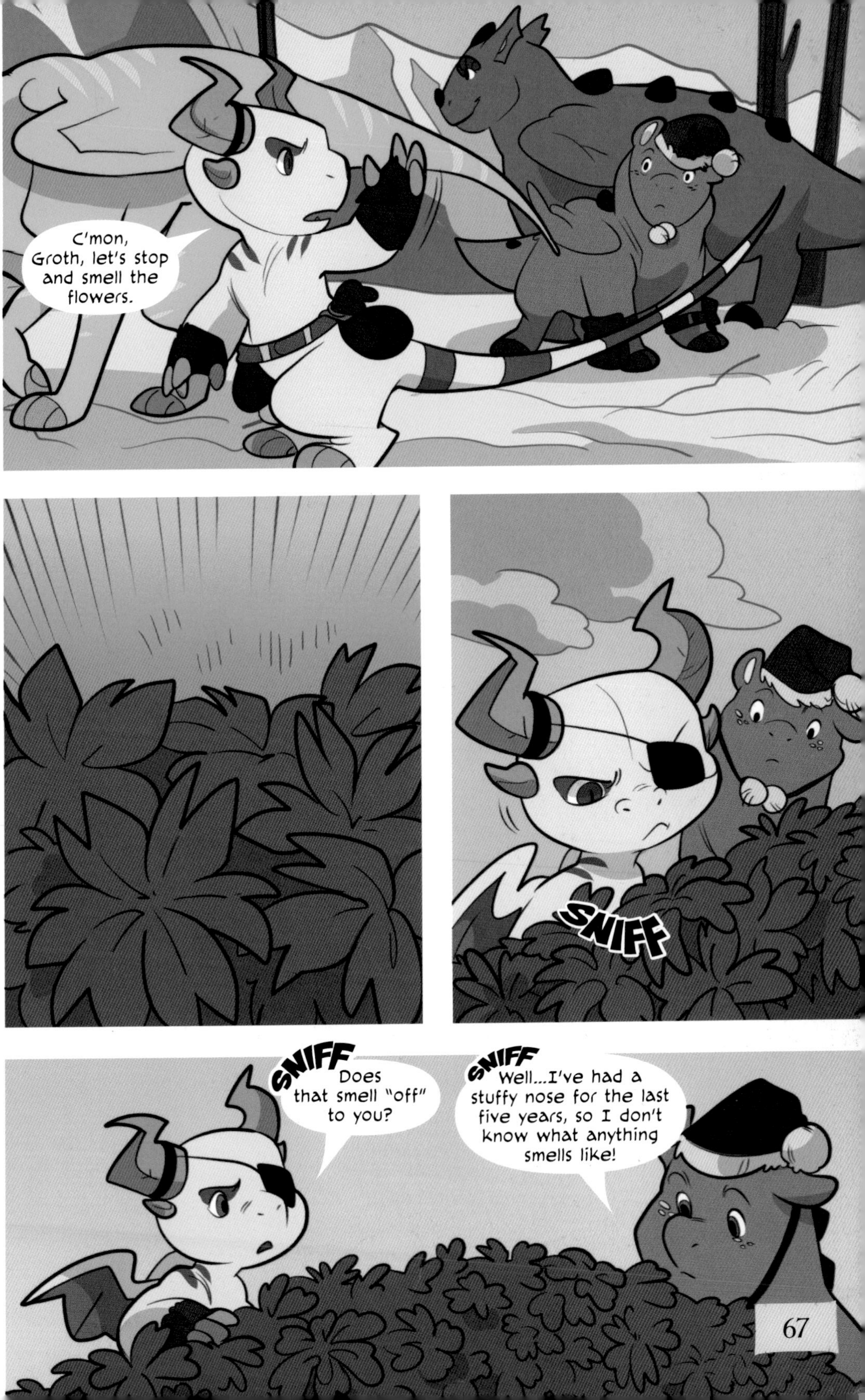
C'mon, Groth, let's stop and smell the flowers.
SNIFF
SNIFF
Does that smell "off" to you?
SNIFF
Well...I've had a stuffy nose for the last five years, so I don't know what anything smells like!

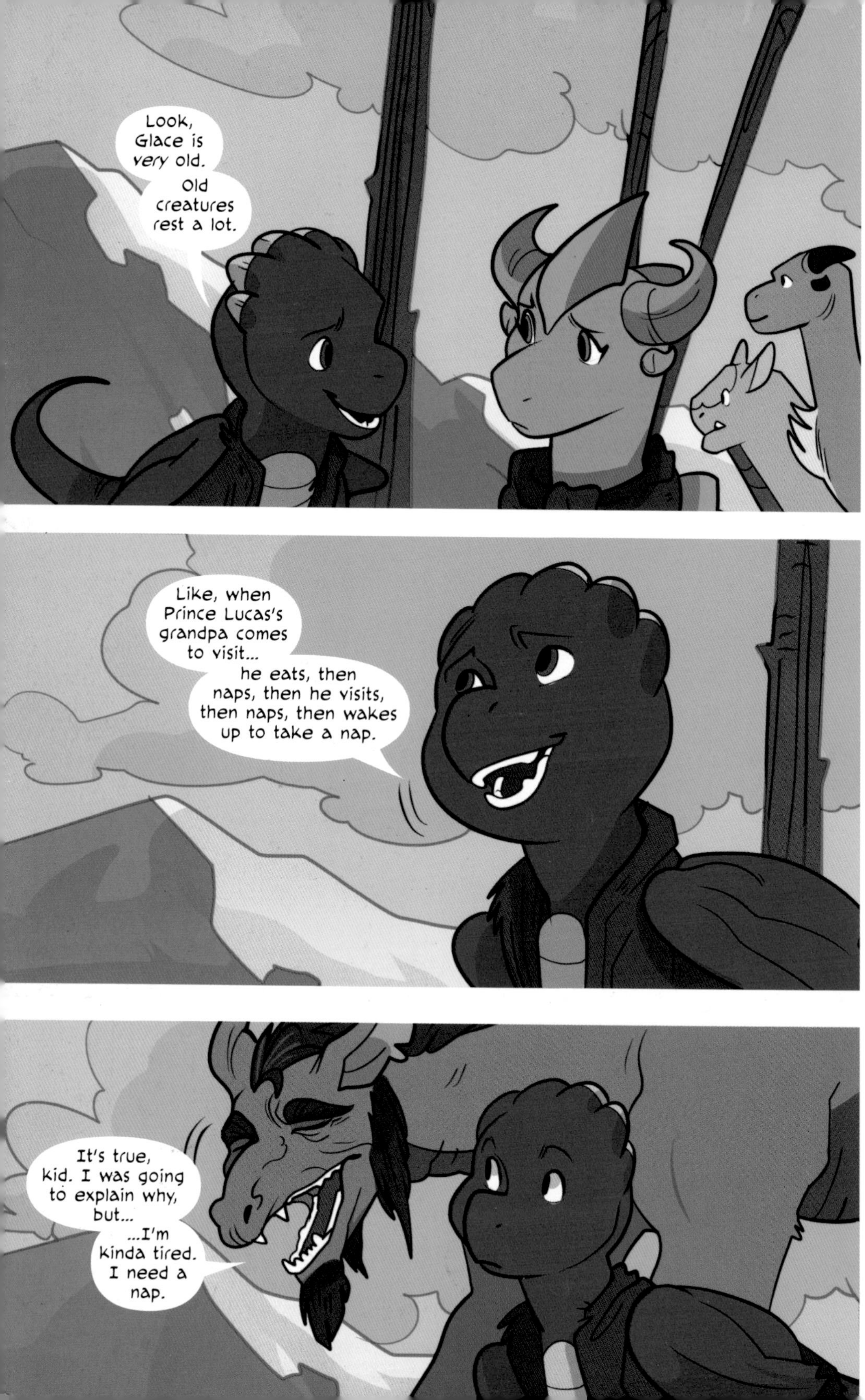
Look, Glace is *very* old.
Old creatures rest a lot.
Like, when Prince Lucas's grandpa comes to visit...
he eats, then naps, then he visits, then naps, then wakes up to take a nap.
It's true, kid. I was going to explain why, but...
...I'm kinda tired. I need a nap.

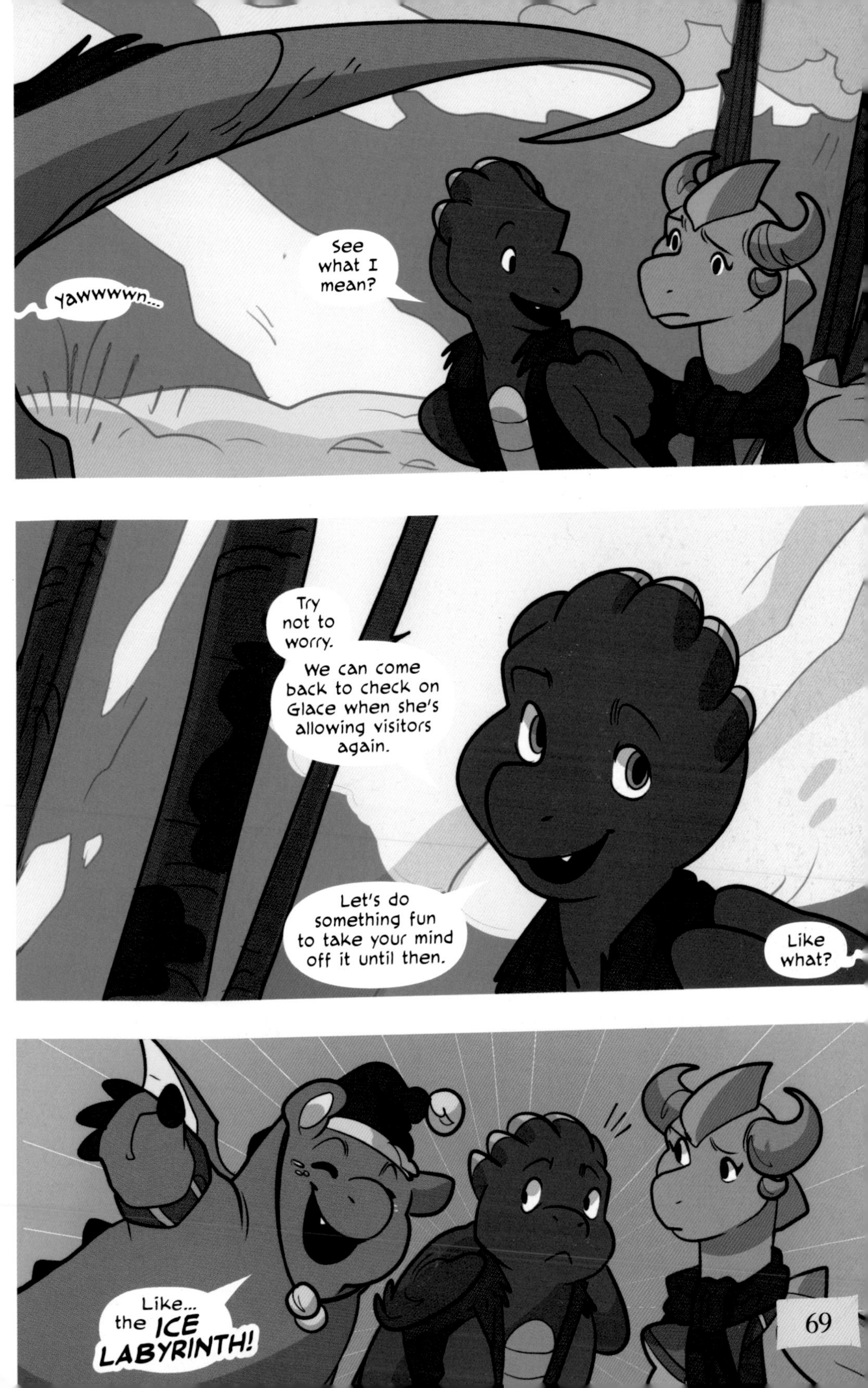
See what I mean?
yawwwwn...
Try not to worry.
We can come back to check on Glace when she's allowing visitors again.
Let's do something fun to take your mind off it until then.
Like what?
Like... the ICE LABYRINTH!

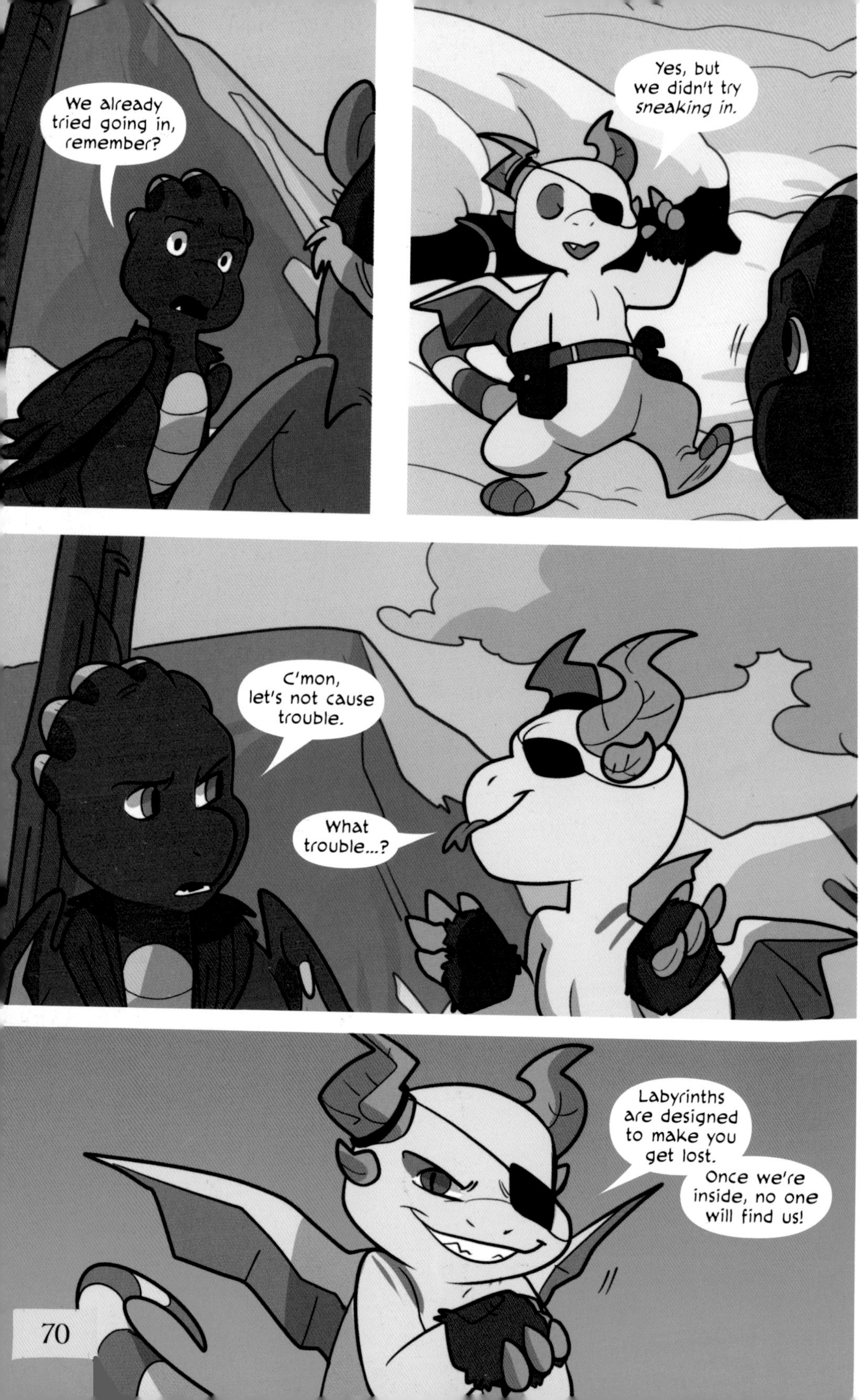
We already tried going in, remember?
Yes, but we didn't try *sneaking in.*
C'mon, let's not cause trouble.
What trouble...?
Labyrinths are designed to make you get lost.
Once we're inside, no one will find us!

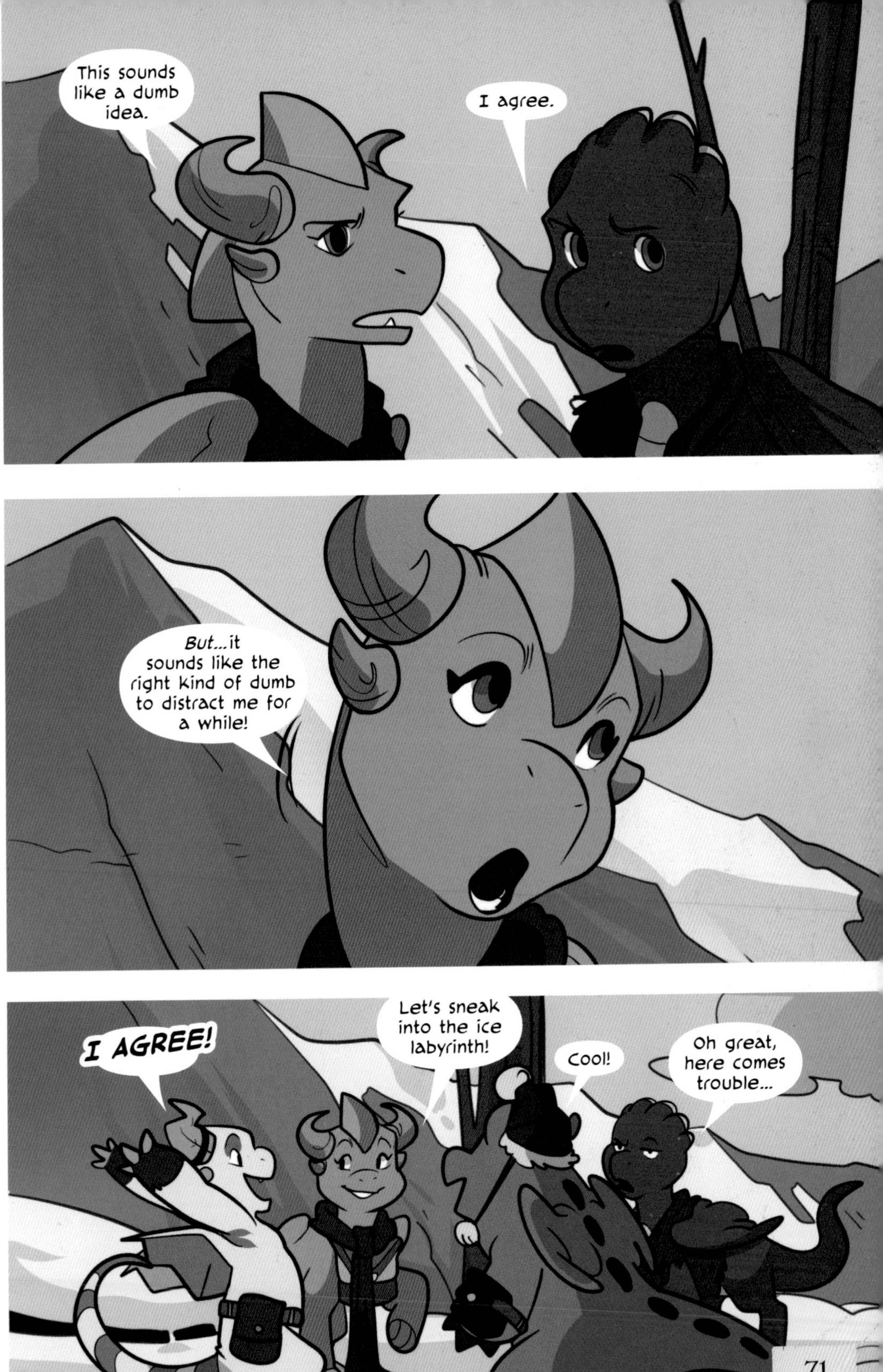
This sounds like a dumb idea.
I agree.
*But...*it sounds like the right kind of dumb to distract me for a while!
I AGREE!
Let's sneak into the ice labyrinth!
Cool!
Oh great, here comes trouble...

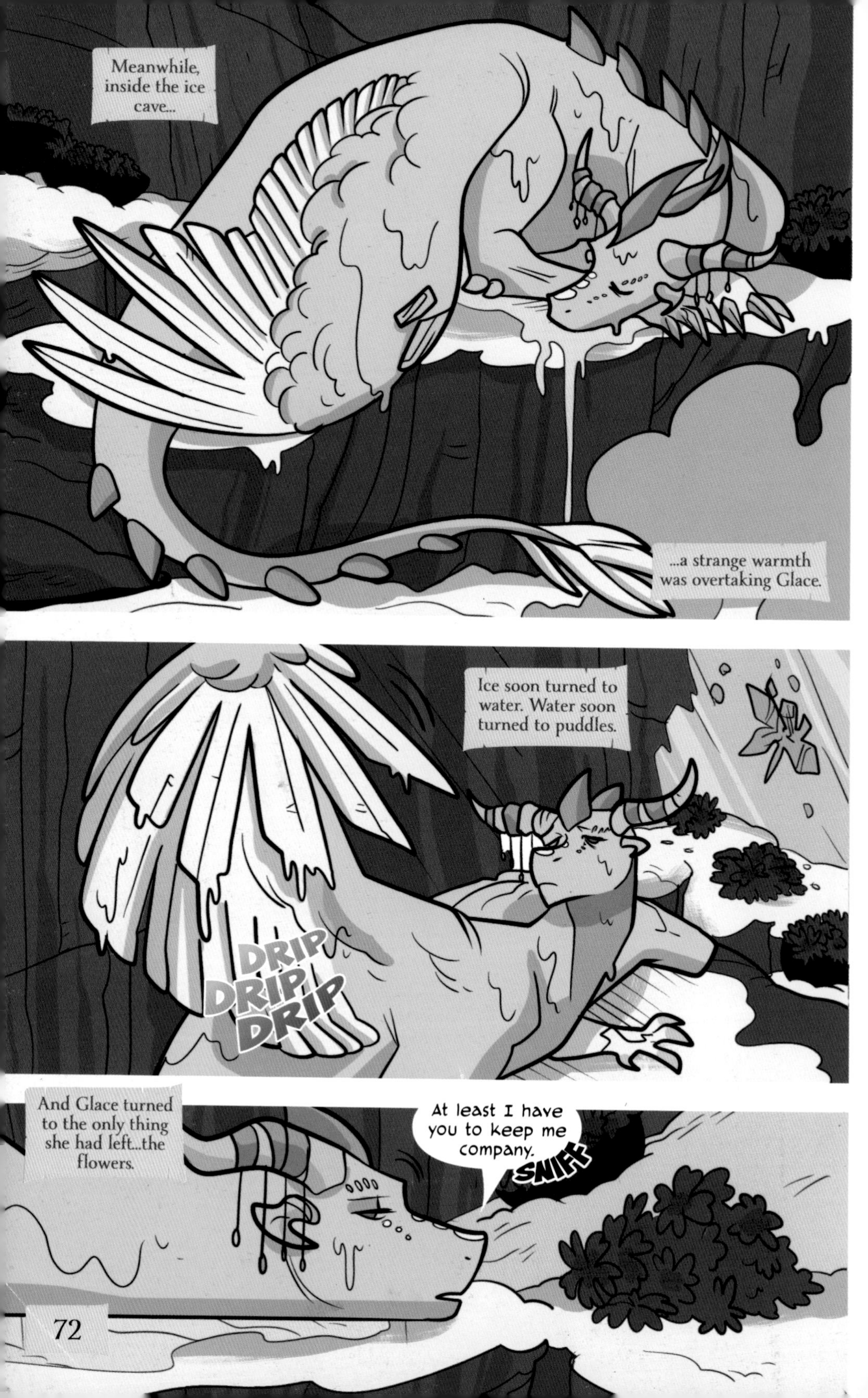
Meanwhile, inside the ice cave...
...a strange warmth was overtaking Glace.
Ice soon turned to water. Water soon turned to puddles.
DRIP DRIP DRIP
And Glace turned to the only thing she had left...the flowers.
At least I have you to keep me company.
SNIFF

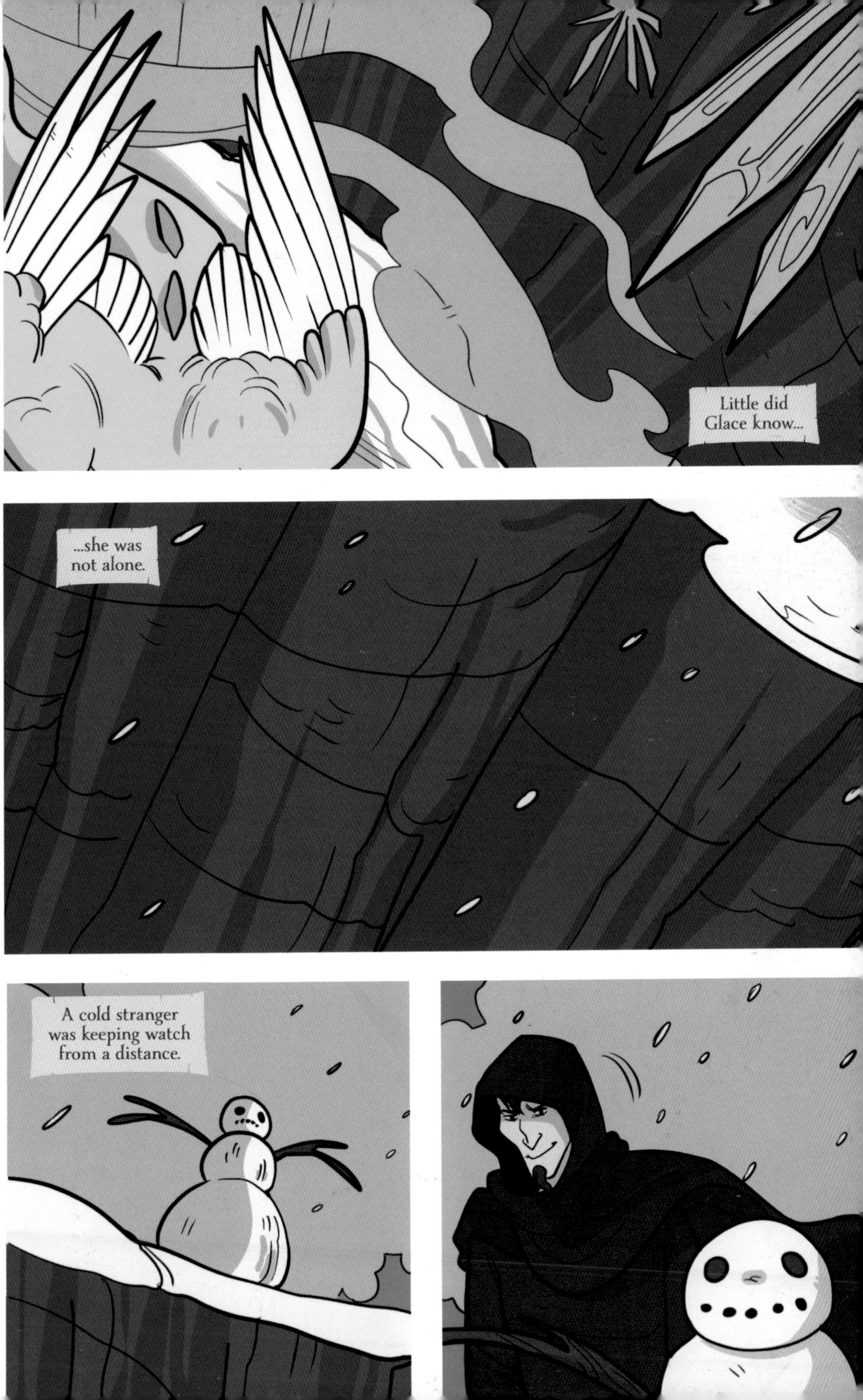
Little did Glace know...
...she was not alone.
A cold stranger was keeping watch from a distance.

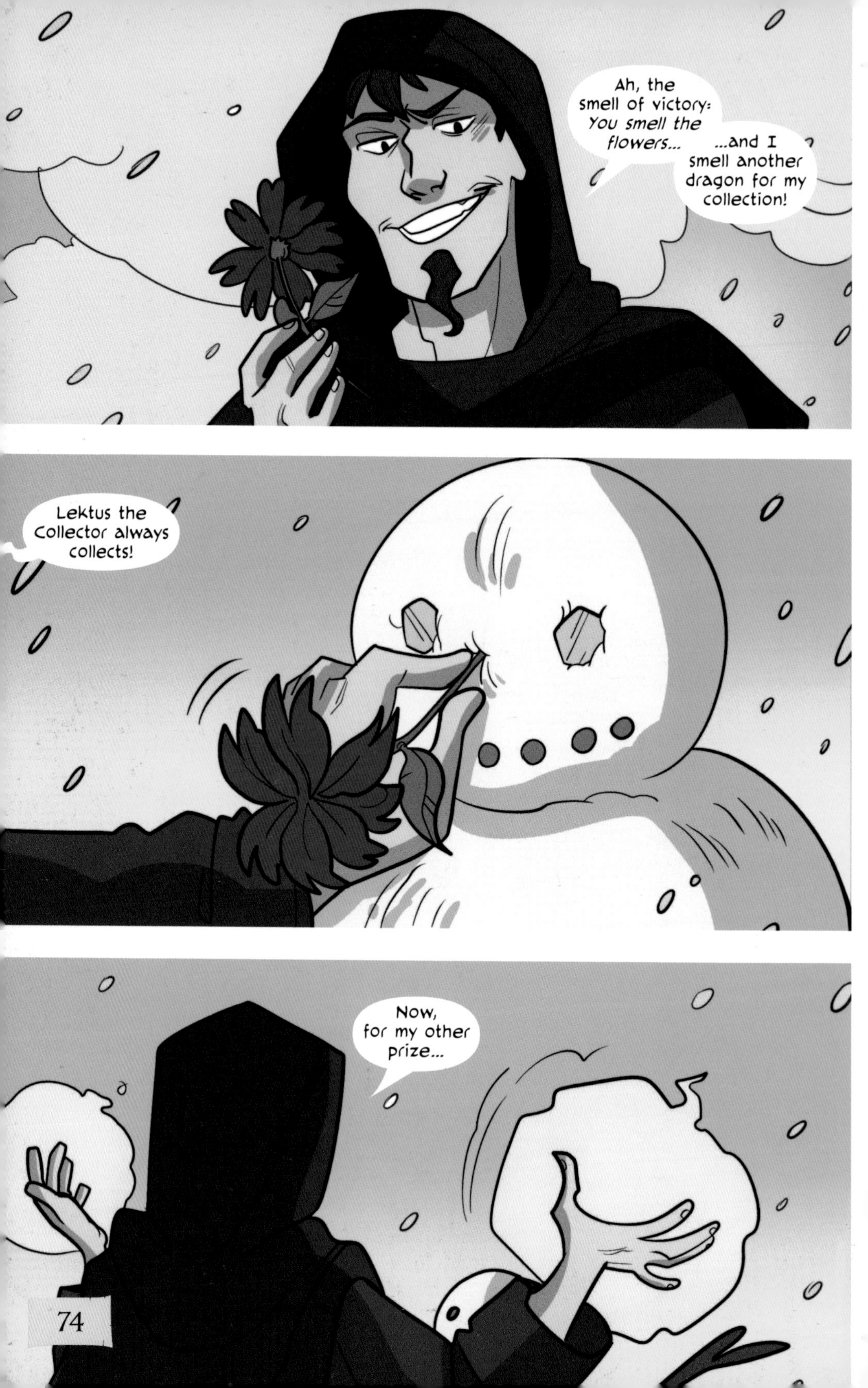
Ah, the smell of victory: You smell the flowers...
...and I smell another dragon for my collection!
Lektus the Collector always collects!
Now, for my other prize...

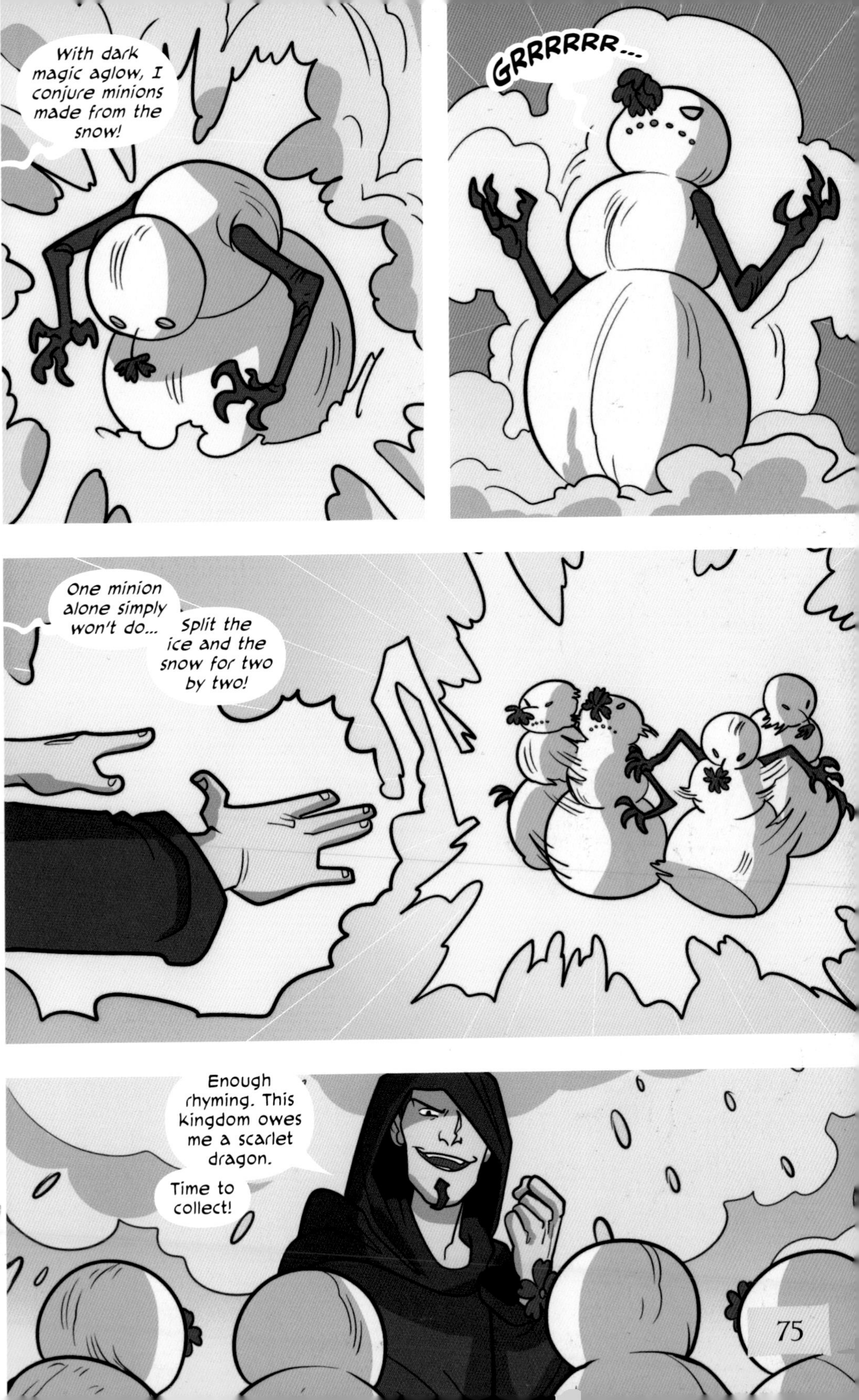
With dark magic aglow, I conjure minions made from the snow!
GRRRRRR...
One minion alone simply won't do...
Split the ice and the snow for two by two!
Enough rhyming. This kingdom owes me a scarlet dragon.
Time to collect!

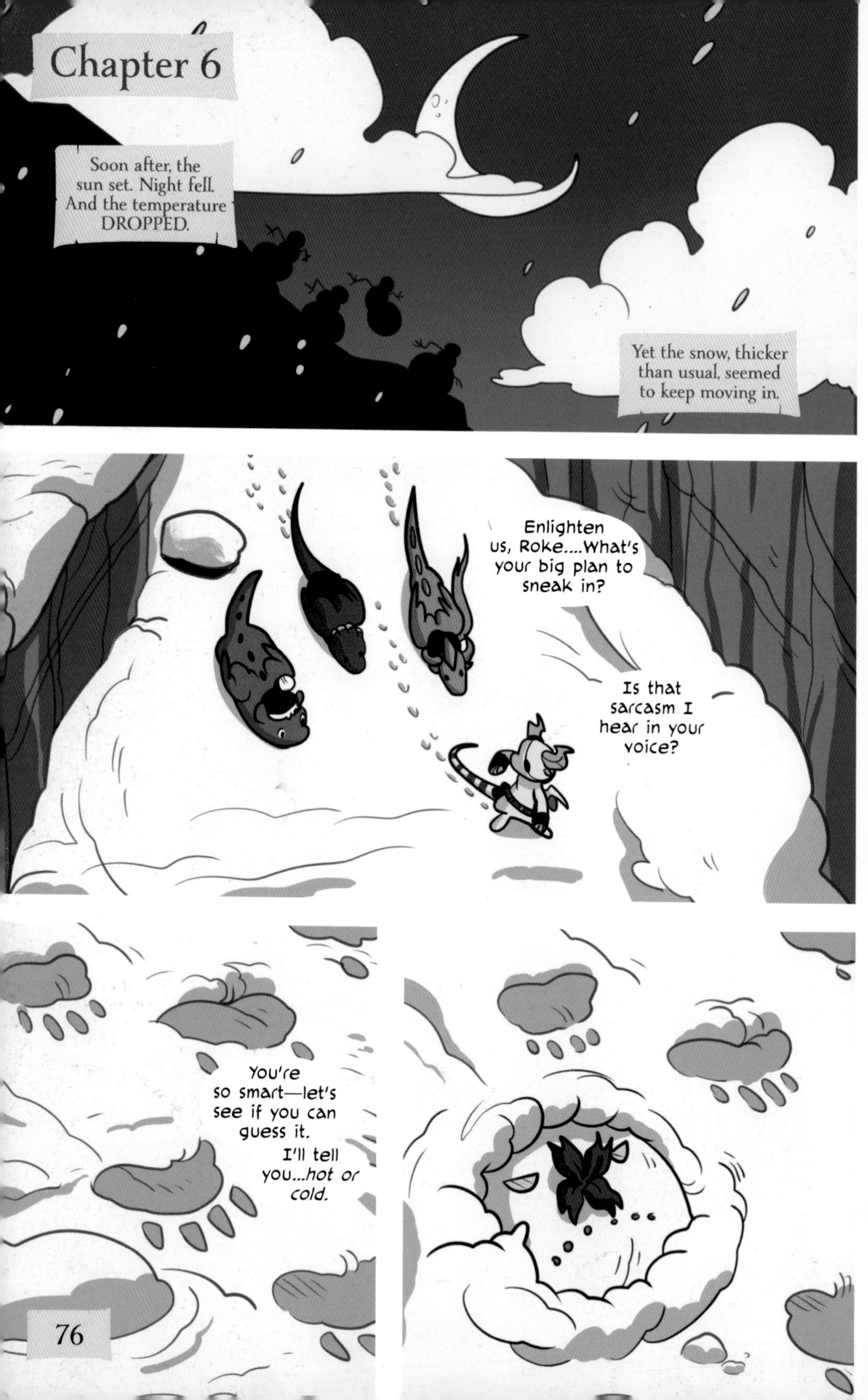
Chapter 6
Soon after, the sun set. Night fell. And the temperature DROPPED.
Yet the snow, thicker than usual, seemed to keep moving in.
Enlighten us, Roke....What's your big plan to sneak in?
Is that sarcasm I hear in your voice?
You're so smart—let's see if you can guess it.
I'll tell you...*hot or cold.*

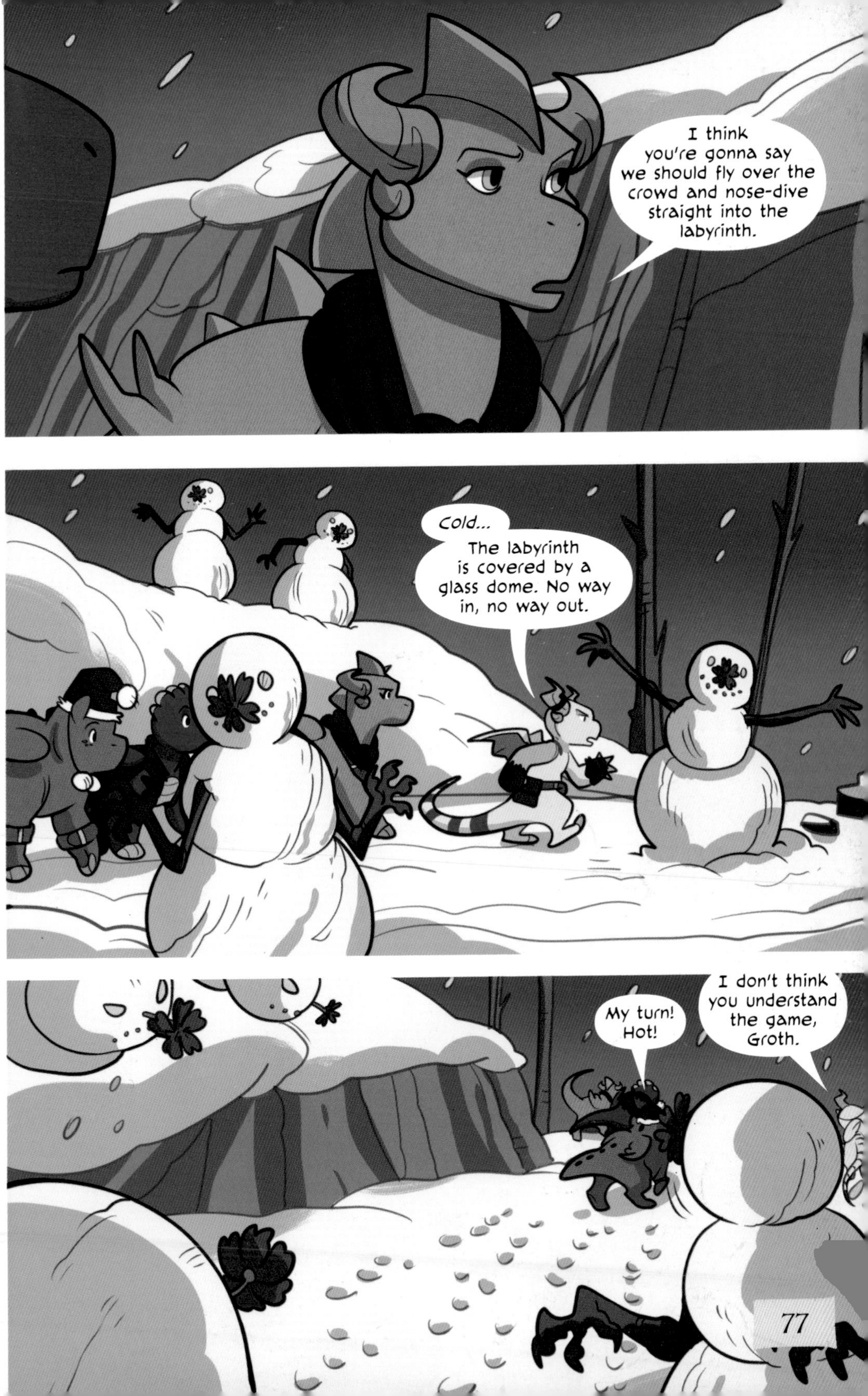
I think you're gonna say we should fly over the crowd and nose-dive straight into the labyrinth.
Cold...
The labyrinth is covered by a glass dome. No way in, no way out.
My turn! Hot!
I don't think you understand the game, Groth.

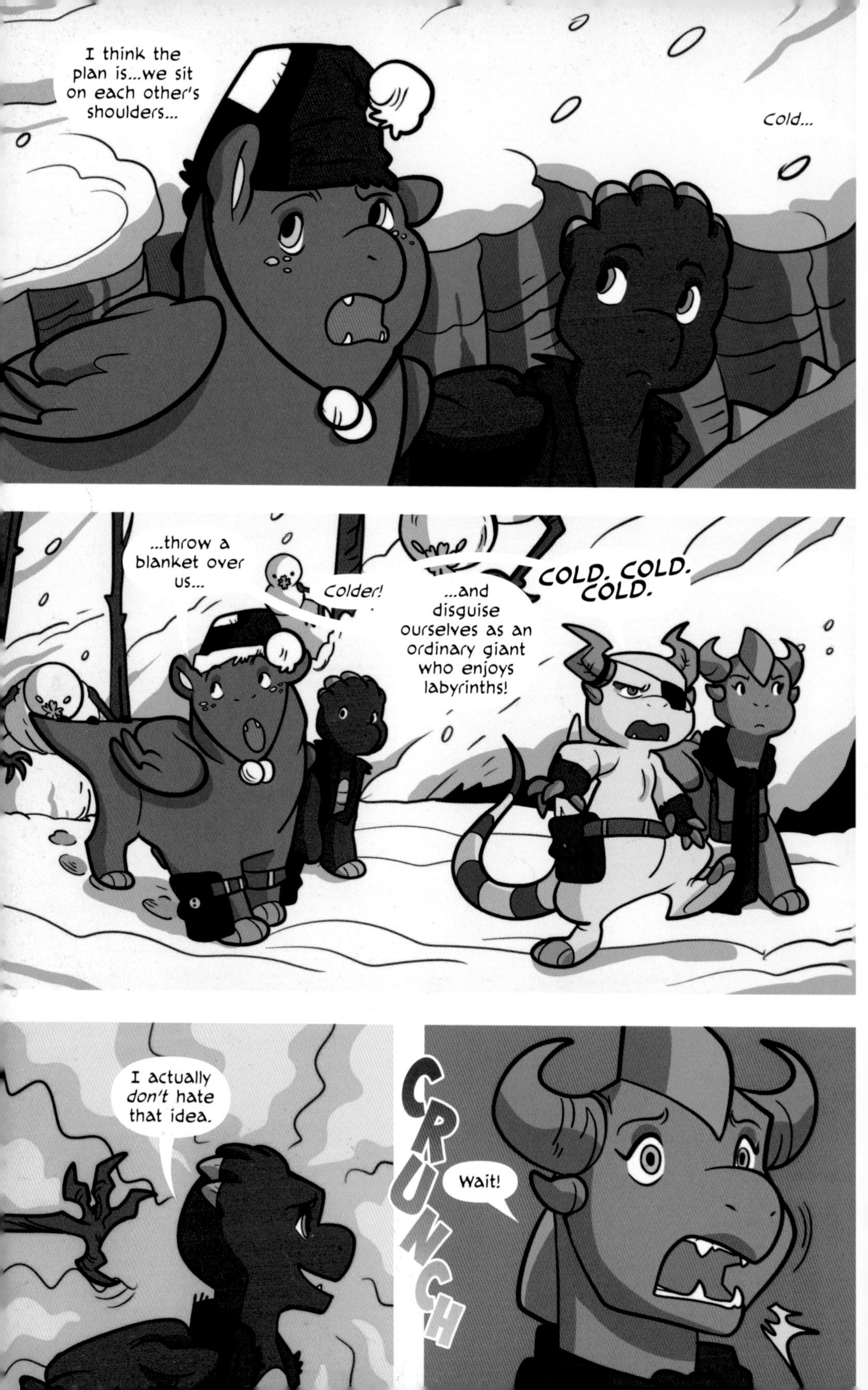
I think the plan is...we sit on each other's shoulders...
Cold...
...throw a blanket over us...
Colder!
...and disguise ourselves as an ordinary giant who enjoys labyrinths!
COLD. COLD. COLD.
I actually *don't* hate that idea.
CRUNCH
Wait!

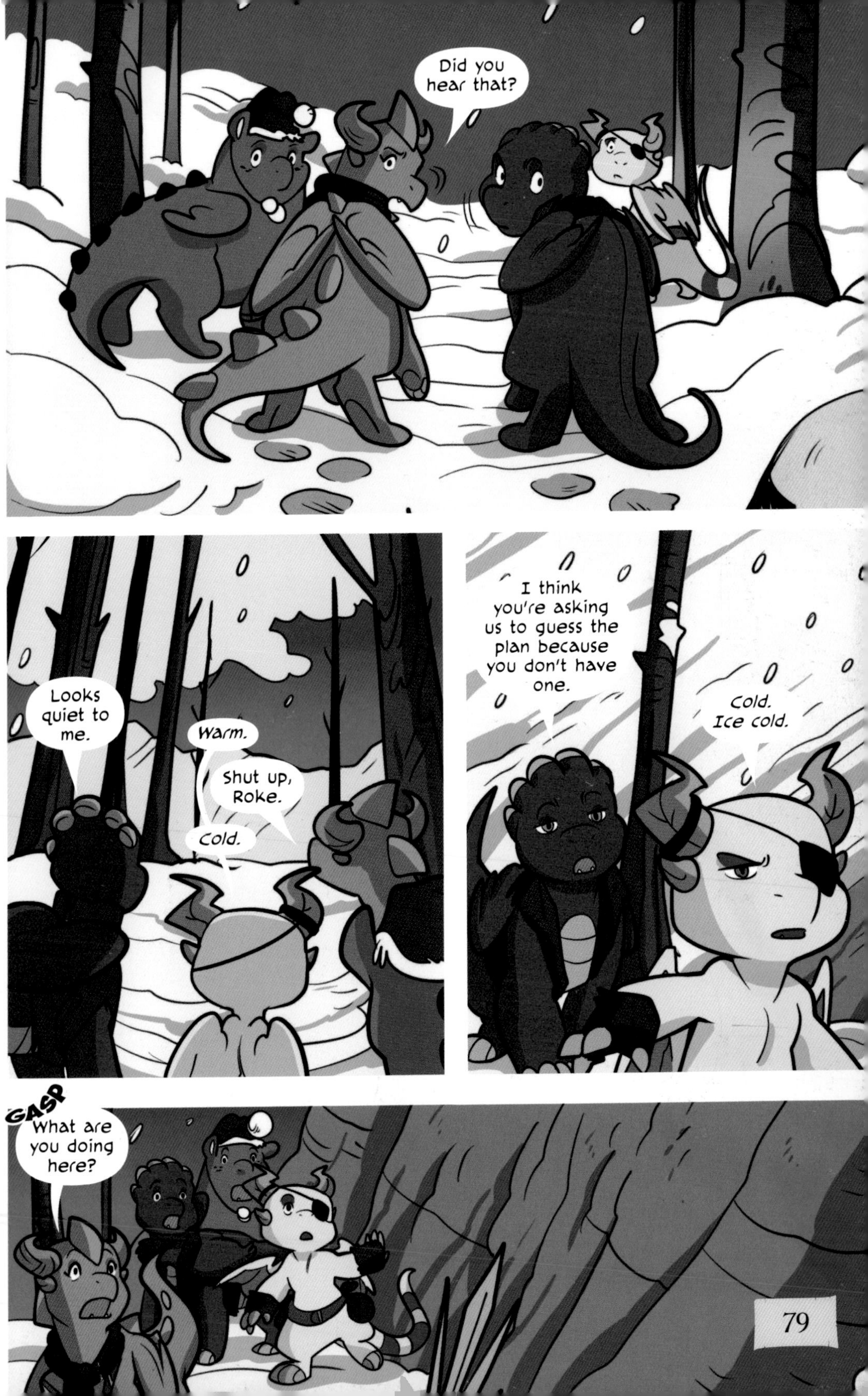
Did you hear that?
Looks quiet to me.
Warm.
Shut up, Roke.
Cold.
I think you're asking us to guess the plan because you don't have one.
Cold. Ice cold.
GASP
What are you doing here?

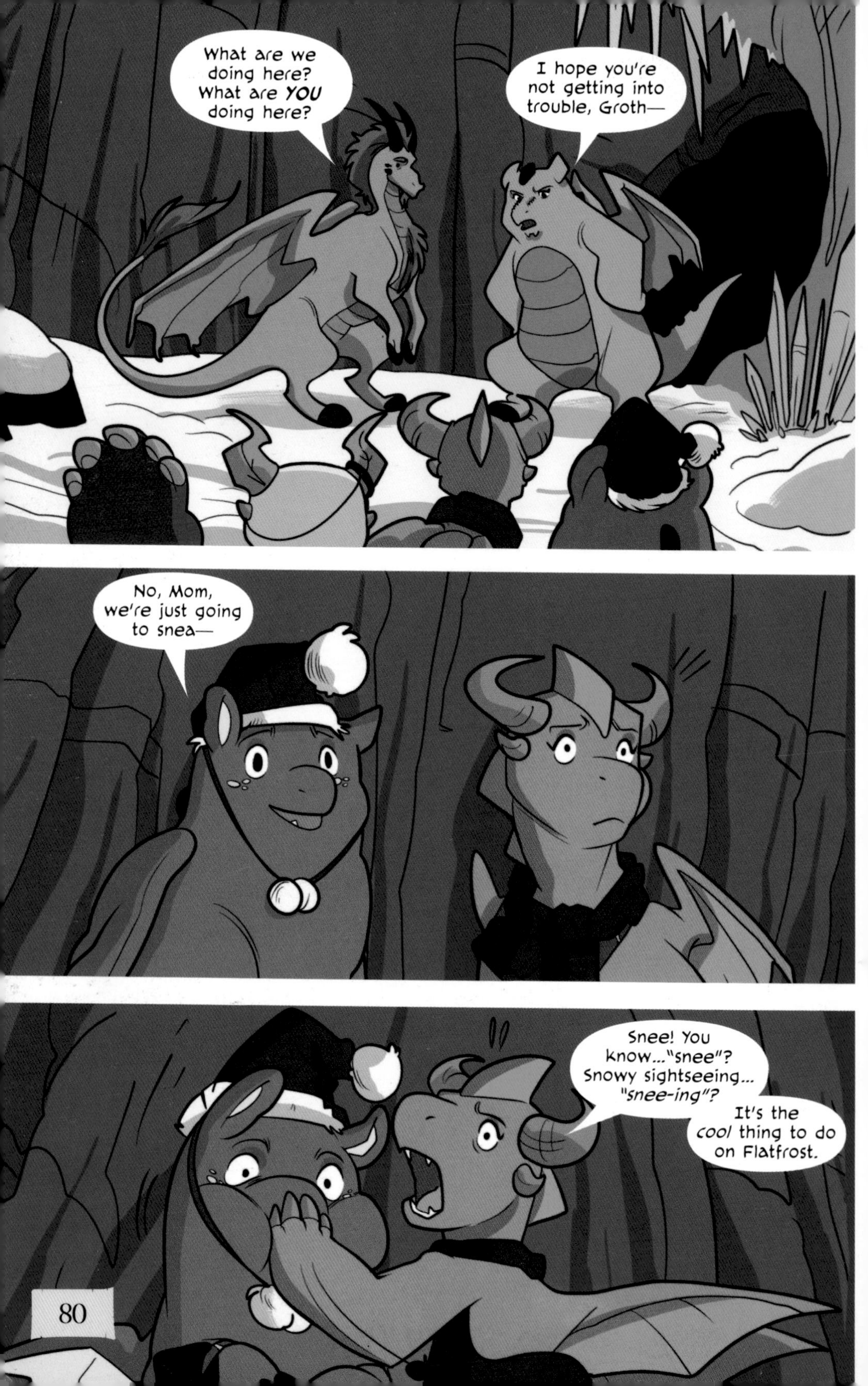
What are we doing here? What are *YOU* doing here?
I hope you're not getting into trouble, Groth—
No, Mom, we're just going to snea—
Snee! You know..."snee"? Snowy sightseeing... *"snee-ing"*?
It's the *cool* thing to do on Flatfrost.

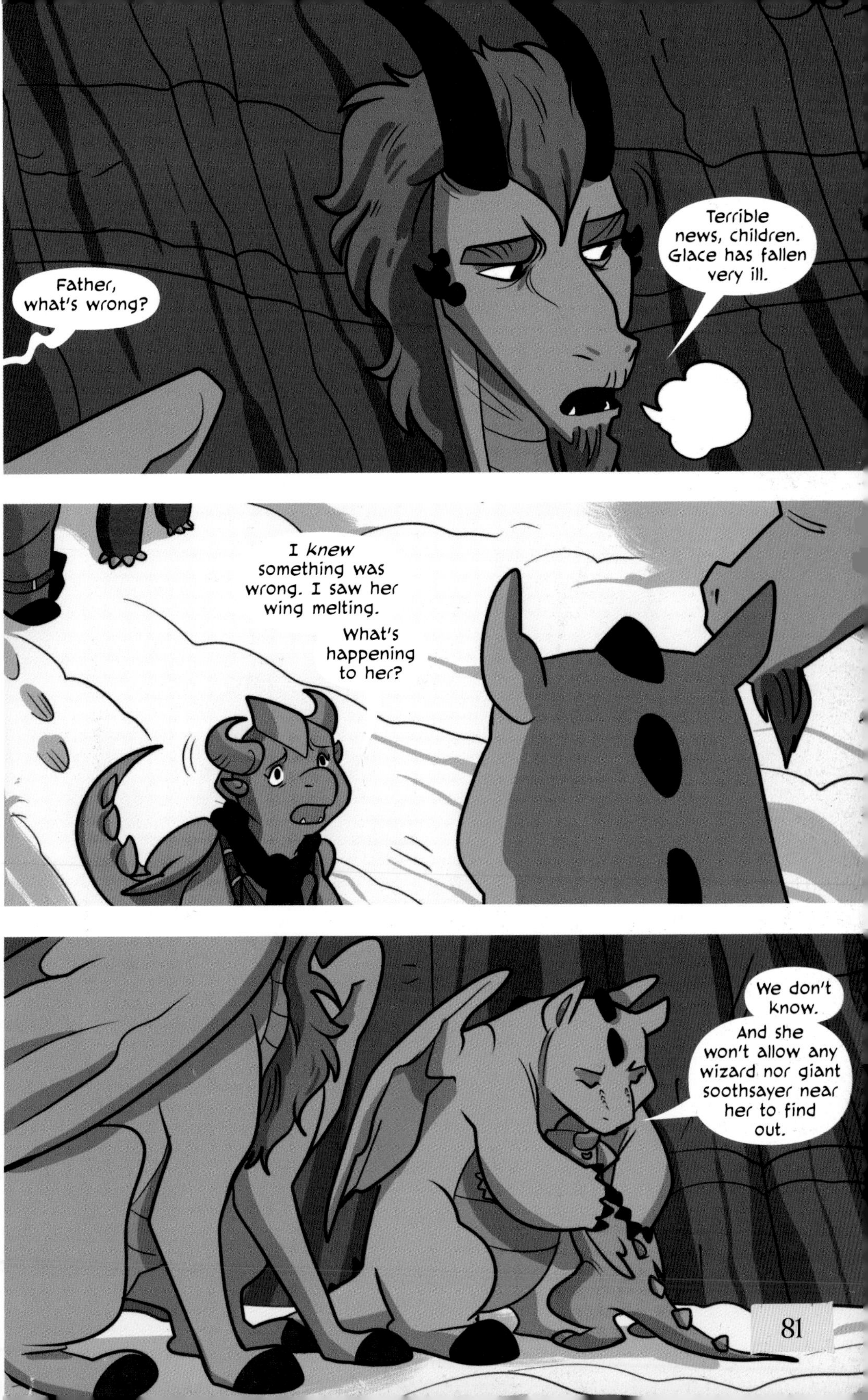
Father, what's wrong?
Terrible news, children. Glace has fallen very ill.
I *knew* something was wrong. I saw her wing melting.
What's happening to her?
We don't know.
And she won't allow any wizard nor giant soothsayer near her to find out.

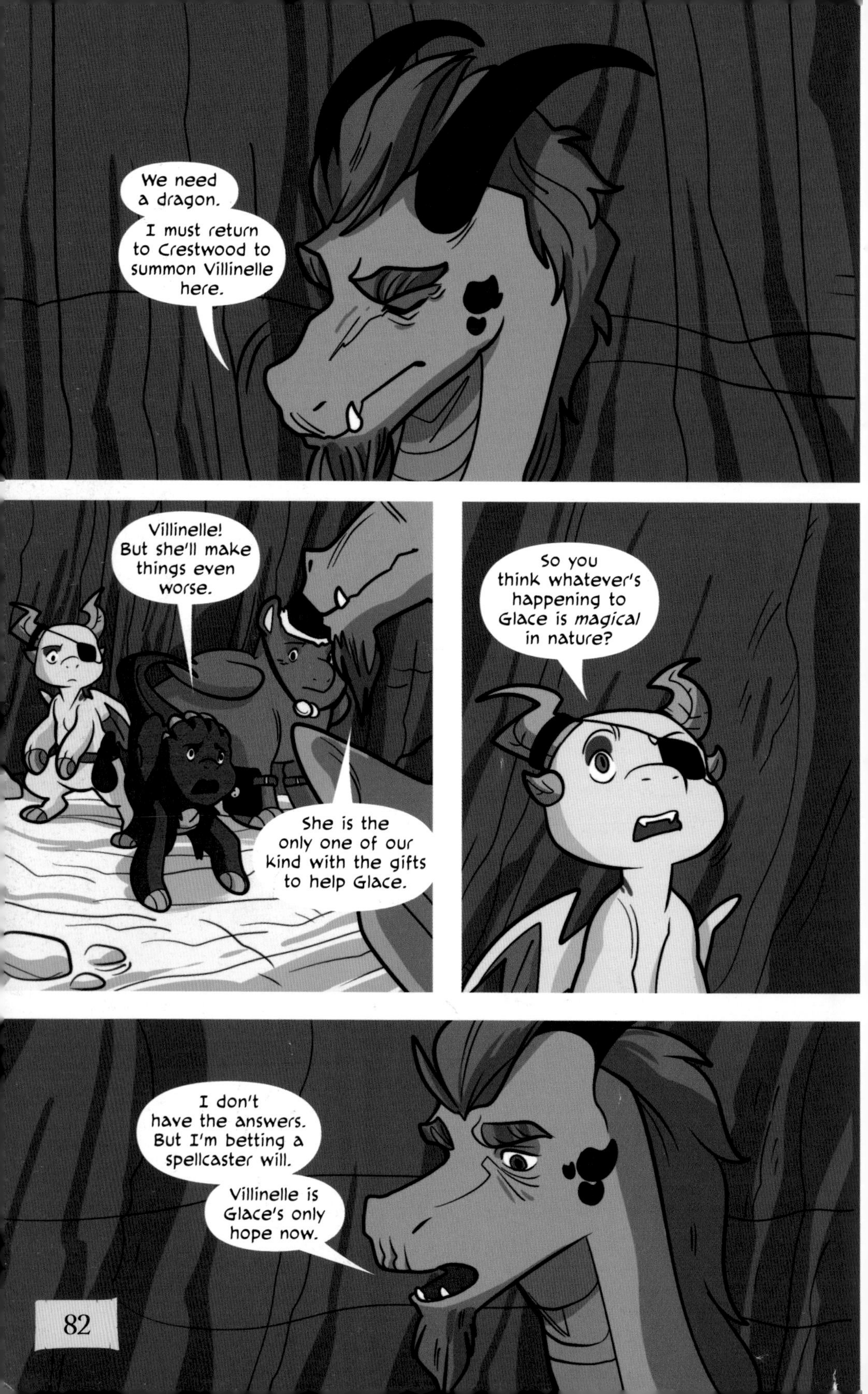
We need a dragon.
I must return to Crestwood to summon Villinelle here.
Villinelle! But she'll make things *even* worse.
She is the only one of our kind with the gifts to help Glace.
So you think whatever's happening to Glace is *magical* in nature?
I don't have the answers. But I'm betting a spellcaster will.
Villinelle is Glace's only hope now.

I think Villinelle should have a closer look at *this.*
It smells bitter...almost toxic.
These flowers were in Glace's cave.
Visitors were bringing them in. I didn't think anything of it at first...
...but there was a giant-lady— ***a flower seller***— handing these out on the mountain.
She was giving them away by the bunch, practically begging us to take them inside. I think she's behind this.
Why didn't you say something before?

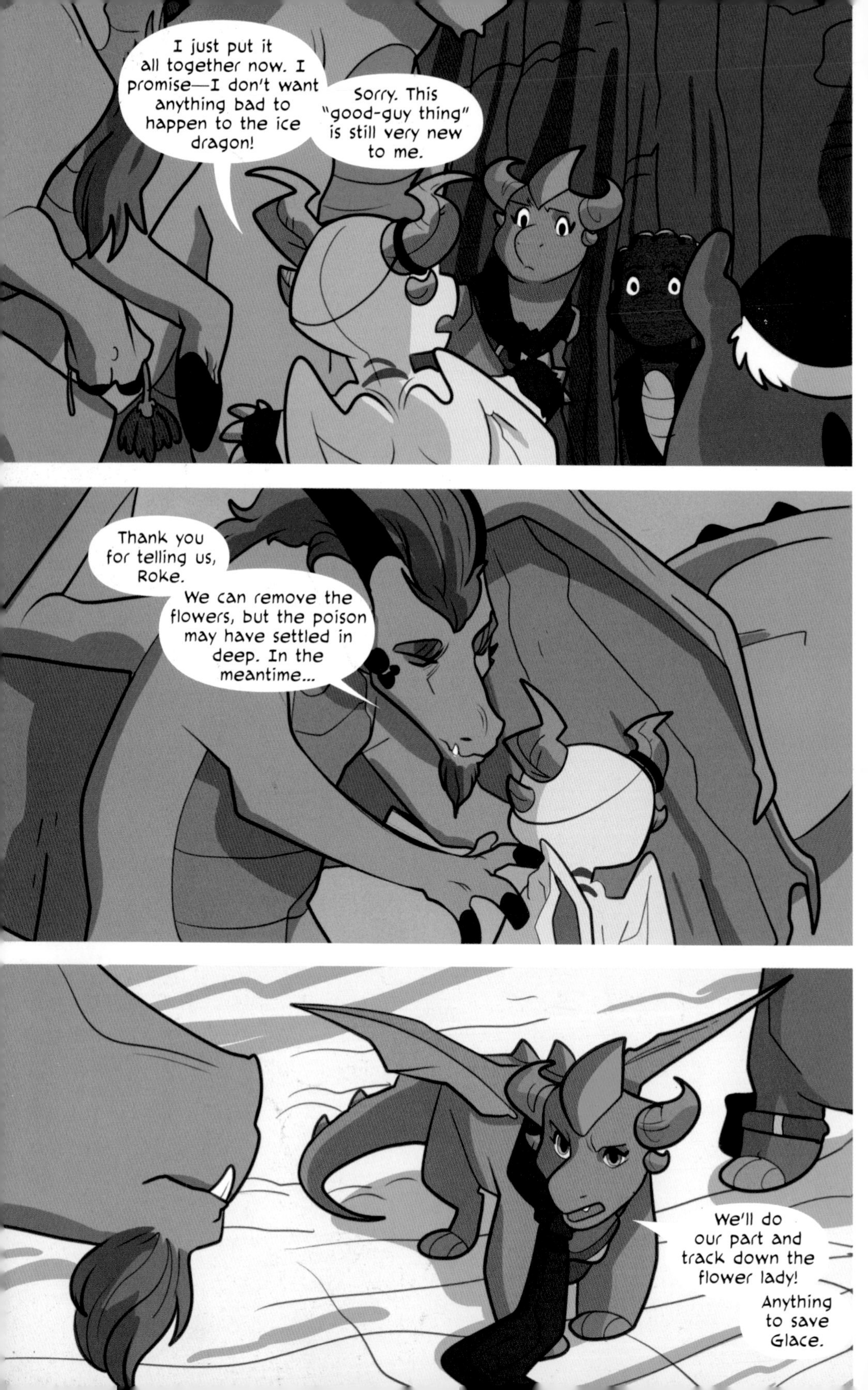
I just put it all together now. I promise—I don't want anything bad to happen to the ice dragon!
Sorry. This "good-guy thing" is still very new to me.
Thank you for telling us, Roke.
We can remove the flowers, but the poison may have settled in deep. In the meantime...
We'll do our part and track down the flower lady!
Anything to save Glace.

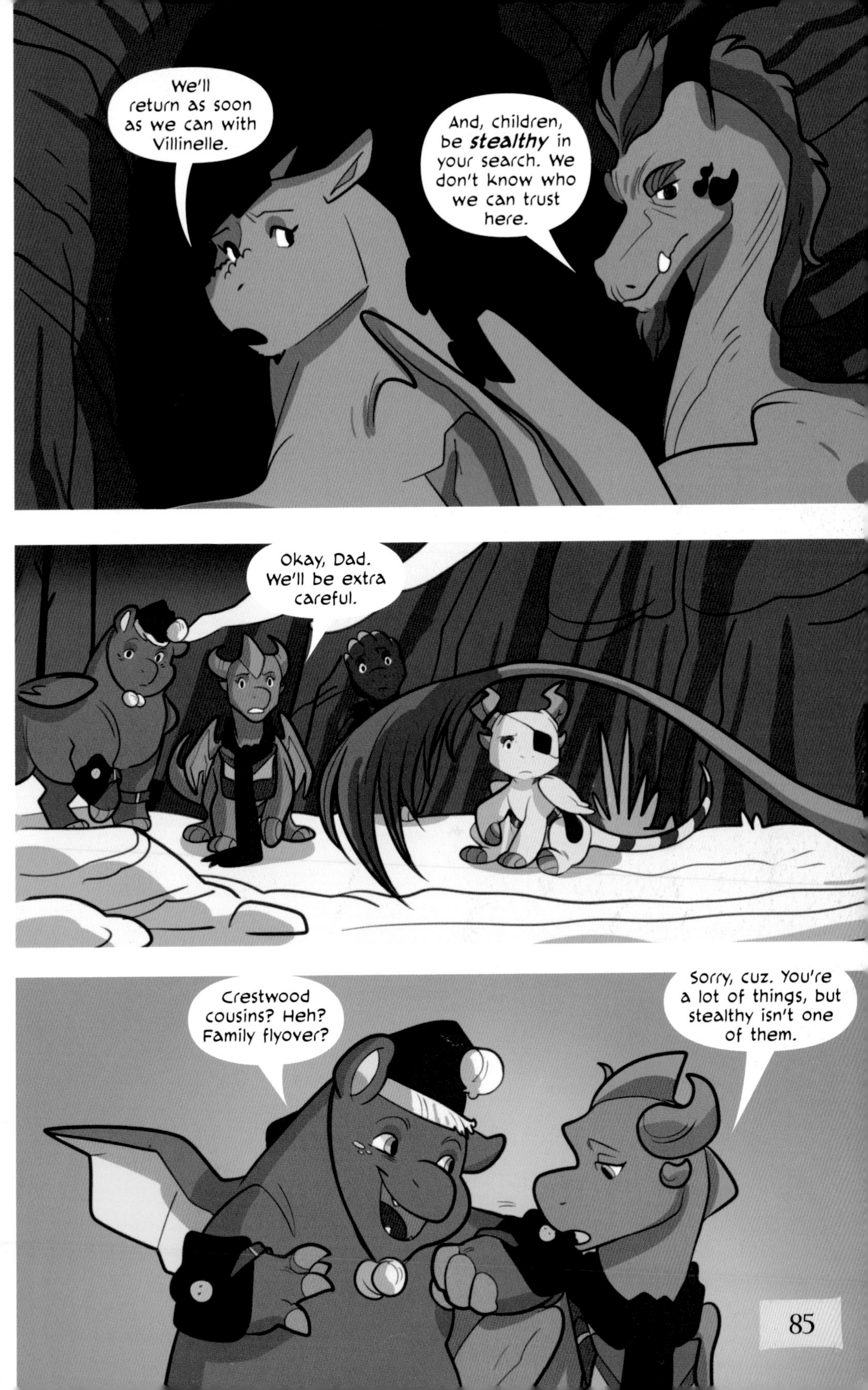

We'll return as soon as we can with Villinelle.
And, children, be *stealthy* in your search. We don't know who we can trust here.
Okay, Dad. We'll be extra careful.
Crestwood cousins? Heh? Family flyover?
Sorry, cuz. You're a lot of things, but stealthy isn't one of them.

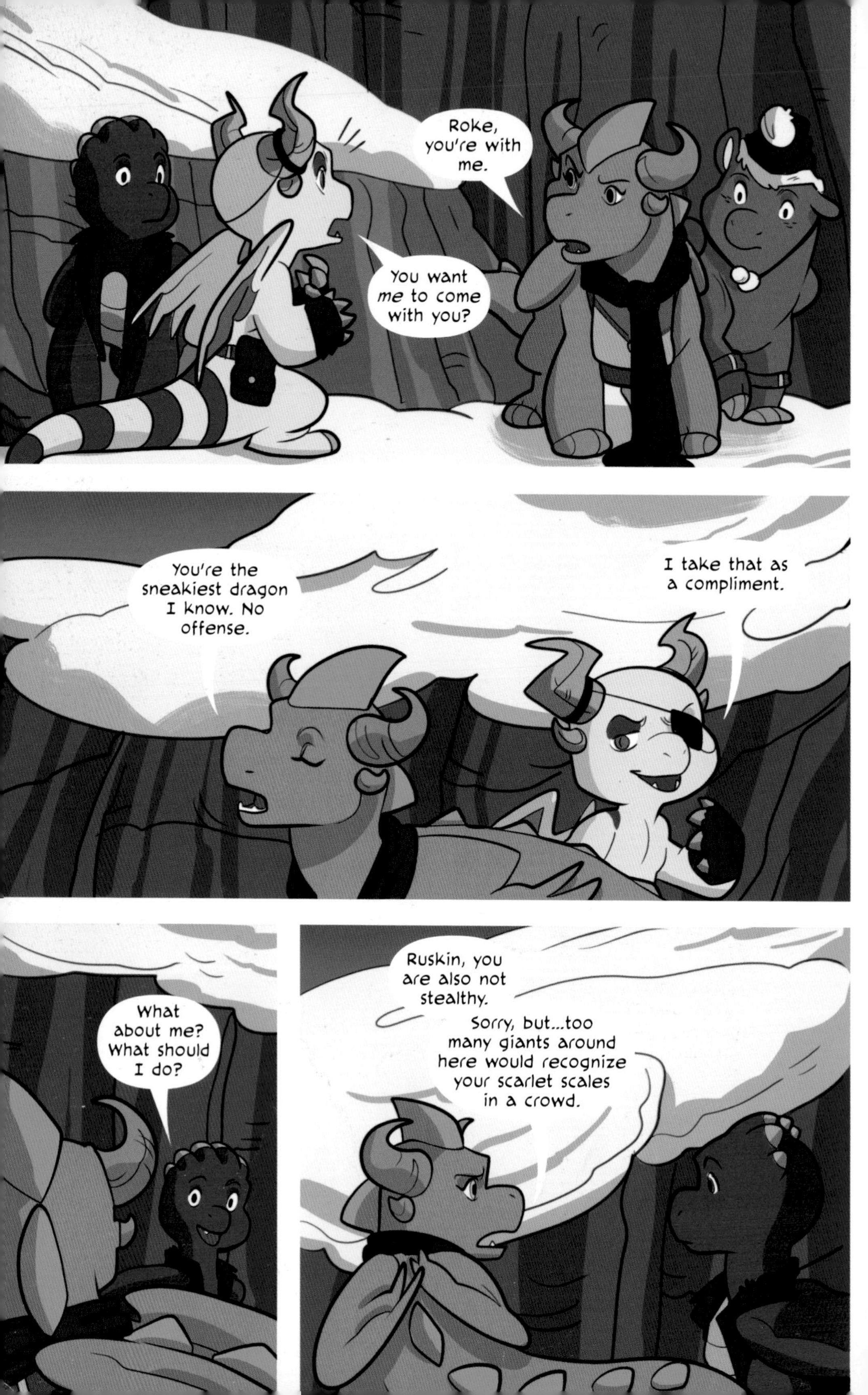
Roke, you're with me.
You want *me* to come with you?
You're the sneakiest dragon I know. No offense.
I take that as a compliment.
What about me? What should I do?
Ruskin, you are also not stealthy.
Sorry, but...too many giants around here would recognize your scarlet scales in a crowd.

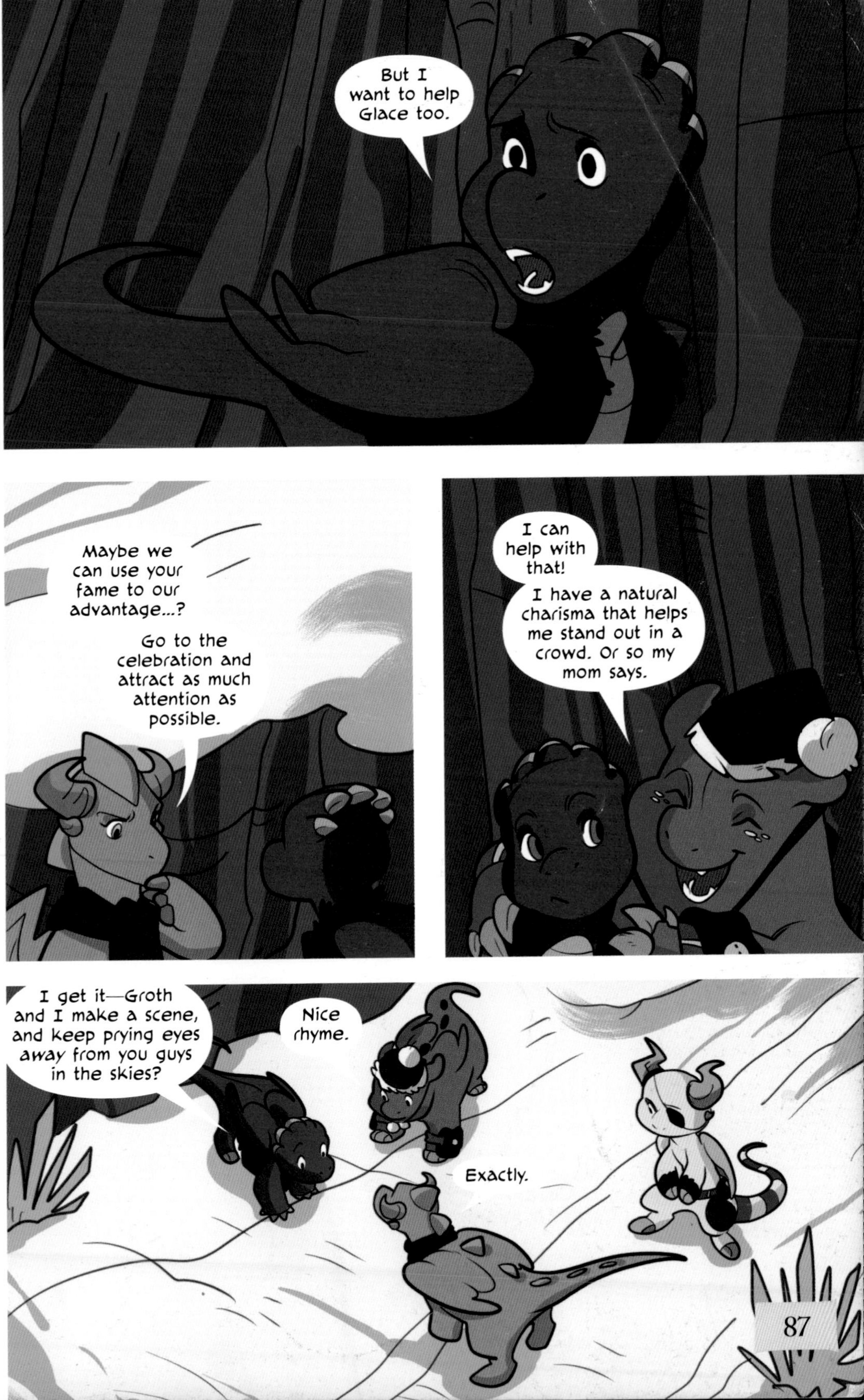
But I want to help Glace too.
Maybe we can use your fame to our advantage...?
Go to the celebration and attract as much attention as possible.
I can help with that!
I have a natural charisma that helps me stand out in a crowd. Or so my mom says.
I get it—Groth and I make a scene, and keep prying eyes away from you guys in the skies?
Nice rhyme.
Exactly.

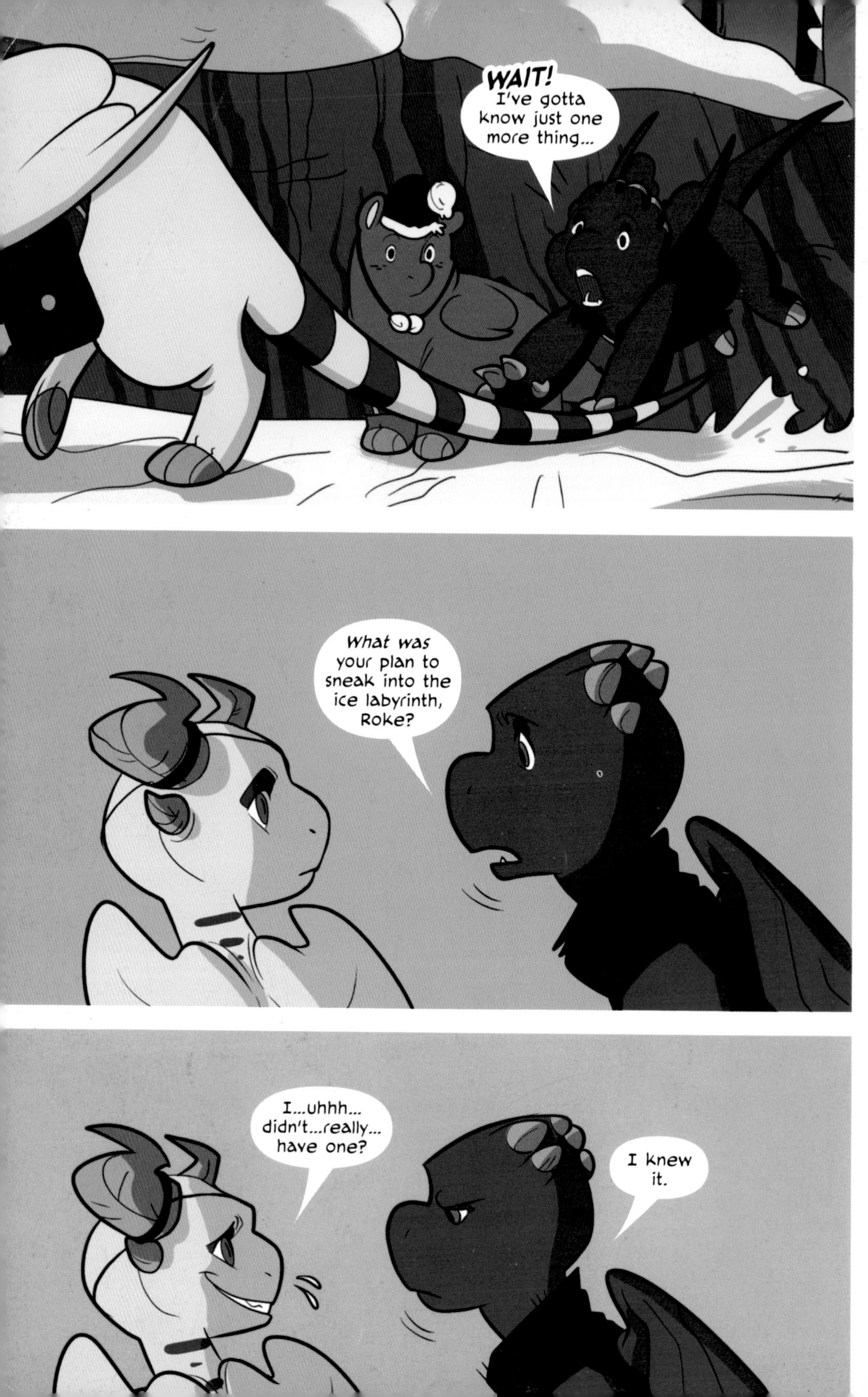
WAIT! I've gotta know just one more thing...
What was your plan to sneak into the ice labyrinth, Roke?
I...uhhh... didn't...really... have one?
I knew it.

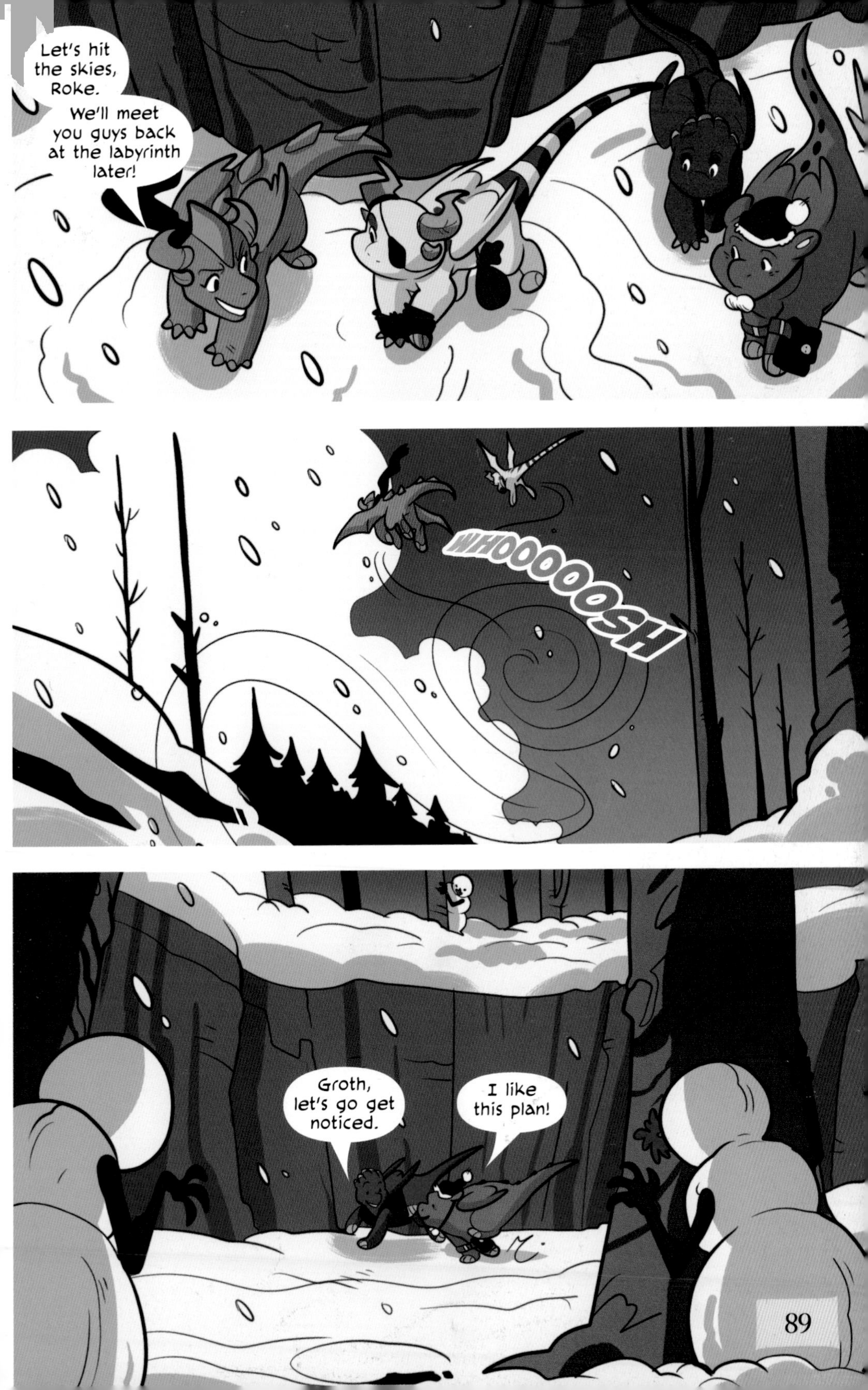
Let's hit the skies, Roke.
We'll meet you guys back at the labyrinth later!
WHOOOOOOSH
Groth, let's go get noticed.
I like this plan!

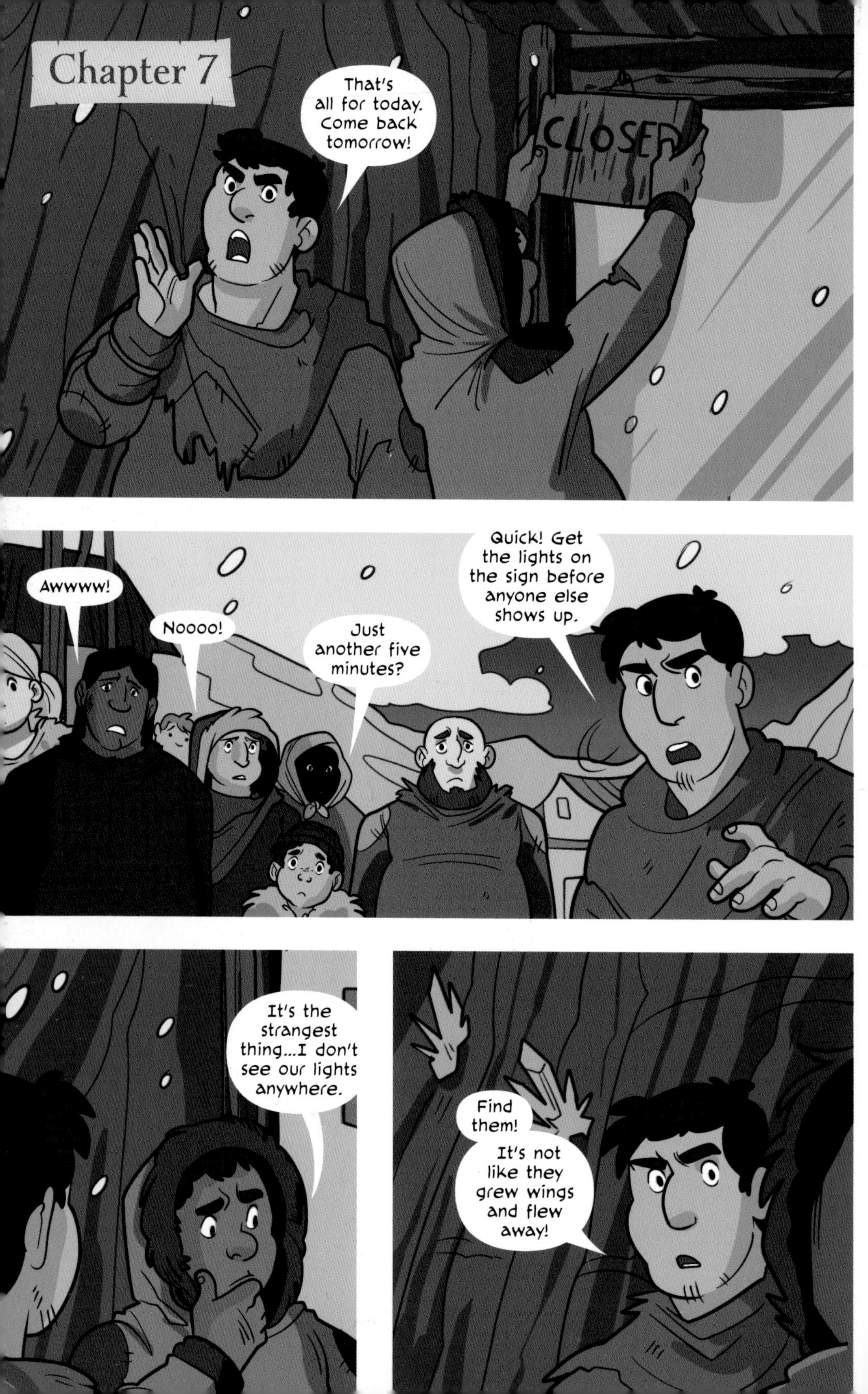
Chapter 7
That's all for today. Come back tomorrow!
CLOSED
Awwww!
Noooo!
Just another five minutes?
Quick! Get the lights on the sign before anyone else shows up.
It's the strangest thing...I don't see our lights anywhere.
Find them!
It's not like they grew wings and flew away!

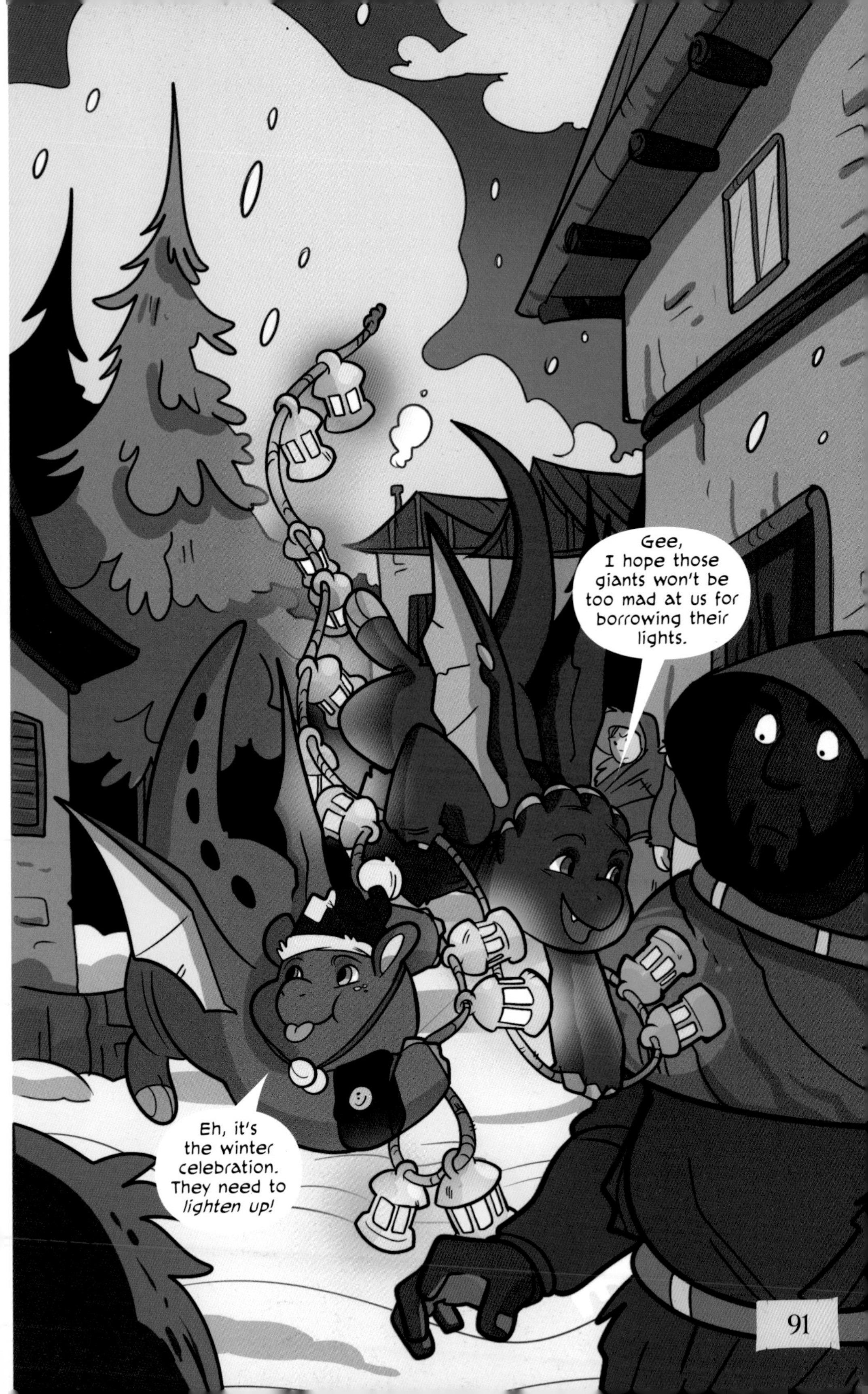
Gee, I hope those giants won't be too mad at us for borrowing their lights.
Eh, it's the winter celebration. They need to *lighten up!*

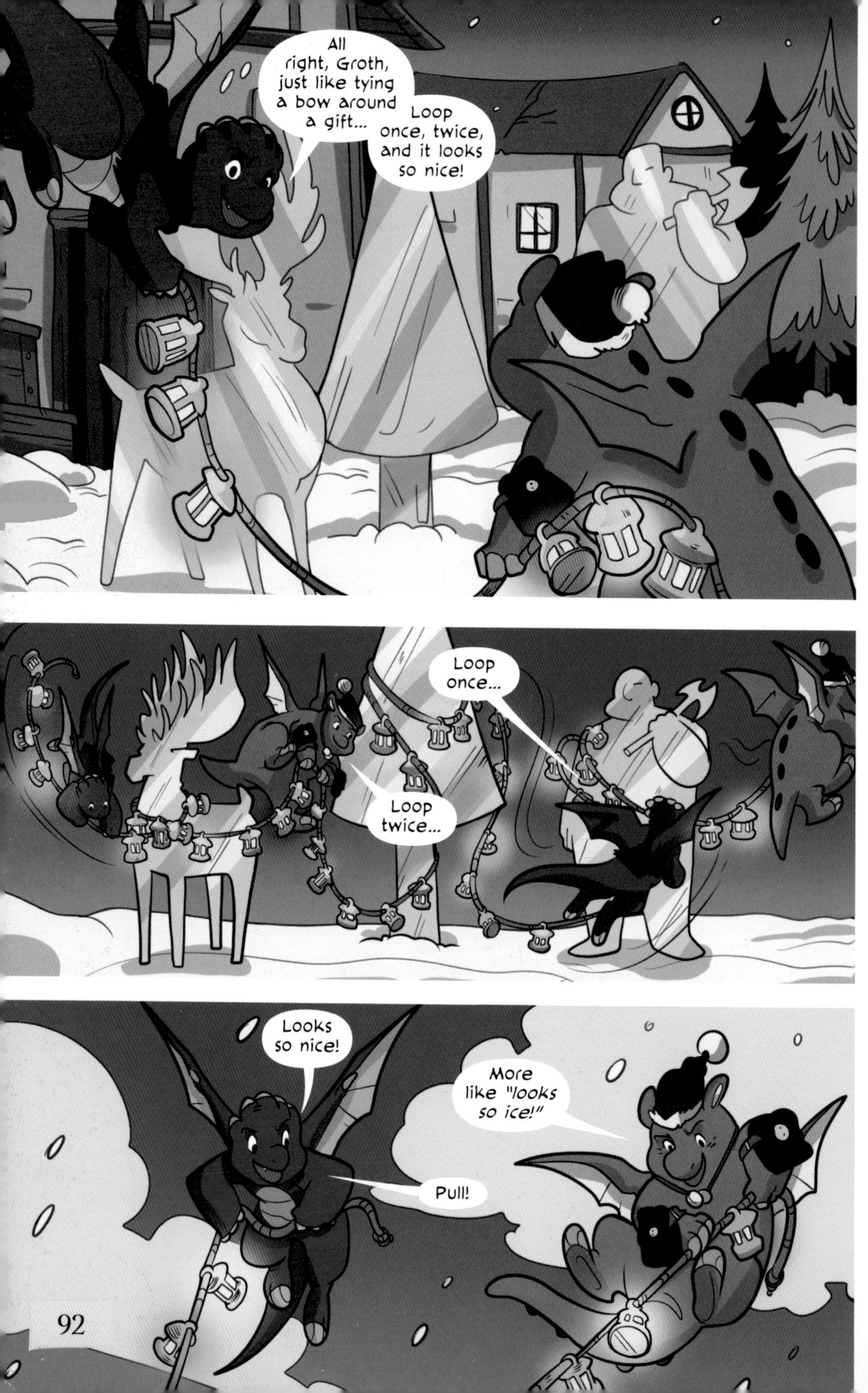
All right, Groth, just like tying a bow around a gift...
Loop once, twice, and it looks so nice!
Loop once...
Loop twice...
Looks so nice!
Pull!
More like "looks so ice!"

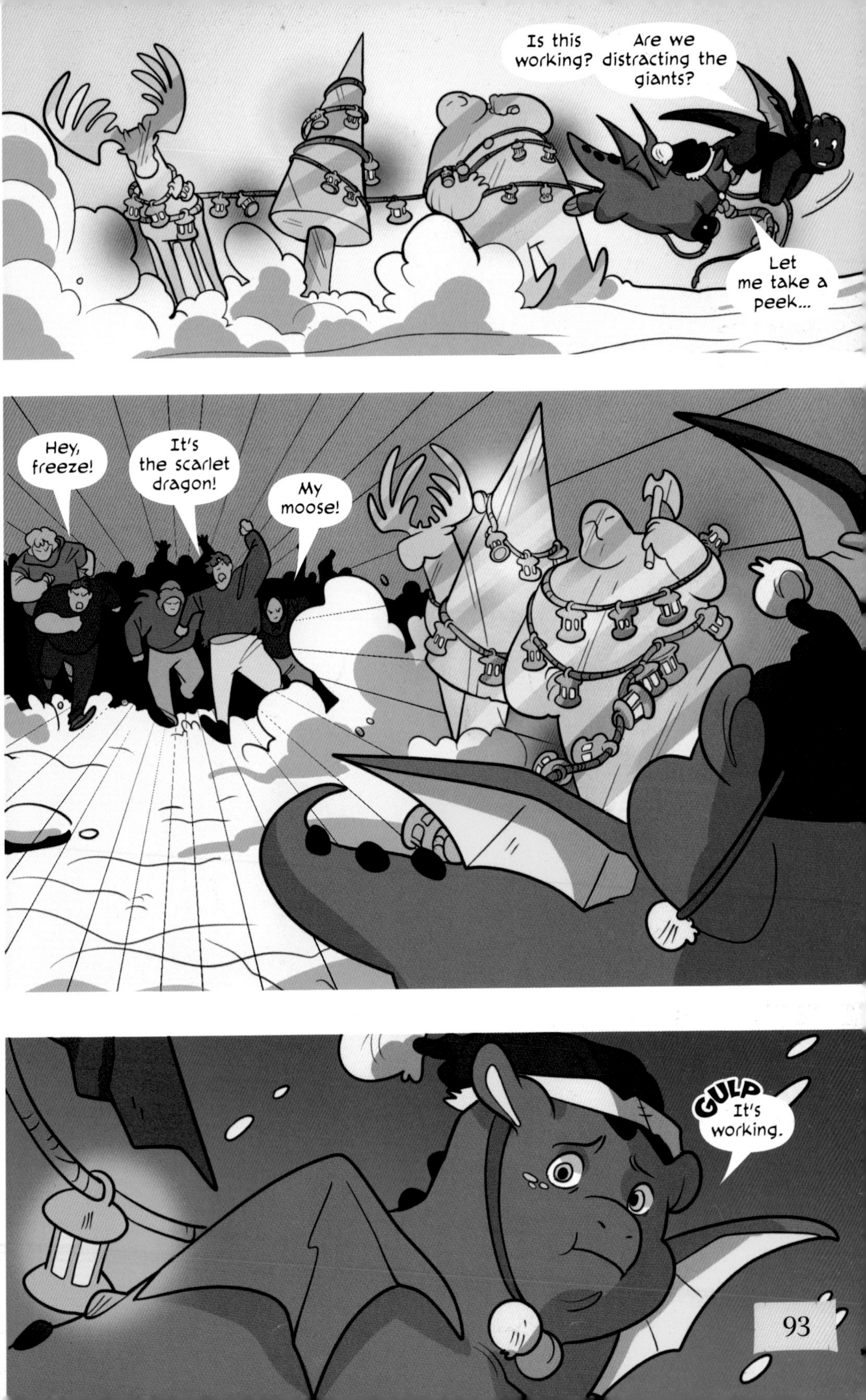
Is this working?
Are we distracting the giants?
Let me take a peek...
Hey, freeze!
It's the scarlet dragon!
My moose!
GULP
It's working.

I don't believe my eyes!

OUR LIGHTS! C'mon, we have to get them back, or we'll never be able to close!

I just want to go home and take a bath!

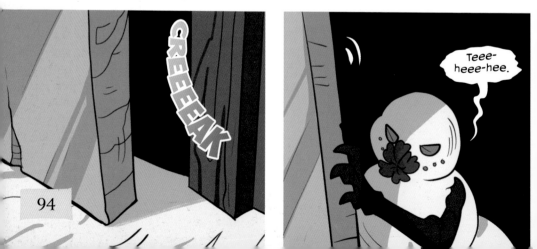

CREEEEAK

Teee-heee-hee.

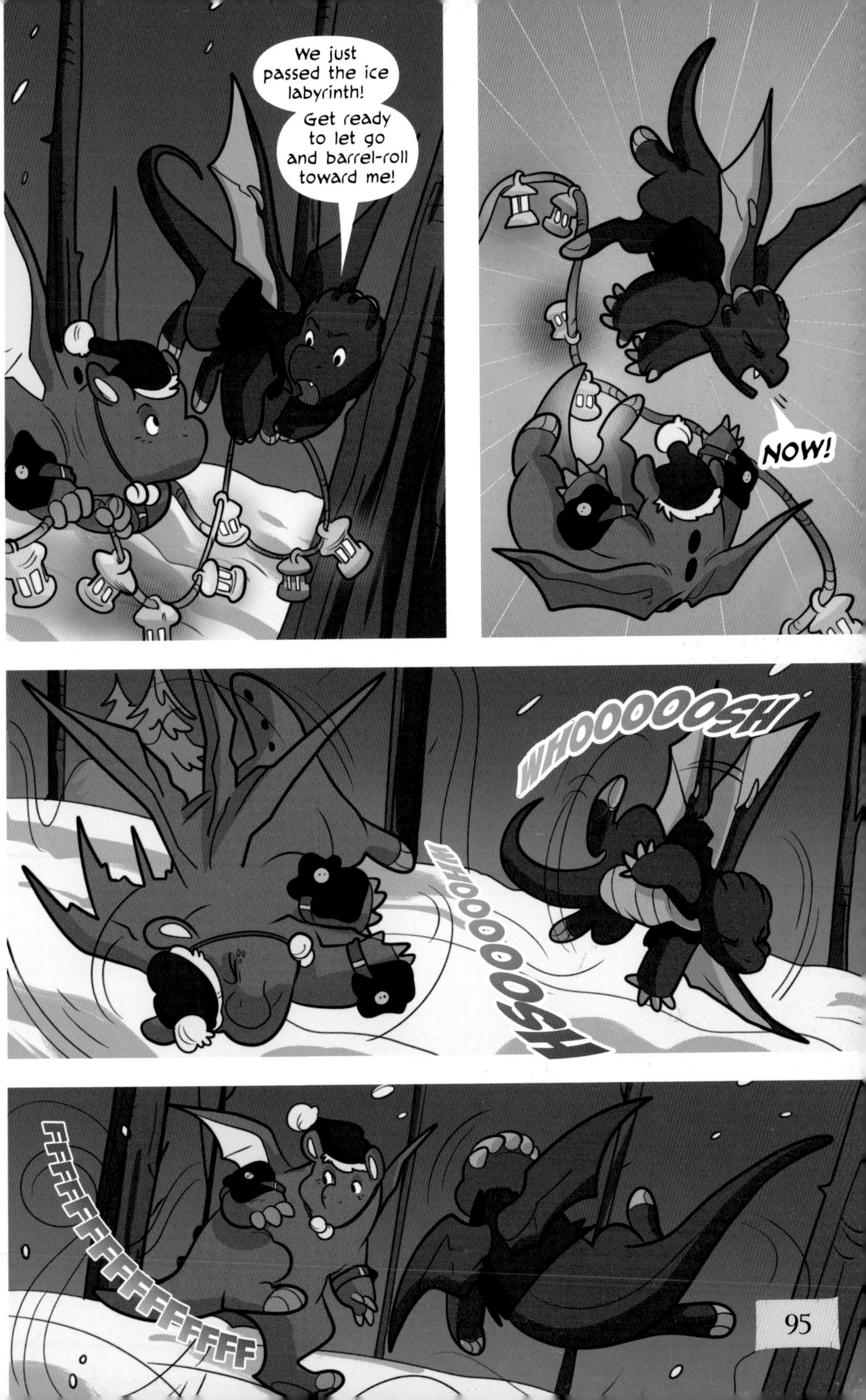
We just passed the ice labyrinth!
Get ready to let go and barrel-roll toward me!
NOW!
WHOOOOOOSH
WHOOOOOOSH
FFFFFFFFFFFFFF

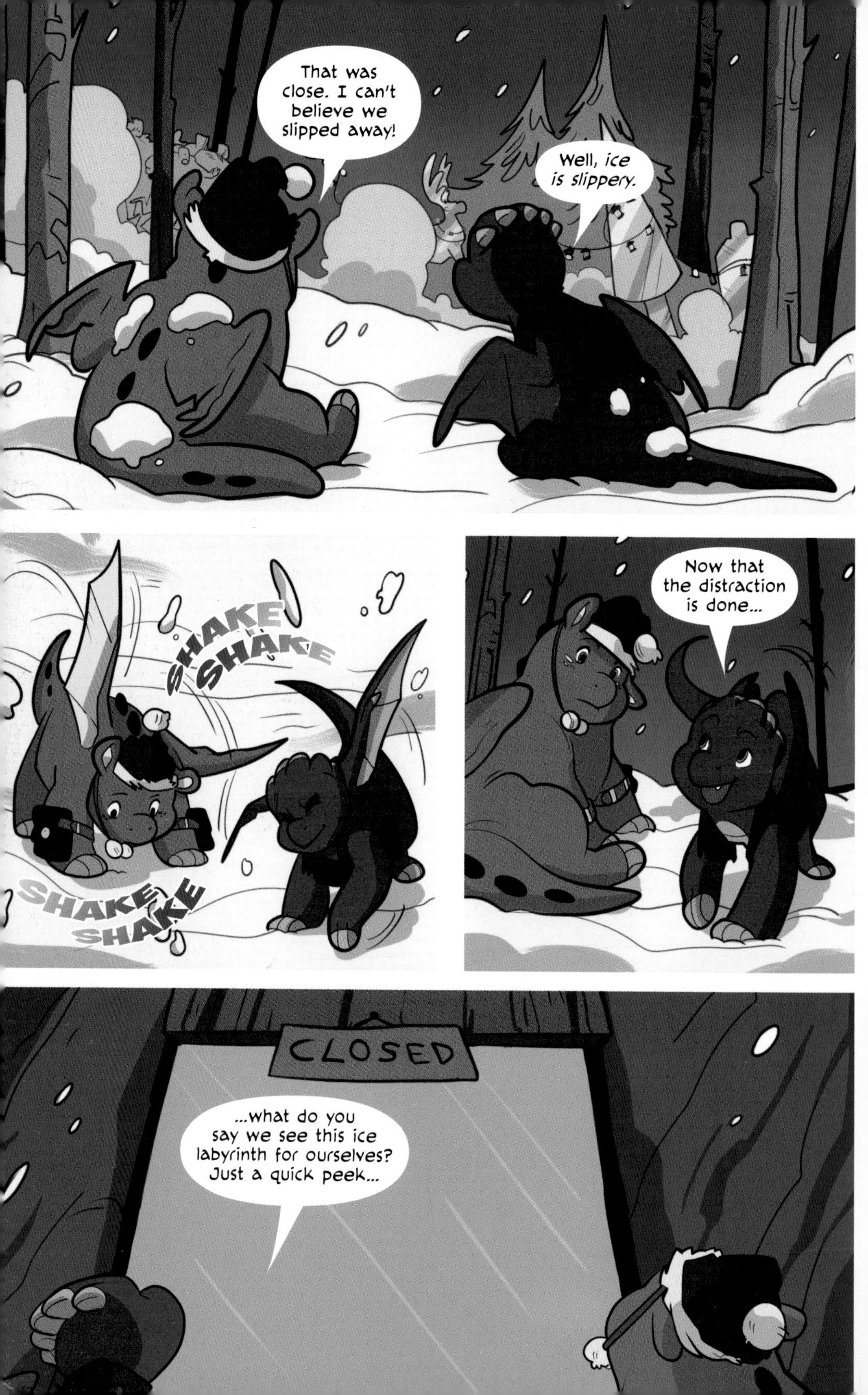
That was close. I can't believe we slipped away!
Well, *ice* is slippery.
SHAKE SHAKE
SHAKE SHAKE
Now that the distraction is done...
CLOSED
...what do you say we see this ice labyrinth for ourselves? Just a quick peek...

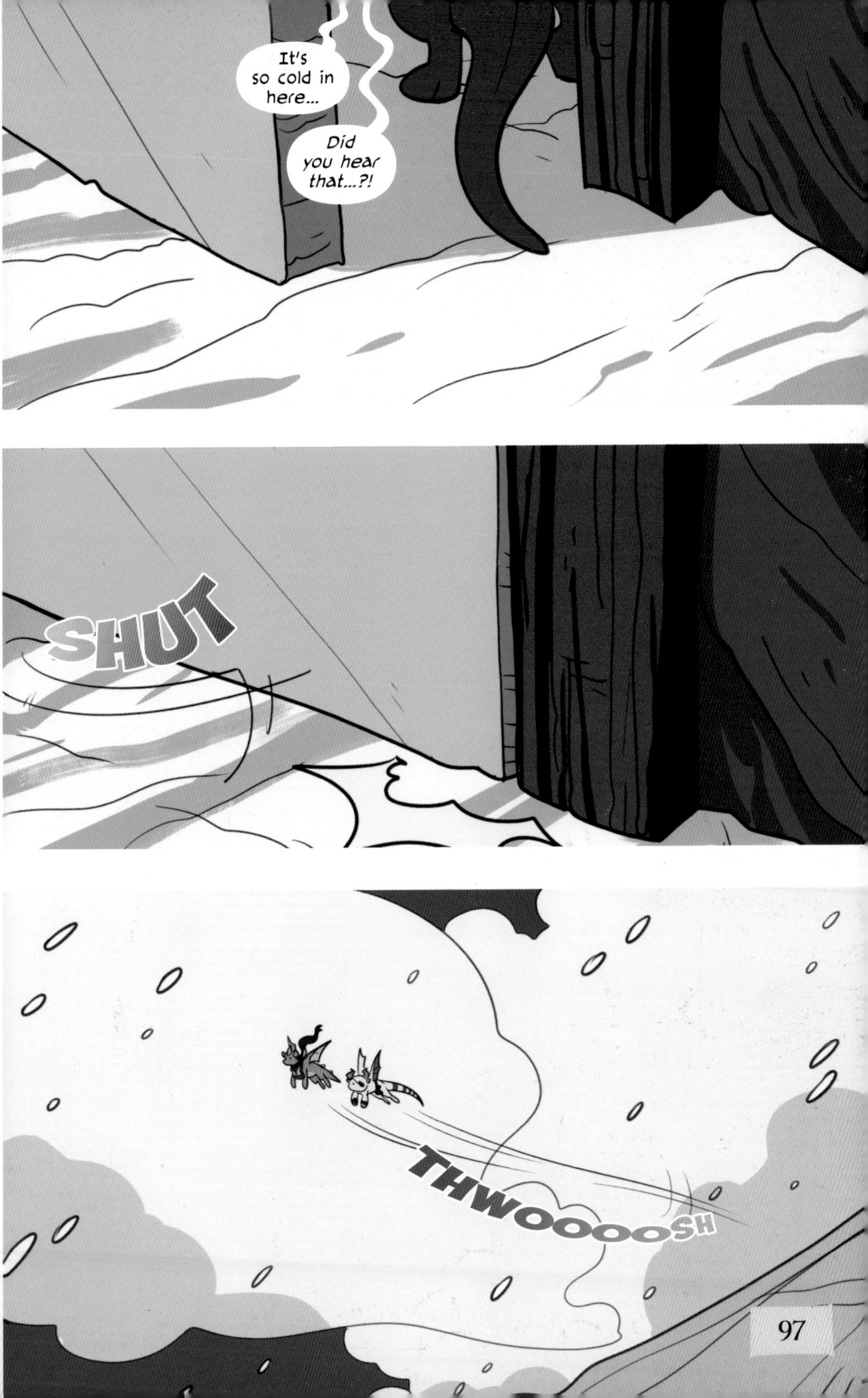
It's so cold in here...
Did you hear that...?!
SHUT
THWOOOOOSH

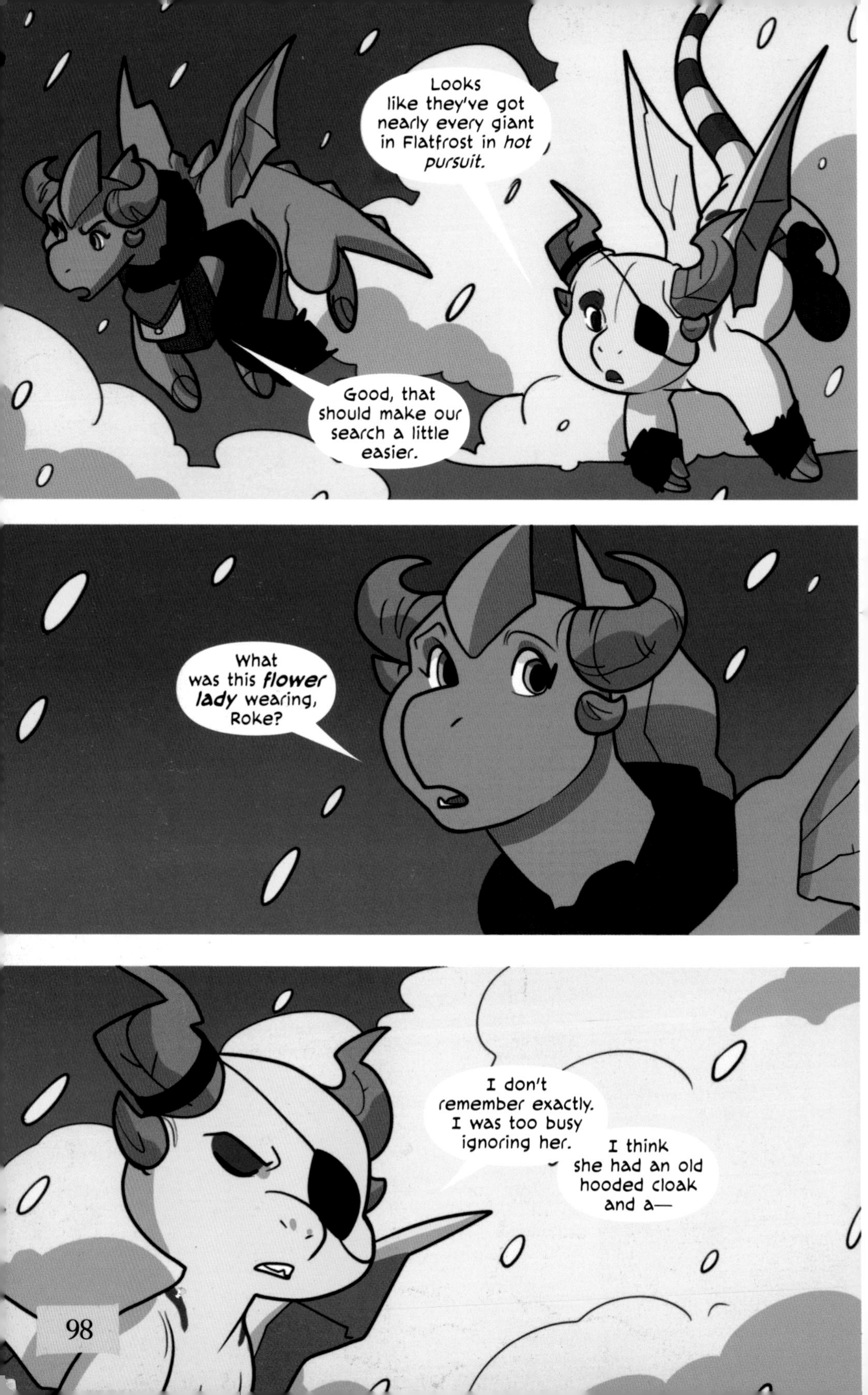

Looks like they've got nearly every giant in Flatfrost in *hot pursuit.*
Good, that should make our search a little easier.
What was this ***flower lady*** wearing, Roke?
I don't remember exactly. I was too busy ignoring her.
I think she had an old hooded cloak and a—

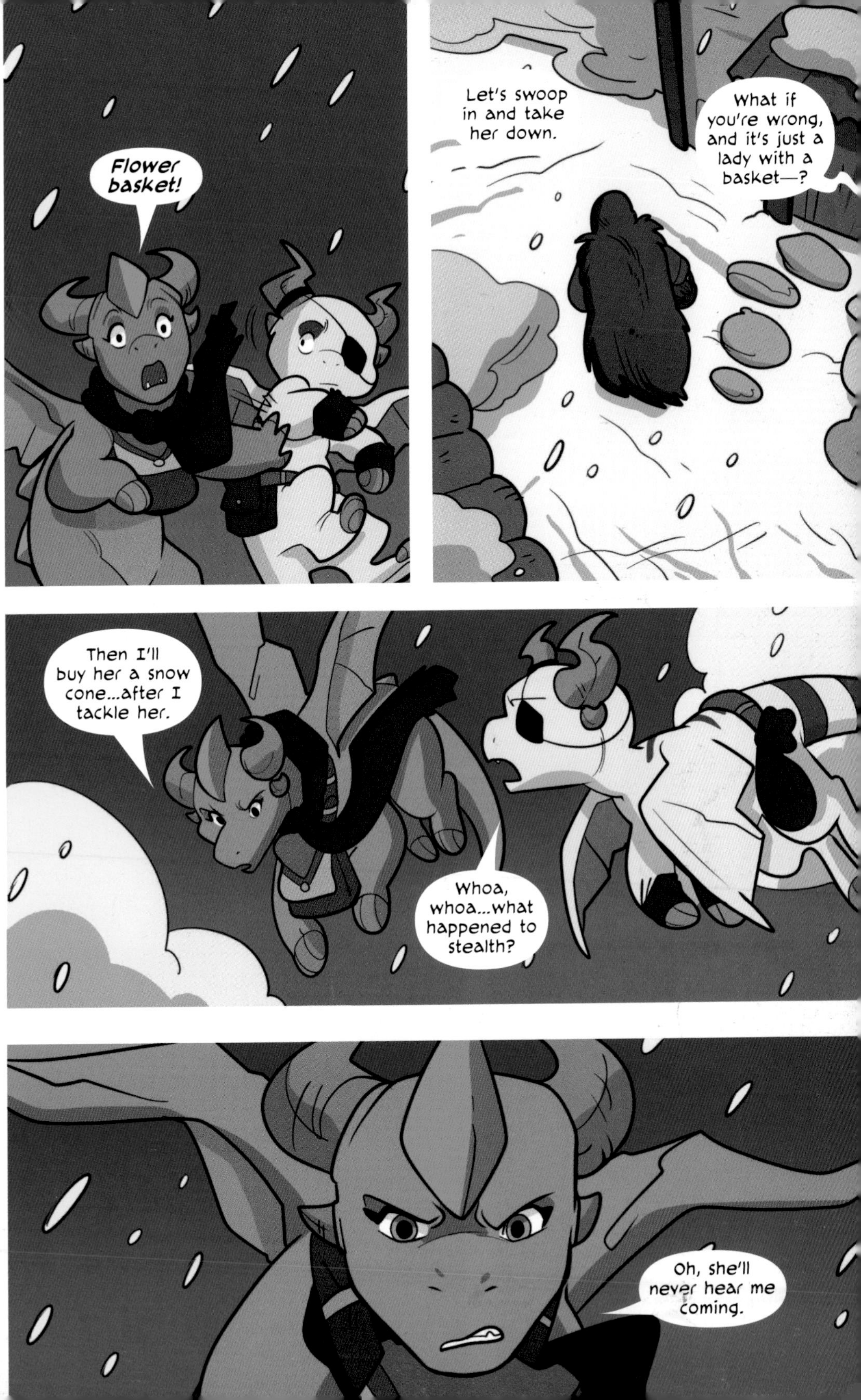

Flower basket!
Let's swoop in and take her down.
What if you're wrong, and it's just a lady with a basket—?
Then I'll buy her a snow cone...after I tackle her.
Whoa, whoa...what happened to stealth?
Oh, she'll never hear me coming.

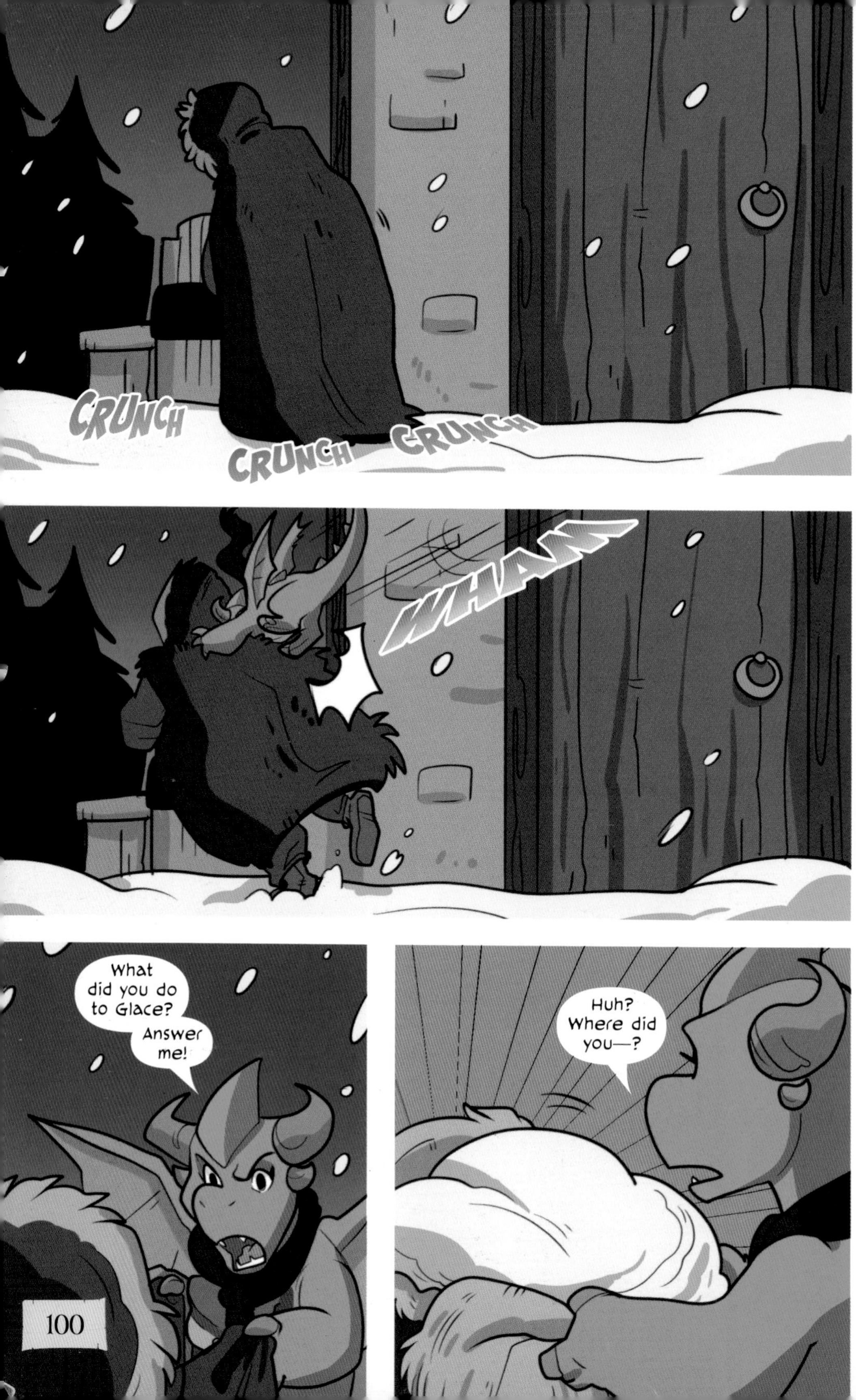
CRUNCH
CRUNCH
CRUNCH
WHAM
What did you do to Glace?
Answer me!
Huh? Where did you—?

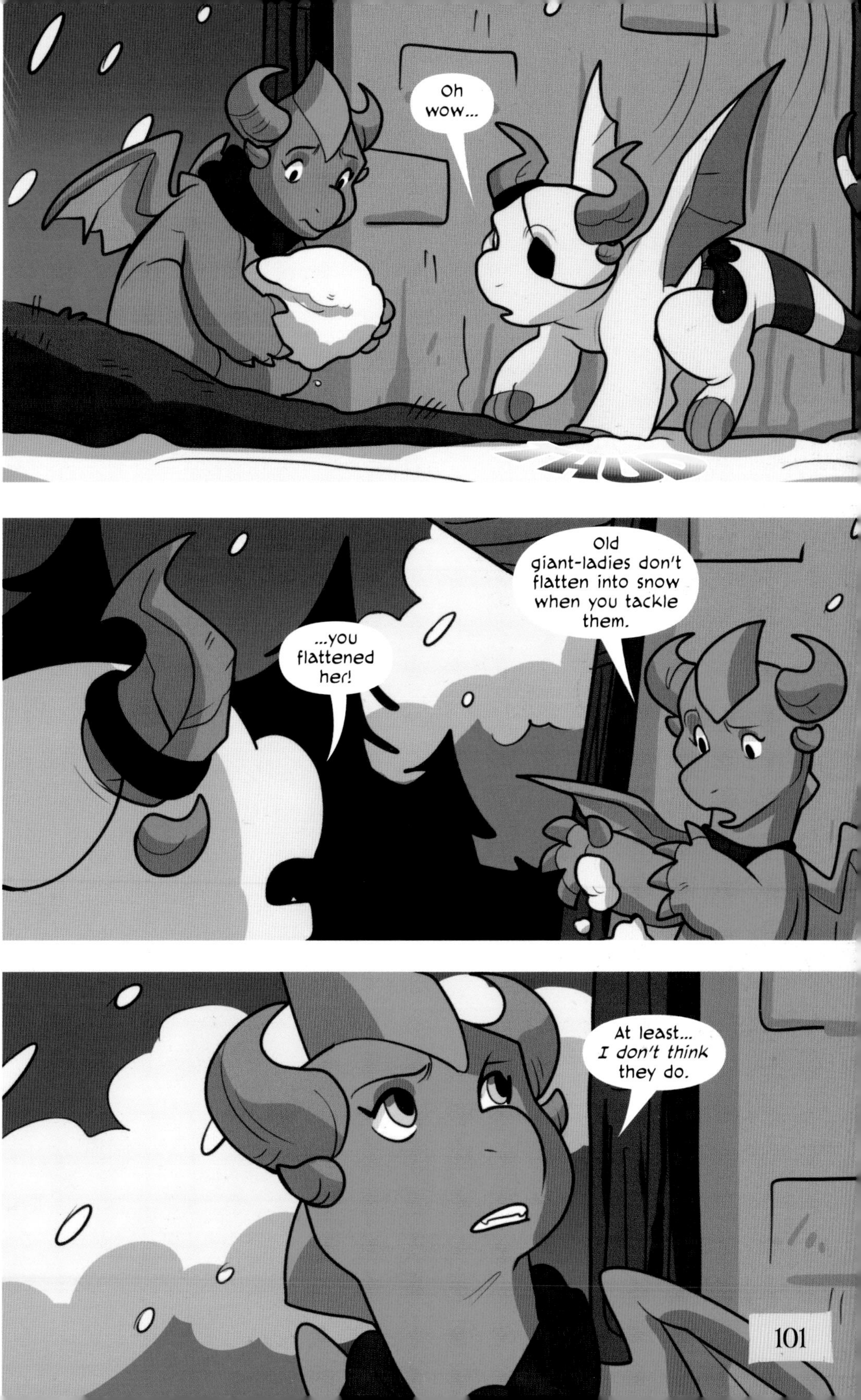
Oh wow...
...you flattened her!
Old giant-ladies don't flatten into snow when you tackle them.
At least... *I don't think* they do.

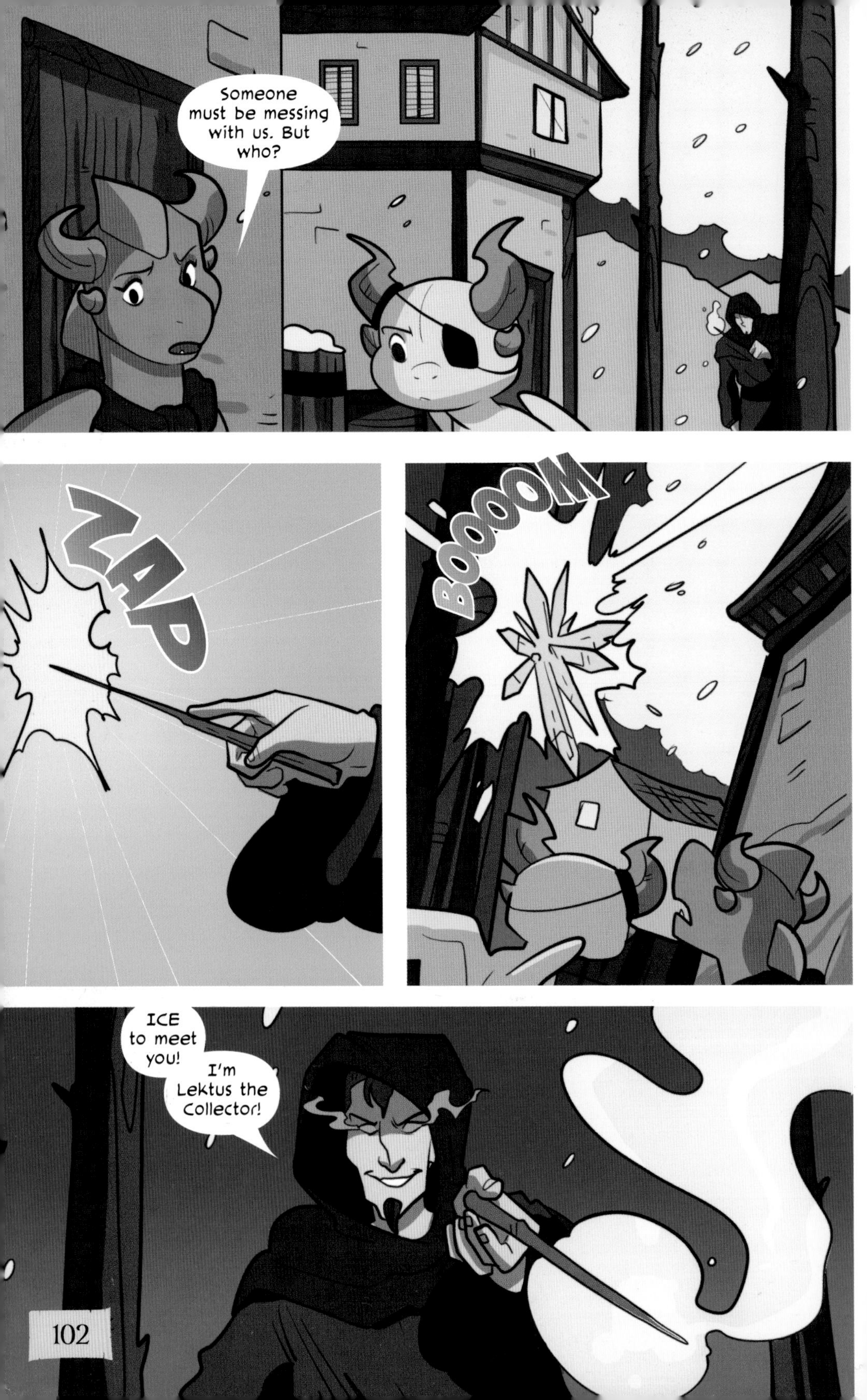
Someone must be messing with us. But who?
ZAP
BOOOOOM
ICE to meet you!
I'm Lektus the Collector!

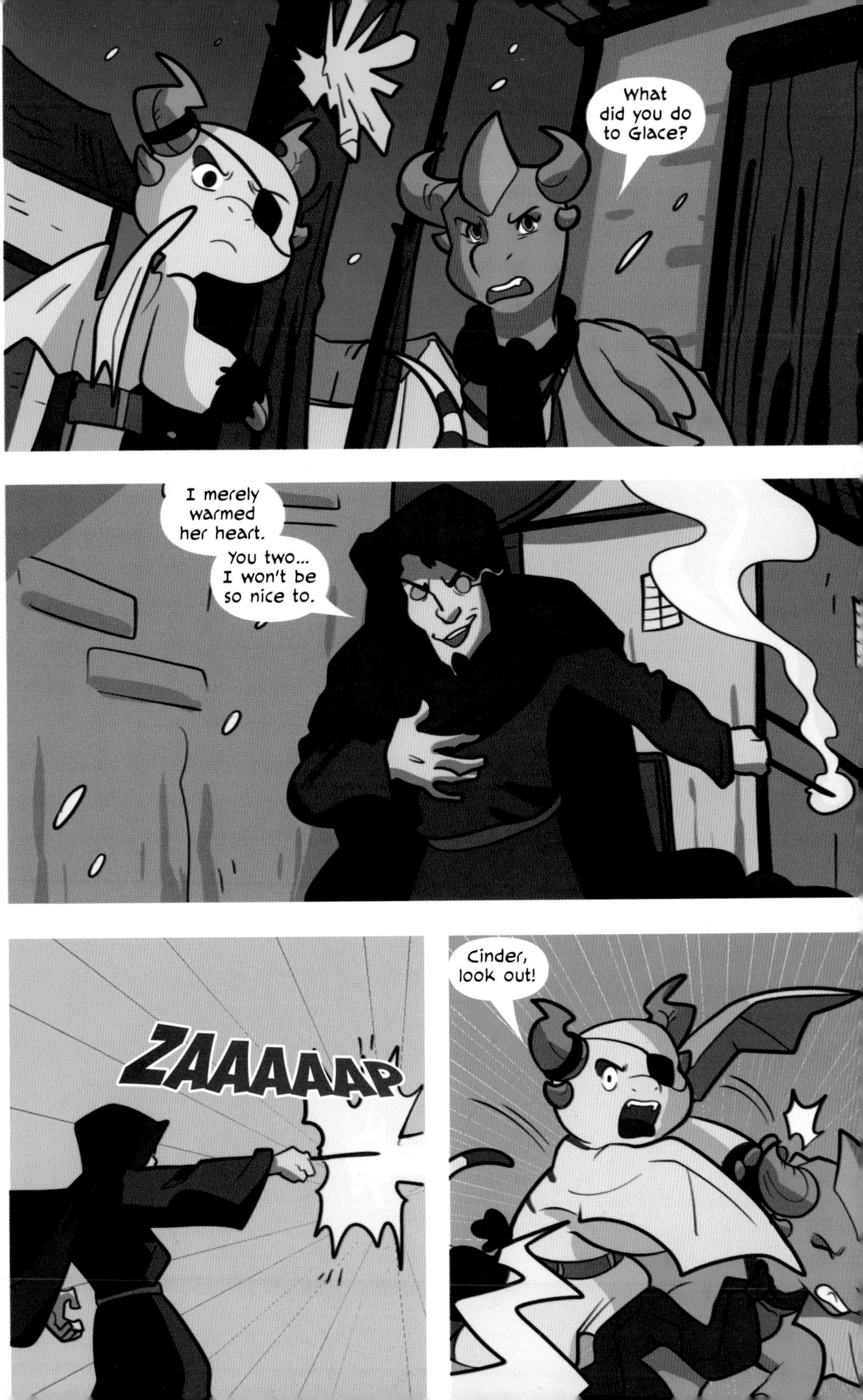
What did you do to Glace?
I merely warmed her heart.
You two... I won't be so nice to.
ZAAAAAP
Cinder, look out!

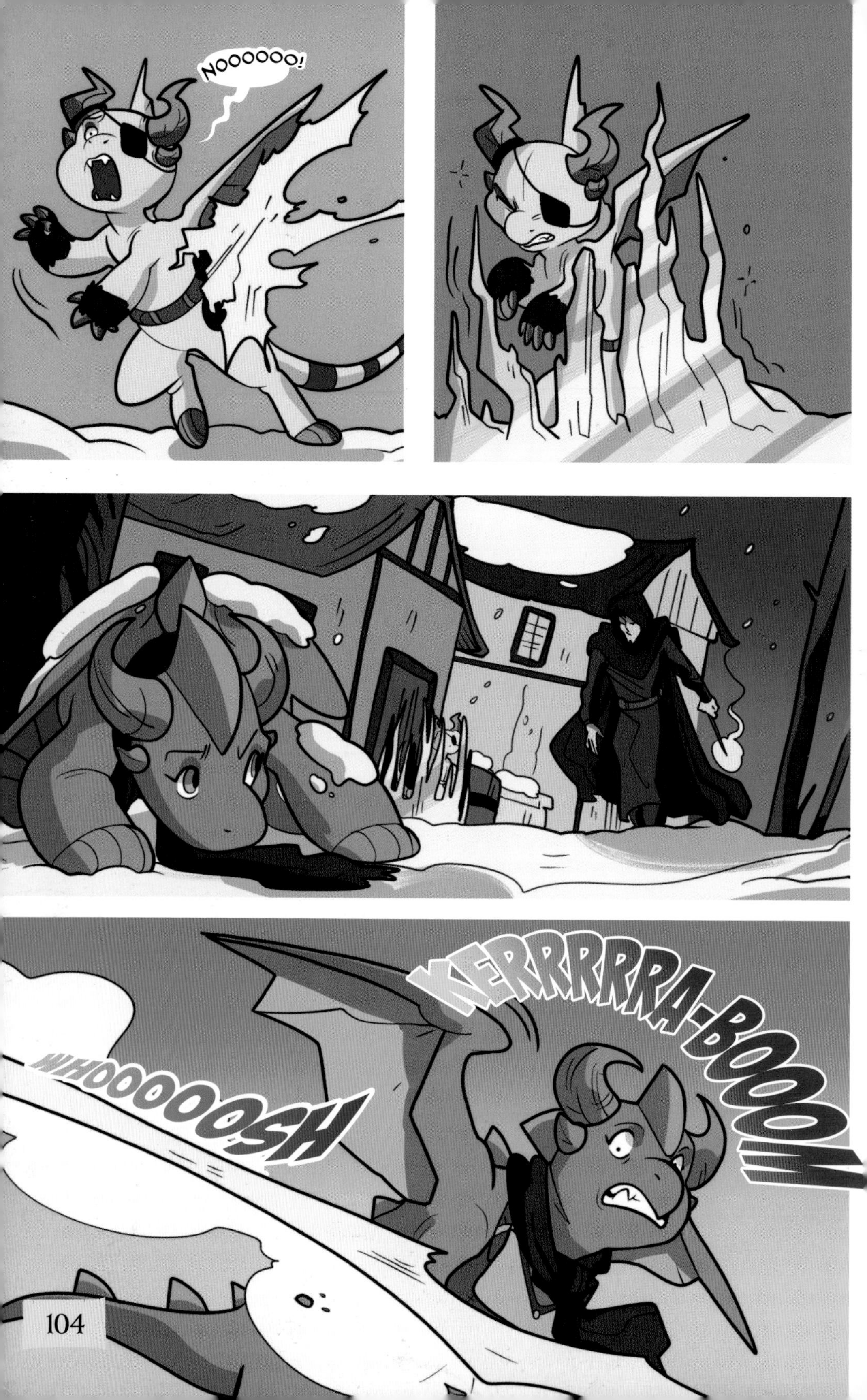
NOOOOOO!
WHOOOOOOSH
KERRRRRA-BOOOM

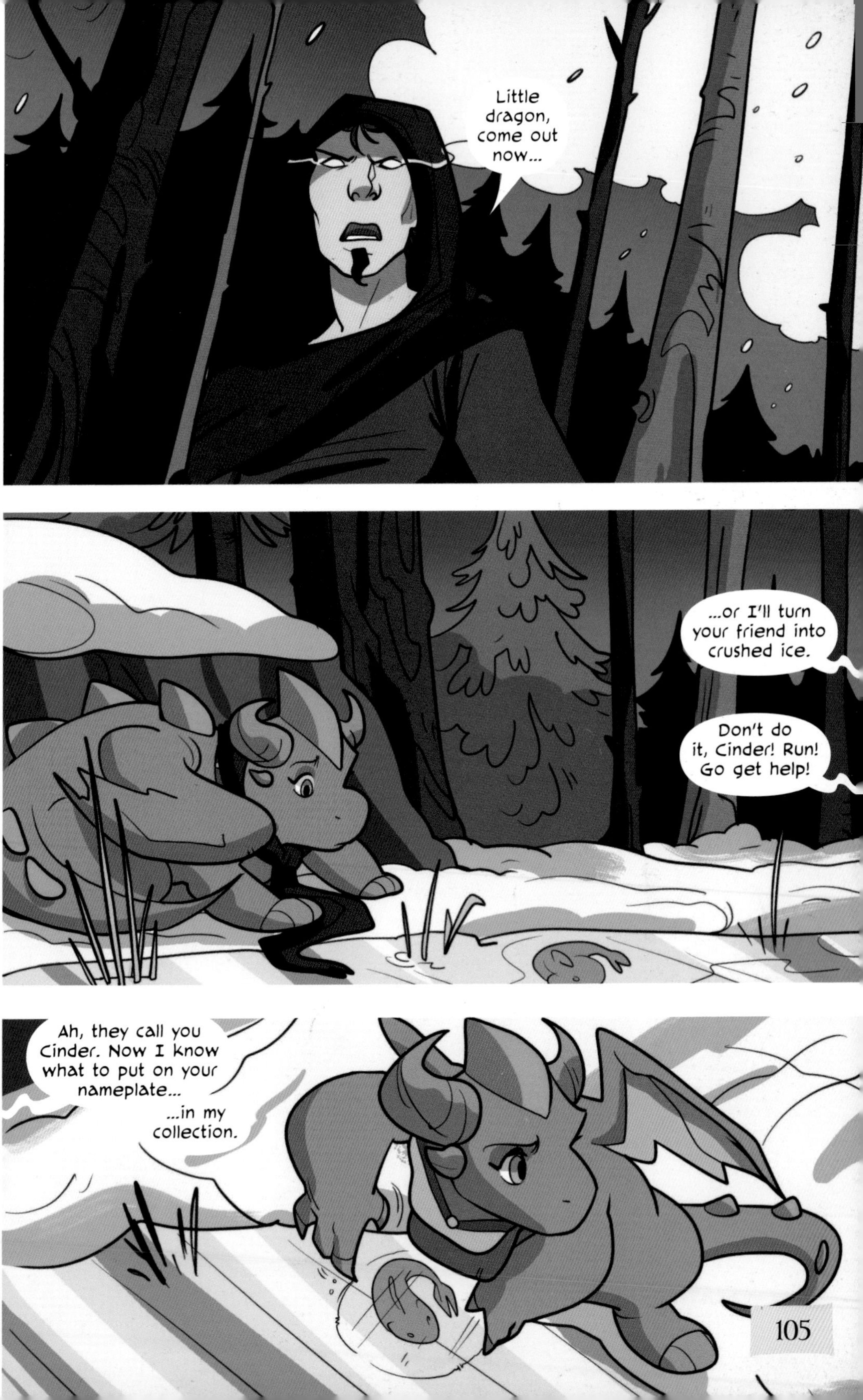
Little dragon, come out now...
...or I'll turn your friend into crushed ice.
Don't do it, Cinder! Run! Go get help!
Ah, they call you Cinder. Now I know what to put on your nameplate...
...in my collection.

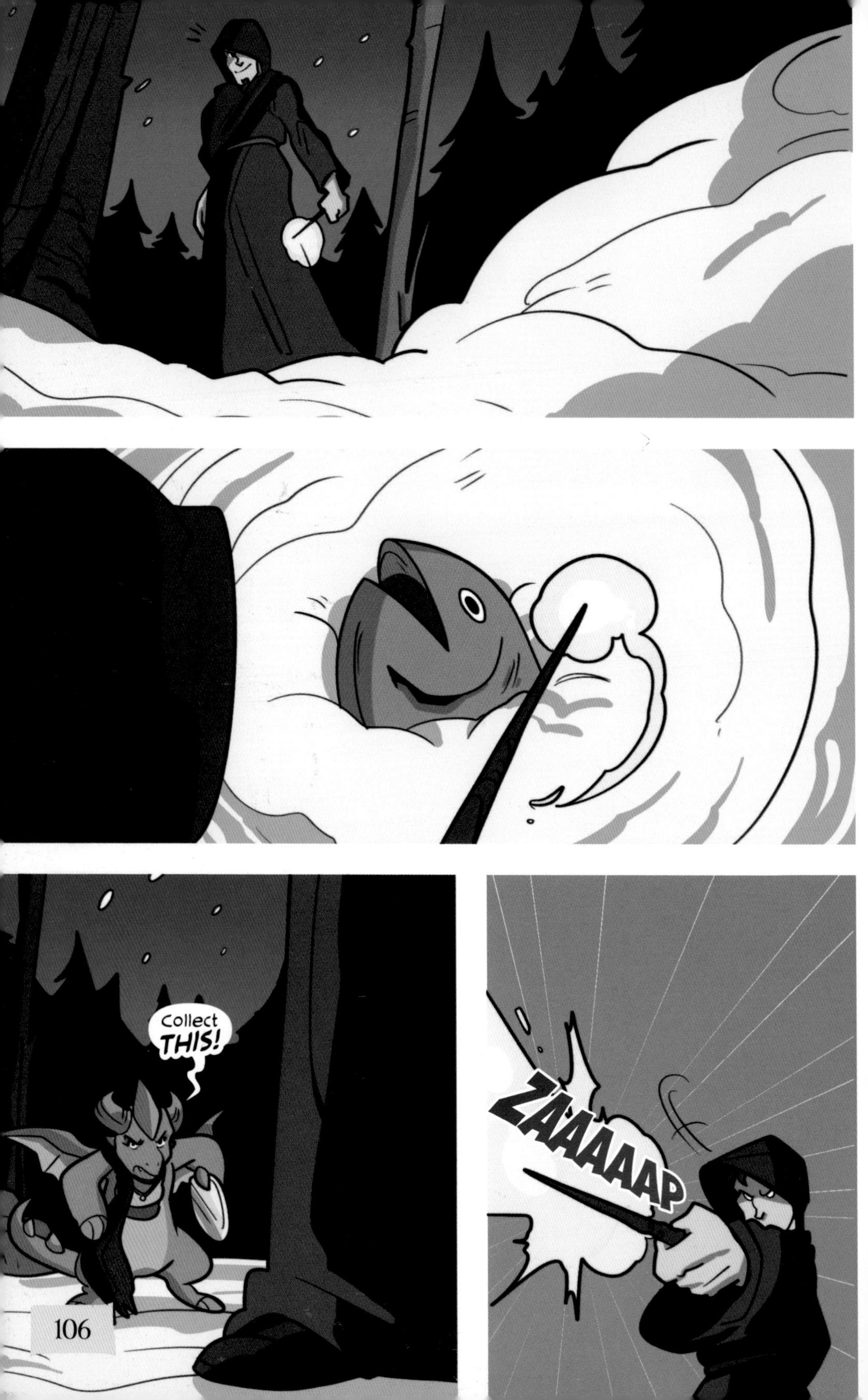
Collect THIS!
ZAAAAAP

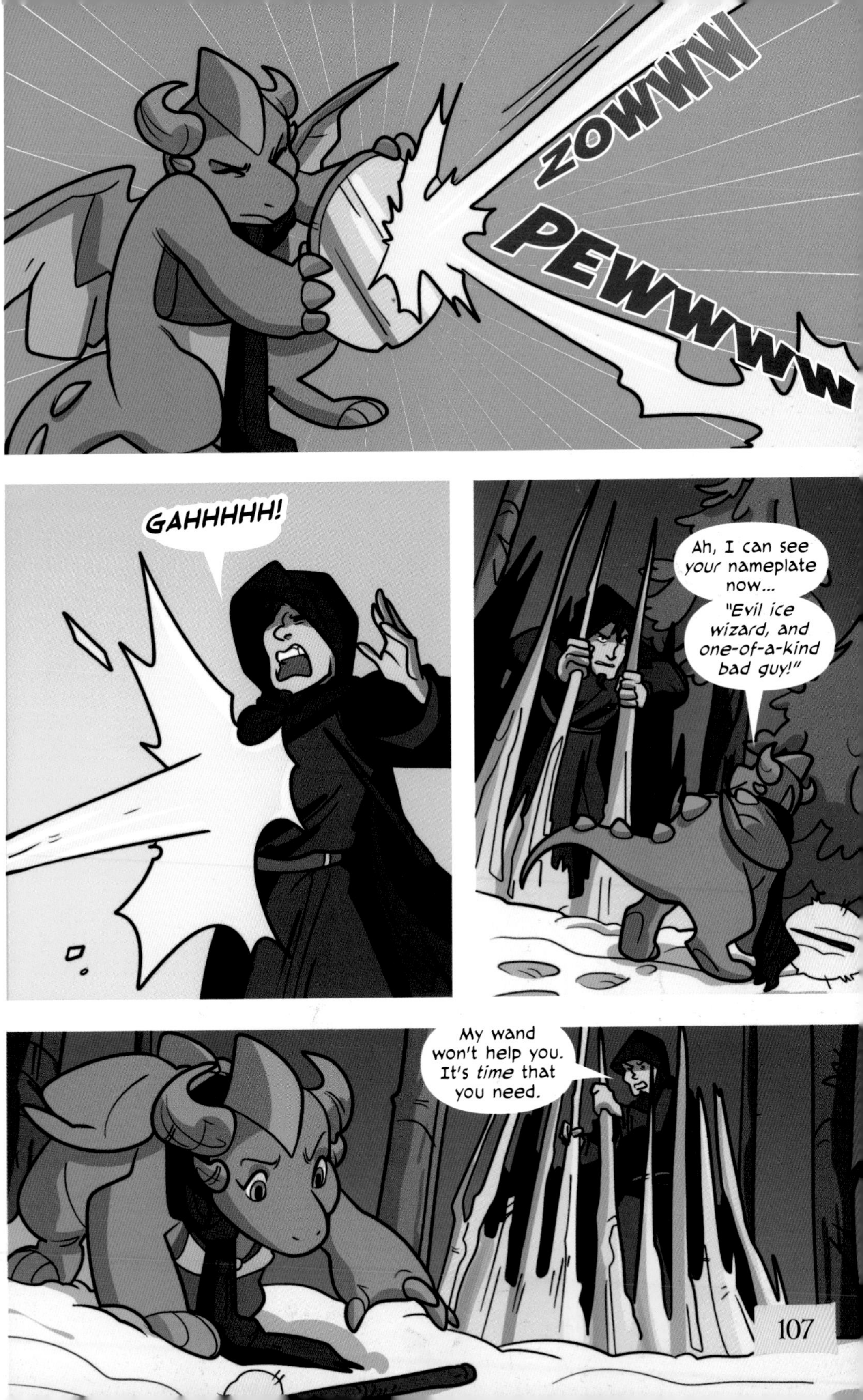
ZOWWW
PEWWWWW
GAHHHHH!
Ah, I can see *your* nameplate now...
"Evil ice wizard, and one-of-a-kind bad guy!"
My wand won't help you. It's *time* that you need.

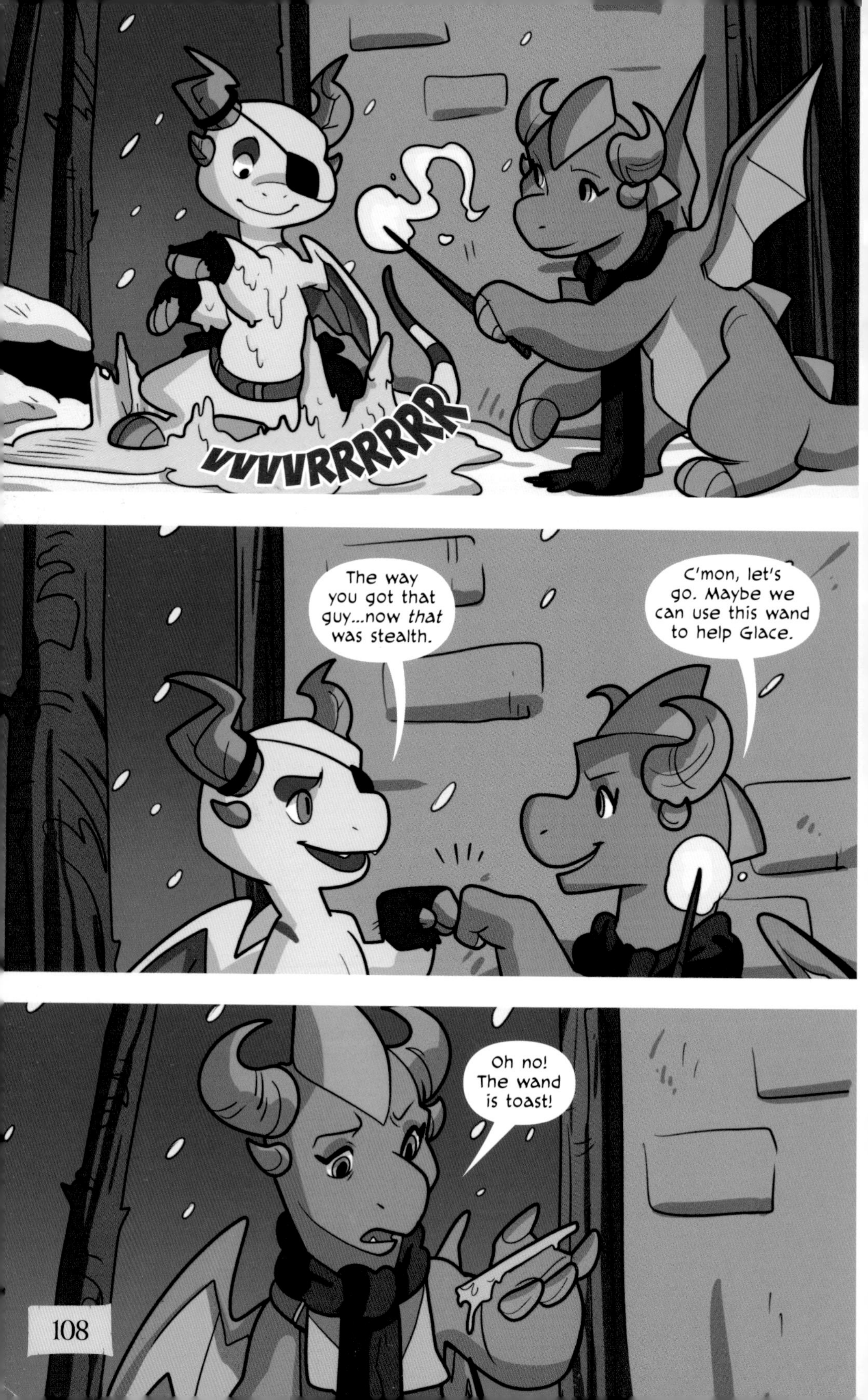
VVVVRRRRRR
The way you got that guy...now *that* was stealth.
C'mon, let's go. Maybe we can use this wand to help Glace.
Oh no! The wand is toast!

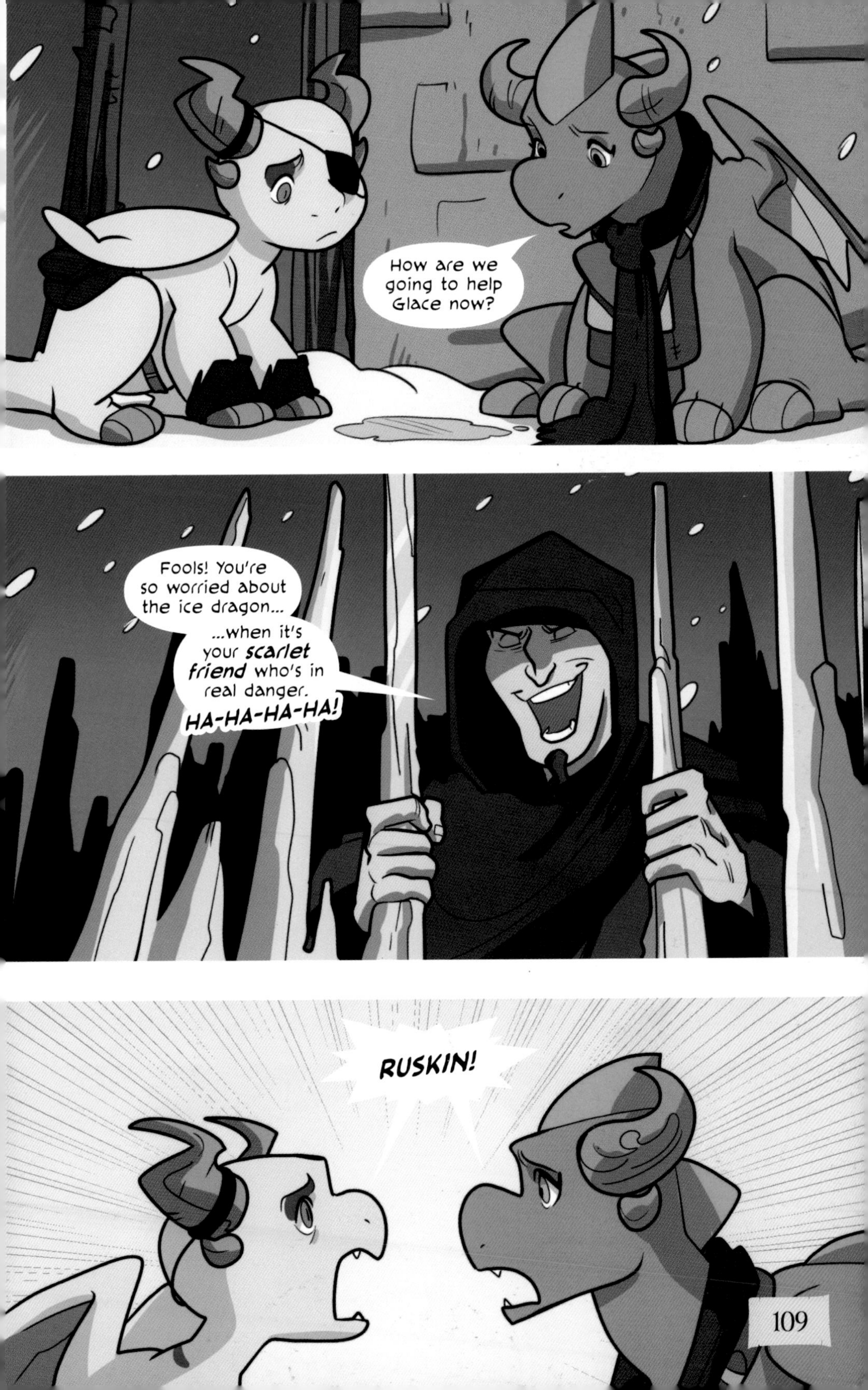
How are we going to help Glace now?
Fools! You're so worried about the ice dragon...
...when it's your **scarlet friend** who's in real danger.
HA-HA-HA-HA!
RUSKIN!

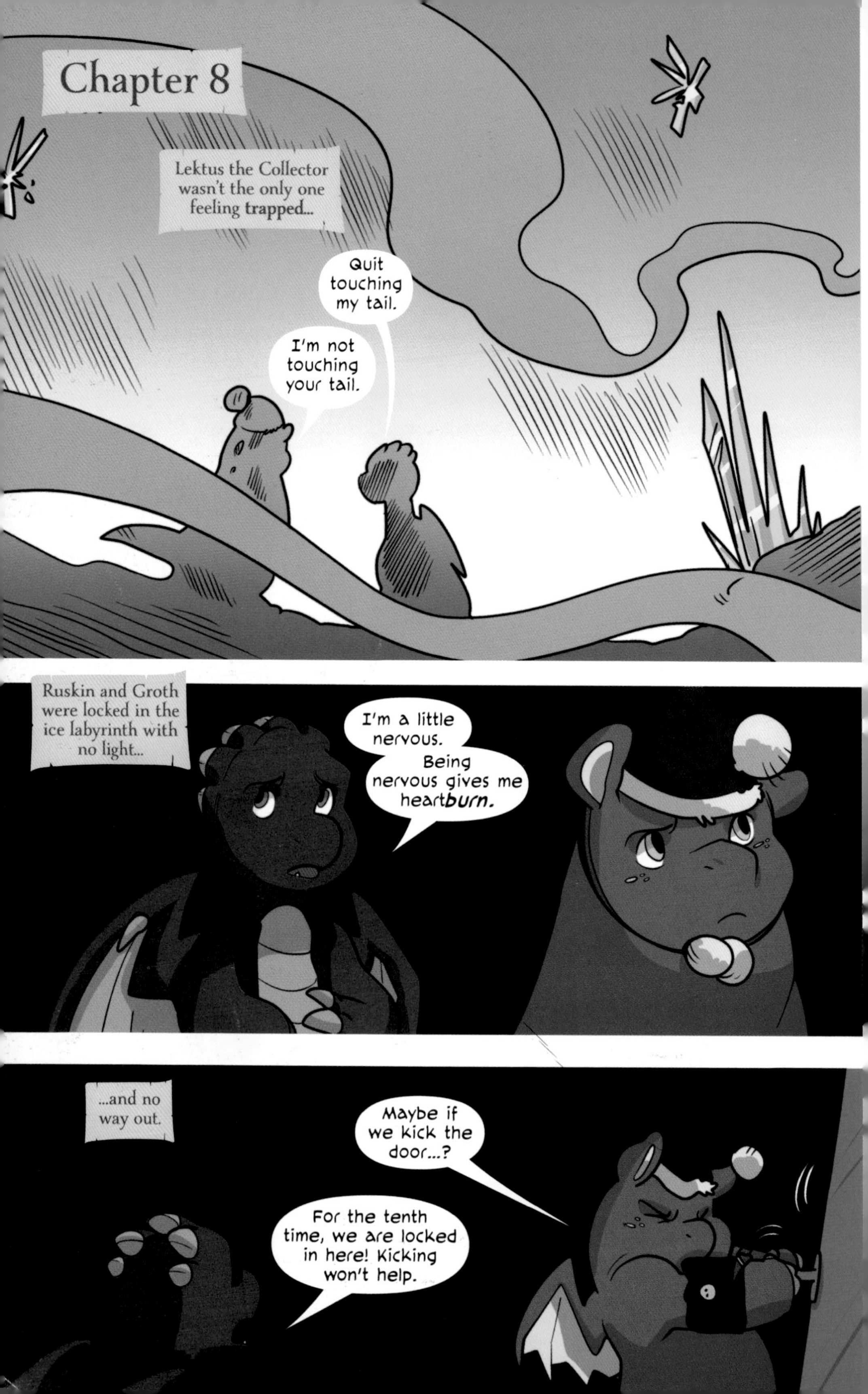
Chapter 8
Lektus the Collector wasn't the only one feeling trapped...
Quit touching my tail.
I'm not touching your tail.
Ruskin and Groth were locked in the ice labyrinth with no light...
I'm a little nervous.
Being nervous gives me heartburn.
...and no way out.
Maybe if we kick the door...?
For the tenth time, we are locked in here! Kicking won't help.

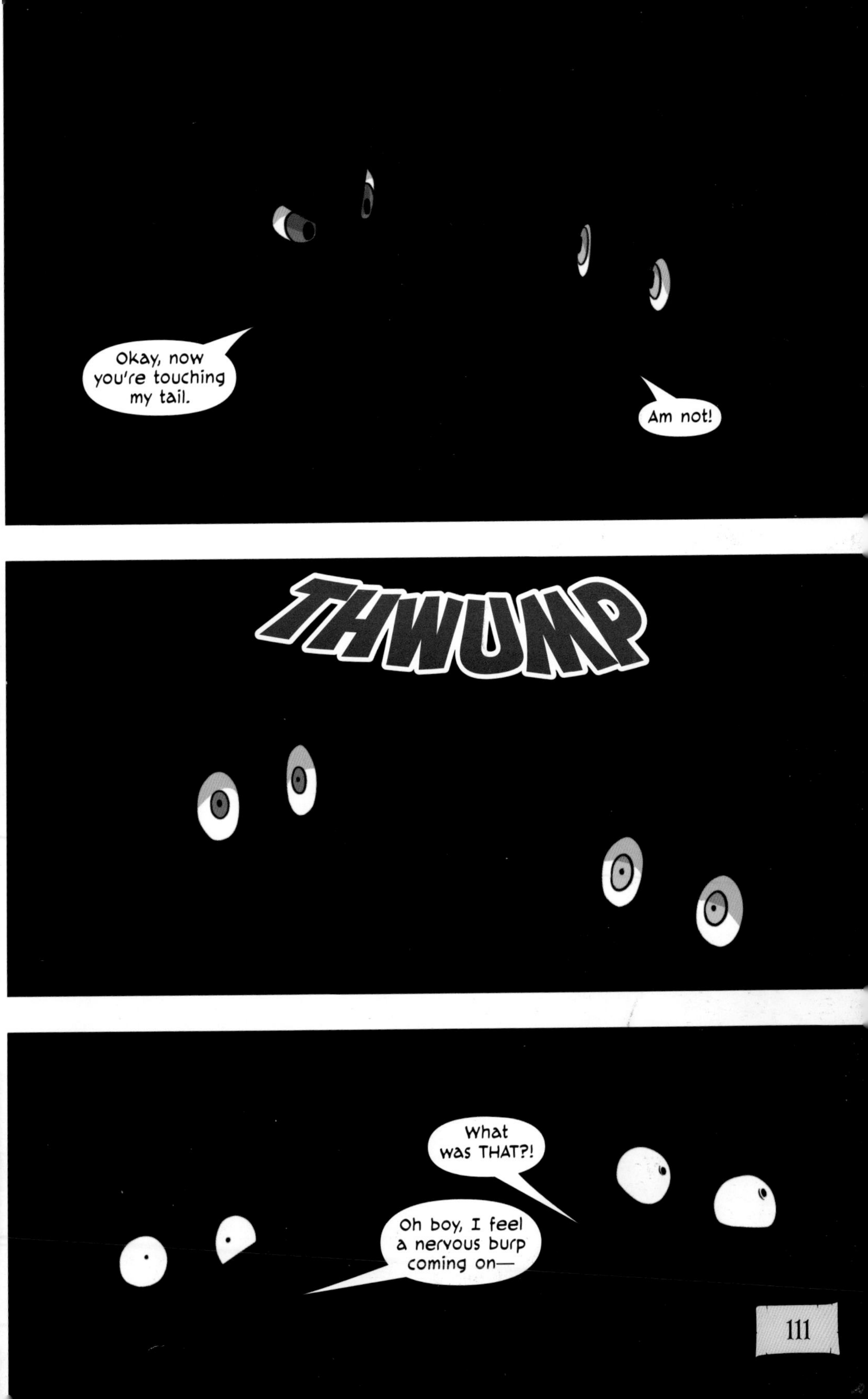
Okay, now you're touching my tail.
Am not!
THWUMP
What was THAT?!
Oh boy, I feel a nervous burp coming on—

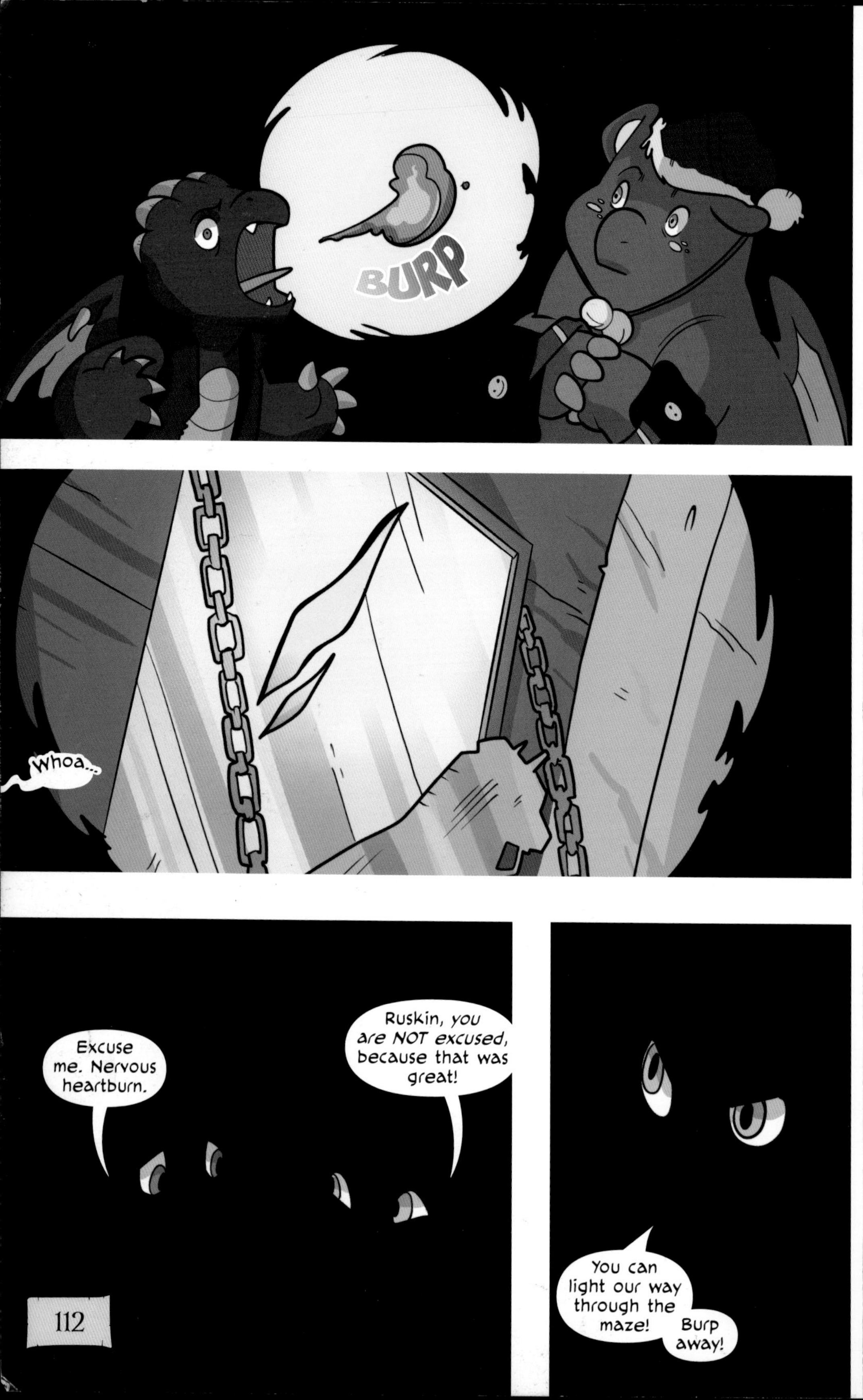

BURP
Whoa...
Excuse me. Nervous heartburn.
Ruskin, *you are NOT excused,* because that was great!
You can light our way through the maze!
Burp away!

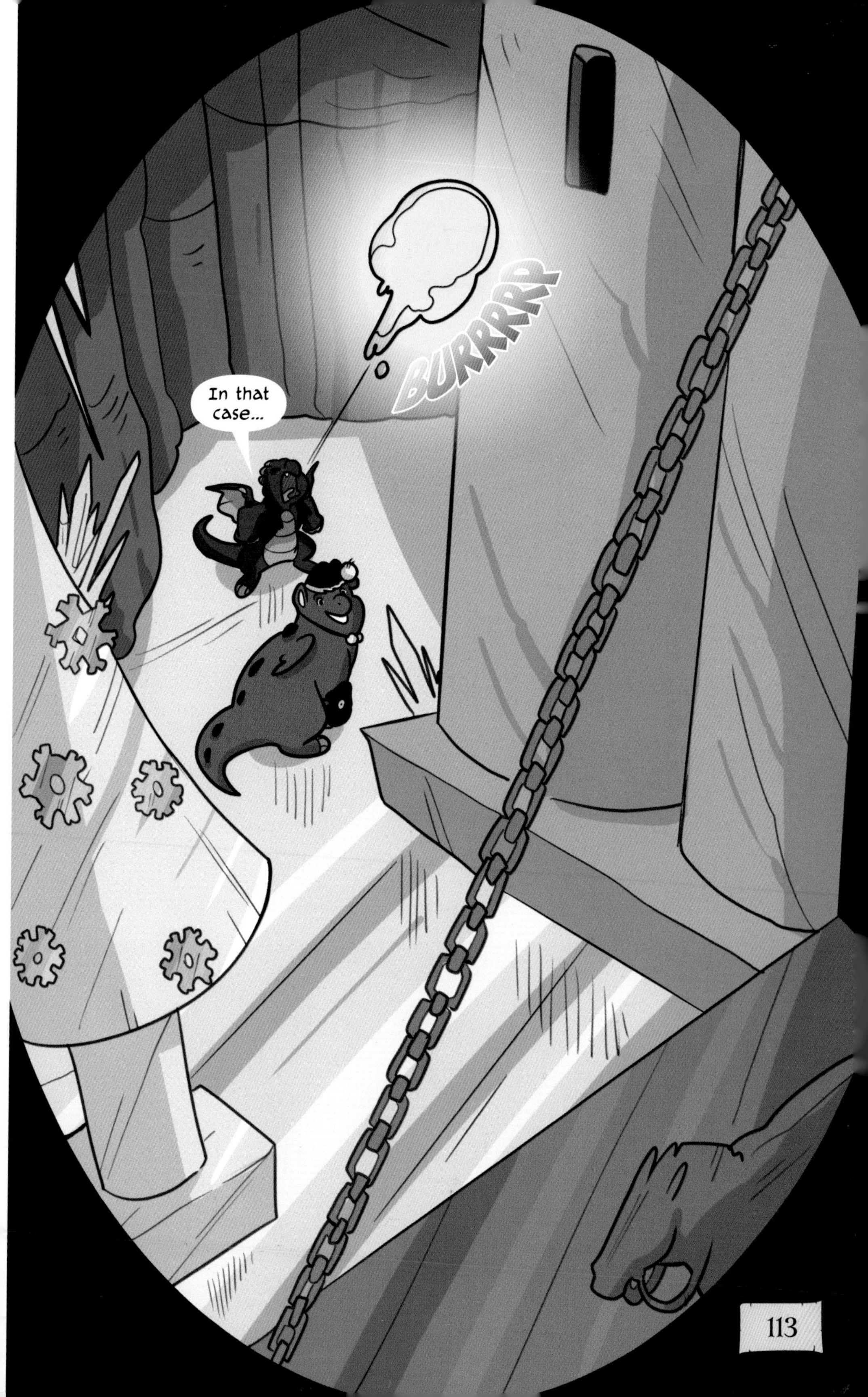
In that case...
BURRRRP

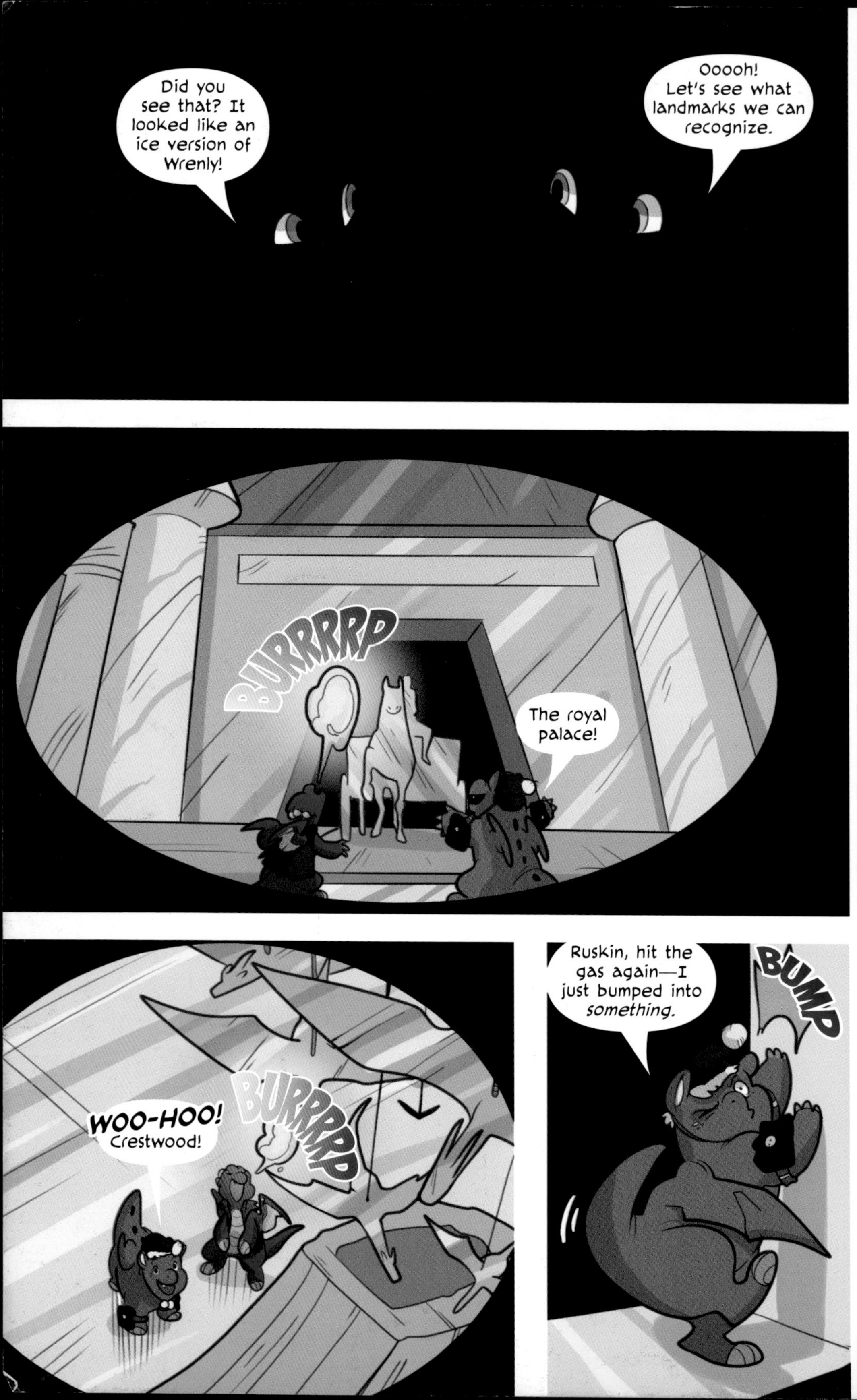
Did you see that? It looked like an ice version of Wrenly!
Ooooh! Let's see what landmarks we can recognize.
BURRRRP
The royal palace!
WOO-HOO! Crestwood!
BURRRRRP
Ruskin, hit the gas again—I just bumped into *something*.
BUMP

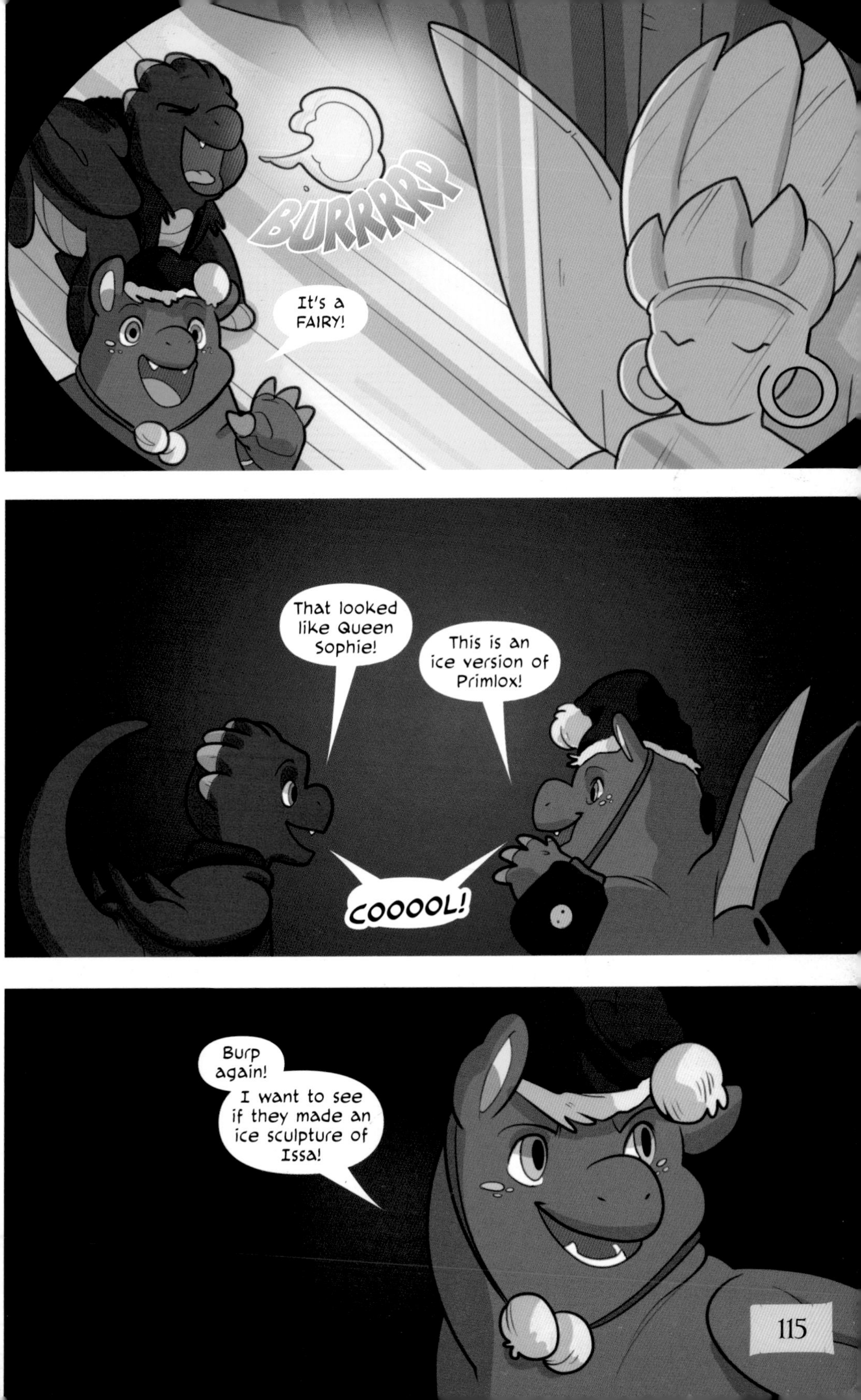
BURRRRP
It's a FAIRY!
That looked like Queen Sophie!
This is an ice version of Primlox!
COOOOL!
Burp again!
I want to see if they made an ice sculpture of Issa!

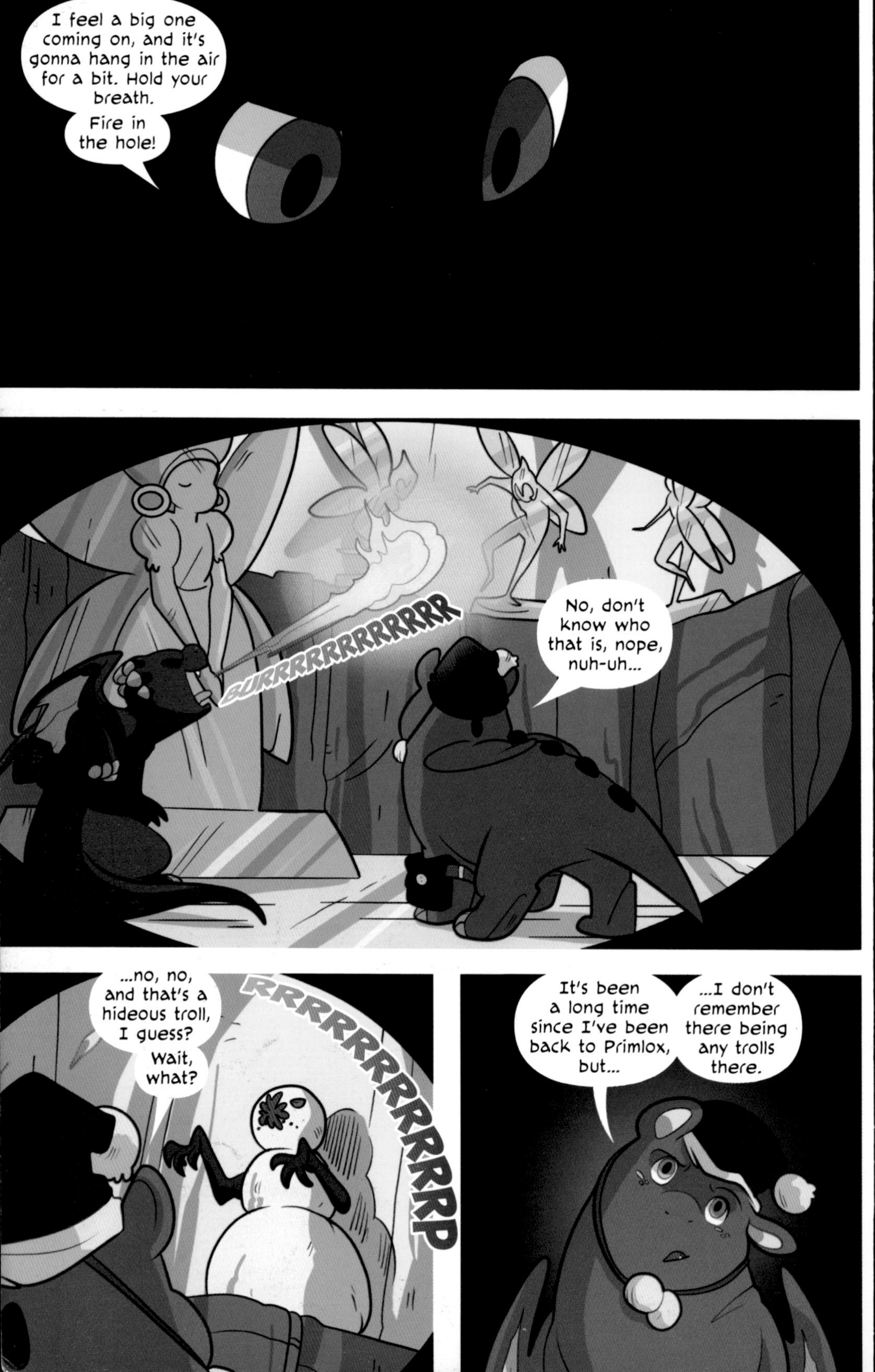
I feel a big one coming on, and it's gonna hang in the air for a bit. Hold your breath.
Fire in the hole!
BURRRRRRRRRRRRR
No, don't know who that is, nope, nuh-uh...
...no, no, and that's a hideous troll, I guess?
Wait, what?
RRRRRRRRRRRRRP
It's been a long time since I've been back to Primlox, but...
...I don't remember there being any trolls there.

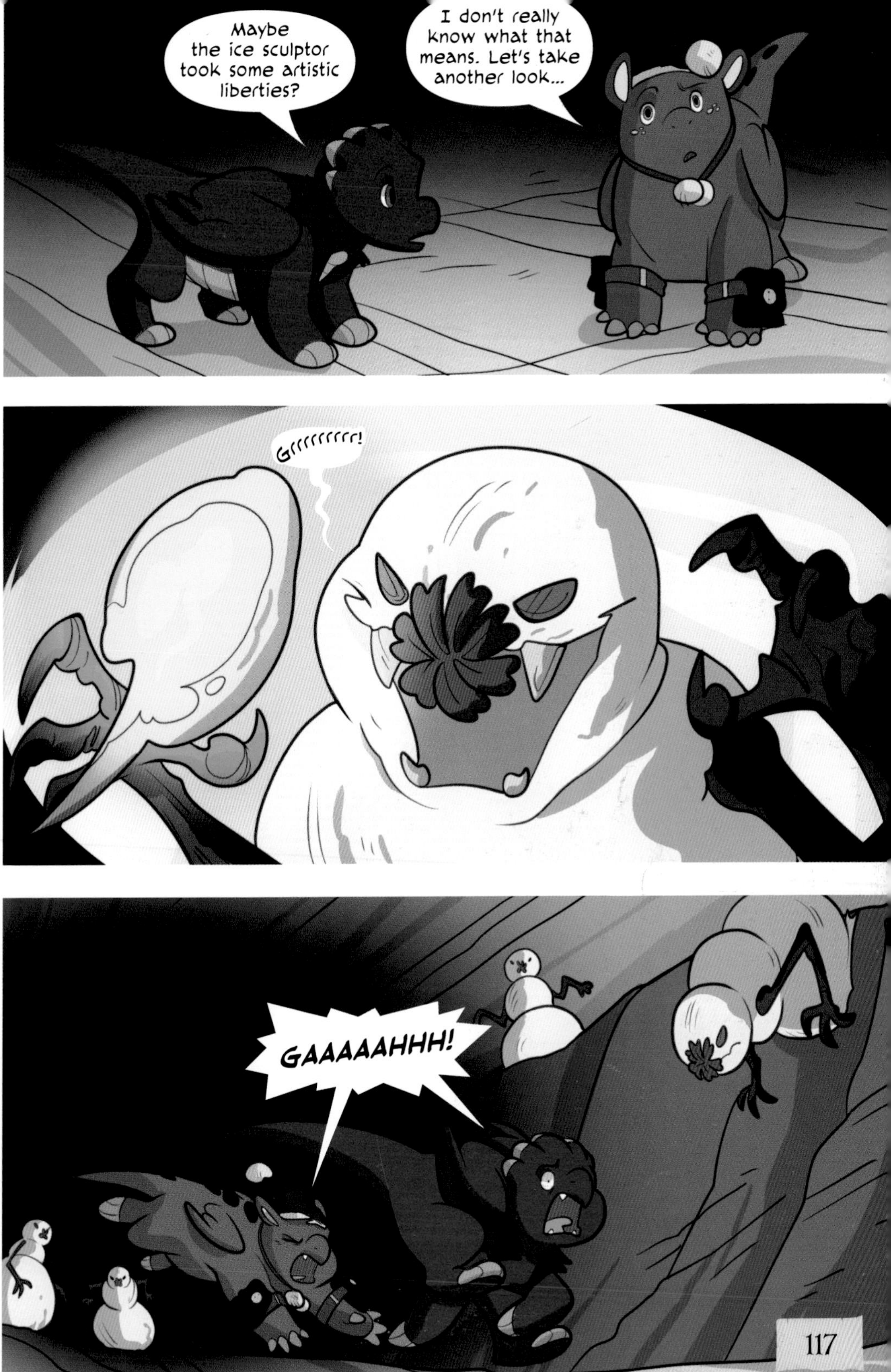
Maybe the ice sculptor took some artistic liberties?
I don't really know what that means. Let's take another look...
Grrrrrrrrr!
GAAAAAHHH!

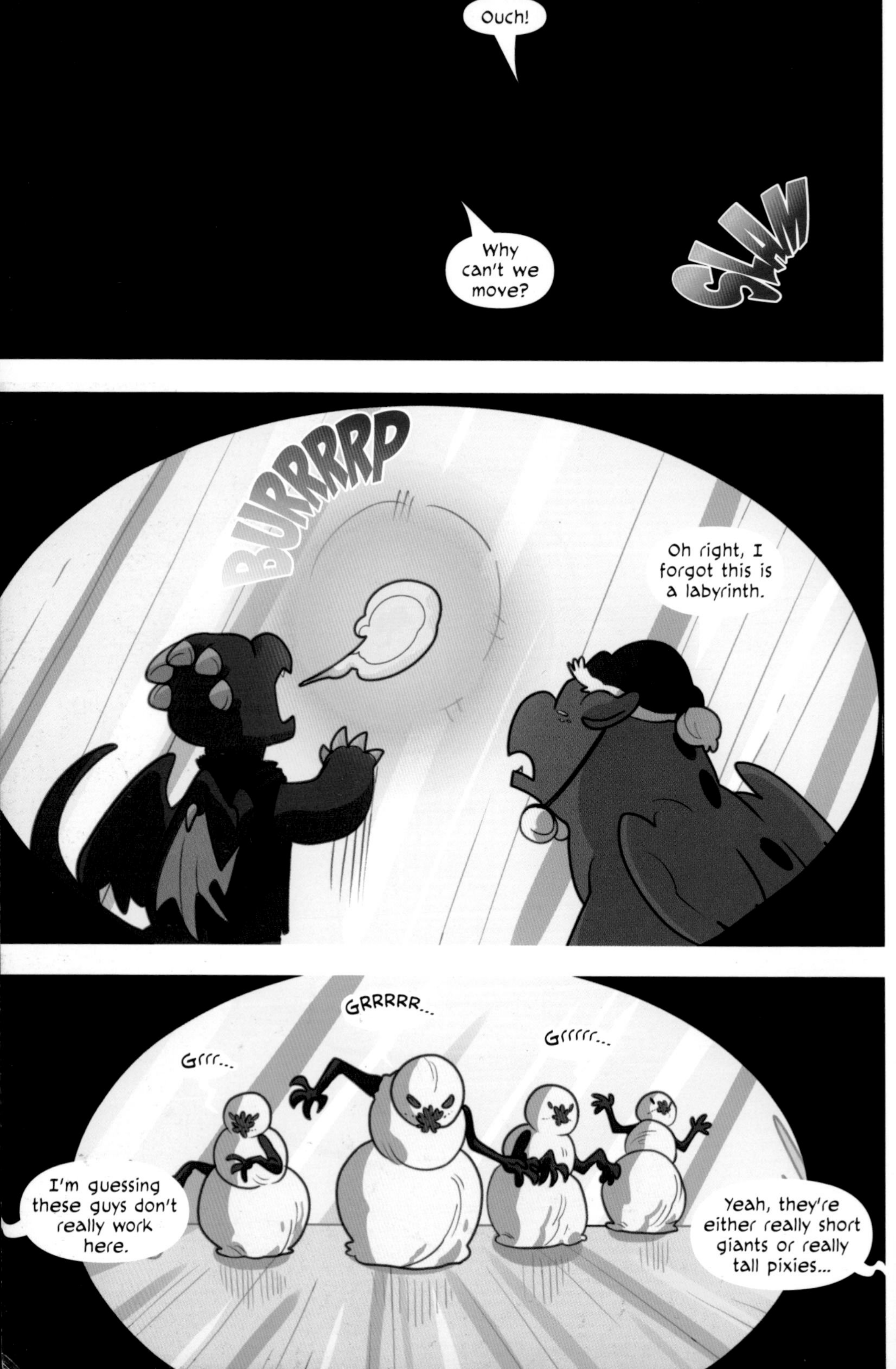
Ouch!
Why can't we move?
SLAM
BURRRRP
Oh right, I forgot this is a labyrinth.
GRRRRR...
Grrrrr...
Grrr...
I'm guessing these guys don't really work here.
Yeah, they're either really short giants or really tall pixies...

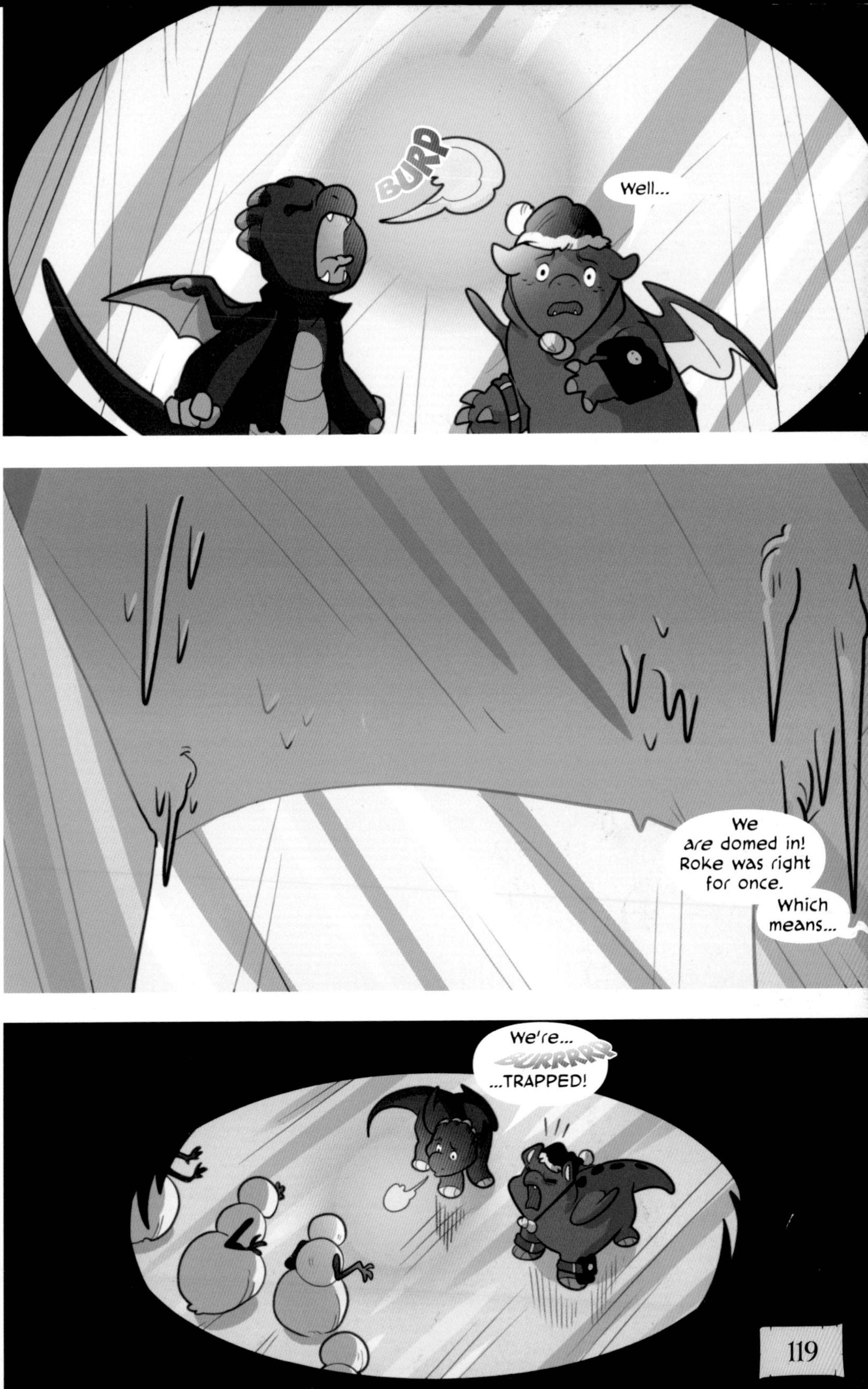
BURP
Well...
We are domed in! Roke was right for once.
Which means...
We're... BURRRRP ...TRAPPED!

Chapter 9

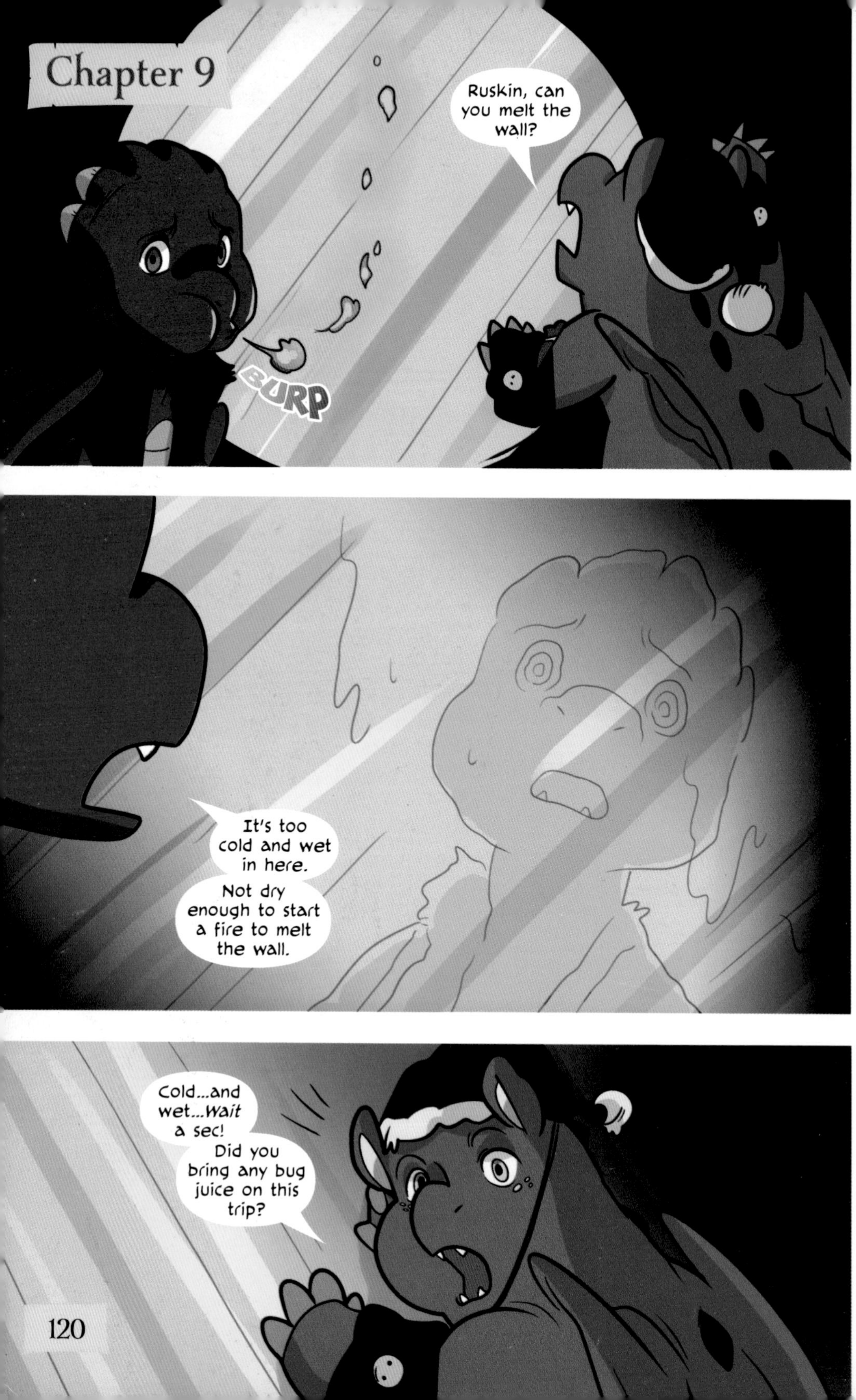
Ruskin, can you melt the wall?
BURP
It's too cold and wet in here.
Not dry enough to start a fire to melt the wall.
Cold...and wet...*wait* a sec!
Did you bring any bug juice on this trip?

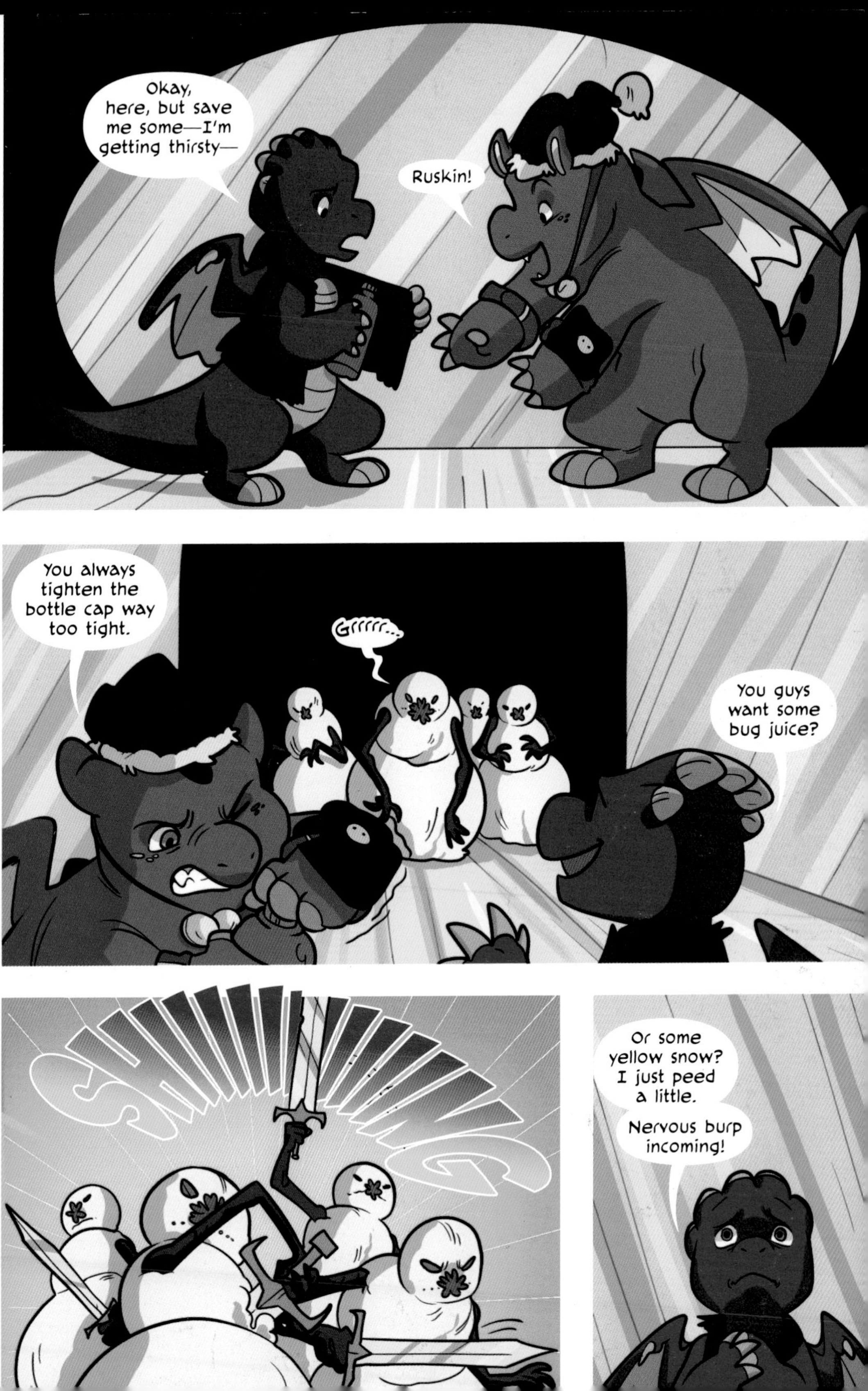

Okay, here, but save me some—I'm getting thirsty—
Ruskin!
You always tighten the bottle cap way too tight.
Grrrrr...
You guys want some bug juice?
SHWING
Or some yellow snow? I just peed a little.
Nervous burp incoming!

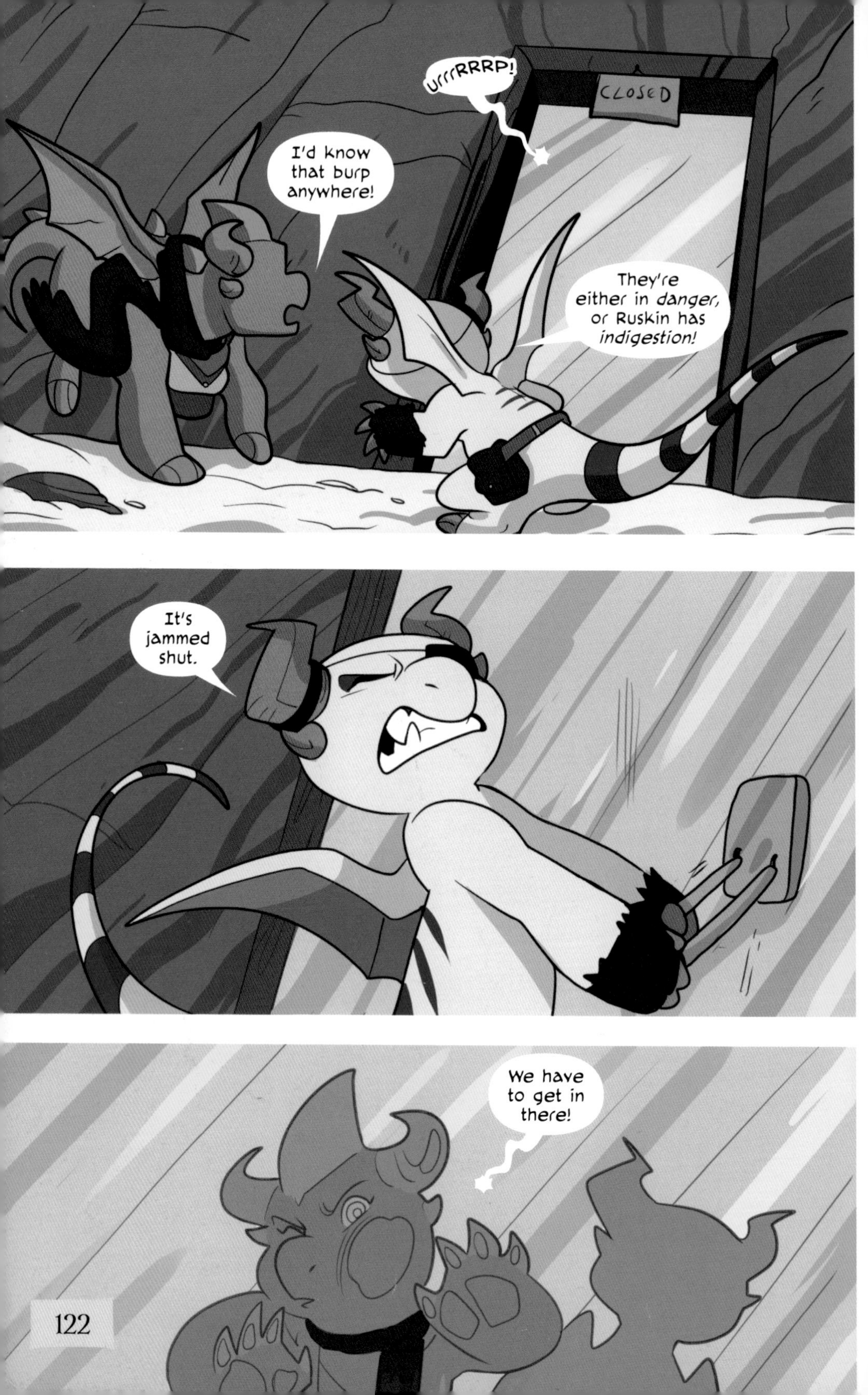
UrrrRRRP!
CLOSED
I'd know that burp anywhere!
They're either in *danger*, or Ruskin has *indigestion!*
It's jammed shut.
We have to get in there!

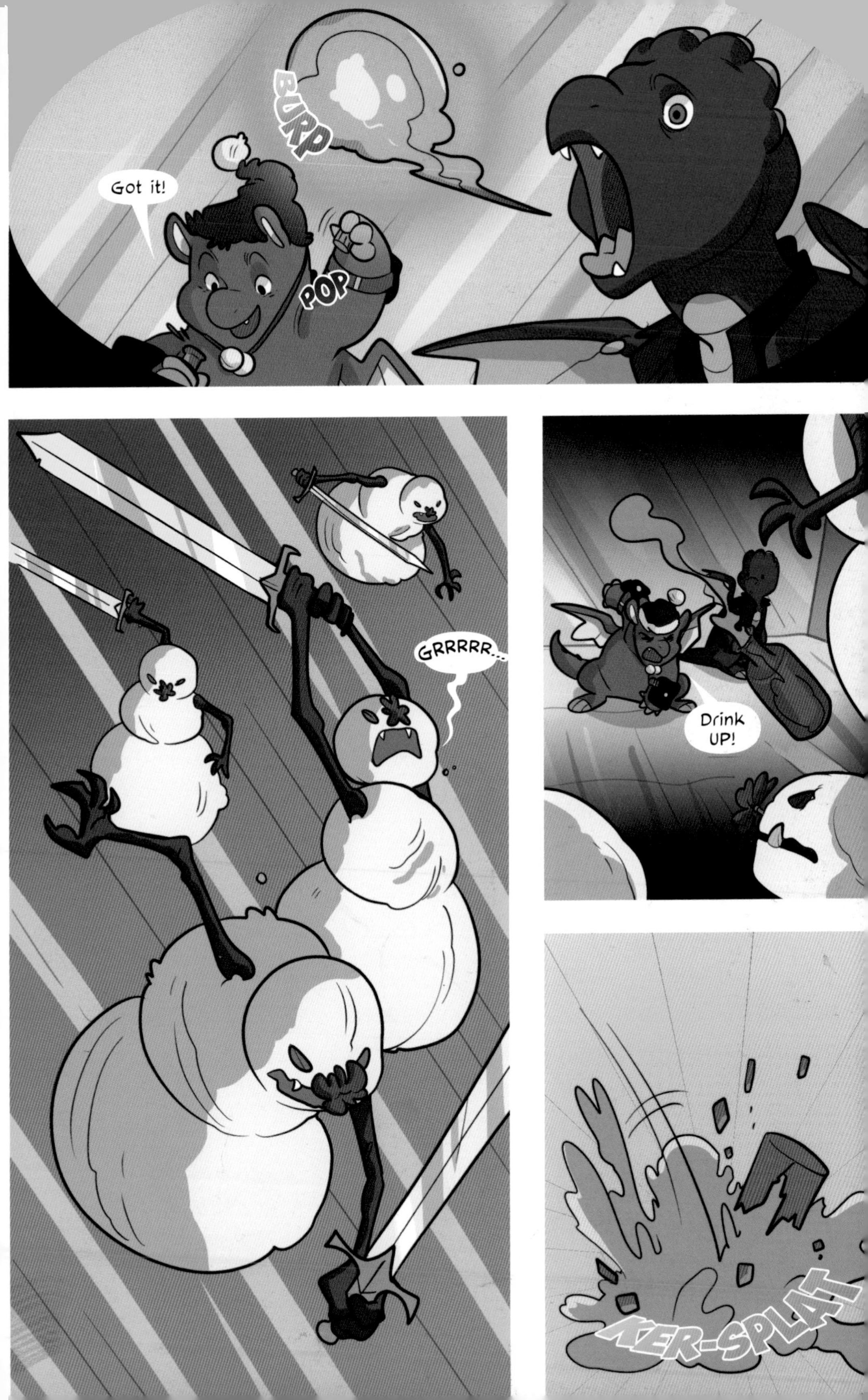
BURP
Got it!
POP
GRRRRR...
Drink UP!
KER-SPLAT

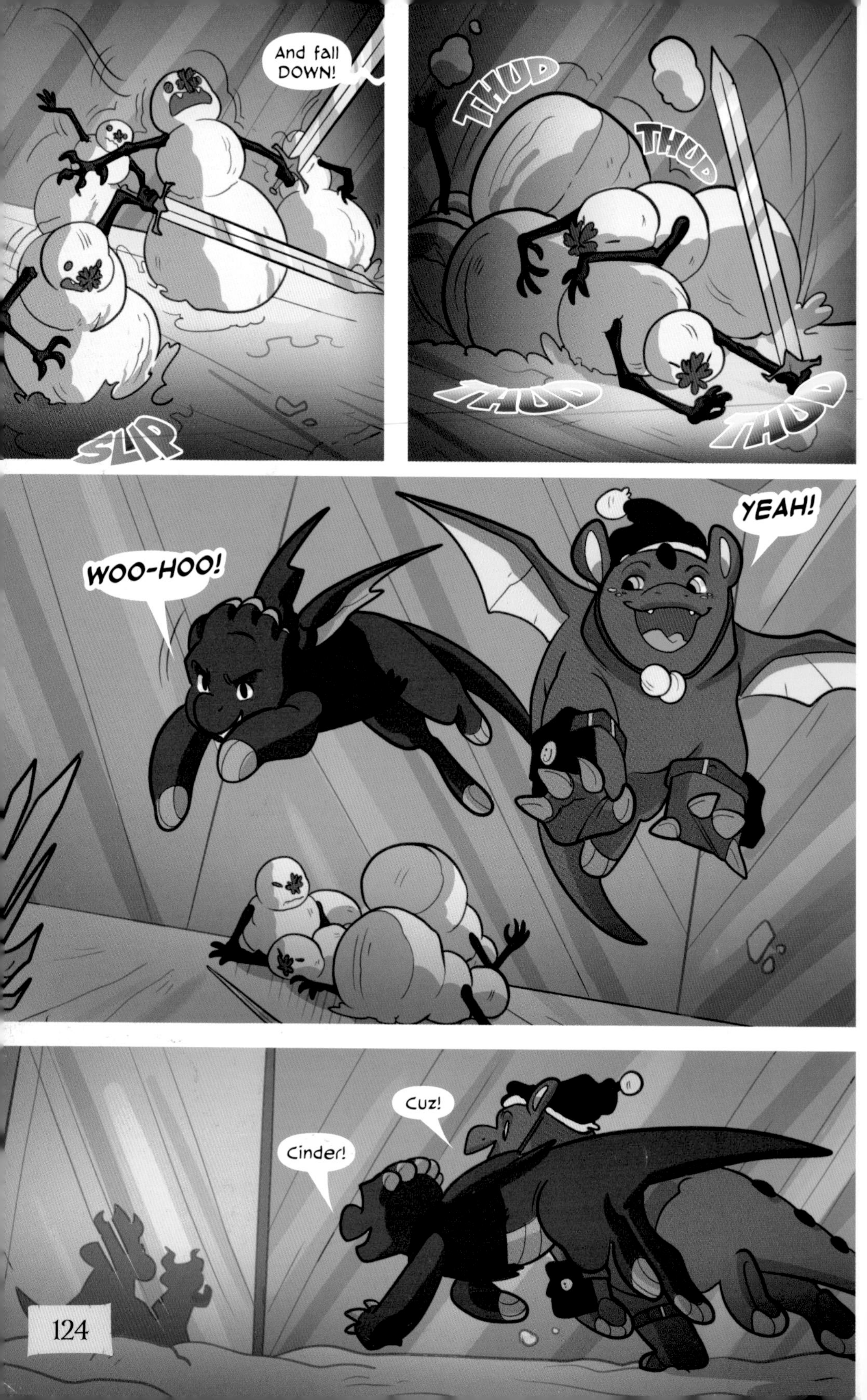
And fall DOWN!
SLIP
THUD
THUD
THUD
THUD
WOO-HOO!
YEAH!
Cuz!
Cinder!

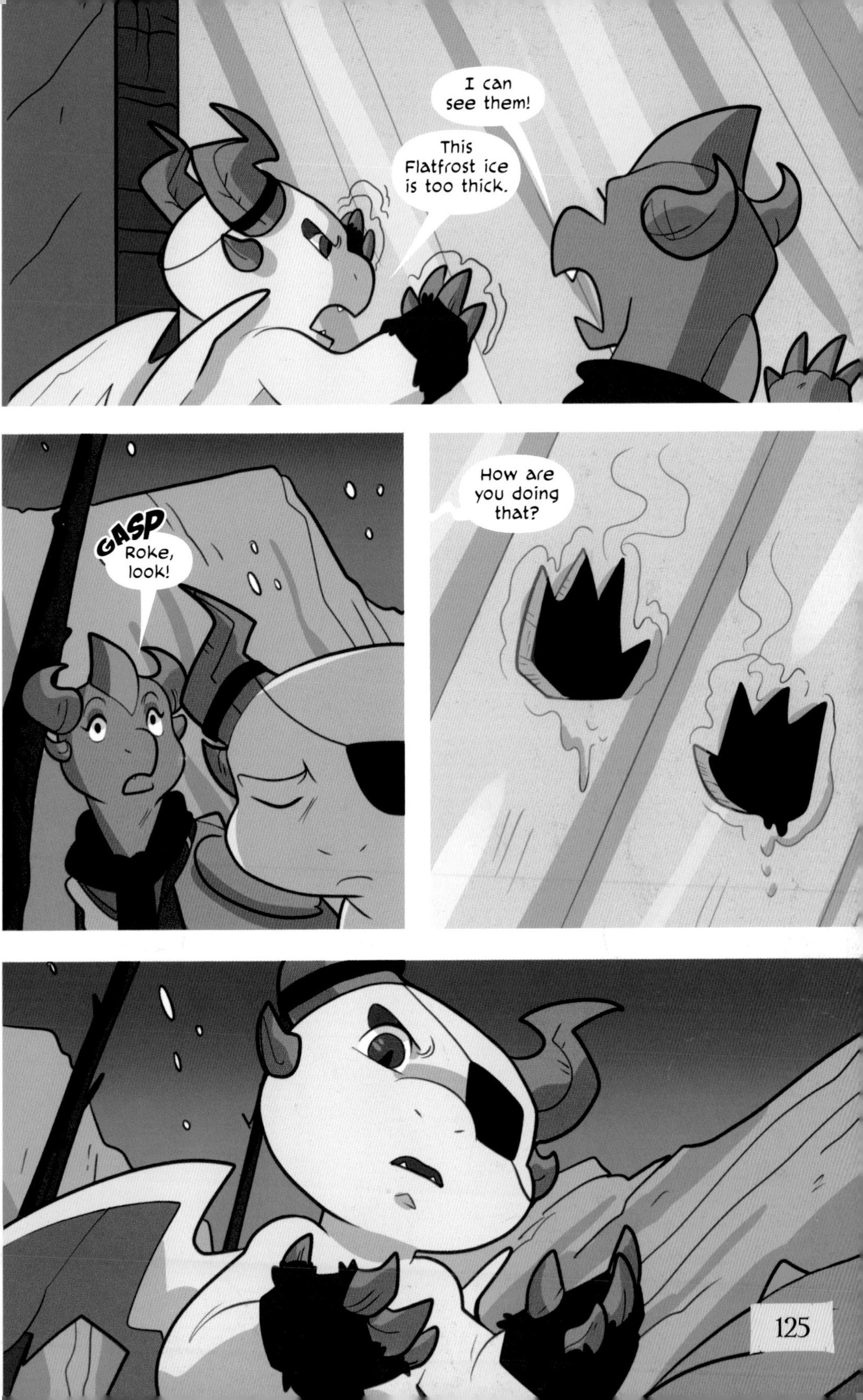
This Flatfrost ice is too thick.
I can see them!
GASP
Roke, look!
How are you doing that?

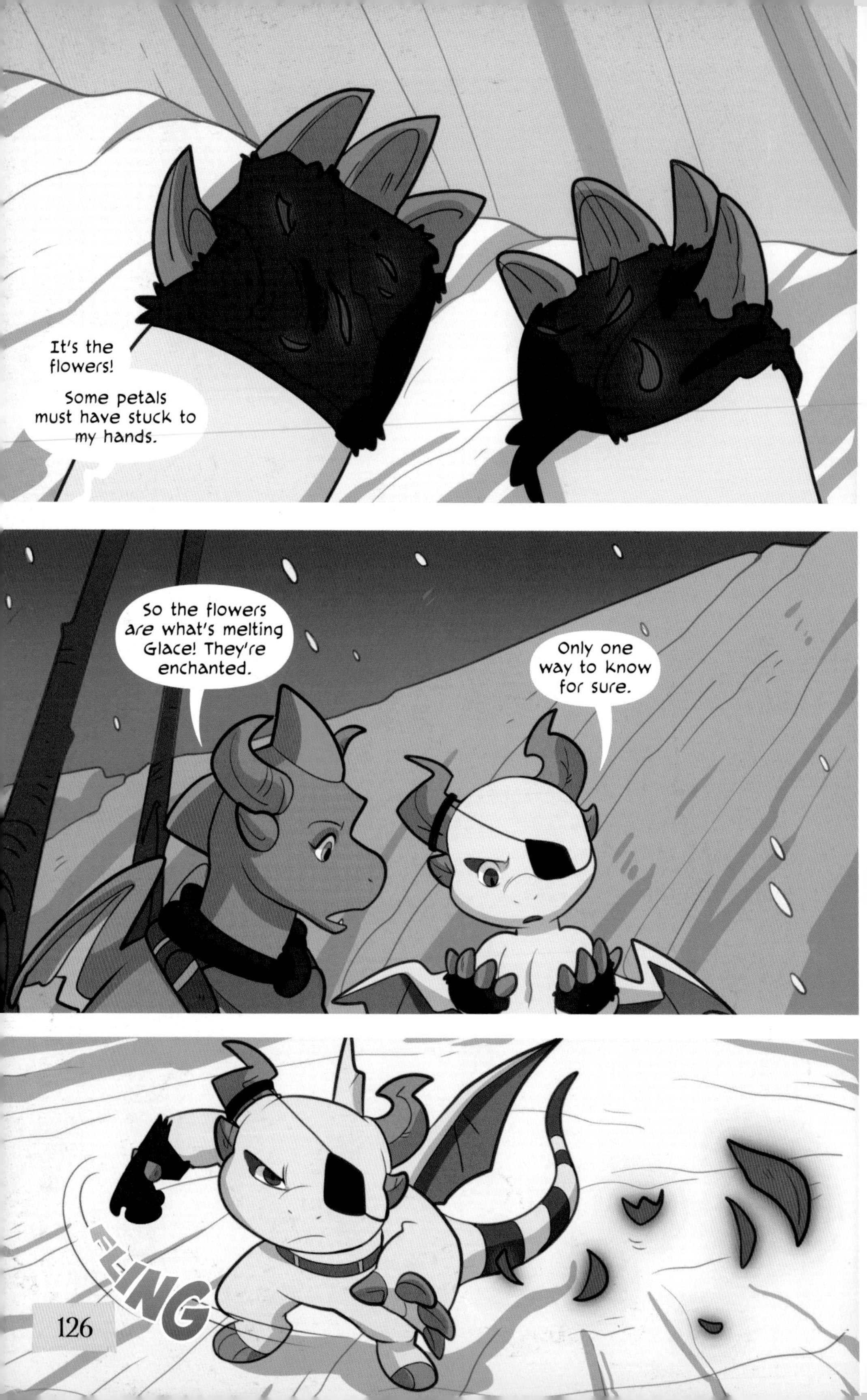
It's the flowers!
Some petals must have stuck to my hands.
So the flowers are what's melting Glace! They're enchanted.
Only one way to know for sure.
FLING

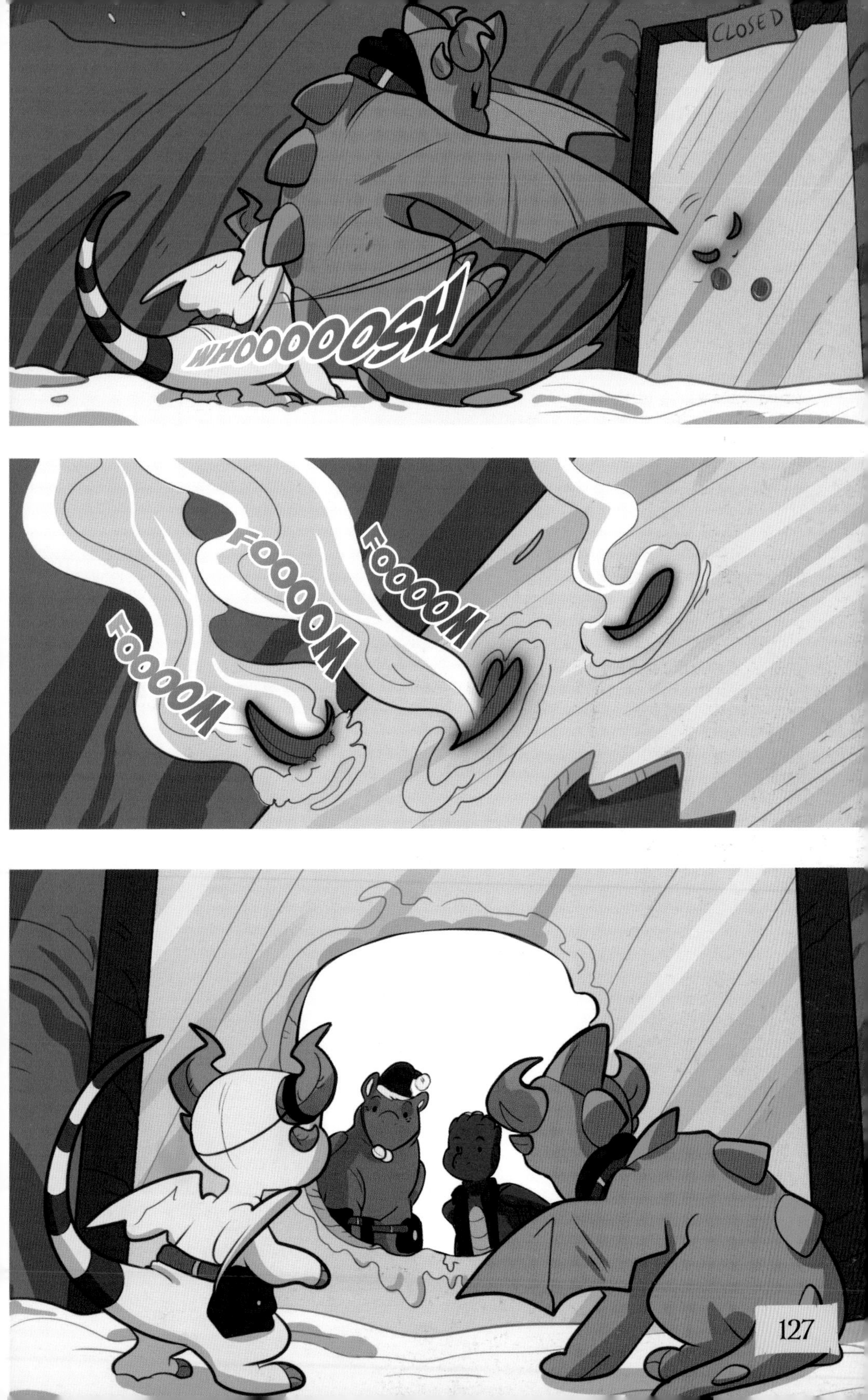
CLOSED
WHOOOOOSH
FOOOOM
FOOOOM
FOOOOM

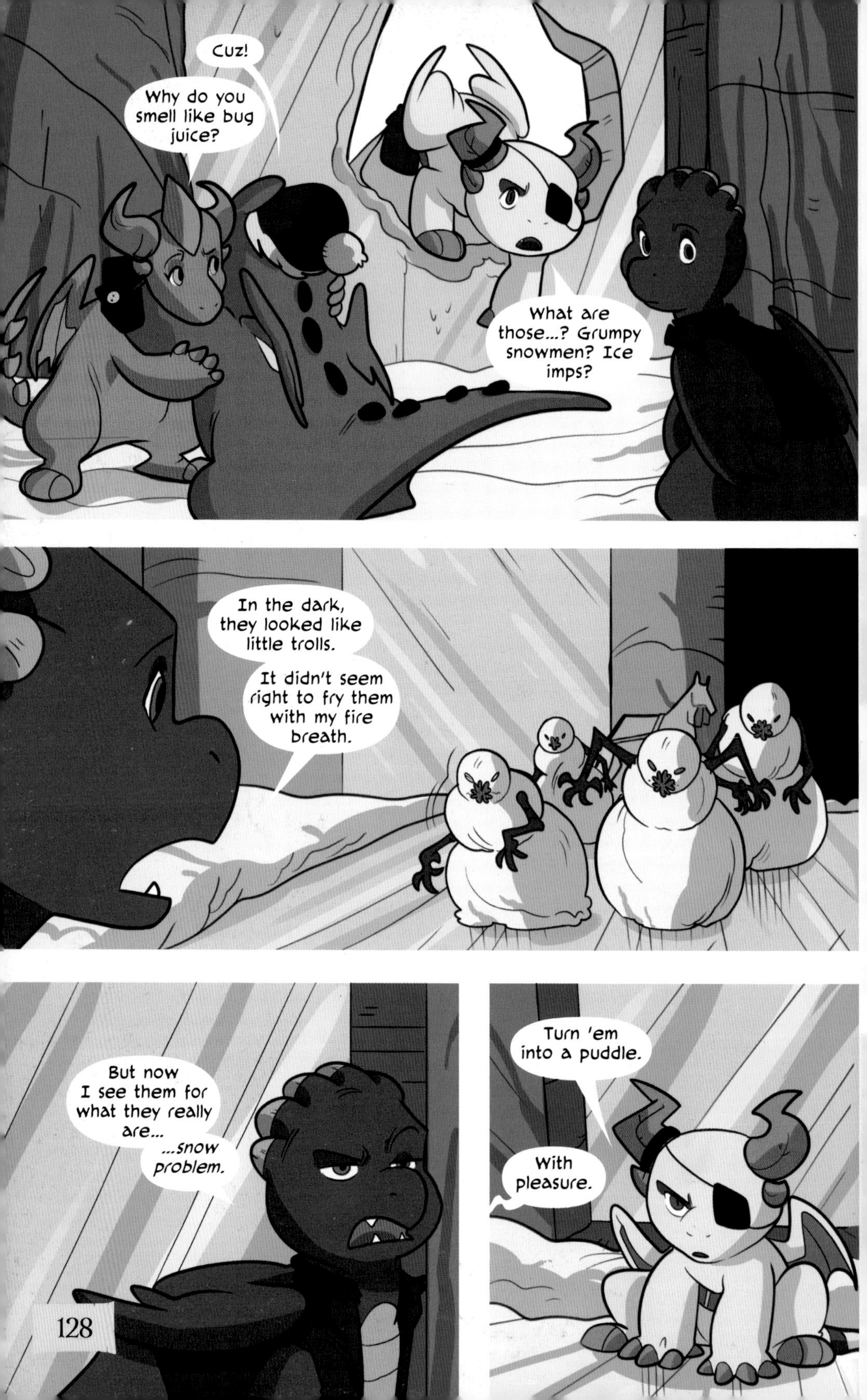
Cuz!
Why do you smell like bug juice?
What are those...? Grumpy snowmen? Ice imps?
In the dark, they looked like little trolls.
It didn't seem right to fry them with my fire breath.
But now I see them for what they really are...
...snow problem.
Turn 'em into a puddle.
With pleasure.

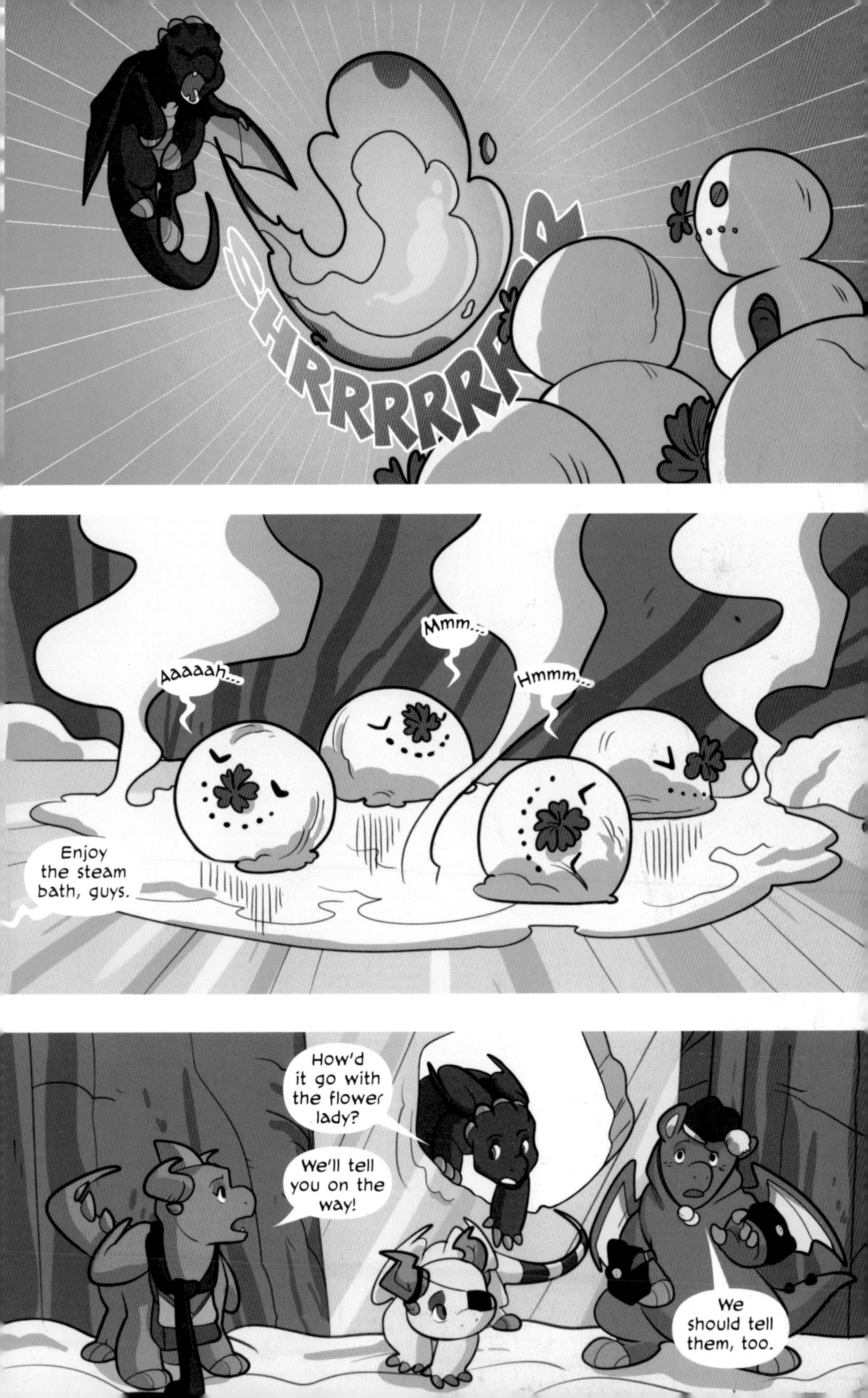
SHRRRRRRR
Aaaaah...
Mmm...
Hmmm...
Enjoy the steam bath, guys.
How'd it go with the flower lady?
We'll tell you on the way!
We should tell them, too.

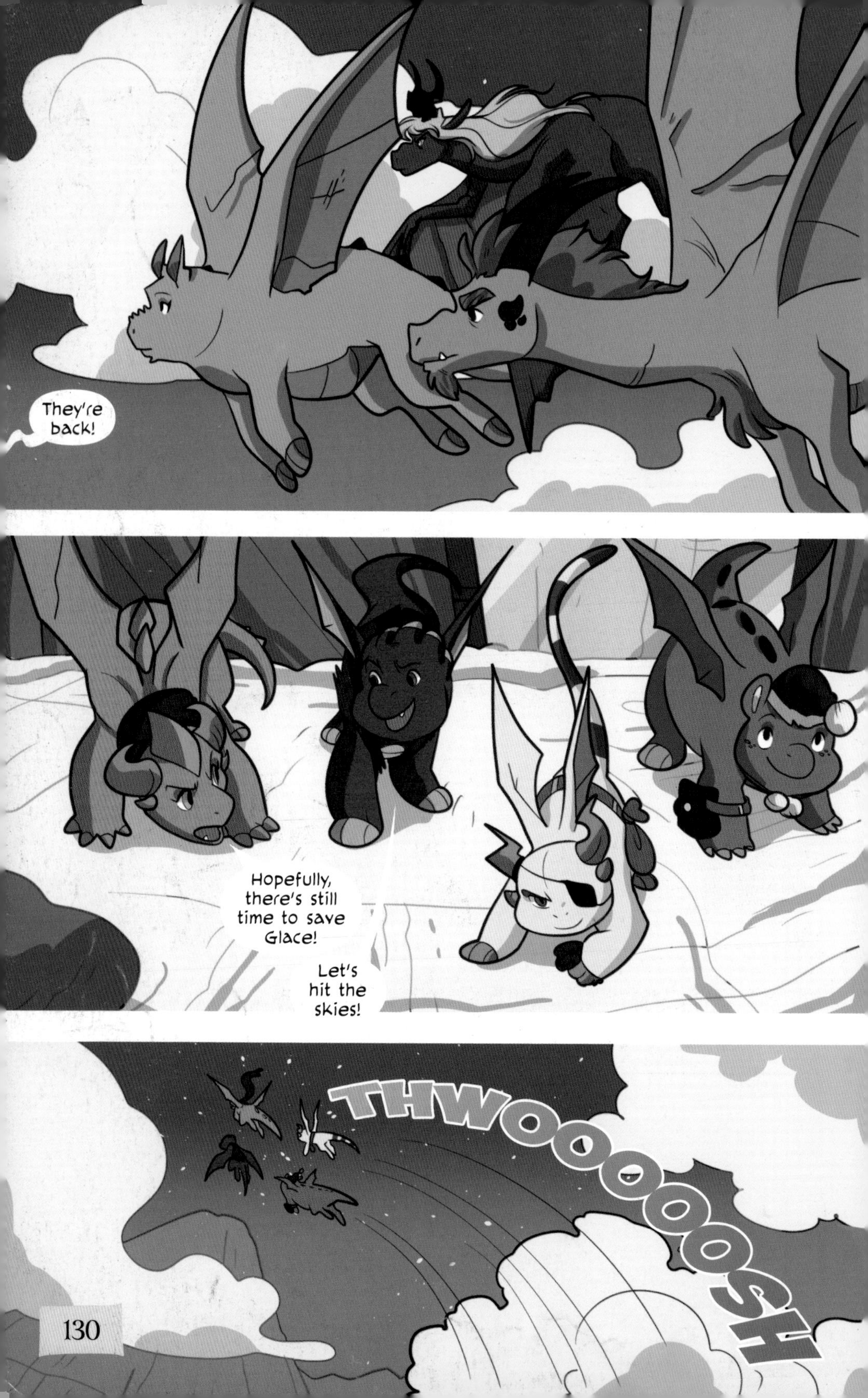
They're back!
Hopefully, there's still time to save Glace!
Let's hit the skies!
THWOOOOOOSH

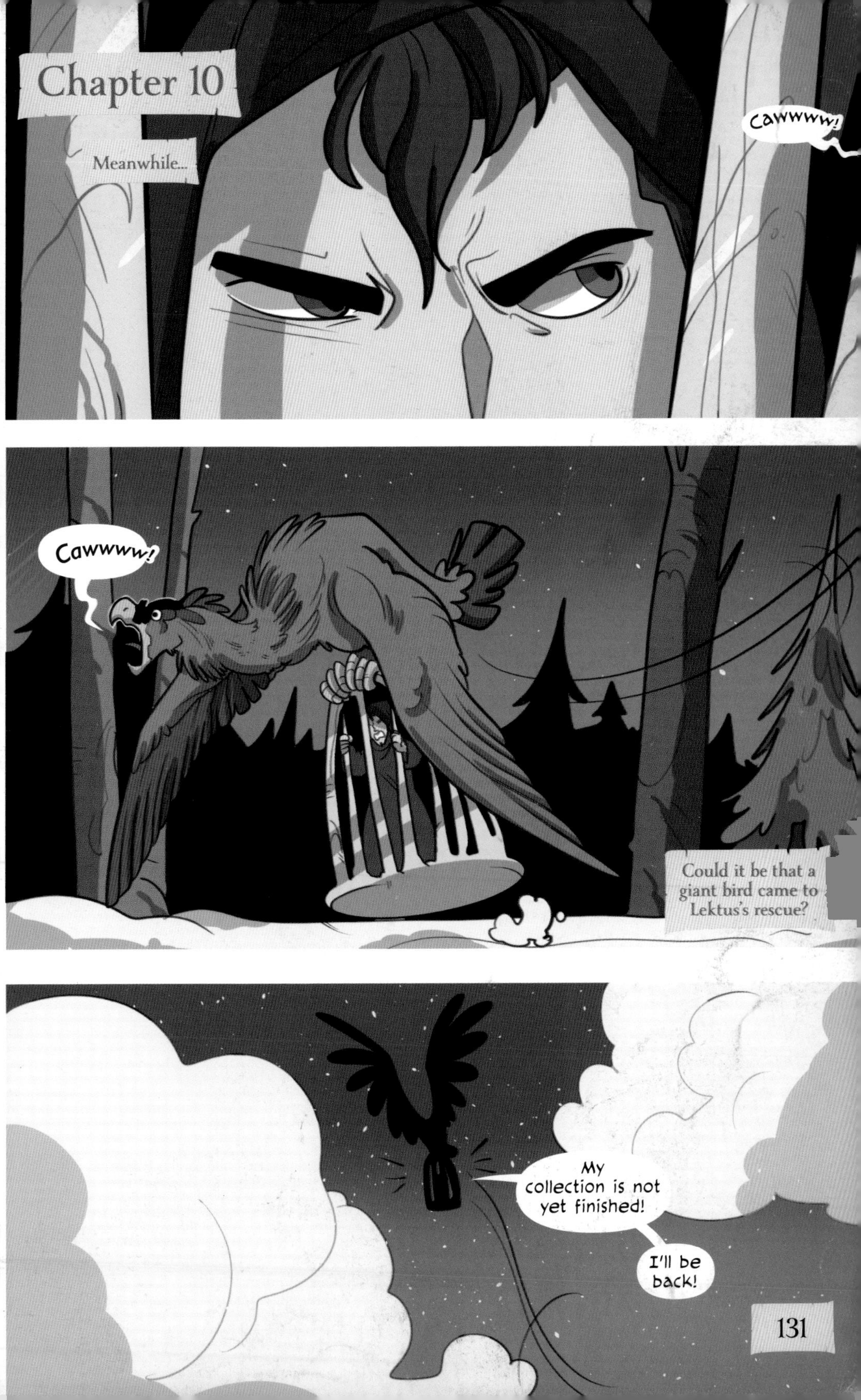
Chapter 10
Meanwhile...
Cawwww!
Cawwww!
Could it be that a giant bird came to Lektus's rescue?
My collection is not yet finished!
I'll be back!

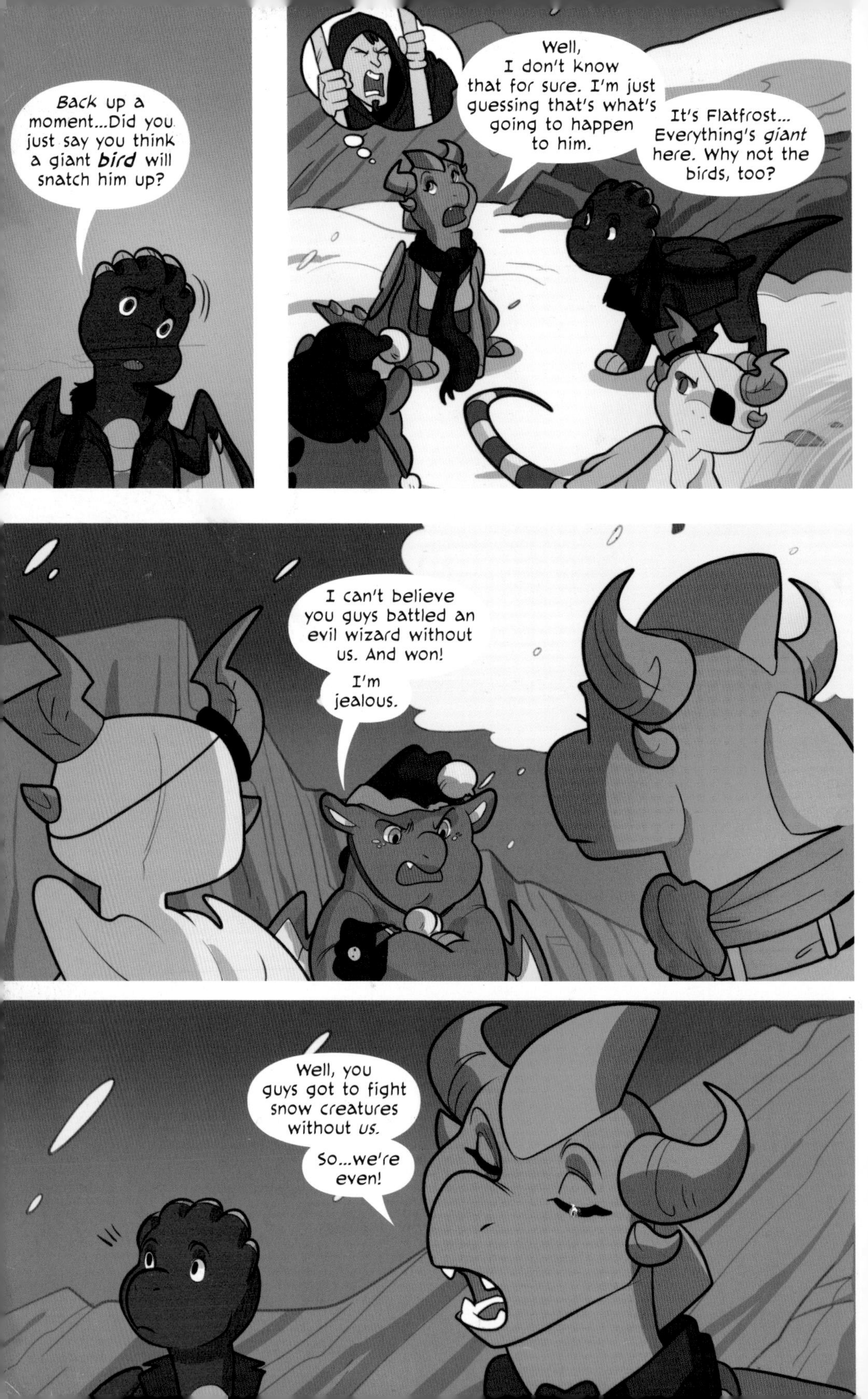
Back up a moment...Did you just say you think a giant *bird* will snatch him up?
Well, I don't know that for sure. I'm just guessing that's what's going to happen to him.
It's Flatfrost... Everything's *giant* here. Why not the birds, too?
I can't believe you guys battled an evil wizard without us. And won!
I'm jealous.
Well, you guys got to fight snow creatures without *us.*
So...we're even!

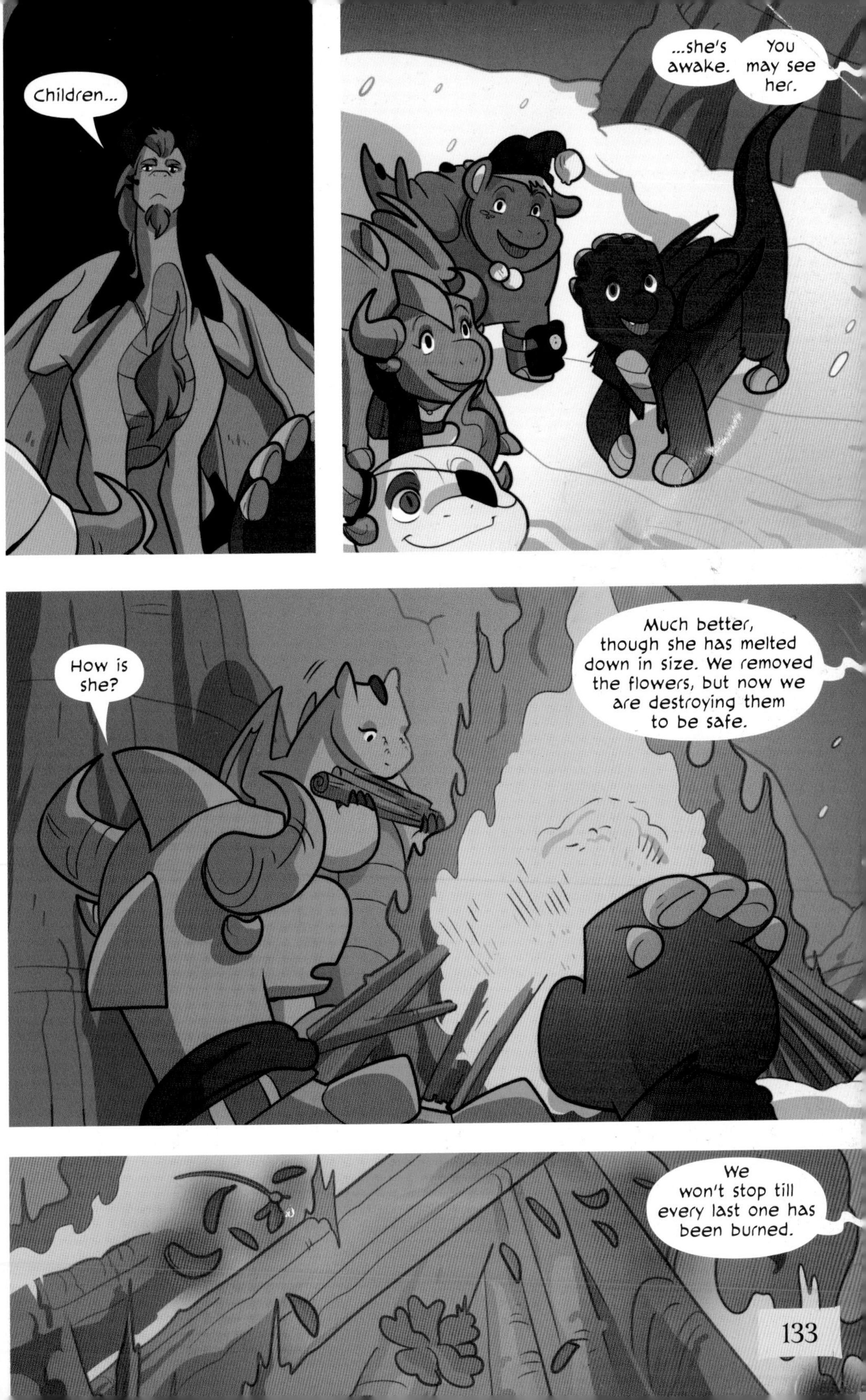
Children...
...she's awake.
You may see her.
How is she?
Much better, though she has melted down in size. We removed the flowers, but now we are destroying them to be safe.
We won't stop till every last one has been burned.

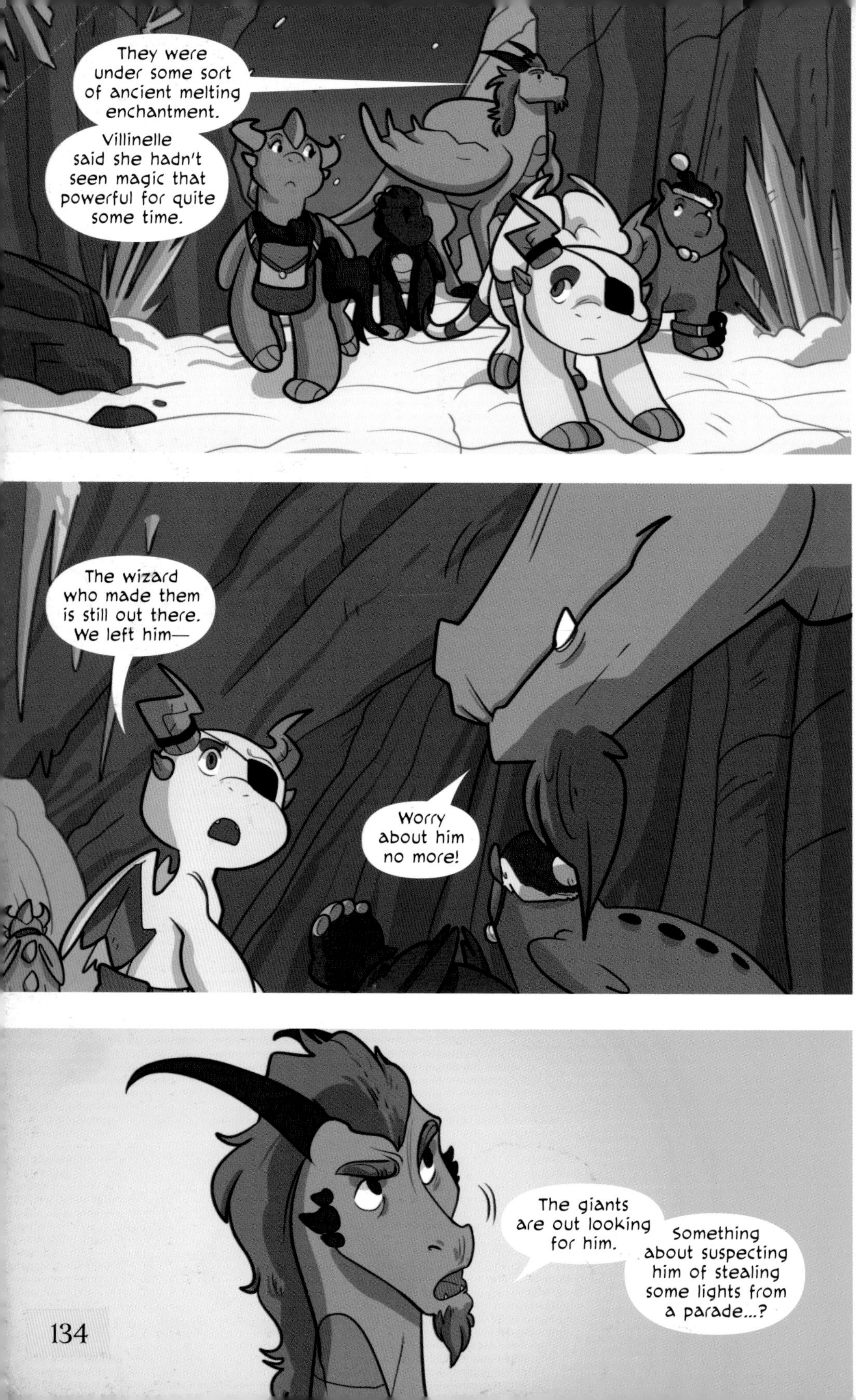
They were under some sort of ancient melting enchantment.
Villinelle said she hadn't seen magic that powerful for quite some time.
The wizard who made them is still out there. We left him—
Worry about him no more!
The giants are out looking for him.
Something about suspecting him of stealing some lights from a parade...?

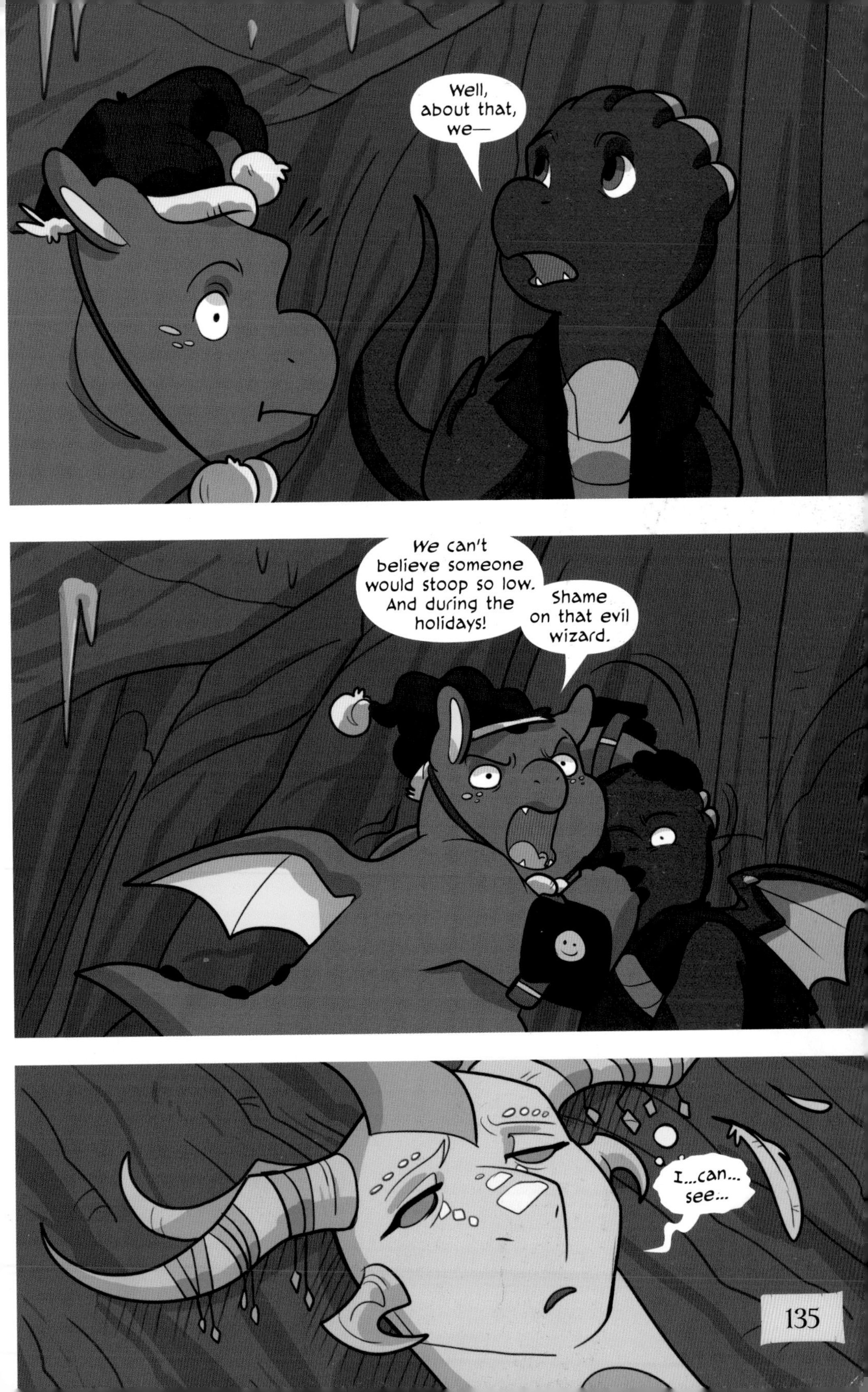
Well, about that, we—
We can't believe someone would stoop so low. And during the holidays!
Shame on that evil wizard.
I...can... see...

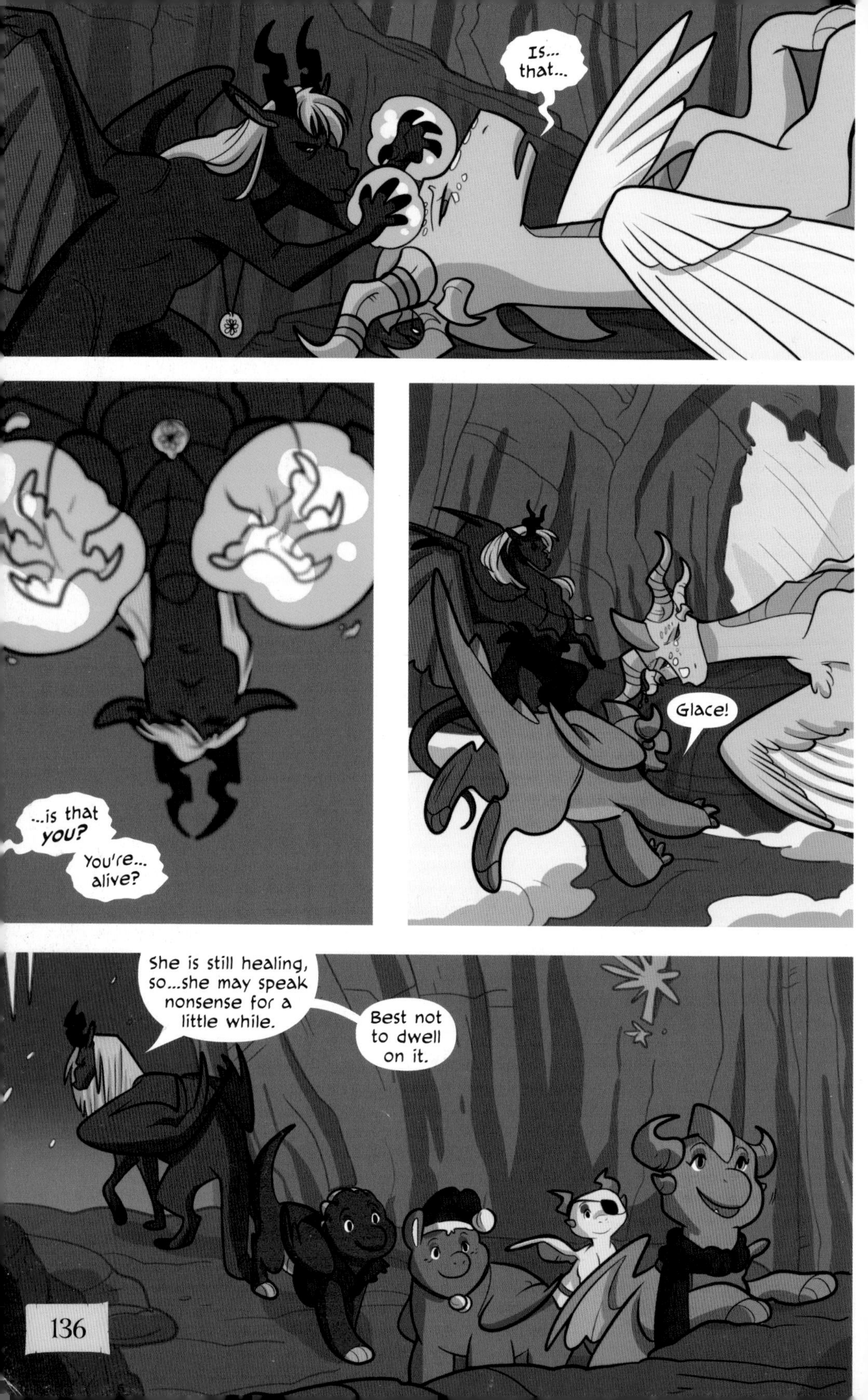
Is... that...
...is that *YOU?*
You're... alive?
Glace!
She is still healing, so...she may speak nonsense for a little while.
Best not to dwell on it.

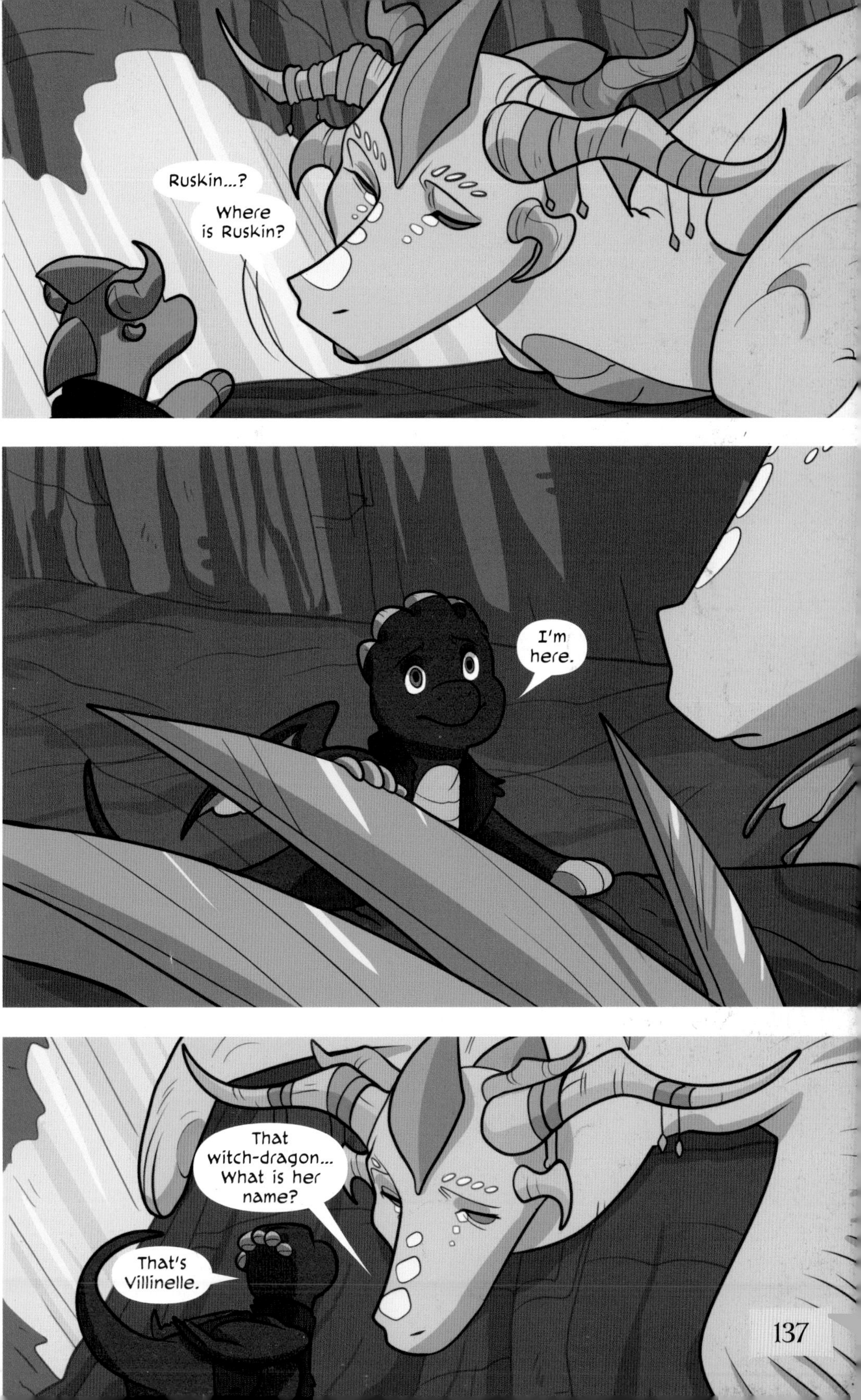
Ruskin...?
Where is Ruskin?
I'm here.
That witch-dragon... What is her name?
That's Villinelle.

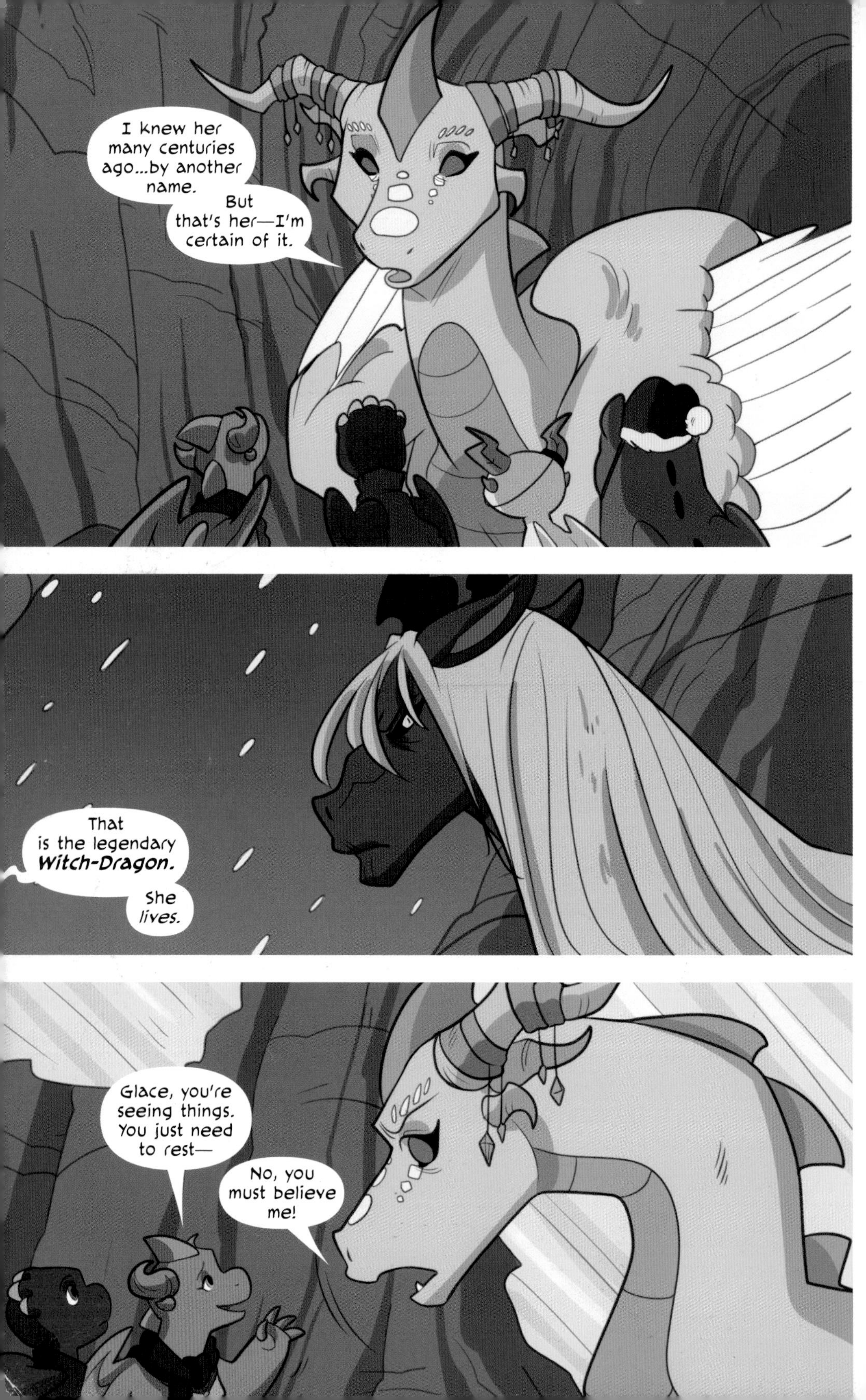
I knew her many centuries ago...by another name.
But that's her—I'm certain of it.
That is the legendary **Witch-Dragon.**
She *lives.*
Glace, you're seeing things. You just need to rest—
No, you must believe me!

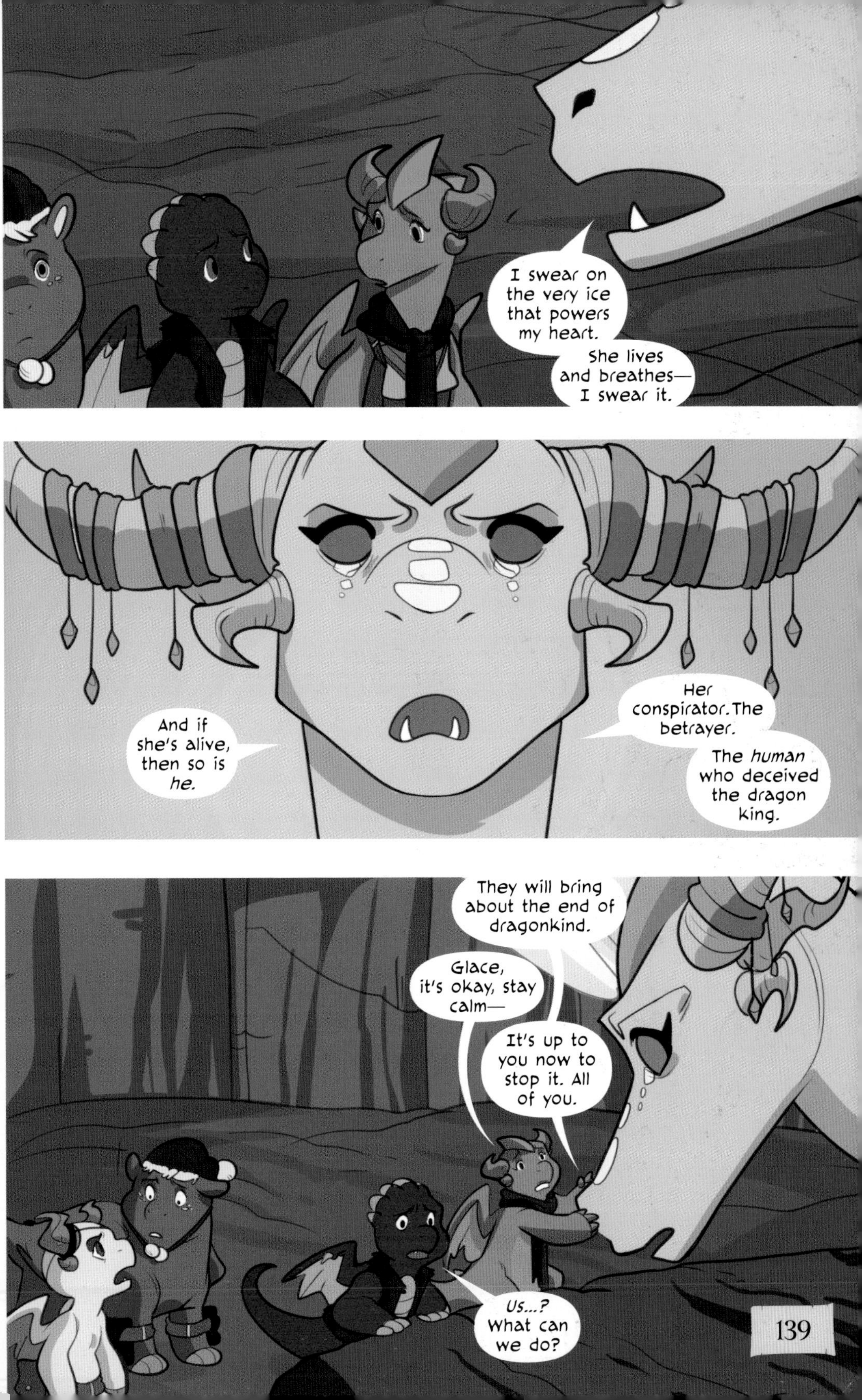
I swear on the very ice that powers my heart.
She lives and breathes— I swear it.
And if she's alive, then so is *he.*
Her conspirator. The betrayer.
The *human* who deceived the dragon king.
They will bring about the end of dragonkind.
Glace, it's okay, stay calm—
It's up to you now to stop it. All of you.
Us...? What can we do?

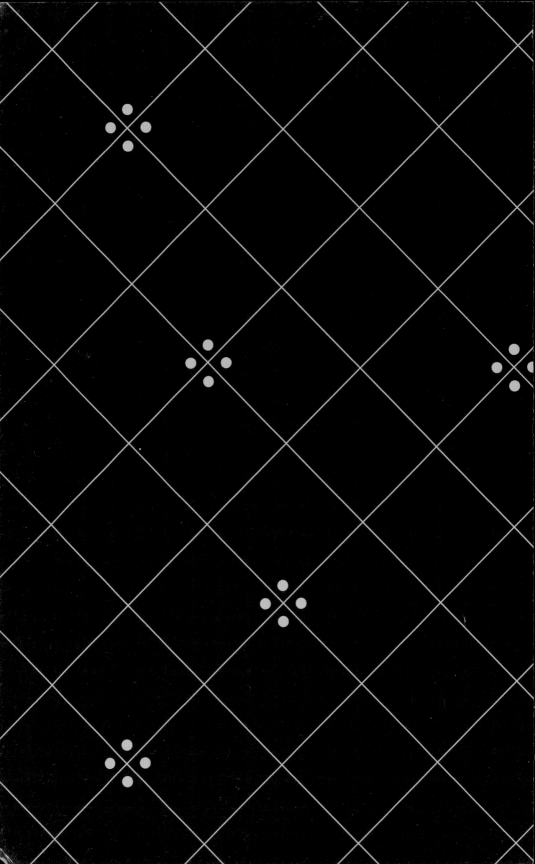

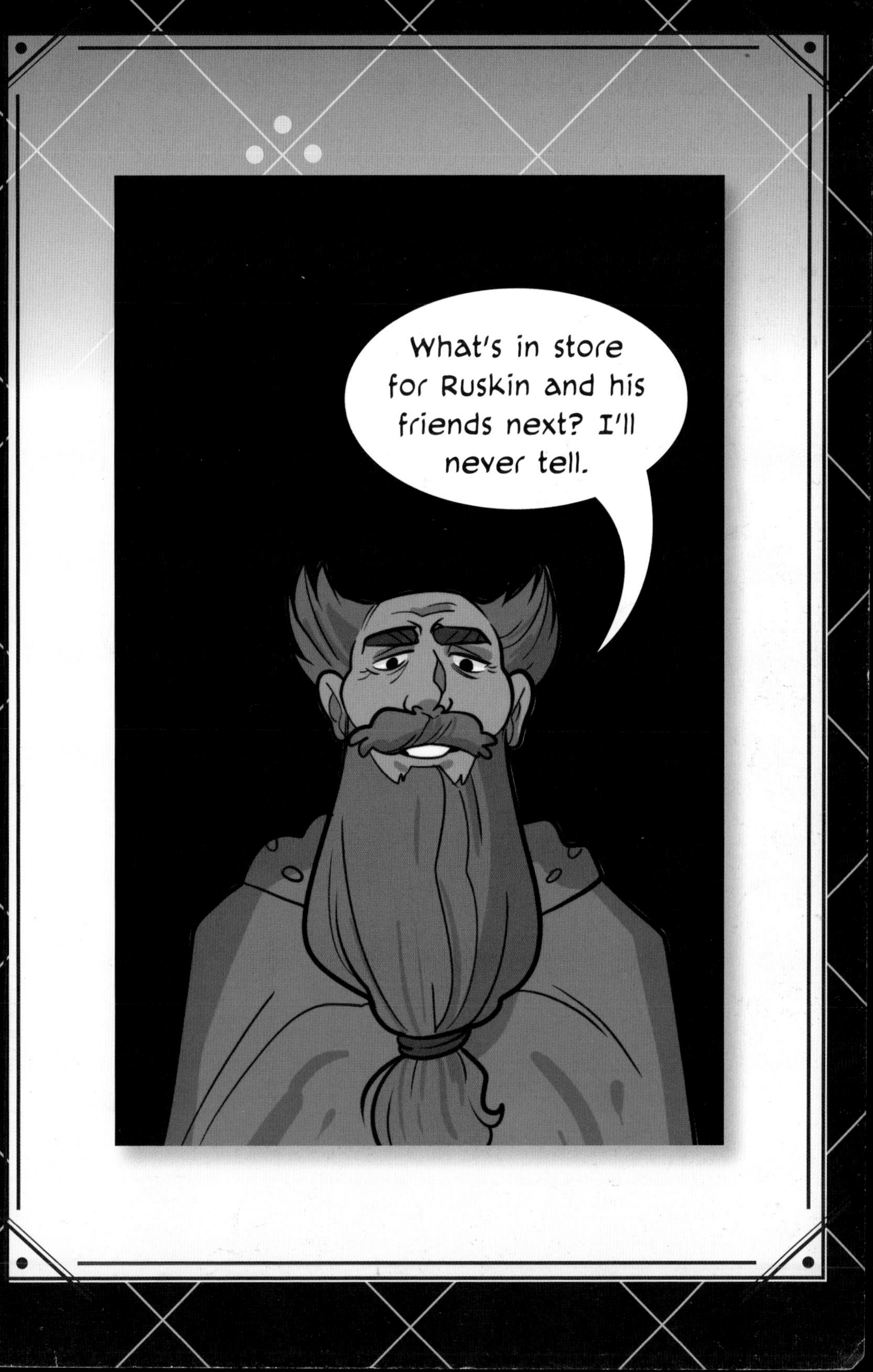
What's in store for Ruskin and his friends next? I'll never tell.

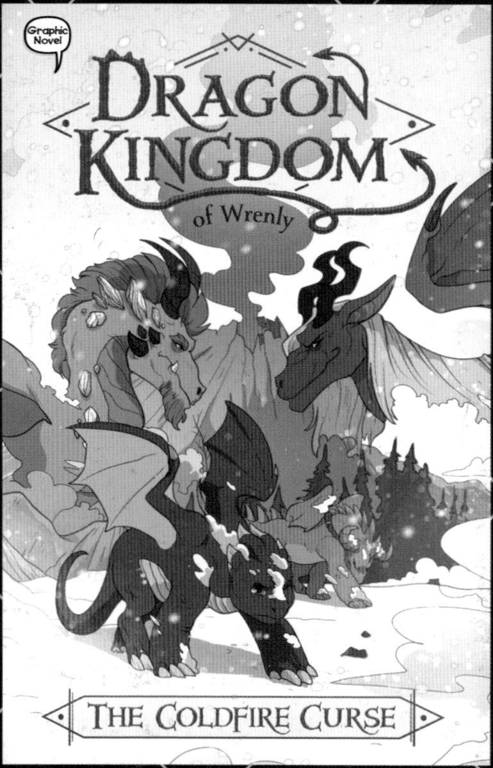
Graphic Novel
DRAGON KINGDOM
of Wrenly
THE COLDFIRE CURSE

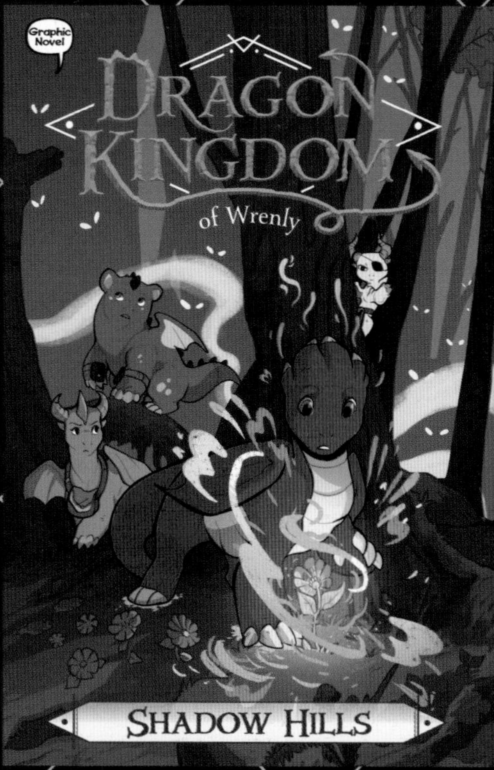
Graphic Novel
DRAGON KINGDOM
of Wrenly
SHADOW HILLS

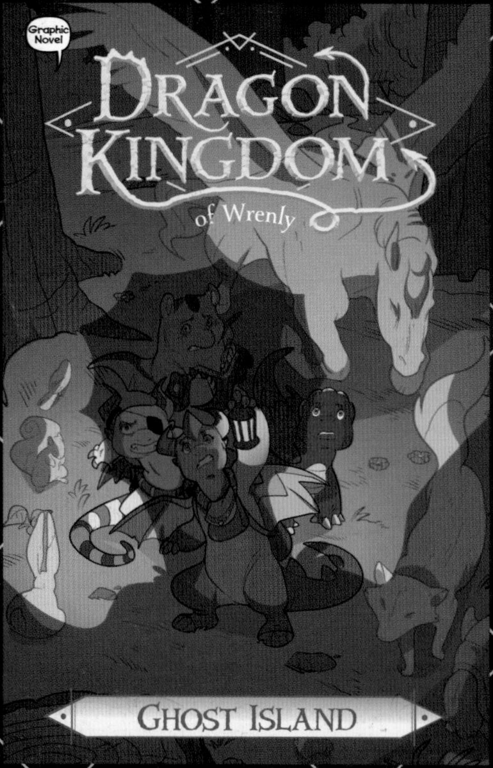
Graphic Novel
DRAGON KINGDOM
of Wrenly
GHOST ISLAND

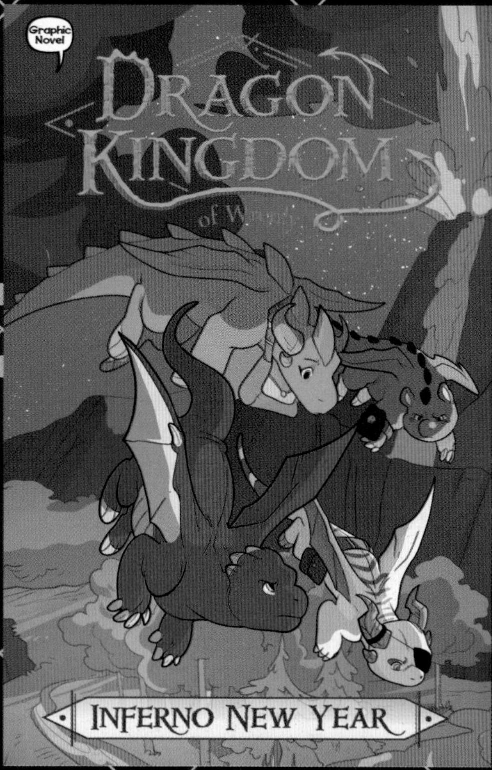
Graphic Novel
DRAGON KINGDOM
INFERNO NEW YEAR

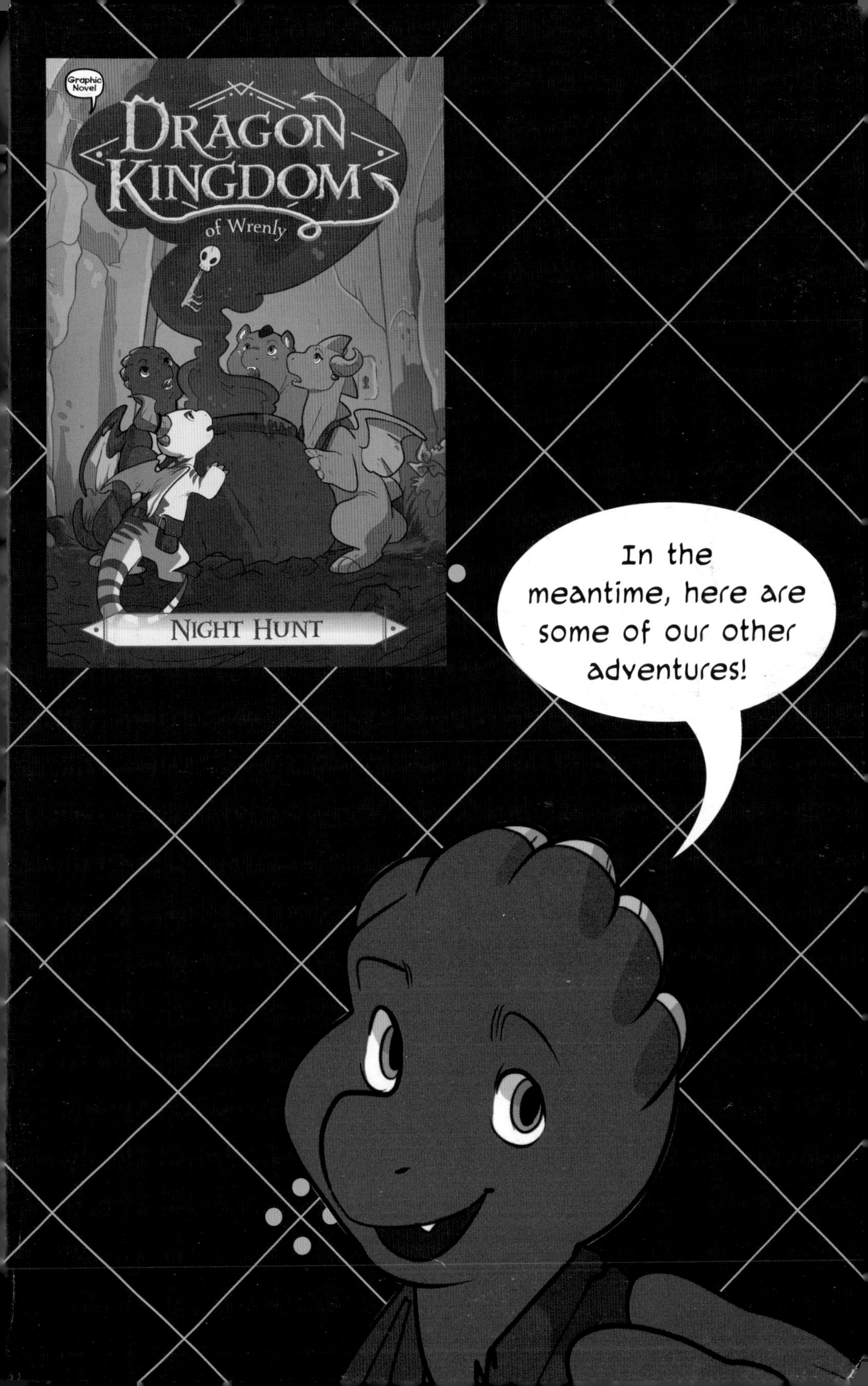
Graphic Novel
DRAGON KINGDOM
of Wrenly
NIGHT HUNT
In the meantime, here are some of our other adventures!